Advance Praise

FOR *IRRESISTIBLE CALLING*

Sean Mitchell's *Irresistible Calling* is the best kind of memoir: lively, confiding, thoughtful, funny, and as broad and searching as the America in which this post-war baby boomer came of age. With family roots deep in the working class and the boost of an elite education, Mitchell is preternaturally attuned to whatever scene he finds himself in, whether it's running a persecuted underground newspaper in Dallas, interviewing A-list movie stars and directors in Hollywood, or enduring the hand-to-mouth struggles of a writer trying to make it in New York. Lucky for us, he's down for it all, and this moving, big-hearted memoir brings a big chunk of our latter-day American history to brilliant life. Do yourself a favor and read this book.

BEN FOUNTAIN
Author of Billy Lynn's Long Halftime Walk *and* Devil Makes Three;
Finalist for the National Book Award

A wonderfully rich, humane, and inhabitable literary memoir. Mitchell's journalistic eye turned inward brings a special clarity and emotional precision to a keenly intelligent life in interesting times among the famous and the appalling on both coasts. I can't imagine a more engrossingly intimate course in American post-war cultural history.

DAVID SEARCY
Author of Shame and Wonder *and* The Tiny Bee That Hovers at the Center of the World

A writer of unassuming intelligence, grace, and sensitivity, Sean Mitchell recalls a career in journalism and its side hustles that hews closely to the arc of writing from old media to new, from the halcyon days of alternative weeklies to the rise and demise of legacy newspapers and magazines, and, inevitably, to the Internet. His unvarnished account is at once compellingly personal and carbonated with revealing, often hilarious encounters with celebrities and their enablers during a period of seismic changes in the culture. I couldn't wish for a more astute companion on this timely journey.

JEREMY GERARD
Author of Wynn Place Show *and* The Man Who Saved Broadway:
Bernard B. Jacobs and the Ascent of the Shubert Organization

The rhythm, the storyline, the object of Sean Mitchell's memoir, takes us from a plain start in a working class Pennsylvania town to the evolving possibilities of Dallas, and then to different realities and outcomes from the East Coast to the West. The search—for a way into and out of journalism en route to books and screenplays—will be of special interest to those of us who traveled a similar path and recognize the Dallas environment in particular. A thoughtful read for anyone pondering their past, their future, and their direction.

ROD DAVIS
Author of The Life of Kim and the Behavior of Men *and* Life in the Time of Hurricanes

Irresistible Calling

Irresistible Calling

A MEMOIR OF
JOURNALISM AND THE ARTS

Sean Mitchell

★ TEXAS WRITERS SERIES

FORT WORTH, TEXAS

Library of Congress Cataloging-in-Publication Data

Names: Mitchell, Sean, 1948- author
Title: Irresistible calling : a memoir of journalism and the arts / Sean
  Mitchell.
Description: Fort Worth, Texas : TCU Press, [2025] | Includes
  bibliographical references. | Summary: "Sean Mitchell was teaching
  English at a private school in Ohio when the New Journalism piqued his
  interest and lured him toward a profession that was much harder to crack
  than he imagined. After an editor in Washington, D.C. finally gave him a
  chance, he found a calling that would require and reveal multiple
  skills: editing an "underground" newspaper in his hometown of Dallas,
  writing magazine length stories about long distance truckers and Z.Z.
  Top, serving as the Dallas Times Herald's first rock critic and then its
  theatre critic, winning national recognition for his reviews. Moving to
  Los Angeles to cover Hollywood for the strangely singular and doomed
  Herald Examiner and then the Los Angeles Times, he profiled stars like
  Clint Eastwood, Ann-Margret and his irascible former St. Mark's School
  of Texas soccer teammate Tommy Lee Jones. While examining the nation's
  preoccupation with celebrity, he wondered if journalists like him were
  part of the problem or part of the solution? Such introspection fills
  this memoir of a young journalist, the only child of two creative but
  very different parents. It harks back to scenes of Dallas in the 1950s
  and '60s, framing a boy's discovery of sports, girls, hootenannies, F.
  Scott Fitzgerald and himself. He saw the counterculture and Vietnam War
  overtake the traditions of the Ivy League, experienced the excitement of
  a big city newsroom, spent a life-changing summer at an institute for
  young critics at the Eugene O'Neill Theatre Center and got close enough
  to Hollywood to blink"-- Provided by publisher.
Identifiers: LCCN 2025022438 (print) | LCCN 2025022439 (ebook) | ISBN
  9780875659312 paperback | ISBN 9780875659404 ebook
Subjects: LCSH: Mitchell, Sean, 1948- | Journalists--United
  States--Biography | Arts--Press coverage--United States | LCGFT:
  Autobiographies
Classification: LCC PN4874.M5125 A3 2025 (print) | LCC PN4874.M5125
  (ebook) | DDC 070.92--dc23/eng/20250521
LC record available at https://lccn.loc.gov/2025022438
LC ebook record available at https://lccn.loc.gov/2025022439

Designed by Katie Howerton

TCU Box 298300
Fort Worth, Texas 76129
www.tcupress.com

For Devin and Susannah

You gotta live by the pen 'cause of what you saw.

VAN MORRISON
"The Pen Is Mightier Than the Sword"
from Keep Me Singing

Contents

PART TWO

PART THREE

JEFF UNGER

Foreword

IN *FUNDAMENTALS OF GOOD WRITING*, an excellent book first published in 1950, Robert Penn Warren and Cleanth Brooks wrote, "To write well is not easy for the simple reason that to write well you must think straight. And thinking straight is never easy."

A special kind of straight thinking goes into crafting the compelling story of your own life, as Sean Mitchell demonstrates in the book you are about to read. First, the writer has to gather, sort, and winnow the Five Ws—the who, what, when, where, and why—about heritage and ancestry, jobs, successes, failures, encounters, travels, and the other assorted minutiae that add up to a life. Once accomplished, that task leads to the even more daunting job of organizing the information in a simple to follow and engaging way.

The straighter the thinking, as Warren and Brooks would have it, the greater the likelihood that the prose produced will read seamlessly, making it easier for the reader to follow and comprehend. Paragraphs will be focused, concise, and foreshadow what's to come; sentences will not require rereading, except, on occasion as is the case with this book, to marvel once again at their beauty. Successfully pulling off this literary magic act, any accomplished writer will tell you, makes it easier for readers, who, E. B. White once wrote, "are in trouble about half the time."

Sean Mitchell is, above all, a straight thinker and a master at his craft, which will become apparent early on, as he tells the compelling odyssey of his early life and career as a distinguished and award-winning journalist and writer. He makes writing look and sound effortless, the same way Roger Federer made hitting a one-handed backhand look simple, Louis Armstrong made playing the trumpet appear easy, and White made essay writing seem like something any of us could do, if we practiced, just a little. Well, it does get easier—provided you practice your trade regularly and diligently for decades, are dedicated to it, and, like Sean, have the extraordinary life experiences from which to weave a masterful story.

I first began reading Sean's work when he and I were colleagues at the *Dallas Times Herald*. Sean's was a unique byline. Below his name was "Critic at Large," a singular honorific that not only signaled his accomplished writing but also his abundant talent as an evaluator of a myriad of art forms—as well as his having won the George Jean Nathan Award for drama criticism.

Whenever I have read anything Sean has written, including this splendid memoir, I am reminded of something Russell Baker said about Henry Fairlie in *The Good Times*, a sequel to Baker's Pulitzer Prize–winning memoir, *Growing Up*. Fairlie was an editorial writer for the *Times of London* when Baker was working for the *Baltimore Sun* as a correspondent in London. Baker said of Fairlie, "Conversation came out of him in fully formed paragraphs ready to be sent to the printer without editing. It was witty, well informed, and more clever than anything I had ever heard in Baltimore."

Sean has Fairlie's gift on the printed page. The author's generous reporting and writing skills are abundantly evident, as is his sense of humor and writer's eye and ear for the cast of characters he has crossed paths with from the East Coast to the West, with multiple stops in between. The writing is as sharp as it is sparkling, the sentences as elegant as they are surprising and original, the recollections as colorful as they are memorable.

His is truly a chronicle of achievement, filled with adventures large and small, and influential friends, mentors, colleagues, and, of course, the extraordinary range of people he interviewed: actors, directors, screenwriters, producers, and others.

It's all but certain that his mother and father would have been pleased by the book and his careful description of their heritage, worldview, and parenting. Sean recalls their deep interest in the arts and cultural affairs and the role his parents played in shaping his own artistic and literary trajectory. The author paints his parents with candor, honesty, and deep admiration for how they lived their lives and what they accomplished. Ultimately, the love the three of them had for one another comes through, despite the inevitable bumps.

Sean Mitchell has written, without a trace of bravado, a diary of a life of accomplishment, documented in a book that is evidence of the author's uncommon grace with words and language.

JEFF UNGER *is a former member of the editorial board of the* Dallas Times Herald, *where he was also a reporter and the newspaper's book editor. A recipient of a Texas Institute of Letters Award for feature writing, he was the director of the news service at the University of Illinois for twenty-three years and taught reporting at the undergraduate and graduate levels.*

Preface

WHEN I WAS STARTING OUT AS A REPORTER, one night I happened to spot Truman Capote standing alone in the lobby of Carnegie Hall before a Josephine Baker concert. I realized I should get a quote from him for a story I was writing about the exotic chanteuse, but my shyness, I regret to say, prevented me from doing so. Only months later, driven by an alter ego, I carried my guitar into Larry McMurtry's used bookstore in Washington, DC, and made him listen to a song I had written about one of his novels. It's hard for me now to recognize these two versions of myself as belonging to the same person. But I know those things happened, pieces of personal history that, while incongruous, must in some ways have defined who I would become. None of us is easily summarized.

The pieces of personal history I have assembled here might otherwise be called a memoir. Memoirs are often written by famous people, and I am not a famous person. I did meet and interview many of them. Writing about myself now could suggest I was influenced by the insistent self-promotion endemic to the world of entertainment and the arts that I covered as a reporter and critic. Yet I prefer to think I wrote this primarily for the benefit of my son and daughter, Devin and Susannah, who, it occurred to me, might one day wonder what I did in my life before I met and married their mother. We married late and were blessed quickly with two healthy, endearing children. But when those children got old enough to do the math, I figured, they could calculate that both their parents had done a lot of living and working before finding each other in time to conceive them. I wanted to fill in some of those missing chapters on my side. I also wanted to illustrate what it was like to be a print journalist and critic before the Internet blew up the business and reduced writers to the status of "content providers."

And so, here is a chronicle of my youth and search for a place in the world, the account of a boy born in a steel town in Pennsylvania after World War II and transplanted at the age of eighteen months to a foreign land, North Texas, where I grew up the only child of two creative but very different parents. Improbably they managed to send me to an exclusive private school in Dallas and then to an Ivy League college where, in both cases, I was ushered into a realm of privilege far from my family's working-class roots. I never resolved that contradiction.

For someone who wrote and published a neighborhood sports newsletter at the age of twelve, it might not seem unusual that I became a journalist, but I had other interests, including fiction, the guitar, and songwriting, and started out as an English teacher. When I left teaching to explore a career in "the media," I had no idea how hard it was going to be to get in the door. The saga of my difficulties is laid out here, along with what happened after I got a lucky break in Washington, DC, returned to Dallas, won a life-changing award, and subsequently made my way to Los Angeles and Hollywood. This is the record of that journey.

Part One

CHAPTER ONE

My Year in the Underground

O N SHELVES WHERE LOCAL WINES ARE SOLD, you can sometimes spot a Hill Country cabernet with the name "Iconoclast" on a label bearing the likeness of nineteenth-century Texas journalist William Brann. The vintage is an homage to Brann and the fiercely independent weekly he put out under that title in the 1890s in, of all places, Waco.

In the 1970s Brann's moniker was revived in Dallas as the banner of its "underground" newspaper, a publication that could be viewed now as an ancestor of the current *Dallas Observer*. I was its editor in 1974, during an unplanned professional detour that brought me back to my hometown, where I had been unable to get hired at the *Dallas Morning News* or *Dallas Times Herald*. I was living then in Washington, DC, and freelancing for the *Washington Star-News*, but during a Christmas visit to Dallas to see my parents, I decided to go by the *Iconoclast* offices to pick up a small check they owed me for reprinting an interview I had done with Kris Kristofferson. I also wanted to meet the editor, a man named Jay Milner, a semi-famous West Texan with a résumé that included the *New York Herald Tribune*.

The presence of Milner, who had taught journalism at Southern Methodist University (SMU), was an indication the alternative weekly was outgrowing the hippie-hugging subculture of hookahs, waterbeds, and stoner FM radio born during the social upheavals of the 1960s and early '70s. Every city had its underground paper, usually a tabloid with florid, psychedelic let-

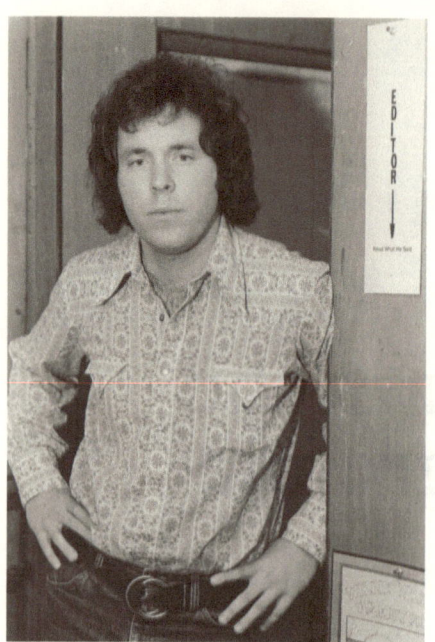

The author at 26, editor of Dallas's underground newspaper

tering on the masthead beckoning to the citizens of Woodstock nation, with articles about sex, drugs, and rock and roll, plus a helping of stick-it-to-the-man politics. During his tenure at the *Iconoclast*, Milner had de-emphasized politics in favor of chronicling the new "outlaw" movement in country music headed by Willie Nelson. *Willie who?* I thought at the time. I'd grown up in a Unitarian house full of the liberal anthems of Pete Seeger and Judy Collins, plus the peace-loving Beatles and rock and roll. Country, by contrast, belonged to the politically backward, my-country-right-or-wrong, Marine-haircut hordes that once flocked to the Big D Jamboree. Merle Haggard's flag-waving "Okie from Muskogee" kind of said it all. How Willie Nelson fit into that world or why his bearded face was on the cover of an underground paper was beyond me.

The answers were contained in a song, "Up against the Wall, Redneck Mother," written by Oak Cliff's Ray Wylie Hubbard and recorded by Jerry Jeff Walker on his contemporaneous "progressive country" breakthrough LP *Viva Terlingua*. Its lyrics about "kickin' hippies' asses and raisin' hell" were a satirical riposte to "Okie From Muskogee"; yet they acknowledged the line in the sand separating Hubbard and Walker and the readers of the *Iconoclast* from fellow citizens who saw long hair on men and beards as a threat to their way of life—an outrage that might require a stomping. When Willie, a Texan and author of honky-tonk hits for Patsy Cline and Ray Price, let his hair grow to his shoulders, left his coat and tie in Nashville, and relocated to Austin, it was clear which side of the line he was on. Cultures were colliding deep in the heart of Texas, and Milner and the *Iconoclast* were on it.

When I got to the tiny office at McKinney Avenue and Routh Street, Milner wasn't there. No one was there but Doug Baker, the wide-eyed, young publisher. He welcomed me into the clutter of the main room, layout boards crammed end to end with strips of ragged-right, camera-ready copy. Baker was a few years older than I was and projected a rumpled essence, his wrinkled dress shirt bunched at his middle and stuffed unevenly into trousers that might have belonged to a suit. His dark hair was uncombed but not particularly long for 1974. You wouldn't place him as the student radical who seven years earlier had started a rough and rowdy newspaper at SMU that was banned by university authorities. After Baker and a classmate took the paper off campus, it evolved into *Dallas Notes*, *Dallas News*, and then the *Iconoclast*.

In the paper's heyday, during the late 1960s, its offices were raided more than once by the Dallas police in search of contraband and things deemed obscene, such as sexually explicit comics. One of its early editors, Stoney Burns (real name: Brent Stein), became a local counterculture hero, taunting the authorities with his white-guy Afro, antiestablishment views, and whimsical defiance. The paper ran a full-frontal photo of a naked man dancing in a downtown parade, and the issue sold nearly ten thousand copies before being confiscated. It published a wire service story, ignored by the Dallas dailies, of the arrest of local Democratic Representative Joe Poole in DC for drunken driving. In return for such journalistic enterprise, District Attorney Henry Wade's office derided the paper's editors as "the scum of the earth" and brought obscenity charges against Burns in a case that would reach the US Supreme Court, where it was judged baseless. But the cops had the final say, arresting Burns for possession of one-eighth of an ounce of marijuana, enough at the time to get him ten years in the state penitentiary at Huntsville. Mercifully, his sentence

The Iconoclast, *May 1974*
AUTHOR COLLECTION

was commuted by Governor Dolph Briscoe, a conservative Democrat. In time, Burns left the *Iconoclast* to start the music magazine *Buddy* and later told me, "The revolution is over. We lost."

BAKER APOLOGIZED PROFUSELY FOR THE OVERSIGHT of my not being paid for the Kristofferson article and then wrote out a check for thirty-five dollars or whatever the amount was.

"How long are you going to be in town?" he asked.

He had just let Milner go over what might be termed "irreconcilable differences," and most of the staff had followed. He had a problem. "Any chance you could come back tomorrow to help us get the paper out?" He said he could pay me a hundred dollars.

This is how I became the editor of *Iconoclast*, the Weekly Newspaper of Dallas. I was planning to return to DC, clutching the faint hope of a job at the failing *Star-News*. But then this happened. I had reservations about the *Iconoclast* and wasn't sure I fit into its Zig Zag culture, but the job, I realized, would allow me to give Dallas another chance, plus put me in a position to offer my father, Gene, a gifted writer without portfolio, an opportunity to contribute columns and reviews (under a pseudonym to protect his employ-

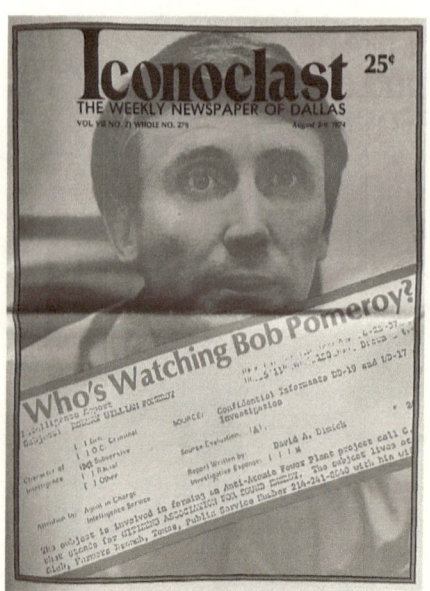

Nuclear Critic Bob Pomeroy, August 1974
AUTHOR COLLECTION

ment at the Dallas Museum of Art).

I would be taking a professional risk by signing on with such a dodgy publication, but I was running out of options, and there seemed to be no middle ground. America was choosing up sides, and, come to think of it, I had been refused service once at Goff's Hamburgers on Lovers Lane, when that proud American, Harvey Gough, noted my short beard and said, "We don't serve hippies." I eventually said yes to Baker and negotiated a salary of $150 a week, comparable to entry-level wages at the dailies. I wasn't sure what I was in for, but I was in.

When I showed up the next week to begin officially as editor, after helping craft the press release announcing my appointment, I found the office only slightly less ghostly than the

3428 McFarlin, second floor upper right, editor's apartment
AUTHOR COLLECTION

night I went by to pick up my check. One key staffer would not be returning, I was told, because he had "gone on the road with Billy Joe Shaver," whatever that meant. An ad salesman had quit, something barely worthy of mention on any given day. On the premises were a receptionist, Pat, who was Doug's wife, and Danny, the production manager and art director. Neither was very cheery nor said much, but their weary expressions carried the message: So, you're the next guy? Milner had been there less than a year; I wasn't sure who preceded him.

Pat and Doug lived in a room behind the main office, amid the back issues and printing paraphernalia. Pat was not thrilled by this cost-saving stratagem, while Doug told me proudly that he lived on forty dollars a week and didn't see why everyone else couldn't do the same, evidence that he was walking the walk of anti-consumerism. He offered me his old one-bedroom apartment on McFarlin Boulevard, near SMU, as part of the editor's package, and I took it. The rent was a hundred dollars a month.

Danny, who oversaw all the artwork and layout, was also in his twenties and, like everyone else at the *Iconoclast*, a refugee from the status quo and dedicated to overturning it. But his overriding concern, I soon learned, was the Kennedy assassination—and the many theories contradicting the official truth that Lee Harvey Oswald had been the lone gunman. The assassination was a unifying topic at the paper and served as a distraction from the daily grind of putting out a muckraking tabloid every week in an unfriendly environment, i.e., Dallas.

Like Doug, Danny exuded paranoia and spoke in a clenched whisper that seemed a sign of fatigue but also reflected an effort not to be overheard, especially if he was discussing the assassination. After one production night that ended, as always, close to dawn, we were seated at the counter of a diner, talking about you know what, when he turned, looked me in the eye, and said softly, "Keep your voice down," nodding in the direction of a stranger sitting by himself a few stools away. The *Iconoclast* had run multiple stories debunking the Warren Commission Report (as Congress would do a few years later), and Danny believed that undercover agents were watching us and possibly had even infiltrated the paper. At one point, he confided to me that he wondered if I might be such an agent. Which possibly affected our rapport.

Although I shared his and Doug's doubt that Oswald had acted alone, to me the idea that our little paper, with no full-time reporters and circulation of a few thousand, could find out what really happened in Dallas on November 22, 1963, was beyond quixotic. We had enough trouble just trying to cover city council meetings.

The office was chaotic, a walk-in clubhouse for lefties and assorted grievance bearers seeking an audience, plus music promoters and the occasional musician. The great guitar stylist David Bromberg walked in one day to publicize his appearance at a Dallas club, and I interviewed him without getting up from my desk. One book reviewer who specialized in philosophy held court regularly. We got academics and poets in sunglasses and athletes who had just discovered the night before they were destined to write a column. The burly leader of the Bois d'Arc Patriots, a community organizing group, barged in one evening and threatened to tear up the office if we didn't do a story about affordable housing in East Dallas. Gene the Wino sat around explaining how some of Dallas's most prominent families were using electronic equipment to monitor his brainwaves.

Meanwhile, there was a lot of work to do and not enough people to do it. We relied on strangers walking in the door with an edgy or outrageous story that would not get a hearing in the mainstream media—like the massage parlor worker who had written a tell-all account about exactly what went on there ("For twenty-five dollars extra, I'll use my mouth") and the airline pilot who brought evidence he was being spied on and harassed for his public opposition to the nuclear power plant being built at Comanche

Peak, southwest of Dallas. We went inside a Dallas swingers club and published letters from a Mexican jail sent by a young gringo claiming he had been framed for drug possession in an extortion scheme. As a tabloid, we needed eye-catching or sensational cover stories like this every week, and I tried not to care that some of them might not qualify as classroom material at the Columbia School of Journalism.

I was writing some of these stories and unsure if, at twenty-six, I was developing my skills as a journalist or being held prisoner in the office of an underground newspaper. The pressure to come up with enough copy every week was punishing, plus I had to manage the freelancers and pull an all-nighter every Tuesday getting the paper out. All this left me little time to think of ways we were going to turn the *Iconoclast* into the *Village Voice* of Dallas, the recurring mantra heard in the office.

Maybe the revolution was over, but the paper's history of persecution by the authorities was not, it appeared. One day a documented FBI informer and agent provocateur showed up to sell ads. Danny recognized his face from photos the *Iconoclast* had run during the trial of "the Gainesville Eight" two years earlier in Florida, where our would-be ad salesman had testified as the government's chief witness against a Vietnam Veterans Against the War group he had infiltrated and tried to goad into violence. It was hard to believe the government cared about the humble *Iconoclast*, but on some level this FBI agent trying to come on staff proved that Doug's and Danny's paranoia was not entirely unfounded. And caused me to wonder, yet again, what had I gotten myself into.

With Milner gone, I had picked up the story of Willie Nelson as best I could, recognizing the progressive country movement as something authentic and new that an alternative weekly could cover better than the dailies. Willie had become a guitar-plucking, weed-puffing sage and shaman, and when his next three-day, star-studded "picnic" arrived in July, staged on the grounds of a raceway near College Station, I went down with a pack of correspondents to document it. Not long after we arrived and were making our way toward the music along with other celebrants, we passed two parked cars on fire, thick black smoke wafting into the cloudless sky. Oddly no one was doing anything about it, as if the cars were just a ritual sacrifice at this tribal rite for long-haired Texans worshiping under the death rays of a midsummer sun. We devoted most of an issue to the event and ran a cover photograph of the crowd, featuring a bare-breasted young woman atop a man's shoulders, her arms raised triumphantly toward the heavens. Ron McKeown, who snapped pictures for the US Army in Vietnam, took the photograph.

With national political columns by Jack Anderson, Ralph Nader, and Nicholas von Hoffman, plus arts reviews and articles by young SMU professors and future media mainstays David Dillon, Glenn Mitchell, and Rod Davis, the *Iconoclast* in a given week offered an entertaining, alternative view of the arts and current events not available in the *News* and *Herald*. But in 1974 Dallas, that was not enough—not enough to pay the bills, anyway.

It cost a quarter and was available in coin boxes around the city and from street vendors, but the circulation figure was anyone's guess, somewhere south of the ten thousand Baker liked to quote, always mentioning the "pass-on rate" when anyone questioned the number. Doug and I shared the goal of wanting the paper to "make it" but not the same vision of how to get there. Doug was a good soul and earnest to a fault but uncomfortable with the humor and satire I thought gave readers another reason to pick up a copy. There was often tension between us, and when my paychecks started to bounce, I wondered how long I could stick with him. Ever the thick-skinned businessman, he would nonchalantly instruct me to wait a day and try depositing my check again.

He had found a few liberal benefactors to help him over the humps, and at least one of them was unhappy we were not breaking big stories of scandal and political corruption. True enough, but we lacked the resources such stories required. We could review X-rated movies and print Jerry Jeff Walker's profane answers to interview questions, but we were not going to expose the hidden power of the oil industry—not paying fifty cents a column inch.

Taffy Cannon, a future novelist from Chicago, walked into the office one day offering to contribute her observations about cherished Dallas institutions such as debutante balls and gun shows. She was talented, and, after a few spec pieces, I convinced Doug to put her on staff at a minimum salary. Reluctantly he agreed, but then her paychecks started to bounce as well.

I hesitated to leave because it would mean Dad having to give up the anonymous column he was writing (for free) with such pleasure and skill, skewering the *Dallas News*, Nixon, religious zealots, management consultants, and other targets that H. L. Mencken would have found worthy. Ah, well. Owed several weeks back pay at the end of August, I submitted my resignation.

A few years later, director Joan Micklin Silver (who had worked at the *Village Voice*) made a lovely film about an alternative weekly called *Between the Lines*, with John Heard, Lindsay Crouse, and Jeff Goldblum as the rock critic. It was set in Boston but looked charmingly familiar to me and I'm sure to anyone who ever worked at a paper like this. Removed from real-life deadlines, drudgery, and economic pressures, an underground newspaper could look noble, romantic, and even fun on film. Which I took to be proof that the brain manages not to remember some forms of pain.

I kept the apartment on McFarlin, an upstairs one-bedroom in what had been a roomy Spanish Revival house, with an outdoor entry through a white stuccoed arch leading to a set of paved stairs and a Monterey-style balcony. When a new landlord bought the property, the rent doubled, to two hundred dollars, but it was still a bargain. I would live there for another seven years and remain ever grateful to Doug Baker for making that possible.

CHAPTER TWO

Accidental Texan

ONE SUMMER AFTERNOON WHEN I WAS FIVE OR
SIX—it must have been a Saturday—I came into the house to
make an announcement. I'd just been next door playing on the
neighbors' St. Augustine grass with Connie, whose dad's name was Wookie.
They were from East Texas.

"It's fixin' to rain," I said.

My father's face tightened, his eyes squinting, as if in pain. "What did
you say?" he said.

"It's fixin' to rain. Wookie said it's fixin' to rain."

"We don't talk like that."

It was an early indication to me that we were different, that I was different from the other kids in our Oak Cliff neighborhood. I never again said
"it's fixin' to rain" or that anyone anywhere was fixin' to do anything.

My parents, Eugene and Lucille, had come to Texas knowing not a
soul and only what they had read in a 1948 issue of *Holiday* magazine tout-
ing the shiny promise of Dallas and Houston. They spoke an unmistakably
nonlocal dialect that could be traced to the steel town of Bethlehem, Pennsylvania, where they were born and raised and where I was also born in that
same year of 1948.

Bethlehem is eighty miles west of New York City, and my dad's parents
had moved there in 1912, one year after emigrating from Liverpool, England,

to Brooklyn. A first generation American of Anglo-Irish descent, my father had grown up poor but attentive to the English language and its proper usage, as if his own father had been Henry Higgins instead of a tradesman from the docklands of Liverpool. He even used the word "proper" in its British locution to describe something genuine, as in "a proper meal" or "a proper vacation." Not something you hear Texans say.

Dad had contemplated San Francisco and Vancouver as possible destinations when planning our escape from the Lehigh Valley. But my mother hated the Pennsylvania winters and wanted someplace warm. Both my parents had grown up the children of working-class immigrants in Bethlehem, but they were not happy there, trapped in lowly jobs in a one-industry town, crowded by their extended families and pinched by parochialism. They were meant for something different.

They met at the Bethlehem Civic Theater one evening in 1944 when my mother, only a few years out of high school, walked into the old brewery building downtown to audition for a play being directed by my dad. She often recalled the moment: He was straddling a chair turned 180 degrees, his short, thick arms stretched forward over the back. He was seven years older.

"Have you done any acting?" he asked her.

The answer was no, and what she didn't tell him was that her father, a crane operator at the Steel, had forbid her from coming here to try out. She was still living at home and had to sneak out of the house. The play was *Double Door*, a now-forgotten melodrama with a role for an ingenue. She got the part.

Gene and Lu at the Bethlehem Civic Theater
AUTHOR COLLECTION

"That opened up a whole new world to me," my mother said. "The people from the theatre were interesting and different, and after rehearsals we'd all go to the Hotel Bethlehem bar. It was wonderful. I think that was the happiest time in my life."

Lucille and Eugene fell in love working together in the theatre in those last years of World War II. Dad missed the war, exempted from military service as the sole provider for his mother, Rose, and two younger siblings. That role fell to him after his father, George, a luckless painter and paperhanger with a drinking problem, disappeared one day when Dad was a senior in high school.

"He couldn't help himself," my mother said about George. "He was an alcoholic. It was a disease.

Marriage, 1946 | AUTHOR COLLECTION

He would drink up his paycheck and come home with nothing. When your dad was sixteen, just graduated from high school, he said, 'I'll do it. I'll take care of the family.' And he went and got a job in the office at the Steel. Then Gerry was able to go to college and Ron, too." (Dad's younger siblings.)

Mom's family on her mother's side had come from Ireland in the 1850s. But her dad's family, the Reisers, were German Hungarian farmers who immigrated through Ellis Island just after the turn of the century. They were lured by Bethlehem Steel, which advertised in Europe that it needed workers and welcomed immigrants.

My parents and their siblings, who struggled through the Great Depression as kids, were the first generation in their families to get a step up the ladder from the bottom later in their lives, lifted by the general prosperity of the United States after the war and maybe some underutilized brainpower. My dad, who should have gone to college and would have done so given the opportunity, continued to support his mother in the wake of Germany's surrender in May 1945. He had sacrificed his own future and become a hero to his younger sister, Geraldine, and brother, Ronald, keeping a roof over their heads after their dad disappeared.

A Signpost to Texas: Holiday *Magazine 1948*
AUTHOR COLLECTION

To marry my mother in 1946, my dad was forced to convert (or revert, in a sense) to Catholicism, as under the rules of the church she was not allowed to marry a non-Catholic. Still, they were denied a ceremony in the church and had to settle for the priest's chambers. When I came along, I was given the Gaelic name for John, an indication of my parents' sympathies in the matter of ethnic heritage.

As the Civic Theater's co-director, Dad had to take time off from work occasionally to attend to theater business, which drew disapproval from his bosses and led to his quitting the Steel after thirteen years. Briefly he took a job for which he was totally unsuited, selling modified highchairs called Babee Tendas door-to-door in the coal regions north of Bethlehem. That did not work out well, and one afternoon while waiting for a woman's husband to come home from the mines and approve a sale, he stopped at a drugstore and saw on the news stand that issue of *Holiday* magazine with the word "Texas" on the cover in an Old West font over a drawing of a gushing oil well surrounded by saddles, steers, an armadillo, and dollar signs. He took it home.

My parents had been living in a house with Rose, which strained relations between my mother and her mother-in-law and likely hastened our departure. The year was 1949. The Mitchells were dispersing from Bethlehem. Gerry had recently married an engineer from Lehigh and would move with him to Toledo, Ohio, taking Rose with them. Ron was back from the Navy and enrolled at Lehigh on the GI Bill. George was still at large, whereabouts unknown. I had just learned to walk, making it easier for my parents to finally get up and go.

Dallas it was, and Dad went first, by Greyhound. Once he found a tiny house to buy amid the postwar housing shortage, Mom and I followed a few weeks later, making the drive south with her parents, Tony and Margaret, in Tony's late model black DeSoto. It was said that I stood up in the back seat the whole way, keen to take in the scenery. No one had yet heard of car seats or even seat belts.

My mother's family was not happy with this turn of events. "They were horrified," Mom recalled. "Such crying. Everybody was crying." None of the Reisers or their progeny had ever moved away from Bethlehem, let alone to a distant sun-scorched frontier. "They thought it was just cowboys and rattlesnakes."

As Tony and Margaret got into their car for the return trip home to Pennsylvania, they bid a tearful goodbye to their daughter and first grandchild and offered a knowing prediction: "You'll be back." But Eugene and Lucille never went back, except on occasion to visit. And so it was that I grew up an accidental Texan, with the sound of the Lone Star state in my ears but my own voice descended from Yankees.

CHAPTER THREE

Chance Encounter

C HOOSING TEXAS WAS NOT THE FIRST OR LAST TIME MOM GOT HER WAY, but "someplace warm" hardly described the hundred-degree temperatures that greeted us on arrival in Dallas in July 1949. I was eighteen months old and have no recollection of this, but my mother told me later that she had to sleep naked with a wet towel draped over her in those first weeks in Big D sans air-conditioning.

The house Dad had found was on Exeter Street in South Oak Cliff and cost $5,000. It was two bedrooms and 750 square feet, all wood, with a single car garage and a nub of a concrete front step where I would sit and wait for him to come home from work. He took the bus until he could afford to buy a used Studebaker. His first job was selling ties at a men's store downtown called Reynolds Penland. During these lean years, a callous hiring boss looked at his thin résumé and told him, "You don't have much to offer, Mr. Mitchell." Which my father never forgot or forgave and later repeated to me as a lesson in understanding the cold, hard reality of the working world.

"There were nights waiting for your father to come home," my mother remembered, "when I was lonely, and I wondered if we had done the right thing. But I was not going back. I thought, *we will make it here*."

Dad did get on at the local Coca-Cola Bottling Company in accounting, but we needed a second income, and after a year Mom found a secretarial job with Lone Star Gas. I was sent to Tiny Tot Nursery School in Oak Cliff, located in a two-story house in an older neighborhood. The proprietor was a large, benign but stern woman who had fleshy upper arms that sagged with reddish, scaly skin. My mental images of that place are hazy, but I know one day I wasn't feeling well, and I had to go into her office, pull down my pants, and bend over so she could take my temperature with a rectal thermometer. The way things were done at the time. Dad would arrive to pick me up after leaving work. I'm not sure how Mom got home.

Oak Cliff was "dry," meaning no liquor sold or served in its environs, at least publicly (thanks to the prohibitions of the Southern Baptist Church), but my parents were years away from having wine with dinner. And we rarely ate out. My mother took me for lunch sometimes to Piggly Wiggly, a pre-Denny's kind of place where I always ordered a peanut butter and jelly sandwich.

Every year in October, when it was still hot, we attended the carnival-like State Fair of Texas with its midway of amusement rides, arcade games, and food booths. I scarfed corny dogs and billowing cones of pink spun sugar known as cotton candy while gazing up at the wonder of Big Tex, a fifty-two-foot likeness of a cowboy dressed in oversized Lee Jeans and a pearl-buttoned Western shirt. His jaw dropped open mechanically to bark the word "Howdy" through a PA system. When you're four years old, that's exciting.

After the move to Dallas, Gene and Lu had to let go of their interest in the theatre. Making ends meet while raising a boy took all their time and energy. Their social life consisted of the occasional evening spent with couples they had met at the local Catholic church in Oak Cliff. Once, for a variety show at the church they adapted a Dorothy Parker short story, which they rehearsed often enough at home that I learned every word apparently and recited it back to them one night, to their surprise. While the three of us were

Getting an early start. | Author Collection

Christmas shopping downtown

at Sanger-Harris, a newspaper photographer snapped a photo of me as a tyke in overalls reaching up to grab a toy on a counter, and the picture ran on the front page of the *Morning News* the next day. Another time, I wandered off from Gene and Lu in a department store and got lost. Mother would often tell this story as her version of every parent's nightmare. But the nightmare didn't last long, and we were somehow reunited before either of us had a breakdown.

Contemplating the meaning of Big Tex
AUTHOR COLLECTION

Dad would get invited to watch the Friday night fights on TV (in black-and-white) with the guys from church at someone's home, and he would sometimes take me along. The boxing was a blur, but I noticed the men all drinking longneck bottles of beer, an early indication that sports and liquor went together.

One afternoon when Connie and I were playing together outside, my mother called me in for my bath. I didn't want to stop playing and asked if Connie could come in and take a bath with me. "NO" came back the emphatic answer from my mother. I deduced there was something wrong with my innocent request, but it was not explained. Around this time, I asked my father what it was about certain women that made Bob Hope start rolling his eyes and panting on TV? I had no idea. This also was not explained.

In 1954, five years after getting to town, things began to change for us. Dad improbably managed to land a job at the Dallas Museum of Fine Arts, Mom took her secretarial skills to the southwestern headquarters of the Eastman Kodak Company near Love Field (then the main airport), and we left Oak Cliff for a better house in Farmers Branch, at the other end of the city. The sequence of these three events is not clear.

Dad had begun taking business classes at SMU's night school downtown to help him with his job at Coca-Cola, and in one of those classes he

Gene and Hermes at Lee Park circa 1955,
with sculptor Heri Bartscht and wife, Waltraud

met a man who would make a big difference in our lives. The man's name was Hermes Nye. His wife, Mary Beasley Nye, had ties to Dallas society and worked as a volunteer at the art museum. Her family owned Whittle Music, a leading music store, where Hermes was being groomed to become an executive—the reason he was taking an accounting class. The Nyes were cultured.

Hermes was a lawyer, but his real love was literature and folk music, made evident the first time we went for dinner at their modest one-story house overlooking Lee Park in Oak Lawn. They happened to have a son my age named Eric, who became a frequent weekend playmate and later a classmate and soccer teammate at St. Mark's. Hermes, who was balding and self-consciously dramatic, with large, searching eyes, got out his guitar and played a few of the old Texas ballads he was collecting and recording for Folkways Records, capturing my mother's attention immediately and planting a vision in her head of something she might want to try herself.

Mary knew about the opening for a business manager at the museum and recommended Dad to director Jerry Bywaters, who eventually hired him after what Mom remembered as an agonizing wait that stretched on for months. Dad did not yet have a college degree, but Bywaters, himself an accomplished painter, possibly credited his background in the theatre or sensed his innate intelligence. It was a different time, Dallas in the 1950s, when everything was wide open. But being recommended by the Nyes no doubt counted for a lot.

My father's glee in getting the job is evident in a letter he wrote to his mother: "This comes as a tremendous relief to me because my jobs in Dallas have not given me cause to rejoice." He proudly enclosed a picture of the museum, housed in a beautiful and stately Art Deco building in Fair Park, the city's first cultural district.

The museum, to a kid, was an enchanted kingdom to be explored, its massive limestone walls and heavy bronzed doors holding in a magical quiet that rose all the way up to the highest ceiling I had ever seen. At the end of the main hall, immediately visible when you came in the front entrance was "El Hombre," a towering modern mural by the Mexican artist Rufino Tamayo that introduced me to the idea of artistic abstraction. The museum's basement was huge and dark, a mysterious repository of dusty crates and boxes—all the art not on display. Sometimes I got to go down there on the freight elevator with Dad or Will Petway, the kindly Black janitor who gave me rides on his hand truck and bought me soft drinks at a machine in the lobby. "You want a Pepper?" he would say before putting a nickel in the machine. Of course, I did, not even knowing that Dr Pepper was a local company, its manufacturing plant only miles away.

I also got to know Teddy, the museum guard, a heavyset white guy with close-cropped red hair and the squared-off handle of a .45 automatic poking out of a holster on the belt that cinched his bulging middle. When I got older, I heard Dad express the fear that Teddy was going to shoot somebody one day.

I was able to take art classes for free on Saturday mornings. Mom did as well, learning mosaic technique with the soon-to-be famous Mexican American sculptor Octavio Medellin. On Saturday mornings the three of us would drive to Fair Park, and Dad would work half a day. When classes were over at noon, we shared potluck lunches with Octavio and his students or stopped at a deli on the way home. Dad loved dried "summer sausage," and at the time, you could get it only at a certain delicatessen in North Dallas.

During the week, if I had a day off from school, Dad would take me with him to the museum, stopping first to pick up the mail at the Fair Park Station post office. It came in a big bundle, bound with string or a thick rubber band, and once in the car, he let me search through the clump of fliers and announcements from galleries and museums for the latest issue of *Sports Illustrated* that for some reason was often in there, like the prize in a Cracker Jax box.

CHAPTER FOUR

The Branch

WHY WE MOVED TO FARMERS BRANCH REMAINS A MYSTERY. The desire to get out of Oak Cliff and to the better side of the river might have been a factor, accelerated by politics: the Oak Cliff Catholics expressed their disapproval of Dad going to work for an institution that was exhibiting the work of communist artists like Diego Rivera and Ben Shahn, and that was all it took to end those friendships. There's the dimly remembered notion of a Kodak salesman with a wife who was a real estate agent pushing the Branch, one of the area's first postwar housing developments. We played our part in the making of suburbia, but Farmers Branch was not convenient to either Fair Park or Love Field.

The new house was the first address I ever memorized: 13010 Holbrook. One-three-oh-one-oh. It was a faintly modern one-story wooden ranch (three bedrooms, one bath, slab foundation), built on land that had previously been cotton fields. There were still crops growing just across the road at the end of the block, and after a thunderstorm you could smell the freshly plowed earth giving off a rich, fecund odor. The house is gone now, replaced by a motley two-story brick Tudor mutation, but in the 1950s it was our home for three years, the place where I started Catholic school, had a group of friends on the street, got bitten in the thigh by a neighbor's collie, and was terrified at the prospect of having to get rabies shots in my stomach. Which never happened.

A Texas welcome to the house on Holbrook

The biggest fear for parents in the first half of the 1950s was the polio virus that spread mysteriously, crippling children for life. I knew Gene and Lu worried about it until Jonas Salk's vaccine was released in 1955. Mom also worried about me getting ringworm from resting my head on the back of the seat in a movie theater and cautioned me not to do that.

TELEVISION! THE BLACK-AND-WHITE TV SET WAS IN THE "DEN" (the third bedroom) beside a built-in bookcase holding a fresh edition of the *Encyclopedia Britannica* that Dad had proudly purchased. Together with my parents I watched *Playhouse 90, Gunsmoke, Perry Mason, Your Hit Parade*, and *Your Show of Shows* with Sid Caesar; by myself I watched *Spin and Marty, Sky King*, and *The Cisco Kid* on Saturday mornings, bracketed by commercials for Kellogg's Frosted Flakes featuring the cartoonish Tony the Tiger growling "They'rrre great!" On weekday afternoons I sat in front of *The Mickey Mouse Club* and the first years of *American Bandstand*, coming from Philadelphia.

I was also smitten by baseball, learning its rules and customs from the *Saturday Game of the Week*, narrated by the irrepressible Dizzy Dean and another former St. Louis Cardinal, Buddy Blatner (later replaced by Pee Wee Reese). One of the first country songs I ever heard was Dizzy warbling "The Wabash Cannon Ball" during a rain delay. I watched intently and became a Yankees fan because they were good and often on TV, plus they had an all-star switch-hitting center fielder from Oklahoma named Mickey Mantle. Dad, being from back east, knew all about their history. When he was a teenager in the 1930s, he swept the floors at a cigar store in Bethlehem where the owner allowed him to see the latest baseball scores coming in on a tickertape and then write them on a chalkboard for the customers.

I imagined myself becoming a major leaguer one day, maybe a Yankee, though I was picking up signals from Gene and Lu that it would have to be coupled with another job, like being an architect or an engineer.

I was too young to feel the impact of Elvis, but I remember when he was on *The Ed Sullivan Show* and grownups talking about him shaking his hips as he played the guitar. Which I didn't understand any more than I understood Bob Hope's jokes about "broads." My parents didn't seem interested one way or the other and avoided any talk about sex.

Shane was the first movie that grabbed me, as the melodramas of Hollywood are designed to do. As a kid, it was easy to be enthralled by a mysterious loner whose gunfighting skills rescue homesteaders from a murderous, predatory cattle baron. Good versus Evil 101. For days afterward I reenacted the last scene of the film in the backyard, crying "Shane! Shane!" just like Brandon deWilde did up on the screen, imploring Alan Ladd to come back and protect us forever from evildoers. The oil business saga of *Giant* was not as affecting, but the fact that it was set in Texas filled me with pride in the place where I was growing up, as did the theme song, "This Then Is Texas," whose lyrics I can still sing. *Just like a sleeping giant / Sprawling in the sun / In one great hand the Rio Grande / in the other Galveston . . .*

The night before I started first grade, we went as a family to see *The High and the Mighty* at the Delman on Lemmon (now gone, like so many old theaters). It starred John Wayne as a courageous copilot with a past who helps land a damaged commercial airliner in San Francisco after a stormy, harrowing flight. I would later cringe at John Wayne's big screen machismo and one-note acting, as well as his knee-jerk patriotism, but that night before I started first grade, he was a hero.

Davy Crockett became an alter ego, based on the eponymous Walt Disney TV show. All my buddies on Holbrook and I had coonskin caps that we wore while reenacting Fess Parker's daring exploits on "the wild frontier," fighting hostile Indians, bears, and bad guys. We took turns shooting each other with toy guns in our backyards and keeling over like they did on TV. From the film *The Alamo* (directed by John Wayne) we learned that Davy perished at the San Antonio mission with all the other freedom-loving Texans overpowered by the bloodthirsty Mexican Army under the command of the villainous general Santa Anna. It was an early lesson in the power of propaganda.

AT THE SMALL TOWN & COUNTRY PRIVATE SCHOOL NEAR LOVE FIELD, there were just two class levels, kindergarten and first grade, and I attended both before moving on to spend second, third, and fourth grades with the nuns at St. Monica Catholic school on Walnut Hill Lane. I had my first communion and confirmation there, but the indoctrination didn't take (unless you consider that I can still recite a "Hail Mary"). We were instructed in the Baltimore Catechism of Christian dogma, which even at this tender age I had questions about. I recall asking a nun, in black robe and white habit, to explain some liturgical detail that didn't make sense to me, and she responded, "That's a supernatural mystery." An answer that explained nothing.

In third grade I was selected to join a small group of kids in the class bused downtown to the public library weekly to take part in a creative writing program, about which I remember very little other than it happened. Ironically, my first prepubescent sexual thought occurred in fourth grade while seated in the pews of the St. Monica Chapel during confession (yes, we were confessing our sins at age nine). As the girls walked back down the aisles after their private session with the priest, I noticed their chests were different; the top half of their plaid jumpers showed small mounds underneath. I hadn't noticed that before. It seemed like a good thing.

It was on the playground at St. Monica that I witnessed my first fight—two Hispanic boys in a furious clench. One was crouched with his right arm extended between the other guy's legs, his upturned hand and fingers making pincer movements toward his opponent's genitals. Yes, in elementary school! One day at recess, a boy asked me if I wanted to play football, and when I declined, he called me a sissy. I had to ask my father later what the word meant. I was already losing my innocence. This was a snapshot of the world that was waiting for me.

With both my parents working, I would get a ride home from school each day via the carpool and be in the house by myself for a couple hours. I thought nothing of it, and there were other kids and adults in the neighborhood. One such weekday in April 1957, I was home alone after school watching *The Mickey Mouse Club* when local news bulletins broke in with reports of a tornado on the ground in Dallas. It was moving northeast from Oak Cliff, through West Dallas and aimed in the direction of Farmers Branch. My parents were frantic, trying to race home, but the roads were clogged with other cars doing the same. I had already heard the advice on TV to get into the tub in the bathroom and pull a mattress over my head. I was trying to figure how I was going to do that when the TV said the twister had lifted back up into the sky. It had been on the ground for forty minutes, destroyed or damaged almost five hundred buildings, and left ten people dead. But it never reached Farmers Branch. Personal tragedy averted, not that I could appreciate the relief my parents expressed when they got home. I was too young to be properly scared.

CHAPTER FIVE

Eric Lane

MONTH AFTER THE TORNADO, WE MOVED A HALF A
MILE EAST TO A NEW HOME IN FARMERS BRANCH,
located in a nothing-fancy development nevertheless called
Valley View Estates. The building permit for the house is dated July 31,
1956, and we moved in nine months later. A variation on the ubiquitous
earth-hugging ranch homes that spread across the blackland prairie of
Dallas and environs after World War II, the houses on our block were budget examples of what would later be called mid-century modern, a sleek
and pared-down style that notably lacked the purely decorative window
shutters so common to the ranches in the neighborhood. Our house instead had nearly floor-to-ceiling panels of glass on sections of the front
and back, with ribbons of aluminum-framed casement windows at the top
of the bedroom walls.

Three bedrooms, two baths, a prominent fireplace that opened on two
sides, hardwood floors, and an electric galley kitchen with a "pass-through"—
all of it coming in at a tidy 1,479 square feet and priced at $19,500. A classi-
fied ad in the *Morning News* in September of 1956 described it as a "Brand
New Contemporary," highlighting the "12-ft. sliding glass doors overlooking
large diamond-shaped patio."

"He got the plans from California," my mother later said about Gail
Ladd, the young contractor with the androgynous name who built the house,

one of eight he did on the block. (She also told me years later he was handsome and made a pass at her.)

The Dallas architect Philip Henderson, whose wife had worked at the museum with Dad, once told me he thought Gene and Lu might have been influenced by visits to Bywaters' house, a flat-roofed single-story gem near SMU created by the most famous of all Texas modernist architects, O'Neil Ford.

The expanse of sliding glass doors embodied the modernist aesthetic of eliminating the barrier separating indoors and outdoors, but the idea was inspired by the Mediterranean climate of coastal California and didn't work so well in North Texas, especially in the furnace heat of summer. Even with central air conditioning, the house got so hot sometimes that Dad would train a sprinkler on the sliding glass doors to cool them off. And forget about using the patio for dining or entertaining. Not until my parents put in a pool many years later could they really use the backyard except for brief stretches of spring and fall.

As was de rigueur, we had lawns of Bermuda grass in front and back that I mowed once a week with a gasoline-powered mower to earn my two-dollar allowance. The smell of fresh cut grass still triggers pleasant thoughts of being out of school, finishing my elementary landscaping chore, and being rewarded with a tall glass of iced tea. My parents, inexperienced at horticulture, at first planted Mimosa trees on the lawns. They must have been cheap. They grew fast but offered scant shade and were easily damaged by my attempts to climb them.

A midcentury modern couple at Eric Lane
AUTHOR COLLECTION

I was still at St. Monica and doing well in class, but I was not happy with the nuns and the rigid discipline they imposed. One night at dinner I must have said as much because Gene and Lu, revealing their tepid ties to the church, asked me, "Would you rather go to public school?" "Yes!" I answered immediately. We were in the Carrollton-Farmers Branch School District, so the next fall, I entered fifth grade at Valwood Elementary, a newly constructed single story horizontal building about a mile distant, on the other side of plowed fields that I sometimes crossed to walk home.

Mr. Shipman, a sallow and simple-faced man, was my teacher in the fifth grade;

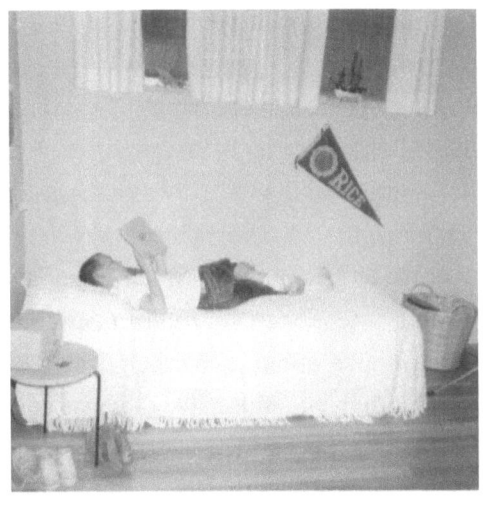

It was a quiet house | AUTHOR COLLECTION

he wore white short-sleeved shirts, frequently with a clip-on bow tie. In the sixth grade I had a smart, strong woman, Mrs. Perry, who commuted from University Park. It was the height of the Cold War, and we had occasional air raid drills, sheltering under our desks as instructed (as if that would protect us from an atomic bomb blast).

I don't remember the offense, but I misbehaved once with a couple other boys and was sent to principal Montgomery's office to be paddled. He was a slim, unthreatening young administrator with slicked-back dark hair who seemed to be bound by duty more than conviction in carrying out our sentence. He offered a few words of opprobrium, then ordered each of us to stand and turn around so that he could deliver two whacks to our backsides with a narrow wooden paddle. He didn't swing that hard, and it didn't hurt much but I might have cried from the embarrassment and sense of guilt. From nuns to corporal punishment.

One of my first memories of Valwood Elementary was a blonde-haired boy in my class named James who introduced me to the word "cum," in a sexual context I only vaguely understood. I also heard that certain girls were "whores," and I tried to reckon with that thought. Sex was still an abstraction but an unavoidable one. By sixth grade, kids were pairing off and "going steady," sometimes even exchanging rings. I got my first girlfriend. Her name was Kathy Houseman, and we sometimes went to movie matinees at the Plaza in Carrollton on Saturday afternoons. I would dare to put my arm on the back of her seat. That was the extent of our intimacy, but I began to associate these early stirrings of physical attraction with songs on the radio like "All I Have to Do Is Dream" by the Everly Brothers.

In the sixth grade, I was chosen to edit the class newsletter, though I can't imagine what news it contained. I remember another, illicit bit of media called a "slam book," which circulated away from the eyes of Mrs. Perry. It was a notebook full of rude and unkind comments class members penned anonymously about each other. I guess it was supposed to be funny, but you wonder that something like that was going on in the sixth grade in Farmers Branch in 1960.

Farmers Branch offered me a glimpse of small-town Texas, even then being swallowed up by the encroaching "Metroplex." While a student at Valwood Elementary, I was introduced to the pageantry and glory of Texas high school football, attending the nearby Carrollton High games on Friday nights, cheering for the Lions and thrilled that their star running back (no. 30) had the name Clint Mitchell. After one victory, I made my way onto the field of thinning autumn-browned grass and caught up with him as he headed for the locker room. He towered above me, sweat streaming down his face, and I shouted my congratulations upward, adding, "My name is Mitchell, too!" I don't recall his response. I think it was brief.

I discovered the sports section of the newspaper and started reading columnists like Bud Shrake, Blackie Sherrod, and Dan Jenkins who had a flair for storytelling and description. Their columns matched my growing interest in sports—baseball, football, tennis, and golf. When the telephone book-sized Sears catalogue arrived, I would take it to my room and stare at the sets of junior golf clubs (and later at the women's underwear section).

To broaden my reading, Dad ordered a monthly subscription to the "We Were There" (at the Oregon Trail, etc.) series, plus Random House's "All About" (Rockets and Jets, etc.) books. I read *Thirty Seconds over Tokyo* and decided to compose my first two-page "novel" I called "The 50th Mission," doubtless cribbed from the earlier title and countless World War II flyboy movies. On a sheet of 8½ by 11 typing paper, folded in half sideways, I drew, with crayons, a dramatic cover of a B-25 bomber headed downward with flames coming out of the engines.

These were latchkey summers, with many of us unsupervised all day while our parents were at work. Mom left me a frozen TV dinner to heat up in the oven every day for lunch. When it was too hot to be outside, we retreated to air-conditioning, often seated on the beige wall-to-wall carpeting at our house, playing Monopoly or Hearts while listening to the cast albums of *My Fair Lady* and *West Side Story*—the first LPs my parents bought for the new cabinet-sized stereo. We didn't think to compare these show tunes to the doo-wop and rock and roll on the radio. It was just music and sounded great. I don't think we watched much daytime television, which was not programmed for kids. I designed a table-top baseball game, using a pencil for the bat, a marble for the ball, and building blocks to stand in for position players. I drew the playing field with crayons on brown wrapping paper.

In the evenings, when it was slightly cooler, we played hide-and-seek under the streetlamps and included the neighborhood girls (who were excluded from baseball pre–Title IX). We also rode our bikes up and down the street, attaching baseball cards to the wheel forks so that they flapped against the rotating spokes and made an ersatz muffler sound. Proof we were cool.

CHAPTER SIX

Modern Living

I T WAS A QUIET HOUSE WITH JUST THE THREE OF US. After Mom took up the guitar, she would practice and play albums to learn songs, but the radio was rarely on. (There was no NPR yet.) We watched the half-hour evening news with Walter Cronkite on CBS or *The Huntley-Brinkley Report* on NBC and then sat down to dinner at 6 p.m., except for the nights Dad had a class, when Mom would pick me up from school and stop at the Dobbs House diner on Royal for burgers and a slice of black-bottom pie, my favorite dessert. Otherwise, she had to whip up something quick and easy after getting home from the office at 5:30. She was not an avid cook, and Dad didn't cook at all. Sometimes we had frozen TV dinners of turkey or "Salisbury Steak," which was hamburger sloshed with a brown sauce. I also remember her frying pork chops, served with instant white rice; hot dogs and sauerkraut; boiled rutabagas, a mysterious (to me) vegetable that Dad loved, as he did the inexpensive Pennsylvania Dutch throwback of Scrapple, a mush of pork scraps and cornmeal fried in a pan.

Those first years on Eric Lane we often ate meals at "the bar," seated in a line on wooden stools and staring straight ahead into the kitchen. This was considered modern living: being able to serve and retrieve food directly via the "pass-through" above the sink, no matter that it discouraged eye contact and conversation during dinner.

At some point we migrated to a dinner table, where Dad held forth about the world and Mom didn't say much, at least not about politics or history. Looking back, I realized Dad raised me to be his conversational companion, marginalizing my mother in our three-way dialogues. She contributed her own reports and gossip but mainly on the state of the rat race at Kodak, where *Mad Men*–era salesmen brandished the status symbols of pricey new homes and automobiles. It was unclear how much Mom disapproved of the rat race as she often lobbied Dad for a bigger, better house—or at least a better neighborhood, somewhere in Dallas. Which would have been manageable at one point.

"Your father didn't care about houses or where we lived," my mother explained to me after he was gone, and she was still living in the house on Eric Lane in Valley View Estates. "He just wanted a place to come home and be with his family and be left alone."

Left alone and unchallenged, I might add. Not trained in the Socratic Method, Dad did not encourage argument with the verdicts he issued about films or politics or people. His verdicts were well-informed, but still I grew up with the uneasy notion that disagreeing with him was a form of disloyalty. It seemed important that we all share his view of things.

As an only child, I had learned to play by myself and enjoyed building toy cities with wooden blocks and a metallic Erector Set. I became fascinated with aircraft and spent hours assembling plastic models of fighter planes in kits marketed by Revell that came from Venice, California. They filled two long shelves in my room. Influenced by the propaganda of World War II movies, I imagined myself piloting one of these deadly supersonic weapons

The Jets, Farmers Branch Little League; I'm kneeling behind the trophy; Goolsbys, father and son, are first two standing far right
AUTHOR COLLECTION

one day—until I reached an age where I learned the gruesome truth of war was different from the simple-minded heroism we saw on the big screen.

Eventually I graduated to the more challenging kits for World War I biplanes made of balsa wood and tissue paper that had to be stretched and glued carefully over the frame, mimicking fabric. I grew so frustrated with one of these, I am embarrassed to say, I put a match to the wing and tossed it smoking into a wastebasket. The wastebasket was metal, but my mother was properly horrified, doused it with water, and warned me never to do that again. I don't think I attempted another biplane.

Gary Goolsby, who lived just across the alley, was a year older than me and something like a big brother. Gary was the ace hurler on our Little League team, the Jets. His father, Isaac Truman Goolsby, worked in a battery factory and was one of the coaches. He drove us to practice in a weathered blue 1950 Chevy pickup that had an acrid smell I assumed had something to do with batteries. "It smelled of the Old Gold cigarettes that he smoked," Gary remembered years later. We had a good team, amassing a record of 15–1, it says on the back of the team photo that I kept.

This was my first year of organized ball. I was eleven, and they put me in center field. All our games were played under the lights at Don Showman Park, across from Valwood Elementary. In the first game of the season, a fly ball soared up into the lights, headed in my direction—my first chance—and when it came down, glanced off the webbing of my glove and plunked me on the head. E-8. Welcome to Little League, kid. I wasn't hurt (physically) and got the ball back to the infield, but Mr. Goolsby ran out to see if I was OK. He was a good guy and a good coach. One day he explained to us why the catcher had to wear a protective cup inside his pants. If you were struck by a baseball "down there," without a cup, he said, you could be "ruined for life." And what a forbidding thought that was, even if I didn't fully grasp its meaning.

I didn't yet have to worry about wearing a cup, but my dad, God bless him, was concerned about the flimsy earmuff-like headgear we were given to protect our noggins when batting. He made a point of finding a sporting goods store that sold the hard plastic batting helmets worn by the pros and bought one for me in the right color, green. The head coach, a young husband with a flattop haircut named Sammy, was not as nice as Mr. Goolsby and got annoyed that my father would question the league's safety equipment.

"I guess your daddy knows better than us," Sammy said when I showed him my new helmet. "I hope you don't get one in the ear."

I didn't want to draw attention to myself as being more fragile than the other boys, but Dad insisted I wear the helmet. And I should have realized the hard hat was way more stylish than the bush league earmuffs anyway. I wish it had made me a better hitter. I struck out a lot and anguished over my failures at the plate later at home. Mom and Dad pleaded with me to let it go. I brooded anyway.

The first words I ever typed were about baseball. It was during my second season in Little League in Farmers Branch, but I wasn't writing about Little League. The Little League games were at night, and during the hot summer days, three other boys in my neighborhood—Gary and the brothers David and Dickie Wells—joined me to play a lawn and driveway version of baseball using a tennis ball hurled against the Wells's broad garage door that served as a backstop. The four of us would impersonate entire starting lineups of the major league teams of the day, pretending to be Mantle and Maris, Spahn and Koufax while providing our own voice-over narration and keeping track of our individual statistics.

Something moved me to want to chronicle all this, an early predisposition to journalism, I guess. I wanted to be a player, but I wanted to be a chronicler, too. I wanted to do both. I decided to publish my own sports section, dubbed *The Valley View Athletic Association Newsletter*, named for our suburban subdivision and full of my accounts of our lawn and driveway games, written in imitation of what I was reading in the *Times Herald*, *Morning News*, and *Sports Illustrated*. Every few weeks I sat down at Dad's Underwood, pecked out the stories, then handed the pages over to Mom to take to the office to mimeograph. She would come back with eight or ten copies that I distributed free to my pals.

BECAUSE OF HIS HARDSCRABBLE CHILDHOOD, my father never got much chance to take part in athletics and was not able to offer me coaching tips, but he was in favor of me playing sports—except for football, which he considered dangerous. For some reason he had a perverse prejudice against physical fitness, which he relegated to overactive self-regard and egotism. He himself was modestly built, about 5'7", with naturally strong arms that had never lifted a dumbbell. I think it's fair to say, from photos of him as a young man, that he was handsome. But personal vanity was verboten. As a kid I remember him describing actors as the people you saw on the street in New York staring at their reflections in department store windows. Which also might seem a perverse judgment for someone who loved the theatre, but that was Dad. None of us is easily summarized.

He bought me the junior set of golf clubs for Christmas but did not think to get me any lessons or even guidance from an adult who played the game. Lessons cost money. But golf was hard. Maybe a natural could have learned the swing on his own. Not me.

With the raw enthusiasm of a kid, I hacked around with my Sears clubs here and there, sneaking on to the women's course at the new Brookhaven Country Club nearby. I also practiced putting indoors on our wall-to-wall-carpeted living room. Somehow Gary and I fashioned a golf hole on a vacant lot in the neighborhood, sank a pickle jar into the ground on the "green," and held a golf tournament, playing the same hole over and over again.

On two occasions Dad gamely volunteered to play with me at a low-cost public course in nearby Denton, where he rented clubs for himself. What I wouldn't give for film of one of those rounds. Neither of us even knew how to grip the club properly, shanked drives left and right, and traipsed off into the rough searching for lost balls. I hate to think we kept score. On one of these outings, I grew so discouraged on the front nine, I announced I was ready to go home. Dad understandably was not pleased and should have said, "We paid for eighteen holes, and I'm going to finish." But he didn't say that. Sweaty and angry, he lugged his clubs back to the pro shop and then, while putting my bag into the trunk of the car, allowed the trunk lid to slip and bang him on the head, which only added to my culpability. We drove home in tense silence. Golf did not become a father-son bonding activity.

We did better with baseball—watching it, that is. Dallas and Fort Worth didn't get an MLB team until the Washington Senators moved down in 1972, but during these years, the late 1950s, Dad took me to Burnett Field in Oak Cliff to see the Dallas Rangers of the AA Texas League and later the AAA American Association. It didn't matter that it was only minor league baseball; the diamond looked beautiful to me: the finely groomed green grass set off against black basepaths and gleaming white chalk lines. Green and black became my new favorite colors. The ballpark bumped up against the Trinity River levee, and in the distance, over the outfield fence and on the other side of the river, loomed the smokestacks from the Neuhoff Sausage factory. I thought I could smell the sausage.

I became a fan of the Rangers and their pudgy power-hitting first-baseman, Keith Little. I think he hit twenty-two homers one season. Or was his number 22? Maybe both. My parents bought me a simple plastic AM radio kit that I assembled and used primarily to listen to the Rangers' games in my room. Sometimes I sat at my desk, which had a plate glass top you could slide photos under—and a businesslike mid-century modern lamp emitting a cool fluorescent light. The play-by-play announcer was a man named Bill Mercer. At the end of the 1960 season, I sat at my desk and wrote Mercer a fan letter. I was thrilled to receive a letter back from him. "I feel greatly honored that you enjoyed our broadcasts of the games this past year and in 1959," he typed on KRLD stationery, adding, "Congratulations on your outstanding baseball feats this summer."

In my second Little League season, with a different team, I played Keith Little's position of first base and somehow made the Farmers Branch all-star team. I guess I wanted Bill Mercer to know that.

CHAPTER SEVEN

Lu

A FTER HEARING HERMES NYE PLAY AND SING, Mom bought a used guitar and began taking lessons at McCord's Music downtown. Her first guitar was a Gibson, but photos from that time also show her playing a classical, nylon string model. She didn't get her Martin 00-18 until 1966. Once she learned three chords and two-finger picking, she was ready to find her way into the folk music revival touched off by Pete Seeger, the Weavers, The Kingston Trio, and Joan Baez. Her only singing experience had been in Girl Scouts, and she said folk music reminded her of the songs she once sang around campfires—and under the streetlamps on summer evenings in Grandma King's Irish neighborhood where the kids knew all the words to "Molly Malone" and "Did Your Mother Come from Ireland?"

She had grown up on the South Side of Bethlehem, where the steelworks were located, along with the enclaves of Irish, German, Czech, and Italian immigrants who came to find work in the mills. At the onset of the Depression, her family was forced to move in with her father's German-speaking parents, then later switched to Grandma King's place on Hillside Avenue through her schooling and the war.

Both families were Catholic, yet neither approved of her parents' union. Tribalism was in force. "The Germans thought they were better than the Irish," my mother explained. "They thought the Irish were trash."

James King, maternal great grandfather and Bethlehem fire chief
AUTHOR COLLECTION

Anthony, my grandfather, though uneducated and a bigot, was not dissuaded by such prejudice when he met Margaret King at a public dance at Dorney Park in nearby Allentown. He was certain he had found his mate. "They were both wonderful dancers," my mother said, "and very much in love." Margaret, my grandmother, was the daughter of a fireman, James King, who rose to be chief of the department. James's father, William King, a "laborer," had arrived in Bethlehem from County Cork in 1853.

The Reisers, meanwhile—George and Elizabeth—my mother's paternal grandparents, were farmers from Vezprem County, Hungary, about forty miles west of Budapest. They were among the wave of Germans who in the second half of the nineteenth century had migrated east into parts of Hungary that had been ruled by the Turks for 150 years. In the decade before World War I, thirty thousand of them left Vezprem County for America. "Poverty and wretchedness" were prominent among the causes of the exodus, one descendant later wrote.

George got a job right away at Bethlehem Steel as a general laborer. Anthony, my grandfather, who came over with George and Elizabeth as a baby, would go to work at the Steel at age twelve as a water boy, refreshing the men who toiled in the intense heat near the blast furnaces.

As the first grandchild in the family, my mother remembers receiving a lot of attention. But crowding into George and Elizabeth's place with their three daughters at the start of the Depression was a hardship, and Grandma Reiser was strict. It was lights out every night at 8 p.m. after she made her rounds, sprinkling all the girls with holy water.

The food was good. Mom remembered Grandma Reiser as a great cook whose dishes were spicy and delicious, made from vegetables and herbs often plucked from the backyard. "She could take whatever was available and feed an army," Mom said. While they lacked formal schooling, the Reisers knew how to grow things, including grapes. They made their own wine—and beer. Curiously, Anthony (Tony), Mom's father, preferred the blander American diet and discouraged Margaret, his wife, from learning any of his mother's flavorsome recipes. Selfishly he severed the savory link to the old country.

Tony was just old enough to miss being drafted and worked through the war operating a crane in the beam yards, lifting red-hot molten molds from the forges to cool. Bethlehem Steel made its share of the ships and ordnance used to defeat Hitler and Hirohito, and he worked enough overtime during the war to be able to buy a two-story row house on the north side when the war was over. This is where I first encountered him (that I can remember), on a road trip east when I was in middle school. I began to see why people in the family referred to him euphemistically as a "character." In truth, he was egocentric, callous, manipulative, and cheap. When Mom graduated from Bethlehem Catholic High School, the nuns wanted to help her get a scholarship to a nearby college, but Tony said, no way. "If anyone in this family is going to college," he proclaimed, "it's going to be your brother." But her brother wasn't interested and became a home improvement contractor instead.

Elizabeth and George:
great grandparents from Hungary

They say the Irish never forget a slight, but if Mom never forgot it, she also didn't harbor a grievance that I could detect. She seemed to make allowances for a man—her father—whose cramped worldview was shaped by going to work at the blast furnaces when he was twelve.

Those first years in Dallas, Mom lacked an outlet for self-expression, but in her soul she must have still been the actress from the Civic Theatre who had worn her hair in the same pin-curled flip as Lauren Bacall. Now, with Hermes as her guide and mentor, she found herself back onstage again, this time playing the guitar and singing folk songs. Hermes introduced her to his audiences at women's clubs and book review groups, and eventually she started to get bookings of her own.

We began attending hootenannies (a new word) at the Nyes's Lee Park house. Men and women with guitars and banjos sat in a horseshoe arrangement at one end of the living room, taking turns performing old ballads from the British Isles and Appalachia, as well as "singalongs" like "This Land Is Your Land" and "Irene Goodnight." I didn't think much about it; it was just something we did as a family, and my mother was taking part in the singing. Around this time, she shortened her name from Lucille to Lu.

In 1959 she and Hermes cofounded, with Miriam Gallerstein, Bart Bernstein, and Segle Fry, the Dallas Folk Music Society, which scheduled a hootenanny once a month at a different member's home, a custom that continued, without fail, for the next sixty years. They also helped bring Pete Seeger to town for a concert at the Knox St. Theater, an event that attracted controversy and threats as Seeger was still blacklisted for refusing to answer questions before the stridently anti-communist House Un-American Activities Committee.

Lucille becoming Lu | AUTHOR COLLECTION

Not only was I aware that Pete Seeger made records (we owned some), but I was excited to know that my mother was helping put on a concert for such a famous person. The politics of it all were yet beyond me; I just knew something important was happening and we were part of it. Mom got abusive phone calls at home, and her boss at Kodak expressed concern about her involvement in such an event. But despite Dallas's reputation as a haven for right-wing fanatics, the evening went off without incident, and Seeger filled the Knox St. Theater, just him and his banjo.

After the show we went to a reception for him at the Nyes's house, and at one point I wandered into a back room where I found the guest of honor seated at a desk typing the lyrics to a song for someone. I looked over his shoulder, staring at the words he was typing. He turned and said, evenly, "Isn't it past your bedtime?" I was pleased the tall, skinny man I had just seen up onstage had spoken to me, but I also figured this was a cue for me to leave the room and go find Mom or Dad.

CHAPTER EIGHT

Trips

W E TOOK ANNUAL TWO-WEEK FAMILY VACA-
TIONS, the three of us, all of them road trips. Commercial
jet travel was not yet common or affordable in the 1950s and
early '60s. We never went to Disneyland or the Grand Canyon, but we did
take a trip back east, to Bethlehem, the Jersey Shore, and New York City in
the summer of 1960. Dad did all the driving, five hundred miles a day, as
planned and plotted in one of those AAA "Triptick" binders with the white
plastic rings holding the mapped pages AAA assembled just for you. The
car was a 1955 Chevy sedan (green with a white roof), bench seats, and no
air-conditioning. The windows would be rolled down to allow the outside
air to rush in. Vehicles did not travel as fast back then, and most of the highways were still two-lane, lined with billboards and the occasional narrative
sequence of red-and-white Burma-Shave signs, advertising a brand of shav-
ing cream in jokey rhymes. The interstates had not yet been cut through the
Appalachian Mountains, and to get to the east coast from Texas you drove
north to Chicago and then east, connecting with the Pennsylvania Turnpike.

Pulling into a motel on the main street of a small Missouri town, we
saw ballplayers sitting on a curb putting on their spikes before heading to
play a game at a low-minors park that must have lacked a locker room.

Once we got to Bethlehem, we stayed with Mom's parents in the
two-story red brick row house Tony had bought on the north side after the

war. I know we saw clusters of Reisers and extended family, and some of them accompanied us on an outing to Atlantic City—my first look at the ocean and the famous boardwalk. In an open-air stall on the boardwalk—when my parents weren't looking—I found a "flip book" that showed a woman casually disrobing in a series of sepia-toned images as you flipped the pages. Damn. I flipped through it again and discreetly put it back, hoping that no one saw me.

But the highlight of the trip was a weekend in New York City, during which we attended a game at Yankee Stadium. I had only seen Yankee Stadium on TV in black-and-white and was unprepared for the glorious shade of green looming at the end of the tunnel we entered to reach our seats down the third base line. Like the first time I saw Burnett Field, only grander and more majestic. The other thing I noticed right away was the prominent Ballantine Beer sign over the scoreboard in the outfield—something I'd never seen on the *Game of the Week* broadcasts, probably because one of the sponsors was a different brand of beer, Falstaff. The Yankees beat the Washington Senators, 1–0, scoring the only run when Roger Maris tripled and came home on a Mickey Mantle sacrifice fly. Whitey Ford pitched a complete game three-hitter. More importantly, I left the stadium with a blue satin Yankees warm-up jacket Mom and Dad bought me at the concessions stand on the way out.

The next day we saw a matinee of the original *West Side Story*, my first Broadway experience, which I found enjoyable but not as memorable as the Yankee game. (I was twelve.) I do remember us walking the shadowy, unwashed streets of the theater district that afternoon, the extraordinary clamor and chaos of it all, the incessant honking of yellow taxis, and the shocking thing I saw in a store window. As we strolled past endless displays of bric-a-brac, I was trying not to stare at my reflection in the glass, remembering what Dad had said about the vanity of actors, but I had to stop to examine—could it be real?—a glazed olive-green ashtray in the shape of a human hand with the middle finger extended in that universal signal of you know what. Right there in the display window! Was that legal? Maybe the police didn't know yet. The image of that ashtray lasted for a long time in my head as a symbol of the vulgarity available for purchase in New York City.

Other vacations and long weekends took us to the Texas Gulf Coast, to San Antonio to see the Alamo, and to Austin for a Texas Folklore Society

Conference that included performances by folk singers (including Mom) and an address by the dean of Texas Letters, J. Frank Dobie, himself a folklorist. I remember the sight of him, puffed out in a billowy white linen suit, standing at a lectern in a large room at the historic Driskill Hotel in downtown Austin. Whatever he spoke about was lost on my adolescent brain.

We also traveled to Mexico in the days when it was cheap and safe. You could drive from Dallas to Monterrey in a day, breezing through customs at Nuevo Laredo and reaching the northern desert industrial capital before dark. As we drove south on the main highway, the mountains surrounding the city began to appear in the distance at dusk. They were the first mountains I had ever seen. We stayed in Monterrey for a week, attending a bullfight and contending with *la tourista*, the gastro-intestinal distress commonly experienced by gringos. Dad and I played golf on an arid, rocky course. It's the only time I ever played with a caddie (as was required). I don't recall that it helped.

On other trips we drove to the Yucatan peninsula to see the Mayan ruins, to the capital of Mexico City, and to San Miguel de Allende, the picturesque birthplace of the Mexican revolt against Spain. Many of San Miguel's eighteenth-century buildings still stand, and bohemian expatriates from north of the border had settled there.

Although they spoke no Spanish, both Gene and Lu were enchanted with Mexico, its people and culture and especially with its art—both the ancient pre-Columbian pottery and statuary in the museums and the folk art on view everywhere—the bold primary colors of buildings and textiles, decorations like candleholders and religious figures made from tin and used materials. I took in the message from my parents that Mexico was a beautiful and soul-renewing getaway from mass-merchandised America. I did not appreciate how unusual it was to be learning from one's parents that a country where English was not the first language and the automobiles were old could have virtues America was lacking. And they were right.

CHAPTER NINE

A Musical Dilemma

I'D HAD NO MUSIC LESSONS OF ANY KIND, but Mom soon enlisted me in her world with the gift of a small bongo drum set. She showed me how to tap out a simple syncopated rhythm that I could use to accompany her on the calypso songs she was learning from Harry Belafonte albums. During a concert at the Fort Worth Art Museum, she called me up onstage to play along on "Tingalayo," a children's song about a donkey. My show business debut. People clapped.

Almost all the music being played on the stereo in our house by now was from the folk revival: The Weavers, Kingston Trio, Joan Baez, the Limelighters, Peter, Paul & Mary, Odetta, Ian & Sylvia, Gordon Lightfoot, Judy Collins, Carolyn Hester, Tom Paxton, Phil Ochs, Bob Dylan, and more. At a young age I was absorbing these sounds and sensibilities and accepting them as I accepted the food Mom put on the table. I began to hear the righteousness in songs celebrating the struggles of the common man like Billy Ed Wheeler's "Coal Tattoo," on a Judy Collins live LP; The Weavers' "Follow the Drinkin' Gourd"; and all of Woody Guthrie. My parents' antiestablishment politics could be heard in the words to these songs, along with the protests of the civil rights movement, which they embraced early on.

That period of the early 1960s, for me, was a bundle of folk music and civil rights activism, based at the First Unitarian Church that we started attending after being invited by the Nyes. Gene and Lu took my departure from Catholic school as an excuse to exit the church altogether and were open to the more liberal environment of Unitarianism, advertised as "a climate not a creed." I became a member of the guitar-slinging LRY (Liberal Religious Youth) that met on Sunday nights and at summer conferences at Lake Texoma, on the border between Oklahoma and Texas. We sang "Kumbaya" around campfires long before it became a cliché.

My mother was getting gigs at the Rubaiyat, Dallas's first coffee house, and the P.M. club on Lovers Lane, but she realized she didn't have the kind of voice that made Joan Baez and Carolyn Hester recording stars. So, she made a shrewd decision: to write and sing her own humorous topical songs, using traditional melodies in the folk tradition. She made a place for herself on the Dallas folk scene gently skewering the mores of conformity and the dubious virtue of televangelists and other celebrities. The first song she wrote was about the larcenous Texas businessman Billie Sol Estes, using the musical template of Merle Travis' "Sixteen Tons."

Dad was not musical, but he was open to the democratic spirit of folk music and supported her joining the army of singers and poets creating this new sound in America far from Tin Pan Alley. Or he was at first. He gladly contributed satirical lyrics to some of her early songs but soon discovered she didn't want his help; my mother preferred sole authorship of her compositions, no matter they might be missing her husband's wit. The two of them were each creative but different, and with my dad lacking an outlet at

Lu's PR Photo, 1965 | AUTHOR COLLECTION

the time for his literary energy, his enthusiasm for Mom's return to performing cooled and even turned to reproach. While a political liberal, he was old-fashioned about gender roles and uncomfortable with the amount of time Mom was devoting to what had become a second, self-promoting career. He called her on it, complaining that this was not his idea of a suitable marriage.

One night, after I was in bed, I heard them arguing in the kitchen about this. I must have sensed the conflict that was building, and it frightened me. I started to cry softly, and they heard me. They came into my room and asked what was wrong. I said I was afraid they were going to get a divorce. They seemed abashed by my observation and reassured me that would not be happening. I think my mother, encouraged by her local success, was being tempted by the prospect of bigger stages, but in the end, she chose the family over fame and agreed to limit her performing to weekends, keeping her day job at Kodak.

The conflict continued nonetheless, and I found myself torn between two creative parents whose differences loomed larger as I grew older, making me wonder how they had ever gotten together in the first place. (The thoughts of a young man.) My dad was bookish and intellectual. My mother, by contrast, was not a reader, preferred art and music to wordy discussions, and was happiest holding forth with a guitar in front of an audience. Politically she tagged along with Dad's lefty views but did not reason her way to them as he did and, truth be told, held an abiding admiration for Panglossian pundits like Dale Carnegie and Norman Vincent Peale.

What was I to make of all this? I suppose most children, coming of age, begin to recognize the separate strains of DNA and personality traits they have inherited from both parents, with the added wish to edit the results. Temperamentally I was more like my dad and certainly absorbed his worldviews and passion for the written word, but I was also drawn to guitars and banjos and clung to folk music as a way of cementing a bond with my mother. Because of Dad's aura and his indifference to music, I felt a twinge of guilt about learning the guitar, as if it were a betrayal of the cerebral life he had planned for me. I was never comfortable performing in front of him, while Mom encouraged my humble musical talent, sharpening my divided loyalties.

When later in high school I developed a troubling case of acne; Dad brushed it off as insignificant, while Mom intervened and got me much-needed help from a dermatologist. I was grateful for that even as I began to see why Dad sometimes complained about her penchant for ingratiation and telling people what they wanted to hear. She was a natural at public relations, and I could see how that helped her win friends and fans, but PR was anathema to Dad, at odds with his stubborn devotion to honesty and integrity. It was left for me to reconcile these divergent philosophies.

CHAPTER TEN

Boys School

T HE FIRST TIME I SAW ST. MARK'S was the day I went there to take an entrance exam. It was the spring before that initial road trip east, and I was in sixth grade at Valwood Elementary. "Mrs. Perry told us we had to get you out of there," my mother explained years later. St. Mark's was a prominent private boys' school in Dallas, but I had never heard of it, and I was not ready to leave my friends in Farmers Branch. My parents could not have afforded the tuition, but they'd seen a notice in the paper about scholarships being offered and persuaded me to go and take the test.

The visit turned my head, beginning with the sight of Davis Hall, the three-story Georgian brick landmark that looked out toward Preston Road from the top of a long U-shaped drive. With other test-takers, I was given a tour of the campus by Ray Hunt, a son of right-wing oil titan H. L. Hunt and then a junior. Not that I knew who he was. He was dressed in the old school uniform of military khakis and showed us, among other things, the new math-science quadrangle that included an observatory and planetarium. Equally impressive was what I saw on a coffee table in the lobby: a neat stack of the latest edition of the school newspaper, the *ReMarker*. Gleaming black headlines spread across sheets of glossy white paper that even smelled special—different from regular newsprint. They did this, here? At a school?

At some point after the test, Gene and Lu and I went back to the campus one afternoon for an interview with the headmaster, Thomas Hart-

Davis Hall in the 1960s | AUTHOR COLLECTION

mann, and director of admissions, Hal Curry. I don't remember what questions they asked me or what Gene and Lu said, but I do remember when the letter arrived in handsome gray stationary informing my parents that I was being offered a scholarship. I took it as welcome news, not fully understanding what that meant or how St. Mark's would change my life.

I entered in the fall of the first presidential election that meant anything to me: the young Democratic senator from Massachusetts, John F. Kennedy, against Richard M. Nixon, who had been Eisenhower's vice president. Like most kids, I parroted my parents' political views and amid the partisanship on display in the student body proudly made my own hand-lettered "John Kennedy" nametag to wear to school pinned to my shirt. Gene and Lu did not encourage this, concerned I might attract hostility from my classmates. They had reason to be concerned: the parents of most St. Mark's boys were well-to-do and Republican. Of the forty-five boys in the seventh grade, I calculated, only four, including me, were for Kennedy. Apparently I was not trying to blend in.

Politics aside, St. Mark's grabbed me full force. Going from sleepy Valwood Elementary, where I had no homework, to the boot camp academics of a prep school at age twelve provided my first experience of culture shock. Suddenly I was in the classroom of John J. Connolly, a product of the Boston Latin School, being called on bluntly by my last name ("Mitchell!") to answer questions about last night's reading of *Beau Geste*, then awaiting his stern judgment of whatever I managed to spit out. Mr. Connolly, a bachelor, had the bearing of a dour priest and ran one of the two small boarding houses available to out-of-town students. After I was involved in a minor altercation of some sort, he ordered me to come to his classroom after school and write

the word "pugilist" in chalk one hundred times on his blackboard. Even punishment was a vocabulary lesson.

The campus was filled with white boys in uniform Banlon shirts and
khaki pants (coats and ties would come later), their arms cradling books if
not slinging briefcases. Slide rules were standard accessories. The classes
were small—twenty or less—and you couldn't hide. That first year I had *two*
English courses: one in literature taught by Mr. Connolly and one in grammar and composition taught by Ludlow North, a dapper young man of the
world with a head of dark brown hair combed back stylishly and a cigarette
dangling from his lips when he was not in the classroom. Mr. North had
gone to Yale; Mr. English, my history teacher, to Dartmouth; Arthur Douglas,
my science teacher, was from England; Frances Shaner, the French teacher,
was from France. Hartmann, the headmaster, was a graduate of Princeton.
This was a new world, where the French honorific "Messrs." was placed in
front of the names of two or more male teachers if referring to them in a
group. I saw it in the *ReMarker.*

I was no longer the smartest kid in the class, and the workload was
onerous, but I soon came to appreciate that I was at a school that might be a
distant cousin of the famous English academies like Eton and Harrow, a day
school version of New England's Andover and Exeter. I had never even heard
of those places before, but the comparisons were in the air at St. Mark's—

romantic notions that I wanted to believe because of how
that would quantify my status
as a twelve-year-old future
Rhodes Scholar if I were to
make the honor roll.

Elitism and snobbery
were baked into such distinc-
tions, but I didn't notice at the
time, any more than I understood that Eton and Harrow
were bastions of the British
Empire, whose ruthless colo-
nialism and belligerence had

St. Mark's Man, 8th Grade | AUTHOR COLLECTION

oppressed peoples the world over (beginning with Ireland) for centuries. No, in my innocence, England was yet the dreamy land of Shakespeare and great writers, the lodestone of wit and higher learning, superior in so many ways to North Texas.

Greg Nobles, who would become my best friend, had also entered in the seventh grade, also on scholarship. His mother, Edna, also worked as a secretary at Kodak and knew Lu. Although Edna and her husband, Paul, voted for Nixon, Greg and I had a lot else in common from the start, including both being ex–Little Leaguers who wanted to play in the infield at St. Mark's.

The scholarship program was in its infancy, and the two of us took our places alongside the sons of the Dallas establishment: Murchisons, Basses, and Cullums, oil and gas tycoons, prominent doctors and lawyers, and both the owner and the coach of the fledgling Dallas Cowboys. Gene and Lu instructed me not to be cowed by my affluent classmates, but they needn't have worried. Status at St. Mark's at the time was derived chiefly from your academic and athletic achievements, overseen by a faculty that was mainly middle class and leaned left-of-center politically. Years later, when Greg and I looked back and reconsidered the pros and cons of attending a school with so many rich kids, we agreed that one of the benefits was that it demystified wealth.

As baseball season approached, I excitedly shared with Dad my expectation to be the starting shortstop on the seventh grade team, and one night after

Greg Nobles, Ann North, and Lud North |
Montclair, NJ, 1968
AUTHOR COLLECTION

listening to my fervid diamond dreams, he whipped out a caution flag. "I hope you're not putting this ahead of your studies. You're not at St. Mark's to play baseball." Ouch. He wanted to hear me voice a similar desire to get a higher class rank. I felt chastened, but of course he was right, and it established my priorities thereafter.

Anyway, Greg got a break in the infield competition when, in the first week of

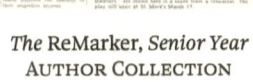

The ReMarker, *Senior Year*
AUTHOR COLLECTION

Joining a distinguished group
AUTHOR COLLECTION

practice, the coach, a gruff young taskmaster who had played center for the University of Delaware, barked, "Mitchell, put on the catcher's gear." What? Much as I loved baseball, I had no desire to be a catcher. I was going to have to wear that cup! I think I cried, but as things turned out, I got to like it and ended up being a catcher for two seasons on the varsity. And Dad came to every game he could.

The full name of the school was St. Mark's School of Texas, and Etonian aspects aside, football ruled, as it did in Farmers Branch-Carrollton and throughout the state. For the first time I found myself putting on a helmet and pads, adding to the regimen of all that was demanding and new. Dad reluctantly went along with it because it was St. Mark's. Mr. English, the tall, broad-shouldered history teacher, had played on the line at Dartmouth and was the seventh-grade coach. Before the first game kickoff, he addressed the team and said, "It's OK to be scared. Once the game starts, you'll forget about it."

Something else new that came with football was showering after practice every day with the other boys and coaches in the locker room's long communal shower. I had no experience being naked with anyone, so this presented another rite of passage that would become a routine part of sports at St. Mark's. The custom was later discontinued, I learned, possibly out of fears of fostering homoeroticism, a term that would have been foreign to us.

I was a reserve halfback on the eighth-grade team and remember coach Hoffman calling me up from the bench in our first game.

"Mitchell, you ready to go in?"

"I think so," I answered, unwisely.

"Sit down, then."

Football required more conviction than that.

The next year, I moved to quarterback, uncomfortably beating out Greg for the starting position after the coach put us through a side-by-side passing competition. It proved to be a dubious honor, being the QB on a winless ninth-grade team, but we did almost tie Jesuit, our big Catholic school rival that must have had at least twice as many players on its bench. And I got to wear jersey number 17, the same as the Cowboys' Don Meredith.

My parents and our family physician discouraged me from playing after that year. I was still growing, and the doc had detected a pinched nerve in my spine. As Greg often told the story, one afternoon the following pre-season, I happened to be walking through the locker room when Tom Jones, who would become famous as the actor Tommy Lee Jones, shouted at me, "Mitchell! Why aren't you out for football?" "I have a back problem," I said. To which Jones retorted, "Yeah, discoloration!" Meaning yellow. What a guy.

Greg and I were about the same size (not future Division I football size, that is) and the same size as Bob Rozelle, a sophomore year addition to our class who would become captain of the football team, play baseball and soccer with us, and join me at college. Physically the three of us could have been triplets and had all been born within days of each other, we discovered. A speedy running back with good hands, Bob was a better athlete than either Greg or me. But he wasn't around in those first years when I was learning that Greg was a better student than I was and didn't have to work as hard to get good grades. He was quick-witted and smooth in a way that I envied. He even had a smooth, unblemished complexion with a light natural tan, where I had unfashionably pale skin that I foolishly subjected to sunburns to get bronzed. Greg didn't have pimples; I had pimples, lots of them.

BECAUSE OF MY LOVE FOR AIRCRAFT, I entered St. Mark's with the vague notion of becoming an aeronautical engineer (a term I learned from Dad, who thought it might be practical). But Mr. North, as well as the challenges of mathematics, set me on a different path. Mr. North was my English teacher four of my six years and later guided us line-by-line through Conrad, Steinbeck, Shakespeare, and even the mystifying plays of Edward Albee. He was taken with the Theatre of the Absurd, new then and surely over our heads, but he made it seem interesting. And he would descend from such heights by regaling us with his adventures in the Navy, where in some unidentified port he got a small blue tattoo on his right forearm that read, simply, "Why?"

He would offer the occasional sly comment on the sex lives of certain characters, pointing out that Curley, the rough-hewn wrangler in *Of Mice and Men* wore a glove full of Vaseline on one hand to keep it "soft for his wife." What that meant exactly, a room full of ninth-grade boys could ponder for the rest of the semester.

From Mr. North I learned how to diagram sentences and the meaning of irony. He was also the varsity soccer coach, though I don't think he had ever himself played. One day in seventh grade, after giving us a piece of paper and the length of class to describe the ceiling of his room, he told me I was a writer.

As mentioned, a significant number of the teachers at St. Mark's (for some reason, not including the math department) had been imported from the East and brought an Ivy League style of tweed sport coat and oxblood

Tom Adams | Portrait by David Terry
COURTESY OF DAVID TERRY

loafers to 10600 Preston Road. Many of them were young and seemed impressively knowledgeable and cultured. Inevitably they became figures of influence. If Mr. North went to Yale, you couldn't help but imagine what a wonderful place it must be.

Tom Adams was another role model, a 6'4" recent Princeton graduate who had played varsity baseball and basketball for the Tigers. He taught history and coached the JV baseball team. He encouraged my youthful literary inclinations by exchanging letters with me over several summers from his hometown of New Canaan, Connecticut, writing mainly about baseball and his favorite team, the San Francisco Giants (formerly of New York), engaging playfully in what would later be called trash talk. "I won't bother to comment on your biased All-Star selections," he wrote in one letter. "When you decide to look at things objectively, I'll consider your opinions worthwhile." Clearly, I had not included enough Giants.

Alternately humorous and intense, Mr. Adams invented the outlandish character of "the world's fastest talker" for the annual talent show, in which he performed in top hat and tails, astonishing audiences with his absurdly rapid vocal delivery, reciting the titles of all the books in the Bible, the train stops between New York and Chicago and a dozen other lists of names in under a minute—a stopwatch clocking him to a tenth of a second. He gave all his time to students, playing touch football and doubles tennis with us on weekends and on occasion drove a carload of us down US 75 to Houston to see the Astros play his Giants when they came to town. Mr. Adams was one of the perks of attending St. Mark's, whether you were there on scholarship or your parents were paying full price.

CHAPTER ELEVEN

That Day and JFK

A FTER GIVING UP FOOTBALL, I TURNED MY ATTEN-
TION TO SOCCER, a sport that was only getting started in
Texas and was played in the winter season opposite basketball.
Soccer held the appeal of being an international sport, evoking the virtues of
the United Nations, the idealistic world body that my family and church supported in a city where it was often reviled. Because so few local high schools
had teams, we played in a men's Sunday league against sides composed of
waiters, hairdressers, and other immigrants from Europe and Mexico. With
only elementary coaching, few foot skills, and no soccer on TV to watch for
inspiration, we relied on our youthful energy and conditioning to compete
against these men who had grown up playing "the beautiful game." Maybe
we learned a thing or two by osmosis.

My first year on the varsity, playing in the back line against a formidable German American team, I collided with their taller and stronger center
forward, whose name was Hans, and fractured my left wrist as I went hard
to the ground. Dad drove me immediately to a clinic, where our family doc
X-rayed the damage and put me in a heavy plaster cast. It kept me out of action for a month, but I wasn't going to let it stop me from going to the airport
to see President Kennedy, who had won that election three years earlier and
in November 1963 was coming to Texas to heal (or mask) a schism in the
state's Democratic Party a year ahead of the 1964 election.

Soccer player; Bob Rozelle in background
AUTHOR COLLECTION

Two teachers offered to drive any interested students to Love Field, where the president and first lady would be landing before heading by limousine to deliver a luncheon address at the World Trade Mart. I went with Clayton J. Tidey, one of those non-Texan Ivy Leaguish dressers and faculty liberals who was a protégé of Hartmann's and would later move to California. When we reached the airport, I managed, even with my cast, to get through the crowd and closer to where Air Force One had taxied to a stop. JFK and Jackie came down the aircraft's steps and passed right in front of where I was standing with others, packed against a low chain-link fence that was holding the crowd back from the runway. Greg was there somewhere and Eric Nye and Jerry Kelley, another future writer. I elbowed my way to a clear view and caught a glimpse of his familiar face and thick brush of auburn hair from about ten yards. Unforgettable. By the time we got back to school, he was dead.

"My first thought was, 'they got him,'" Eric recalled, "H. L. Hunt and the Birchers."

Not everyone at St. Mark's was upset, given the political tenor of the time, but an assembly was called by Mr. Berrisford, and school let out early. I had a rare date that night to see Peter, Paul & Mary, a concert that was cancelled. At home, my parents bemoaned the hatred for Kennedy in Dallas, made visible by a full-page ad in the *Dallas Morning News* that day attacking Kennedy's foreign and domestic policies and accusing him of being soft on communism. The ad was paid for by a member of the John Birch Society.

On Sunday we were watching the continuing news coverage at lunchtime on a portable black-and-white TV when we saw Jack Ruby shoot and kill Lee Harvey Oswald in the basement of Dallas Police headquarters. Did that really happen? Still in shock, we watched JFK's funeral the next day, beginning with the horse-drawn wagon bearing the flag-draped coffin through the streets of the nation's capital toward Arlington National Cemetery. It's the first time I can remember seeing my dad cry. "They were too good for this country," he said with a tearful, tragic finality as images of arriving dignitaries and heads of state from ninety countries filled the small screen. However sentimental, that pronouncement stuck in my fifteen-year-old mind, as it told me virtue was not always rewarded—in fact could get you killed—in America.

CHAPTER TWELVE

No Crusaders, Please

T HE TWO ST. MARK'S HEADMASTERS FROM MY YEARS, Thomas Hartmann and Christopher Berrisford, were men I liked and admired, for different reasons. Hartmann had a friendly, earnest face, a balding dome of fuzzy gray hair, and a sunny, All-American disposition. Berrisford, youthful, stocky, and no-nonsense, was a graduate of Oxford and more taciturn, but when he spoke, his words carried the sound and imprimatur of Great Britain. Once, I walked into his office with a pencil wedged behind my ear, a habit I had acquired. Without saying a word, he reached forward and flicked away the pencil—a judgment, I think, that St. Mark's boys were not to be taken for shipping clerks.

Hartmann and Berrisford were both men of their time, restricted by the conservatism of the community yet each progressive in his own way. Hartmann was a Democrat and JFK supporter who oversaw the initiation of the scholarship program; Berrisford brought in the first Black student and two years after we graduated, amid the political unrest of the era, refused to fire a teacher who had burned a tiny American flag in class to demonstrate the power of symbolism. The board then fired Berrisford.

That first Black student, Lee Smith, entered in 1964. There were no students of color in the nearby public high schools either. Dallas was a segregated city. A few of us in the Class of '66 joined the NAACP Youth Council and ventured on occasion to the South Dallas home of activist Juanita Craft to sit around a table and converse with Black high school students. I'm not sure it occurred to us to ask why there were not more students of color at St. Mark's. Or why the nine members of the Dallas City Council, elected at large, included not a single dark face.

We were trained at St. Mark's to fit into the ranks of the "well-educated," learning the right cultural references, accepted icons, and methods. But, like most kids our age in schools of every type across the country, we were not taught how society really worked, about the way power and influence were exerted, about the role money played in politics and the world in general. We were taught the official story and smart ways to talk about it.

St. Mark's was nondenominational but had an Episcopal chaplain, a link to its merger with an Episcopal school years earlier. Each school day began with a fifteen-minute chapel service that included an organ-powered Protestant hymn like "A Mighty Fortress Is Our God." Nevertheless, roughly 20 percent of the student body was Jewish. And in my class were two other Unitarians: Eric Nye and Dick Wincorn, both soccer players. Dick also sang with The Bountymen, my folk group.

I discovered my real religion at St. Mark's in the form of literature, both in and out of the classroom. *All Quiet on the Western Front, The Red Badge of Courage, The Grapes of Wrath*, and other novels impressed me as being ultimate expressions of the human condition, containing spiritual truths, relayed to us by Mr. North and others. (By senior year we would get to James Baldwin.) When Mr. Connolly discovered that some of us were inspecting a copy of *Catcher in the Rye* before eighth-grade Latin class, he cautioned us that we were not ready for such a book and should wait to read it. Oh, but I *was* ready, enthralled by Holden Caulfield's sensitivity, alienation, and critique of society. He even went to a prep school! He was speaking to me.

My budding disaffection was no doubt spurred by my father's habitual aversion to the movers and shakers of Dallas, but my vantage point, like his, was from inside the gates of privilege. We went home every night to humble Farmers Branch, but during the day and sometimes on weekends we mingled with the monied class—him at the art museum and me at school. St. Mark's was located on the northern end of Preston Road, a historic track through the heart of Dallas and its better neighborhoods, which over time I came to feel was my turf and preferred habitat. Even if I didn't live in one of those ivy-covered mansions, I believed I might someday.

This was fantasy, oblivious of the economic resources required to make such luxury possible—resources I would later see as emblems of oligarchy and inequality. It was another aspect of the class confusion into which I had been hurled. Senior year I wrote a short story for the campus literary magazine, the *Marque*, about the shallowness of the people at a party I attended in the sprawling backyard of one of those houses. And yet I remained attracted to the scenery.

I started writing for the *ReMarker* early on when editor Lewis MacAdams let me turn in a few paragraphs about middle-school sports. I looked up to Lewis, a senior, who set an example by quarterbacking the football team while also writing a sports column. He went on to Princeton and then became a poet and journalist on the West Coast.

The *ReMarker* editors ahead of me were a distinguished group that I hoped to join, but you needed the current editor's endorsement plus the approval of the administration. In the spring of my junior year, Robert Hoffman, the outgoing editor (who later helped launch the *National Lampoon* at Harvard) called me at home to tell me I would be getting his endorsement. Yet, there might be a problem, he said, without elaborating.

"You need to talk to Whitey."

Francis "Whitey" Marburger was Assistant Headmaster and also the assistant varsity baseball coach. Rumor had it he had once played in the low minors somewhere back east. At the beginning of practice, he would bang the cup between his legs with a fungo bat and yell, "Mitch! You got one of these on?" He was the only teacher who called me "Mitch," a baseball moniker.

I made an appointment to see Mr. Marburger and waited in the first-floor hallway for five minutes while he finished a session with a boy I suspected was in academic trouble. I wasn't in trouble. Or was I? I'd had Mr. Marburger for eighth-grade English, in addition to baseball. He wasn't as interesting as Mr. North. He had a plain poker face and short-cropped, prematurely white hair. He didn't joke around a lot. When he was throwing batting practice, if I flinched at an inside fastball, he'd grumble, "A buck if I hit you, Mitch, a buck if I hit you."

He never had to give me any money.

"Have a seat, Mitch," he said and got right to the point. "There's a chance you're going to be editor of the *ReMarker* next year, but I have some concerns." Uh-oh. "You're not going to be one of these crusaders, are you?"

There it was. Which said plenty about Mr. Marburger's journalistic priorities and his knowledge of me. I wasn't prepared for this and don't remember how I answered (probably not honestly), but I somehow passed muster, and a few days later was named editor for the upcoming year. Greg was elected president of the student council.

The newspaper fed my natural instincts to be a chronicler, documenting the life of the school in words and pictures, with opinions if we dared. I looked forward to the late nights we gathered on the third floor of Davis Hall every three weeks to get the paper out. Greg contributed a humor column, and I got the sports column I coveted, modeling it after Blackie Sherrod's in the *Times Herald*, surveying the school's sports scene with some lip while trumpeting our historic 33–1 basketball team. I devoted one column to describing the sensory overload inside Houston's new Astrodome, the nation's first indoor baseball stadium, then being hyped as "the eighth wonder of the world." I had seen it firsthand on one of those trips to Houston with Mr. Adams.

We had no formal training in journalism and only an unhelpful faculty advisor whose squeamishness imperiled the *ReMarker*'s tradition of editorial independence. Mostly, I looked to the *New York Times* for guidance. I admired its front page italicized banner headlines and copied that style for our layouts. I had unusual access to the *Times* because of a paper route I shared with classmate Frank Wiedemann, delivering the *Times* and the *Wall Street Journal* by car to homes in North Dallas every morning before school. This was made possible by an enterprising grad student at SMU who, long before satellite printing plants around the country, arranged for the *Times* and *WSJ* to put bundles of early editions on an overnight flight to Love Field, arriving at 5 a.m.

I hated getting up at dawn, but I was proud of what we were doing to make some money, and I often grabbed one of the papers to read if there was time and it wasn't too cold. Frank was a soccer teammate, fellow aesthete, and future psychotherapist, and I sometimes went over to his beautiful modernist house after school because he had his own stereo in his room.

Imagine. We listened to Beatles albums and 45s by the Righteous Brothers, sharing our frustrations with the crimped social life of a boys school, not realizing how good we had it.

CHAPTER THIRTEEN

Extracurriculum

BEFORE OUR VOICES CHANGED, Greg and I sang in the St. Mark's Boys Choir, presided over by Mr. Johnson, the school organist, who would wander around during rehearsal and lean in close to each boy to detect if you were singing on pitch. I always lowered my voice when I felt him approaching. We performed at Evensong, a holdover Episcopal service held in the chapel on certain Sunday afternoons, and once we went down to the studios of WFAA Channel 8, the local ABC affiliate, to record a concert of carols to be broadcast on Christmas Eve.

Growing up around hootenannies and the sounds of Gordon Lightfoot and Buffy Sainte-Marie, I had learned to play the banjo and guitar, Mom offering elementary instruction. With four other upperclassmen I formed a folk quintet called, in the fashion of the day, The Bountymen, imitating The Kingston Trio and The New Christy Minstrels. We sometimes added as backup singers the Seltzer sisters—Christie, Laurel, and Terrel, from the LRY and nearby Thomas Jefferson High—who made us sound better, plus they were good-looking. Not sure how many gigs we played— the St. Mark's talent show, a Christmas concert, a birthday party or two. The most gifted member of the group was Chris Kershaw, who played a twelve-string guitar, would later turn pro composing commercial jingles, and have a son, Clayton, who became the Cy Young-award-winning pitcher for the Los Angeles Dodgers.

The Bountymen: Dick Wincorn, the Author, Louis Blumberg, Chris Kershaw, David Laney
AUTHOR COLLECTION

Mom worried that my going to an all-boys school was stunting my so-cial development, and early on she enrolled me in Dick Chaplin's dance stu-dio at Preston Center—and drove me there faithfully from Farmers Branch every Tuesday night to learn the fox trot, waltz, and other social dances with "young ladies" from wherever. I never saw any of my dance partners out-side of Tuesday night, and when it came time for my first big social event, the Sophomore Class Dance, I asked Georgeann Higgins, a family friend and the daughter of painter Wilfred Higgins, a former colleague of Dad's at the art museum. By junior year, I had found a girlfriend at Hockaday, the girls school counterpart to St. Mark's—Beth Thomas, who was friends with an-other girl from Hockaday Greg was dating. The four of us sometimes went to foreign movies like Federico Fellini's *Juliet of the Spirits* at the Fine Arts Theater in Snider Plaza. This was evidence we were culturally advanced for high schoolers, even if I didn't understand the films.

After I drove Beth home, we would sit on the floral couch in her living room and politely make out, with her parents down the hall in their bed-room. My natural inhibition was not helped by knowing that her father was head of the Upper School at Hockaday.

Like most teenagers, I was self-conscious about my looks, troubled by a "moderately severe" case of acne as diagnosed by the dermatologist Mom found. Adolescence was hard enough without looking at my bumpy red face in the mirror every day and wondering when that would finally go away. Although guys were not yet lifting weights and showing off their "guns," a lot of us who played multiple sports were, by necessity, in good shape. Mr. North made us run a mile before soccer practice every day. Junior year, when our baseball games for some reason were broadcast on the embryonic KVIL-FM, the Dallas sportscaster Frank Filessi sat so close to the field with his portable press box, I could hear him say, "Sean Mitchell, the wiry third baseman, stands in at the plate . . . " Was I wiry? Was that a good thing or a bad thing? Anyway, Frank Filessi said so.

We never won the conference title in baseball, but in my final season, when I was again the catcher, we did manage an improbable victory over 3A powerhouse Waxahachie, beating a starting pitcher who was so fast there were college and major league scouts at the game—not a common sight at St. Mark's. The Waxahachie hurler would be drafted by the Philadelphia Phillies, but that afternoon he walked me, and I got around the bases to score the only run in a 1–0 win made possible because we also had a formidable starter, Rick Wittenbraker, who would go on to play baseball and basketball at TCU. It was a highlight of a disappointing year in which our volatile coach, Ken Brown, got so angry during a late season game that he threw a Billy Martin–style tantrum, stalked off the field, tore up the locker room, and never returned to campus. In the years to come, more team members remembered Coach Brown's furious exit than the upset victory over Waxahachie.

NOT COUNTING A CERVEZA I HAD ONCE AT A RESTAURANT IN MEXICO WITH MY PARENTS AND ERIC NYE, I did not drink alcohol until senior year. The class ahead of us, the Class of '65, were notorious hell-raisers and boozers, making beer runs to Oklahoma for cases of Coors, a brand that was not yet available in Texas and, therefore, exotic. By the time we were seniors, you could get Coors in Dallas, even if we weren't old enough to buy it legally. The older brother of a classmate was kind enough to procure it, and some of us had fake IDs.

It wasn't like we drank a lot, but more than once I took part in so-called commando raids, when a half dozen of us, athletes all, well-oiled on Coors and Lone Star, would sneak onto the Dallas Country Club golf course late at night and run hundred-yard dashes down the fresh-cut dewy fairways like a pack of sprinters, shouting and hollering. Sheer high school lunacy.

After reading *The Great Gatsby* and *This Side of Paradise* for Mr. North, Greg and I and a few others became enamored of F. Scott Fitzgerald, romanticizing his troubled and tragic life hidden beneath a sheen of elegant prose. And we figured, if he drank gin, then we should, too. Moving on from Coors, we sampled it, with tonic or 7-Up, tempted to believe it was a necessary component to the writerly wisdom of his books. We were clueless about alcoholism and the toll it took on him and other writers. We were seventeen.

I often heard Gene and Lu hark back fondly to their days in the Bethlehem Civic Theatre, but I managed to avoid any dramatic productions at St. Mark's until a new co-ed student acting company was established on campus the summer before my senior year. It was led by a charismatic young Canadian named Anthony Vintcent, who christened the group The Harlequin Players. Vintcent had arrived at the school one February day en route to Mexico on a three-speed bicycle, stopping in Dallas to see where Kennedy had been shot. He was low on funds and inquired about a job. A disgruntled English teacher had just quit, and Berrisford hired him on the spot.

He had done some teaching in Montreal and had a keen instinct for the stage, as would become apparent in the boffo productions he mounted for the drama club during the school year and then in the Harlequin Players. His elegant accent and mien seemed to be stamped Oxford or Cambridge and stood out on a campus in the middle of North Dallas. Considering that

Never wanted to be a catcher until I got to like it.
AUTHOR COLLECTION

I would become a drama critic, the chance to spend a summer under his tutelage was invaluable. He cast me as the tender-hearted prize fighter in Saroyan's *The Cave Dwellers* and as the boy in Tennessee Williams' two-hander *This Property Is Condemned*, but my most important role might have been as stage manager for the show where I sat at Vintcent's side during rehearsals, jotting down his whispered directorial notes as a scene progressed—notes that he would be giving later to the actors.

Many Harlequins later found their way to regional theaters, Broadway, Hollywood, and even the London stage, a testament to Vintcent's uncanny way with young people. And there was always the example of Tommy Lee Jones, whom Vintcent had cast against type as the narrator in Dylan Thomas's Welsh verse drama *Under Milk Wood* and coached to a performance that amazed audiences.

Cave Dwellers, with Martha Pietzsch
AUTHOR COLLECTION

Writing about Harlequins years later for a reunion, I summoned a memory of that transformative season:

Outside, the nights were so hot and muggy you could have walked down Preston Road naked at 2 a.m. and still felt warm. That image in fact occurred to me late one night after a show, a sign of imminent debauchery or merely a symptom of the sensory expansion released by the whole experience, evidence that theatre was not something you only saw with your eyes and processed with your mind but felt on your skin. Tony talked about ritual and ceremony, and on that night, alert and sleepless, I felt I understood for the first time what he meant and how our little group was connected to some larger, eternal human need to act out stories to claim our place on earth, as primitive peoples had done, maybe even here in the jungle heat of north Texas summer.

AN UNSPOKEN MESSAGE AT THE SCHOOL WAS: GO EAST, young man, after graduation if it could be arranged. New England was the promised land. Dad believed in the eminence of the Ivy League, managing to overlook its ruling-class history and preferring to think the Ancient Eight

Tony Vintcent: Straight Outta Montreal
COURTESY OF HARLEQUIN PLAYERS

had evolved after the war into something more like a meritocracy, attracting the best and the brightest with lots of financial aid. I wanted to believe that, too, plus I was drawn to its almost quaint tradition of enrolling true student-athletes. And, well, Mr. North had gone to Yale, Mr. Adams and Mr. Hartmann to Princeton, Mr. Whatley to Harvard, and Mr. Hoffman to Brown. In the periodicals section of the school library, I sometimes picked up the *Yale Football Newsletter*, reading the coach's account of last week's game against Columbia or Cornell, the home team's drives up and down the gridiron diagrammed in blue-and-white.

Spring break junior year I loaded into a Ford station wagon with Greg, Frank Wiedemann, and Warren Foxworth, and drove east to check out the Ivy League and associated colleges. Years later, we marveled that our parents let us do this. We started with picture-postcard Princeton and trudged on through dirty ice and snow to visit Yale, Harvard, Brown, Wesleyan, Amherst, and Middlebury. We stayed overnight at Brown, where a likable junior named McElroy showed us around and made a strong impression on me. On the return trip home, we drove around the clock, each of us taking turns at the wheel of the station wagon so as not to have to stop at a motel. We searched the radio dial for Top 40 stations along the way, and each one seemed to be playing "I'll Never Find Another You" by The Seekers.

Although I had respectable SAT scores and good grades in English, history, and Spanish, my report card in math and physics presented an obstacle to my getting into any of those colleges we visited. After the report card came out, Dad sat me down with a list of good but less selective colleges he had found after some research. His mood was somber, and all I could think of was how I had screwed up by allowing my adolescent dislike for Mr.

Callahan, the physics teacher, to ruin everything. I realized I had to consider the schools on Dad's new list, but I'd been thinking about Brown since our visit there, and in the fall of senior year, in consultation with the college counselor, I decided to apply early decision, indicating it was my first choice. When a Brown admissions officer came to campus to interview prospective candidates, he told me not to expect early admission, but that if I kept my grades up, I had a good chance in the spring with the pool of regular applicants. The *ReMarker* had come out that day, and he had taken the trouble to read an editorial I had written and commented on it. His name was Eric Brown. I was encouraged. Maybe I was going to go east after all.

CHAPTER FOURTEEN

Gene

ALL THROUGH ST. MARK'S, A LOT OF MY EDUCATION TOOK PLACE OUTSIDE OF ANY CLASSROOM and came directly from that dogged student of history and language, my father, Eugene Woodrow Mitchell. (He never liked the name Eugene and preferred the abbreviated "Gene.") It was from Dad that I learned the story of the Mitchells and their curiously divided allegiance to Ireland and its historic nemesis, Great Britain. He explained to me that while his mother and father were born in Liverpool, their parents were from the west of Ireland—Galway.

Both Rose and George grew up in Liverpool households that honored Irish Republican heroes like Charles Stewart Parnell, Wolfe Tone, and Michael Collins, men who had fought for Ireland's independence from Great Britain. Rose even knew the words to some patriotic Irish songs. Yet, later, in America, she and her husband saw themselves as British expatriates and subjects of the queen. After immersing himself in Irish history, Dad chose to identify with the downtrodden Irish rather than their English overlords. I once asked Dad how Grandma Rose could salute both the Crown and its enemies, the Irish rebels, and he threw up his hands. He didn't know himself.

Liverpool was full of Irish immigrants because of its proximity, 136 miles across the Irish Sea from Dublin; hence the term "Liverpool Irish" that applied to members of the Beatles as well as my ancestors. My great great grandfather, Thomas Mitchell, was born in Galway in 1803—the same year

Ralph Waldo Emerson was born in Boston— and had emigrated to Liverpool in the early 1840s with his wife, the former Mary Devaney, and five children. The years leading up to the Potato Famine. The youngest of the five was an infant, Michael Mitchell, who would become a merchant seaman, marry Bridget Peacock, and father twelve children of his own, including Rose's future husband, my notorious grandfather George.

Pushed by poverty, George and Rose set out for America in 1911, after their first child, Frances, was born. George went first, working his way across the Atlantic, stoking coal on a passenger ship bound for New York, then didn't bother to show up for the return voyage, just as his brother Frank had done before him. "He was a wetback," Dad would say provocatively about his father, employing the derisive term Texans use to describe Mexican immigrants who swim across the Rio Grande. He wanted to make the point that white Europeans like us had also once jumped the border.

Rose soon followed, booked in steerage on the Cunard liner RMS *Coronia*, arriving legally at Ellis Island on June 26, 1911, accompanied by her two-year-old daughter and pregnant with a boy, Georgie, who would die at the age of seven in the 1918 influenza epidemic.

The four of them lived in the Bushwick section of Brooklyn for a year before the promise of a steady job for George lured them to Bethlehem, where a department store was looking for a full-time painter. But the job came with a proviso: "No Irish Need Apply," i.e., no Catholics. And so, the Southern Irish Mitchells abandoned their native Catholicism and became Protestants by the time the horse-drawn van arrived to move them from Brooklyn to Bethlehem, courtesy of George's new employer. My father was born four years later in Bethlehem in 1916, during World War I—his middle name, Woodrow, a nod to the president who had taken us into that war.

Rose thought that a small town might discourage her husband's binge drinking. She was mistaken. George apparently never got over leaving Liverpool and on occasion, after a few pints, would sing out, "We are outcasts in a strange land!"

George's maladjustment was aggravated by the death of his firstborn son, Georgie, in the influenza pandemic, which produced a cruel and irrational resentment toward his other, surviving son, my father. The day my dad graduated from high school, the drunken George spied him in a new jacket Rose had scrimped and saved to purchase for the occasion, and, in a scene out of Eugene O'Neill, grabbed him by the lapels, shouting, "Now I bet you think you're too good for me!"

Eugene Woodrow Mitchell | Author Collection
(Larry Reese, *Dallas Morning News*)

"He tried to tear the coat off me," Dad remembered, ever emotional in the retelling. The benighted George ripped the lapel's seams before storming out the door, never to return. Fortunately, Rose knew how to sew.

"When your father was a young boy," George's brother Frank (my dad's uncle) wrote to him in a letter years later, "he fell off a wall and had a concussion of the brain. He was not expected to live. This may be the reason for certain events."

In the class of 1934 Bethlehem Liberty High yearbook, Dad listed his hobby as "reading," but he had taken the nonacademic commercial course at the behest of Rose, a product of the British class system. Dad didn't realize he was eligible to go to college until years later, in Dallas, when a registrar at SMU's night school asked him why he wasn't enrolled in a degree program since he was getting As in all his courses. He didn't earn his degree in business administration from SMU until he was fifty, but if not for starting at the back of the line, he might have become a professor of literature or history or found his way into the professional theatre. He subscribed to magazines like the *New Yorker*, the *New Republic*, the *Reporter*, *I. F. Stone's Weekly*, the *Nation*, and *Harper's*. I was too young to read them, but he would talk at dinner about an article he had read or something that had happened in history that people didn't understand—that the Potato Famine in Ireland had been made worse by the heartless colonial practices of the British, that the rise of Fidel Castro in Cuba was in response to the tyrannical reign of dictator Fulgencio

Batista. He was drawn to stories that illustrated the treachery and stealth of the rich and powerful, who were, I gathered, the enemy of ordinary people like us. His observations were often freighted with a moral fury that I doubtless inherited and tried to modulate.

A pacifist and democratic socialist at heart, Dad proudly considered himself "working class" and perversely clung to the label even after securing a place among the gentry at the art museum. FDR was his hero. Roosevelt and the New Deal, he believed, had saved the nation from the damage done by unfettered capitalism, maybe forestalling another revolution. And coupled with FDR was the emergence of unions to protect working people from the abuses of their wealthy bosses. More than once I heard him recall the glorious day the plant workers went on strike at Bethlehem Steel for better and safer conditions, clashing with mounted police in a violent scene that Dad had watched from a high office window, a witness to history.

With a tear in his eye, he would then repeat the two words, "They won."

At the end of August 1963, Dad took a week's vacation to paint the interior of the house and asked me to help him. I gladly accepted the responsibility, which involved learning how to use a paint roller. It was the beginning of the house looking like an art gallery, white on white on white, even the wall paneling and stone fireplace. Among the oil paintings hanging on those white walls were works by Wilfred Higgins and Otis Dozier, leading Texas modernists who discounted their prices to my parents out of friendship.

The day of the historic Civil Rights March on Washington—three months before the Kennedy assassination—we were painting the living room, and Dad put the small portable black-and-white TV on a folding chair so that we could watch as we worked. An estimated quarter of a million people were gathered on the Mall to demonstrate for jobs and freedom. In front of the Washington Monument, Peter, Paul & Mary sang "If I Had a Hammer" and "Blowing in the Wind," Joan Baez led a chorus of "We Shall Overcome," and Dylan did "When the Ship Comes In," a song The Bountymen would learn. When Martin Luther King rocked the world with his "I Had a Dream" speech, we might have put down our rollers.

Dad's love and devotion nevertheless came bundled with a mercurial temperament that I had to sort out. Evincing a Mitchell family trait, he slipped occasionally into dark moods that were hard for a kid to understand,

and when I asked my mother, she would knowingly confide that the clouds would pass, and we simply had to wait until the next day. Usually, she was right, and I learned to accept the changeable weather of his personality.

His excitable disposition did prove an impediment to teaching me how to drive, however. After taking me out for an initial, nerve-wracking session in his used British-made stick-shift Morris Minor, he decided that I needed a calmer and more patient instructor. Such a person was found in family friend Byrd Helligas, the worldly and gregarious assistant minister at the Unitarian Church who presided over the Liberal Religious Youth group each Sunday night at his residence next door to the sanctuary. It was at Byrd's house where many of us saw the Beatles make their historic appearance on *The Ed Sullivan Show* in February 1964.

Byrd was happy to help and let me take the wheel of his vintage VW bug while he offered defensive driving tips and shared memories of landing on a beach in Italy during World War II. I would forever remember Byrd's advice to watch the front left wheel of a car passing on the right for signs the driver might be pulling into your lane. I got my license at sixteen.

Driving lessons and black moods aside, Dad was ultimately an optimist, always rebounding from a depression or setback, bright-eyed, and ready to roll. "Sometimes it's a good feeling just to be alive," he told me once. "It's enough to see the sun come up; it's enough just to be in the world." This simple truth, from someone who had been blocked by circumstance from pursuing his dreams, resounded with me as I reached the age when one begins to examine the nature and meaning of happiness.

CHAPTER FIFTEEN

Providence

YOU FIND YOURSELF CONFRONTED WITH THE STAR-
*TLING FACT that you are being initiated into an institution that is
more than two hundred years old. Everything here has been happening for a very long time. French troops were housed in University Hall during
the Revolution!*

This is from a letter I wrote home giddily at the end of Freshman Week,
September 18, 1966. University Hall was the stately four-story Georgian edifice
and national historic landmark that bordered the main College Green, ringed
by eye-catching examples of eighteenth-and nineteenth-century architecture.
Along with two other members of my St. Mark's class, I had made it to Brown,
one of the "lesser" of the eight Ivy League colleges: meaning the five that were
not Harvard, Yale, or Princeton. (Greg was at Princeton.) Brown was one of the
nation's oldest universities, founded before the Declaration of Independence,
in 1764, and I was thrilled to be here, enchanted by the notion I would be trans-
figured by history and academic tradition. When my father dropped me off
with Bob Rozelle at the beginning of Freshman Week, after a three-day drive
from Dallas, I sensed I would be attending Brown not just for me but for him as
well. Before we left for Providence, he took me to Neiman's to buy a soft plaid
winter topcoat. I'd never needed one of those before. Such was the anticipation.

*You ought to see the halftime shows here. The band wears brown blazers
and white pants, but it's not like the ones you see in the Cotton Bowl because the*

Freshman at Brown | AUTHOR COLLECTION

guy narrating the action makes jokes the whole time. It's really different.

So read the description of my first Brown football game, against the University of Rhode Island, which Brown somehow won. Ivy League football was considerably down market from the Southwest Conference I had grown up with, and Brown was often overmatched.

I had been unduly influenced by Fitzgerald's 1920 novel *This Side of Paradise*, set at Princeton after World War I, and couldn't help but notice that life in Mead House, my freshmen dorm, did not much resemble Fitzgerald's world (or the fantasies it inspired). The interior walls of our rooms were made of cinder block—painted and practical but not what you imagined for living quarters in the Ivy League. Because of overcrowding, some doubles had been turned into triples, with bunk beds hogging the modest space. There were engineers, hockey players from Canada, science majors, and unfamiliar East Coast accents in the halls. Providence itself, once you wandered away from the brick sidewalks and elms of College Hill, was rundown, cheerless, and gray, a stark contrast to the sunny and clean (if antiseptic) city I had grown up in. Being from Dallas, I discovered, implicated me in the murder of JFK. "Does everyone there own a gun?" I was asked accusingly more than once. I quickly got defensive about the place I had been so ready to escape.

But in general, I was eager to feel the affiliation of my new tribe: Brown. What did those five letters mean exactly? Outside Marvel Gym the athletic image of Brown was represented by a seven-foot bronze sculpture of a grizzly bear named Bruno. At St. Mark's we had been lions, at Brown we were bears. I was making the adjustment.

In my room assignment I was fortunate to have only a double and be paired with a big-hearted Korean American Methodist minister's son from

Honolulu named Dale Lee, who planned to major in American civilization—or American Civ. He introduced me to Hawaiian music and culture, including the great crooner Don Ho, whom I'd never heard of. He had brought the LPs with him. In return, I mounted on the wall above my bed several album covers bearing the likeness of Lightnin' Hopkins, the legendary Texas blues man—my initial attempt at interior decoration.

It was because of Dale that I met another student from Hawaii, Douglas John, who showed up at our door the first day of Freshman Week looking for Dale because Dale had kicked a game-winning field goal for Iolani School against Doug's Punahou team the year before. After Doug spotted my guitar case, the two of us discovered that we both knew all the songs on Simon & Garfunkel's *Wednesday Morning 3 a.m.* album and were soon recording "He Was My Brother" and "Bleecker Street" on a cassette player in the third-floor bathroom to get reverb. Doug had a seriously good baritone with a gift for harmony and looked a little like Roger Daltrey of The Who. Over the next four years, he and I would sing and play here and there, mostly in dorm rooms and lounges. Once, we performed at a Providence coffeehouse on open mic night. I don't remember how we were received, but I remember the pants I wore: gray and red plaid flannel with cuffs, something I'd seen in *Esquire*. We were not yet hipsters.

With five thousand undergraduates, Brown was modestly sized compared to most state universities, but coming from a small high school as I did, it seemed plenty big and impersonal. Clearly it would be much harder to stand out in the crowd here, and the crowd included graduates of the eastern boarding schools, the offspring of famous families, sons of publishers and politicians, and high achievers from all over—young men untethered by parents, liquor laws, and dress codes for the first time, many trying on new identities each week. There were sockless preppies in khakis and topsiders; jocks from the South in pink polo shirts; coat-and-tie men from fashion layouts; and the first evidence of long hair, jean jackets, and bell-bottoms. My own wardrobe consisted of corduroy slacks and button-downed Oxford cloth shirts (that I ironed myself to save money), two tweed sportscoats, and a single pair of cordovan Bass loafers.

The biggest man on campus was not a square-jawed, blonde-haired athlete or future senator but a disheveled nerd from New York City named

Ira Magaziner, who was busy constructing a reform movement that would transform the 202-year-old university's curriculum. He would go on to win a Rhodes Scholarship and one day lead the Clinton Foundation, but at the time he was "that guy" you might spot crossing the Green, looking like Ichabod Crane (as Bob once described him) yet possessing an intellect and imagination of a higher order.

Though a lot of my fellow students were from New York and the Eastern Seaboard, many were from everywhere else: St. Louis, Chicago, Portland, Los Angeles, Atlanta, Seattle, Rome, Costa Rica. There were 650 men in my class, plus an additional 250 women at Pembroke, the adjoining women's college soon to be absorbed by Brown. This gender imbalance made social life a challenge, especially freshman year. To meet women from nearby women's colleges, including the Seven Sisters, required attending "mixers," or open house dances at the schools, events that attracted carloads of men from other colleges as well. It was a crude mating ritual that required boldness, determination, and prior fortification with alcohol. And if you succeeded in finding a dance partner, you often had only moments to get to know her before asking her to come to Brown for an entire weekend—an impractical and even crazy idea that made you wonder if the deans at these supposedly elite institutions approved of this?

I shared these experiences of initiation into college life in correspondence with classmates from St. Mark's like Greg, Dick Wincorn (Stanford), and others who wrote back with their own reports. Between classes I often detoured through the long hall that held the student mailboxes in the basement of Faunce House, the student center, because there were multiple deliveries during the day, and it was easy to see through the tiny glass door on your box if any new mail had arrived. Phone calls were infrequent because each dorm only had one pay phone per floor that had to be shared with thirty other guys. Plus, you needed the coins to feed it.

I WENT TO BROWN HOPING TO PLAY DIVISION I SOCCER, working construction on the LBJ Freeway (I-635) in Dallas that summer before freshman year to get in shape. I planned to join the list of St. Mark's athletes who had made it to the next level and was willing to make that a priority over the Brown Daily Herald or trying out for the theatre, which might have

Undefeated. I'm seated in first row, between future All-American Herman Ssebazza and goalkeeper Robert Borthwick (holding ball)

made more sense. Unlike high school, you couldn't do both; soccer practice lasted three hours, five days a week, and on top of that I worked at the "Ratty," or refectory, bussing plates and trays. I figured I could rejoin journalism later. The theatre I never got around to; my shyness held me back.

Brown was a perennial frontrunner in Ivy League soccer, but I was not prepared for how high the level of play was, nor in my Texas innocence did I realize how many of the guys trying out for the freshman team had been recruited, mostly from Long Island, Maryland, and New Jersey, where the high school game was more advanced. As a walk-on, I managed to make the squad as a midfielder and saw some playing time during our undefeated season but sitting on the bench was humbling after being captain of the team at St. Mark's.

Following a victory over Yale in New Haven, I reported home that *I didn't think I would have had any trouble starting for Yale*. Accurate or not, it reflected my ambivalence about landing at a collegiate soccer power. I also noted in the same letter that Bob Rozelle was faring better on the freshman football squad, where he had been turned into a wide receiver and in their game against Yale had caught nine passes in a 23–20 loss.

There seemed to be a lot of musicians here, and the names of student bands were evocative of time and place: The Rhythm Method, the Slithy Toves, Uranus and the Five Moons. I bragged to my mother about the number of top folk singers who came to campus, people like Tom Rush, Mark Spoelstra, Judy Collins, Phil Ochs, and Harry Belafonte. Greenwich Village, I wanted to think, was not that far away. I hitched a ride to Brandeis, up the road in Waltham, Massachusetts, to get my first look at Simon & Garfunkel in the flesh. I took a notebook and tape recorder just in case I might score an interview. Ha.

The air turned cold in October, and I walked to classes on wet pavement covered by red and yellow leaves pasted in place by the frequent rain. The novelty of my first true autumn was invigorating and my courses demanding. I signed up for a creative writing class with the novelist R. V. Cassill and found him unfriendly and unhelpful. He praised a short poem I wrote and reproduced it for class discussion but otherwise offered little in the way of encouragement or direction. My intermediate Spanish instructor was strictly by the book and focused narrowly on grammar rather than the conversational skill emphasized at St. Mark's; European history was much better, with a compelling lecturer, but the section leader was a pompous ass from Oxford who said an A would only be awarded for something "publishable." In Philosophy I, or whatever its name, I happened to land in a small class being taught by a ranking professor in the field of metaphysics, but his humorless, gray-faced demeanor failed to spark my interest in the historic texts of Spinoza, Hobbes, and Kant.

One day in class, Professor Cassill asked us to respond to the inscription on Soldier's Arch, a memorial to the forty-two men from Brown killed in World War I and located downhill from an equestrian statue of the Roman emperor Marcus Aurelius. In addition to the names of the fallen, a line from Ralph Waldo Emerson is carved into the limestone: *Tis man's perdition to be safe / When for the truth he ought to die.* At the time, it struck me as confounding and confusing, knowing that Emerson had been a Unitarian. A few years later I would have said: Is that what those guys in the trenches were thinking?

For the major short story the course required, I submitted what I'm sure was a sophomoric treatment of the life I imagined for a young professional soccer (or *futbol*) player in Mexico City. I'd be curious to read that story now, but maybe it's best it was lost years ago.

When Christmas vacation arrived, many of us flew home for the first time after months of adapting to our new habitat in Rhode Island. As the Braniff Airlines 707 taxied to the terminal at Love Field, I looked out the window and saw the familiar lights of Dallas beckoning to me in the December night. It made me think of Nick Carraway's recollection in *The Great Gatsby* of his youthful trips home to Minnesota at Christmas, changing trains in Chicago before pushing north happily into "the real snow" of the upper Midwest, his native land. In my mind, I was updating that scene some fifty years later in a part of the country that rarely saw snow or anyone traveling on trains.

Reuniting with my St. Mark's friends, as well as Gene and Lu, proved more emotional than I anticipated, a bittersweet reminder of what I had left behind. I knew—we all knew—this was just a dalliance with the past before getting back to our new lives, but when I returned to chilly, dreary Providence after the holiday, its otherness seemed more pronounced. As I steeled myself for final exams, for the first time I was truly homesick and wondered if I had made a mistake in coming to Brown. I even entertained fantasies of transferring to Texas or SMU.

Unlike some guys in Mead House, I had not done any serious drinking that first semester, but after completing my last exam, I brought wine and beer back to the room, and with Dale and a few others, drank indiscriminately into the night, adding whiskey, gin, and whatever else we could find to top off the celebration. The next day, I had a hangover so bad I went to the infirmary for pain medication.

A couple nights later, some members of the freshman soccer team asked me to join them to go watch a home hockey game against Dartmouth. (Brown and Cornell were the Ivy hockey powers in those years.) I tagged along with the group as we walked the icy streets of January to Meehan Auditorium and watched Brown triumph in a sport that was foreign to me. Embedded with the cheering home crowd, I felt oddly numb and detached.

Then came the grades. In my four courses I got 2 Bs and 2 Cs, for a 2.5 GPA—disappointing, especially a C in history, a subject I had aced at St. Mark's. The only solace was learning that the freshmen class average was even lower, meaning I had finished above the middle. (This apparently was before grade inflation swept higher education.)

When I let it sink in that I had survived the first semester, I snapped out of my malaise and put any thoughts of transferring out of my head. This place was hard and humbling, but I wasn't giving up on it. The dirty ice of winter, I learned, could be followed by fresh snow, blue skies, and sunshine, days when just walking across the quad in a bright chill made you happy. I looked forward to the arrival of spring (not yet realizing how late it comes to New England) and in the meantime, saw the prospect of a better living situation the next year. I was anti-Greek bro culture before coming to Brown, based on examples I'd seen in Texas, but the fifteen or so fraternities here were housed in the regular dorms and offered the refuge of a familiar group inside the larger university.

At an open house during the spring rush, I met Alan Fedman, a future government lawyer from Tulsa, a class ahead of me, who I discovered had attended the same high school as one of my best friends from the South-west LRY—and even knew him. Serendipity. Alan and I had the Southwest in common, a similar sense of humor, and found an instant rapport. The house was Lambda Sigma Nu and seemed to be an eclectic mix of humanities majors, actors, musicians, politicos, and preppies. I was tempted by another fraternity where Doug was headed, along with some soccer players and the future filmmaker Ross McElwee, who had become a friend. I got bids from both houses, but on the last day to return a bid, still unsure of my decision, I strode down into the lower quad, where both fraternities were located, and (drum roll) at the point the paths diverged, I took the one to Sigma Nu—because of the upperclassmen I had met there and because of Alan. Two decades later, he would be the best man at my wedding.

CHAPTER SIXTEEN

Up for Grabs

I DIDN'T TRY TO PLAY BASEBALL AT BROWN because (1) it was too cold and (2) in high school I had trouble hitting the curveball. I figured soccer was my sport, however daunting. That first summer back in Dallas I worked at the Eastman Kodak warehouse by day and at night helped organize pickup games with former St. Mark's teammates who were playing in college and trying to stay in shape. We managed to schedule a match against a mostly Hispanic club team at the University of Texas, driving down to Austin on a Sunday in July. The temperature was close to 100 degrees at game time, and they beat us 7–1. The only thing notable about it was that our single goal was scored by Kyle Rote Jr., son of the SMU football great and future star of the Dallas Tornado (of the North American Soccer League) who was learning the game and asked to play with us. I had the assist, which might have been a career highlight.

Back in Providence in the fall, embracing the cool of September, I was assigned to the JV team and started as a winger. I enjoyed that—my best season. At Sigma Nu I ended up with a roommate from Andover whose nickname "Burundi" signified the nation in Africa where he had lived because of his father's job with the Agency for International Development (said by some to be a front for the CIA). Before Burundi, he had lived in Greece. He was tall, blonde, and good-looking, with the long fluffy sideburns of a Victorian dandy, pouty lips, and the bearing of someone who had grown up with servants. He played squash. His name was William Barringer, and, charming snob that he was, he liked to tease me that he'd gone to "a real prep school," unlike the country day knockoff I attended. He also observed, only half in jest, that I had "a working-class face," which, compared to him, I guess I did. I indulged his haughty jibes, and we got along fine, maybe because I saw him as another aspect of my education, someone whose patrician background and worldview were so different from my own but worth knowing about. Possibly he accepted me on similar terms.

There was no hazing, but after our first semester, sophomore year, the twenty members of our pledge class were summoned one evening to be scolded by an officer in the fraternity, a cerebral Philadelphian, who informed us we were not cutting it academically. We learned that a friendly competition existed among the fraternities for highest average GPA each term, and that our class's first semester grades had dragged Sigma Nu down from its previous attainment of second place. Oh, please, I thought. At least no names were mentioned, and I don't recall the subject ever coming up again.

Already it is apparent that living in a fraternity house will be superior to the freshman year setup, I wrote home sophomore year. There was a TV room, a large lounge on the first floor with a baby grand piano (and Jeff Carter, a guy who could play "Satin Doll" on it), a cool, dark bar in the basement for weekend parties and, well, weekend parties. We had our own dining room off the main area of the Ratty—the same *oh, no* cafeteria food but a more congenial space to sit and look at it, lingering for post-meal discussions about such topics as whether Brown should lower admission standards for football players or if we should aspire to fame in our lives. In that instance, I remember a guy named Tim suggesting the best kind of fame would be a sort limited to cognoscenti, like being a professor well-known in his field. I would recall the good sense of that years later when interviewing actors in Hollywood.

In addition to the "brothers" (we rarely used that term) who spoke at house meetings as if auditioning for roles on Capitol Hill, the membership included a United States senator's son and the son of the governor of Illinois. A few guys smoked pipes, and a few qualified as snobs, but idiosyncrasy was accepted and affectation indulged. There were characters like Peter Schoeffer, a son of Park Avenue who carried himself with a roguish European élan that earned him the nickname "the baron." The preppies were easily identified by the topsiders they wore without socks even in the freezing Providence winters. And we had un-preppies, modeled by jean-jacketed upperclassman Bob Arnold, a visage out of Jack Kerouac's *On the Road*.

The house was full of music. After home football games, our own jazz trio would play for cocktail parties in the lounge—Carter on piano, Bill Hart on drums, and a bass player from nearby RISD (Rhode Island School of Design), the school where David Byrne formed Talking Heads. Bill Griffith, a future New York lawyer from Houston, composed the scores for original undergraduate musicals; Al Basile, a de facto member of the house, wrote the lyrics. Al was also in Cassill's class and a horn player who would later tour with the swing band Roomful of Blues.

Though I continued to sing and play with Doug—his fraternity wasn't far away, on the same lower quad—some nights I jammed in our lounge with Michael Hahn, a keyboardist who had grown up in Rome, wore a beret, and would go to work for the State Department as a cultural attaché. We were often joined by Doug Gillespie, a future architect who played trombone in the ironic Brown marching band and could power us through Chicago's signature tune "Beginnings."

I drove to mixers with Alan, who had a car. One night, on the way to Wheaton in his yellow-and-black Camaro, we listened avidly to the Beatles' new double LP *The White Album* (on cassette) and agreed that we would be analyzing the lyrics for decades to come. I believe we gained that insight after smoking a few *numbers*, or "joints," hand-rolled marijuana cigarettes.

Sigma Nu had its own lingo, some of it shared with the greater university community. If you did too many *numbers*, you got *wrecked* or *destroyed*. If you *bagged a lecture* (cut a class), you could ask someone who did go what the major *cepts* were—the concepts or ideas expressed. If

Alan Fedman | AUTHOR COLLECTION

you parted ways with a date at any point during a weekend, you *faded* on her—or she faded on you. If someone did something stupid, house member Chris Dunn reminded me, you would arch your eyebrows and proclaim sarcastically, *Oh, good!* In the same way, *Get serious!* expressed some level of incredulity, as when John Wayne won the Oscar for *True Grit*, beating out Dustin Hoffman and Jon Voight from *Midnight Cowboy*, and when Nixon announced that he had a plan to end the war.

Bill Barringer, my Phillips Andover roommate, early in the term explained his course selections to me with the casual assurance that defined him: he chose classes based on which ones were most likely to net him the highest GPA so that he could get into Harvard Law School. He had a plan. It made me wonder: Did I have a plan?

During Freshman Week, Doug had sized me up and asked, "Are you one of these angry young men?" He later denied ever saying this, but if I imagined it, it was because it was true and spoke to the differences between us: his father had been an Air Force general, and Doug was in ROTC. He was a gifted joke-teller, comfortable in his own skin, and would one day launch a successful law firm representing oil and gas companies. I wanted to be a writer, even if I wasn't sure what kind of writer. I longed to express my experience of the world and the people in it as Salinger and other novelists had done, but how exactly did one learn to do that? Verlin Cassill's class wasn't helping much.

Peter Schoeffer
AUTHOR COLLECTION

Bill Barringer in his cast
AUTHOR COLLECTION

Sigma Nu, Junior Year: A House Divided | AUTHOR COLLECTION

I had tacked up over my desk an article from the (London) *Times Literary Supplement* about Britain's leading "men of letters," bannered with photos of William Empson, F. R. Leavis, I. A. Richards, and T.S. Eliot. Except for Eliot, I had never heard of any of them, but the term "men of letters" sounded like something I should know about and maybe aspire to. Edmund Wilson was the American version, but I didn't yet know much about him either. In fact, the era of the "men of letters" was ending just as I discovered it.

And then there was Bob Dylan, pulling me in a different direction altogether, his urgent, enigmatic rock and roll poetry breaking down the wall between high and low culture, his homely Midwestern twang establishing a new vocal standard in pop music. I had learned the two-finger picking necessary to play "Don't Think Twice, It's Alright," but I wasn't sure about his blues-based ungrammatical lyrics ("Ain't no use to sit and wonder why, babe …") that broke all the rules of English I had learned. Again, "low" culture was being elevated to "high." Dylan and other visionary rockers had transcended mere entertainment, supplanting literature and theatre with a new form of truth-telling performance art. I began writing songs on the guitar, inexpertly modeling Dylan and Paul Simon while musing that the Ivy League was the last place Dylan would be found dead. Sometimes I imagined myself the troubadour in Simon's "Homeward Bound," alone and aloof in a railway station, destination unknown.

Everything was suddenly up for grabs. The history-laden Brown tradition I had planned to appropriate was being overtaken by forces outside the university. Doug, Dale, Bob, and I had arrived on College Hill in the fading autumn of Harris tweeds and Weejuns and would depart in Levis and motorcycle boots. Or at least I would. We began freshman year attending Sunday afternoon sherry hours with our resident adviser and a semester later were smoking marijuana and listening to "Surrealistic Pillow."

Sigma Nu's yearbook photo my junior year bore witness to the shift. All forty of us were arrayed in front of University Hall, split into two groups—one side well-groomed and attired in traditional tweeds, blazers, and ties; the other scruffier, lined up in jeans and sweatshirts, with a few Army surplus jackets visible. (Alan and I were in that group.) Senior year the change was complete, and the fraternity photo was staged to resemble the cover of the Beatles' *Sgt. Pepper's Lonely Hearts Club Band* album, with many of us clad in vintage clothes from thrift shops and a peace symbol pasted on the bass drum.

CHAPTER SEVENTEEN

Rumination in the Air

I HADN'T MET MANY FAMOUS PEOPLE when I drove out to the Providence airport one afternoon with other members of the class council to pick up the Black comedian Dick Gregory, whom we had invited to campus. I was excited, knowing he was someone my parents admired, and I wasn't prepared for his indifference to us. He was angry, just like in his act, and did not seem at all interested in the admiration of the three earnest white college boys who had come to fetch him in a VW Beetle. Maybe he expected a better car. On the ride back we got to talking about the news, and when I quoted an article I had just read in the *New York Times,* he turned and gave me a withering look. "The *New York Times?*" he growled. "You can't believe everything you read in the *New York Times!*" Really? At nineteen, I thought you could. I had never heard anyone say that before, certainly not an important person.

We also booked Jimi Hendrix, and I sat in the lobby of Faunce House spinning "Purple Haze" and other cuts from his first LP on a portable stereo while selling tickets for $2.50. The day of the show I went to Marvel Gym for the load-in in the afternoon and saw Jimi and the band arrive in a sedan pulling a small U-Haul trailer with their equipment. (The days before limos and big money.) Glancing backstage, I saw someone in the band tying off his arm with a tourniquet, then lifting a syringe. I looked away.

I didn't meet Jimi, but I did meet another pop star of the era who showed up at Sigma Nu one night and put on an impromptu concert in our lounge. "That's Donovan," someone said to me when I noticed a crowd had gathered downstairs. What? No. Yes. The "English Dylan" (Scottish actually), Donovan was in town for a concert the next night and had ventured to campus with the promoter, who knew our social chairman. His songs "Catch the Wind" and "Sunshine Superman" had been major hits in America, and by the time he got his guitar out, the lounge was packed. Before he left at 1 a.m. I went over and talked to him, foreshadowing what I would one day be doing for a living. He was friendly and optimistic and told me he believed *the younger generation of the world will overpower the forces of hate and aggression,* I noted in a letter. Hippie wisdom!

With a head of long springy curls and tie-dyed clothes, Donovan looked every inch a hippie, the name lately given to the growing number of disaffected young people "dropping out" and dressing differently to signify their belonging to a new tribe (or fashion trend). We were not hippies at Brown, only hippie sympathizers, those of us drawn to the rebellion of the counterculture, made visible in the way we decorated our rooms with sheets of floral paisley India block prints on the walls and posters of the New Wave French film star Jean Paul Belmondo and Beat poet Allen Ginsberg. A suitable setting for toking up to the Beatles' *Magical Mystery Tour* or one of the cosmic California bands.

Spring break that second year in Providence I joined Bob and two other classmates on a budget tour of the Mid-Atlantic states, the four of us packed

My Room at Sigma Nu
AUTHOR COLLECTION

India Block Prints on the Walls
AUTHOR COLLECTION

into yet another VW bug, an old one Bob had inherited from his brother Allen. We had no money and slept on the floors of fraternity houses, saw George Washington's Mount Vernon and Thomas Jefferson's Monticello, and took in some early season Brown baseball games against the University of Virginia. On the drive back, we crossed Chain Link Bridge into Washington, DC, and stopped at a liquor store, where the clerk informed us that Martin Luther King had been assassinated in Memphis and that riots were breaking out in major cities. We got back in the car and kept driving.

When summer came, Bob, through family connections, got us jobs as baggage handlers for American Airlines at San Francisco International. Greg managed to land a gig with a San Francisco inner-city youth advocacy program, and the three of us, along with Bountymen guitarist David Laney (coming from nearby Stanford), squeezed into a small third-floor apartment at the base of Nob Hill in that summer after the Summer of Love. I don't know what we ate for three months (none of us could cook), but we bought six-packs of El Rancho beer for a dollar and attended concerts in Golden Gate Park and at Bill Graham's Fillmore West, digging the psychedelic light shows and smoking grass to the sounds of Janis Joplin, Jefferson Airplane, and The Grateful Dead. We had reached Mecca.

But not without a warning. The job at the airport required Bob, David, and me to load dead soldiers from Vietnam onto 707s bound for hometowns across America. They arrived at SFO packed in long gray plywood boxes labeled "Human Remains," ready for transfer to domestic airlines. We had to crawl up into the cargo hold to secure them with the rest of the luggage, all the while wondering who was inside and what they had died for. It wasn't uncommon on an August morning to see one of those gray coffins resting on a mobile conveyor belt out on the runway, glowing in the golden Bay Area sunshine, waiting for its plane to arrive. An incongruous and unsettling sight.

No doubt influenced by Steve McQueen in *The Great Escape*, I bought a used Suzuki 150 motorcycle to ride down the peninsula to the airport each day. Bob sometimes rode on the back. Once I rode it across the Golden Gate Bridge in a rainstorm to a party in Tiburon.

California wowed us, and we weren't the only ones. When I got back to Brown in the fall, I discovered another classmate had been in San Francisco and was wearing a watch on each wrist, one set to West Coast time.

I WAS MAJORING IN ENGLISH, taking courses in English and American literature, Shakespeare, poetry, and satire, plus electives in art history and anthropology. Because distribution requirements still obtained, I took an introductory course in geology with John Imbrie, an expert in the ice ages and a wonderful teacher who introduced us to the theory of continental drift. In my own field I was probably not ready for the course in "persona" taught by the eminent poet Edwin Honig, who routinely unloaded cryptic statements like "There are too many words."

For an assignment in a Shakespeare course, I adapted a section of *Richard III* to the present, substituting Richard Nixon for the treacherous English monarch, in imitation of the way Barbara Garson had substituted LBJ for Macbeth in the off-Broadway hit *MacBird!* For an independent study project with Professor Charles Nichols, I wrote a forty-five-page paper on the complete works of Norman Mailer, whose *Armies of Night* had captivated me with its personal account of an anti-war march on the Pentagon—an early example of the New Journalism that would eventually lure me into the profession. (I dare say, decades later, I found the book unreadable.)

In and out of class I read John Barth, Kurt Vonnegut, Thomas Pynchon, Joseph Heller, Sylvia Plath, Ken Kesey, Bernard Malamud, Jerzy Kosinski, Philip Roth, and Saul Bellow—yes, mostly men. Some of them came to campus to speak.

Rumination was in the air. In a navel-gazing letter I sent to my parents years later during a frustrating job search in New York, I looked back on this impressionable time and recalled, *The more I learned about art and philosophy and psychology, the less clear my future seemed, the more futile all human endeavor seemed.*

My closest friends and I were beginning to question the standard definitions of success, not unlike the aimless eastern college grad played by Dustin Hoffman in the film *The Graduate*, released at Christmas my sophomore year. New concepts of existentialism and cultural revolution had reached us, beyond the classroom. One of the titles we were sharing was a radical academic treatise called "Man's Rage for Chaos," by Morse Peckham, that advocated experiencing the arts from a new, behaviorist point of view.

Bob Rozelle
AUTHOR COLLECTION

Dale Lee & Monica MacAdams in Sigma Nu bar
AUTHOR COLLECTION

To earn spending money, I moved up from working at the Ratty to waiting tables at the Faculty Club alongside Bob and eventually landed a job on the reference desk at the main John D. Rockefeller Library, known as "the Rock." My best gig. I learned to ski in Vermont, driving up to Burke Mountain, below the Canadian border, with Bob and Doug and others, staying in a low-cost time-share in St. Johnsbury. Once, Doug and I played and sang for lift tickets in the bar.

My social life got a boost when my cousin Monica MacAdams, of Toledo, Ohio, daughter of Dad's sister Gerry and her husband, Richard MacAdams, joined me at Brown sophomore year. She was the sister I never had—and welcomed. I got to know lots of her friends and dated a few; she was a frequent visitor to Sigma Nu and caught the eye of my roommate from Andover, who, incidentally, broke his leg skiing over Christmas vacation junior year and had to move to a first floor single, leaving me with the fourth-floor double all to myself.

On my twenty-first birthday I returned from the library to find Monica waiting for me in that room with a big, white-frosted cake, champagne, and a group of friends to mark the occasion—a surprise party evoking a scene from Evelyn Waugh's *Brideshead Revisited*. I held on to that memory for years and another one from a chilly night we were riding in a car with some others, heading down the Hill in search of food after hours when Hendrix's new cover of "All Along the Watchtower" came on the radio. It was a moment of no particular significance except that when I looked over at Monica, moving in her seat to the rhythm of those percussive chords, blond hair framing her face, something clicked—the shutter on life's Nikon, preserving the image forever. We had grown up five states apart and seen each other only a couple of times as kids, but we were together, in college, in New England. This had really happened.

Junior year, Sigma Nu decided to do away with its Greek letters, whose shelf life and traditions had expired. Other fraternities were doing the same, cutting their ties to anachronistic national organizations. In the contest to come up with a new name for the house, my good friend and future poet Tom Linklater (we were in Honig's class together) and I did some research into Brown history and discovered that two of Brown's most distinguished writers, S. J. Perelman and Nathanael West, in the 1920s had edited a campus literary magazine called *Casements*, the name taken from a line in the English Romantic poet John Keats's "Ode to a Nightingale": *Charm'd magic casements, opening on the foam of perilous seas...*

Casements might seem a bit precious now, but we were charmed by the link to Brown's literary past, no matter how obscure. Obscurity was likely a plus. And there was an additional irony: neither Perelman nor West would have been allowed into a fraternity at Brown in the 1920s because both were Jewish.

Another contender to replace Lambda Sigma Nu was Gaspee College, recalling the name of a British customs schooner boarded and burned in Narragansett Bay by Rhode Island colonists in 1772 in a lead-up to the Revolution. Gaspee College was proposed by Jeff Carter, another Philadelphian, keen student of the Colonial period and the guy who played "Satin Doll" on the baby grand. A class ahead of Tom and me, Jeff was also a good friend, but the protracted deliberations grew fraught, and when the membership finally chose Casements by a narrow vote, he didn't speak to me for weeks.

Fifteen years later, when Jeff ran for the New York State Assembly as a Republican against Jerry Nadler, I sent him a check for twenty-five dollars, noting this was the first time I had ever contributed to a Republican but that I was making an exception in his case to acknowledge that Gaspee College might have been a better name after all—even if it *was* the name of a British ship. By then, he seemed to have forgotten the whole thing.

CHAPTER EIGHTEEN

The War at Home

A S UNIVERSITY STUDENTS, WE QUALIFIED FOR II-S DEFERMENTS that exempted us from serving in the war being fought by our government against communism in the distant Southeast Asian nation of Vietnam. But every night we watched televised reports of the carnage, with body counts, on the network news.

Presidents Eisenhower and Kennedy, captives of Cold War mythology, had allowed the United States to get entangled in a former French colony's battle for independence, but it was President Lyndon Johnson, failing to grasp the political and military realities on the ground, who agreed to commit half a million US troops in defense of "freedom." I was embarrassed Johnson was from Texas and cringed whenever he addressed the nation on television. First, we had killed Kennedy, next we gave America this countrified warmonger whose achievements in civil rights were being obscured by the smoke from napalm bombs incinerating rural villages half a world away.

Professors began to speak out against the war in protests held on the College Green, and celebrity anti-war figures like Oregon senator Wayne Morse and *Slaughterhouse-Five* author Kurt Vonnegut came to campus. The acclaimed Open Theater visited with Jean-Claude van Itallie's anti-Vietnam play *America Hurrah*. The Brown drama department staged *Lysistrata*, by Aristophanes, in which the women of the warring Greek city states withhold sex from their husbands as leverage to negotiate peace. The actors had strapped on wooden "erections" poking against their togas to make the point.

By senior year the odious Richard Nixon was in the White House, widening the war he had falsely promised to end. Death counts were rising. We had changed the name of the fraternity, but who had time to notice? On November 15, 1969, three days after the revelation by reporter Seymour Hersh of the Mai Lai Massacre, a couple carloads from Casements headed down I-95 to Washington, DC, to join an estimated crowd of half a million gathered to demand a ceasefire. Surviving snapshots show that our group included Barringer (in an Army surplus jacket by now), Chris Dunn, Tom Linklater, and Michael Hahn, among others. A march down Pennsylvania Avenue culminated at the White House, neatly encircled, and barricaded by large tour busses. Nixon was inside watching on television and perhaps saw Pete Seeger sing John Lennon's "Give Peace a Chance." For the only time in our four years, Brown beat Harvard in football that afternoon in Providence. Somebody with a transistor radio shared the news as our group headed up Constitution Avenue toward the Department of Justice, the acrid smoke from tear gas canisters reaching us.

Two weeks later, on the night of December 1, I huddled with others in the tube room of the fraternity to watch a live broadcast of the new draft lottery ordered by Congress to fill the ranks of soldiers needed for the war. At Selective Service headquarters in Washington, DC, a congressman from the Armed Services Committee reached into a large glass canister and plucked out, one by one, Bingo-style, the blue plastic capsules representing all the days of the year—and by extension the birthdays of all men aged eighteen to twenty-six, numbering their draft eligibility, 1 to 366. The lower your number, the more likely you were to be drafted. Numbers higher than 200 were considered safe.

I suppose you followed the draft lottery on the tube last night. I'm Number 164, which means I won't automatically be drafted, but there's a good chance that I will. The lottery was the main topic of conversation yesterday, with everyone sharing their numbers. The fact that a few people are completely off the hook while others are certain of being drafted has created an undeniable atmosphere of tension.

No way I was going to Vietnam. I had already thought about teaching after college, inspired by the models of teacher-coaches at St. Mark's. Not

Gathered in Protest: Tom Linklater, Michael Hahn, Chris Dunn, Bill Barringer, Bill Miller, Drew Steckatee

AUTHOR COLLECTION

March on Washington, 1969

AUTHOR COLLECTION

only would teaching allow me to earn a full-time salary at last, but it would cancel ten percent per year of the federal loan debt I had incurred at Brown and—not insignificantly—spare me from duty in the Mekong Delta. Just like students, teachers qualified for deferments, at least for now. California was still in my blood, and I started compiling a list of the state's private schools, which generally did not require a separate teaching credential as public schools did.

MY FINAL SEMESTER BEGAN WITH AN OMEN. Professor Andrew Turnbull, the noted Fitzgerald biographer and Thomas Wolfe scholar, whose course I was planning to take, committed suicide on January 10. I had been looking forward to learning more about my favorite author from someone who knew him as a young man and had edited his collected letters. It was not to be. The *New York Times* obituary said Turnbull died of carbon-monoxide poisoning in his garage in Cambridge, Massachusetts. He was forty-eight. (Fitzgerald only made it to forty-four.)

Around this time, I experienced my first ego-bruising romantic heart-break. A Pembroker and friend of Monica's I had been dating threw me over for none other than . . . Bob Rozelle! Upon learning of this development one Saturday night, I bought a fifth of Dewar's Scotch, got some ice and a glass from our basement bar, planted myself on a leather couch in the first-floor lounge, and drank Scotch on the rocks until I passed out. It was the only time I ever did anything like this.

When I read that the Irish playwright and novelist Samuel Beckett had once been employed as James Joyce's secretary, I wrote to Norman Mailer in care of his publisher asking if he might have a similar position available. Not sure how that would have qualified for a draft deferment, but I never heard back from Mailer.

Guys with high draft numbers, which included Bob, were planning postgrad summer excursions to Europe. That would not be an option for me. Or for my old friend Eric Nye, who enlisted in the Navy after Oberlin rather than be drafted. I began applying for teaching jobs in California and in February drove to Washington, DC, for the annual convention of independent schools, that also served as a job fair. There I met the headmaster of Cincinnati Country Day School (all boys), who was looking for an English teacher and invited me out to see the school.

Cincinnati? I was hoping for Monterey or San Francisco. I had never been to Cincinnati, but two weeks later I was being picked up at the airport by the head of the English Department, a barrel-chested thirty-three-year-old New Yorker named Charlie Goetz.

"So, you want to be a writer?" Goetz said to me cheerfully on the drive in, having read something I must have written to Patrick Boardman, the headmaster.

Did I want to be a writer? Was there a right or wrong answer? "Yes," I said, hoping not to sound egotistical but figuring I might as well be honest. I couldn't tell whether Goetz approved of my answer or not.

When we got to the campus, bare-bones single-story buildings squatting on a leafy, pastoral acreage, he gave me a tour, introduced me around and, with no warning, thrust me into teaching a seventh-grade class. At the end of the day, he offered me the job—seven thousand dollars a year. I said I needed to think about it. I didn't say I was waiting to hear back from California. Goetz said they needed an answer in twenty-four hours.

Spring break at Brown started the next day, and I was booked with a few classmates on a budget flight from New York to London chartered by the rugby team—my first chance to see England. On the plane to New York that night, I reviewed my options. I wasn't sure about Cincinnati Country Day, but if I turned them down and didn't get any offers from California, I would have to bet on getting a physical deferment to keep me out of the military.

London was a thrill and a revelation. We landed sometime after midnight, and once we bused into the city, some of us walked the cobblestone streets til dawn in a state of blissful jet-lagged intoxication. Were we really here? Where was Donovan? Where were the Beatles? Carnaby Street? In the next week I saw my first West End theatre: Peter Shaffer's *The Battle of Shrivings* with John Gielgud and the London production of *HAIR*, whose musical narrative included a reminder of what could happen to draftees sent to Vietnam. I would take away fond memories of the verdant Hampstead Heath as well as psychedelic visions of Westminster Abbey and St. Paul's Cathedral, the result of swallowing tabs of mescaline with my classmate Bob Barnes in preparation for a day on the town. It was fun but also strange enough that I never wanted to do that again.

SPRING WEEKEND, THE CLOSEST THING BROWN HAD TO MARDI GRAS, took place on the last weekend of April each year, when it might or might not be warm outside. The musical acts that came and performed on multiple stages in the quads were the rock and folk headliners of the day: Janis Joplin, The Young Rascals, James Brown, The Shangri Las, The Lovin' Spoonful, Linda Ronstadt, James Taylor, Gordon Lightfoot, and on and on. Bacchanalia defined, the last party before heading into term papers and finals. This year was a little different, in that the term papers and finals would never come, even for those of us about to graduate.

On May 4, 1970, a Monday, I drove with a few other potential conscripts to an Army base near Providence for our obligatory draft physicals. I had accepted the job in Cincinnati, but the US Army still wanted to see if I was physically fit for deployment—in the event Nixon eliminated teaching deferments, as he had threatened. I don't remember all the tests performed on us that afternoon in the dank and dreary Army building, but I do remember the final interview in the buff with a doctor who asked me to stand up and turn around. He was looking at a letter from the family physician in Dallas who had treated me since ninth grade for the pinched nerve in my back, making me eligible for a 1Y deferment—not the full disqualification of 4F, but it meant I would not be called up short of a national emergency.

A graduation like no other | AUTHOR COLLECTION

Personally, I felt no guilt about choosing not to take part in an illegal war being waged on a nation of terrorized farmers on the other side of the Pacific. And I felt sympathy for guys who didn't see through our government's lies or lacked the means to circumvent them.

"You're out" is what the doc said after examining me. He said it quickly, without inflection, and to make sure I heard him right, I asked him to say it again.

I didn't get much time to enjoy my reprieve. When we got back to campus, it was buzzing with the news that four students had been shot and killed by members of the National Guard at Kent State University in Ohio. And nine others wounded. All had been peacefully protesting the recent US invasion of Cambodia that signaled an expansion of the war. The deadly response from the Guard was unthinkable and intolerable. Also unthinkable was continuing with college as usual even with graduation a month away. Something drastic had to be done.

Within hours three thousand students massed on the Green and after hearing a round of speeches from the steps of Sayles Hall, voted 2–1 to go on strike, the numbers tabulated by counting who walked through one or the other of the Green's main entry gates on George Street. No more classes. The faculty cooperated by voting the next day to make final exams and term papers optional. Some people went home, but many stayed and joined various committees and groups exploring ways to pressure the White House and Congress to withdraw our troops from Southeast Asia. As a member of the Economic Boycott Committee, I attended a contentious assembly at Harvard, where representatives from all the New England colleges attempted and failed to reach an agreement as to which industries and products should be boycotted. I took this as a real-life lesson in political science.

Our graduation was a teach-in, with workshops in Vietnamese history and foreign policy taking the place of cocktail parties and other festivities. The feeling was that the crisis of the war and the imperative to stop it preempted letting any good times roll. Gene and Lu came and were in accord with all of it. Monica, who had spent her junior year in Scotland, returned for the occasion and helped me not care that I didn't have a date. The fabled Campus Dance had been cancelled in any case. Members of my class wore white armbands and peace symbols over the dark sleeves of our gowns as we marched through the main Van Wickle Gates and down College Hill to the Colonial era First Baptist Meeting House—one Brown tradition we honored.

America had changed during my four years in Providence, and the university itself had been shaken by the anti-war movement, protests against the trustees' investments in apartheid South Africa, and a perceived racial tokenism that led to a walkout by Black students demanding more representation in the student body. My grades improved enough to get me on the Dean's List twice and I found time to write for a magazine of current events with the Latin name *Res Publica* started by Ira Magaziner. I made the varsity soccer team junior year but did not see much playing time on a squad that included an All-American from Uganda and a future member of the US Olympic team.

Years later, filling out an alumni satisfaction survey, I said I regretted not making friends with any of my professors at Brown. That didn't happen, for whatever reason. Maybe it was the school, maybe it was me. But I also said in that survey that I was grateful for how much I had learned outside the classroom. For me the great gift of Brown was the student body and the opportunity to be part of it—humbled, challenged, informed, and entertained by so many intellectually curious and talented people. If that sounds like a promotional announcement, I hasten to add there were exceptions, like the brothers of a fraternity close to Sigma Nu who rolled a piano out onto their terrace one afternoon and drunkenly hacked it to pieces with an axe. This, too, was Brown.

Not sure if I spotted any of those guys at our fortieth reunion, when members of the class assembled once again for the procession down College Hill to the First Baptist Meeting House, some carrying signs that read "Peace" and "Love." Members of the current graduating class of 2010, who had preceded us down the Hill and now lined both sides of the street, were high fiving us as we passed by. I was moved. Did they know about us? Did they know we had tried to stop the war? They weren't even born yet.

CHAPTER NINETEEN

Banks of the Ohio

"**M**R. MITCHELL." Those two words had a new sound, coming out the mouths of high school students, audible evidence that I was indeed now a teacher only weeks after exiting the Van Wickle Gates on College Hill. I had been accepted into a six-week summer program for new teachers at the Mount Hermon School in Northfield, Massachusetts, where veteran educators mentored us as we stepped in front of a classroom for the first time. It was a useful introduction to what lay ahead in Cincinnati, plus the group of young teachers was a harmonious bunch, forging a tight social circle almost immediately. The group included Ray Hornblower, a star halfback at Harvard during my era, and his wife, the future journalist Margot Hornblower. On weekends we drove in a caravan to Tanglewood in the Berkshires and shared picnic dinners on the lawn as we listened to James Taylor, Chicago, The Who, and the Boston Symphony Orchestra.

I got particularly close to one teacher in the group, Bethany Holley, a soon-to-be Mount Holyoke grad. In my four years at Brown, I had not managed to have a serious girlfriend and now wished I had met Bethany at one of those mixers. She joined me for a ten-day road trip through Mexico at summer's end, an adventure that included a harrowing nighttime descent along a winding two-lane road from Durango through the mountains to the West Coast resort of Mazatlán. The beach was great, and we stayed for three days, but I kept thinking we were lucky to have arrived at all after my failing to inquire in advance about the difficulty of the Sierra Madre highway, with its switchbacks and steep drop-offs, navigated in unlit darkness because I had misjudged the distance.

At the close of the trip, when we reentered the United States at El Paso, we ran straight into the teeth of Nixon's War on Drugs. While customs agents strip-searched us, others took apart the interior of my VW. We had been careful to toss any contraband before reaching the border, but the El Paso Gestapo gleefully found a few cannabis seeds on the floorboard under the back seat, the residue of guys from the fraternity rolling joints in the car senior year, I deduced. As I was being interrogated under the glare of a single dangling lightbulb, just like in the movies, the Mexican American customs officer brandished a small manilla envelope containing the evidence. "And you're going to be a teacher?" he shouted at me accusingly. Eventually they let us go, but I worried he might phone ahead to Country Day and warn them about whom they had hired.

When I arrived in Cincinnati a week later, I was relieved to discover this had not happened. But it was hot, and the one-bedroom apartment I found in a nondescript new complex on Duck Creek Road had no air-conditioning. It was unfurnished, and all that I had with me were my clothes, books, and whatever else I had squeezed into my Volkswagen. So began my life as an adult.

I borrowed a cot from Charlie Goetz, the man who had hired me, until I could get to Sears and buy a bed. My mother flew up with a suitcase full of inflatable chairs, the first of many uninvited appearances she would make in the years ahead to help me furnish a new place. She always brought good cheer to these sometimes-challeng-

Mr. Mitchell | Author Collection

With Bill Simon at Country Day | AUTHOR COLLECTION

ing situations, and over the years I absorbed her mantra about being able to improve even the humblest abode with imagination and some art. It was a gift she gave me. Even if she were not there, ever after when I moved into a new space, I would feel her sunny presence as I unpacked, assuring me that everything was going to be OK.

She also gave me three recipes so that I wouldn't starve: spaghetti, oven-barbecued chicken breasts, and I forget the third one. But I hadn't yet learned to cook, and that first year I often relied on a nearby Bob's Big Boy for dinner. Sometimes at the end of the month, when my bank balance was scraping zero, I went to the restaurant at the Holiday Inn because they accepted my Gulf Oil credit card, the only one I had.

Yes, I was an adult, twenty-two years old, but that put me only four or five years ahead of the students in the two senior sections of World Literature I was assigned as a rookie. I drew on my experience at St. Mark's and the examples of Mr. North, Mr. Whatley, and others as I made my way in the classroom and tried to keep things interesting, teaching books I had never read—like *Man's Fate, Remembrance of Things Past*, and *The Upanishads*. I also had sections of ninth and tenth grade—all of it testing my prejudice that teaching was not a skill acquired from taking courses in education (as public schools required) but rather derived mainly from one's knowledge of a subject, as private schools favored. I quickly came to see the flaw in this idea and that some skill was involved beyond a knowledge of literature and grammar. It was a skill I was going to have to acquire via on-the-job training because I was already here, behind a desk at the head of the class: Mr. Mitchell.

This was a world I knew and was comfortable with, the privileged world of private secondary schools, where the teachers were often interesting characters and sometimes distinguished, the classes small, the standards high, the parents had money, and everyone knew everyone. It resembled an organized faith, and Cincinnati Country Day was an Ohio chapter, located in the sylvan suburb of Indian Hill, east of the city. I want to say I fit right in, but it wasn't that simple in the fall of 1970. The generation gap that was splitting the country apart was on view at CCDS and marked me and other young teachers as potential threats to the status quo. Our hair was longer, we dressed differently and held antiestablishment views that were troubling to some older faculty.

After an assembly where a Cincinnati policeman had warned the upperclassmen of the dangers of drugs, flagging marijuana as a gateway to heroin, a furor arose in the teachers' lounge when a few of us questioned the cop's assertion. We offered as proof our own firsthand experience. Some senior faculty expressed shock at our admission that we had smoked grass, and one of them reported us to the headmaster. I was summoned to Boardman's office to explain myself and chose not to share with him my "Midnight Express" incident at the border.

I clashed with the football coach, who didn't understand my opposition to the Vietnam War. He also didn't understand soccer and in particular my proposal, after I became the varsity coach, to move soccer from the frigid winter season to fall, competing with football. A schoolwide referendum was held, and the proposal was defeated, much to the coach's relief. (Years later soccer became a fall sport at CCDS.)

In any case, the students made it worthwhile. They were smart and motivated and curious, many of them. They kept me on my toes, and I enjoyed teaching and getting to know them. The second year was smoother and more rewarding; I got to design my own courses and was no longer the new kid on campus. At soccer practice, if we were a man short, I joined the scrimmage, often playing goalkeeper. One evening I drove with several upperclassmen to Antioch College, an hour north in Yellow Springs, to hear the avant-garde jazz pianist Cecil Taylor.

I moved to Mt. Adams, the closest thing Cincinnati had to Soho, a hilly district with the art museum and resident theater, plus older apartments and pubs. Johnny Bench supposedly lived up here somewhere. Bill Simon, the other young English teacher, helped me get a first floor "shotgun" flat directly under the one he occupied with his wife, Janet, in a funky building that was said to have housed Union troops during the Civil War. It had lots of cockroaches but also lots of character, perched on a bluff overlooking downtown and just steps from The Blind Lemon, a bar and restaurant named after the Texas bluesman Blind Lemon Jefferson.

Friday afternoons, Bill and I, Charlie Goetz, Garven Dalglish (the whole English department), and Ted Stein, who taught French, often gathered at a bar in Mt. Adams with a view of the Ohio River, celebrating the end of another week with pitchers of Stroh's and Hudepohl beer. I was still at a loss in the kitchen but now got invited upstairs to eat with Bill and Janet, who knew how to cook. I was also invited to dinner at the home of Ted Stein and his wife, Judy, a former nurse Ted had met while finishing his post–med school residency at Case-Western in Cleveland before deciding he didn't want to be a doctor and landing a last-minute job at CCDS. Ted was one of the smartest people I would ever know, a remarkable polymath and sweet soul who, after his two years at Country Day, returned to Yale for a PhD in English and became a college professor. He published a book on Wordsworth and was a serious poet himself. We kept in touch after Cincinnati, exchanging long letters and emails until the end of his life.

These were the years of "The Big Red Machine," the name given to the great Cincinnati Reds baseball teams led by Johnny Bench and Pete Rose. They played at the brand-new Riverfront Stadium, and I attended my only World Series game there that first October when the Reds took on the Baltimore Orioles, my ticket courtesy of a school parent. Faculty members also got occasional free tickets to concerts by the Cincinnati Symphony Orchestra that performed in a historic red brick music hall completed in 1878. I began to pay attention to classical music for the first time.

By the second year I had traded in my VW for a new melon-colored Fiat Spider convertible, which I parked on a Mount Adams street in the harsh

David Searcy: Writer and singer I met at Ft. Burgwin
DAVID SEARCY (JOHN LUNSFORD)

Cincinnati winter and drove to school along a river road with the top down in warmer months. In the morning, I tuned to a classical station whose deejay would shout, "It's morning in Vienna, mama!" before dropping the needle on Mozart; I drove home listening to Neil Young, Elton John, George Harrison, and Buddy Miles on FM rock radio.

I felt secure enough now to think I might want to make a career of teaching and coaching. But then, other factors intruded. Boardman, who had recruited me, was ousted by the board and replaced by the head of the upper school, a man I did not care for—nor he for me. My friend and colleague Bill Simon, a Columbia graduate who had campaigned for Eugene McCarthy, broached the idea of protesting the high-handed action of the board by organizing a faculty strike. One day at lunch off campus he offered me a bracing Marxist analysis of our situation: we were toiling as indentured servants, educating the offspring of the capitalist ruling class.

The strike never happened, but his sobering critique gave me something to think about even as I was starting to feel an itch to do something more creative and escape the cloistered environment of a prep school. I wanted to try my hand at fiction or journalism, maybe film school—something out there beyond the classroom. I was reading *Rolling Stone*, *Village Voice*, and Willie Morris's *Harper's* and thought I might want to do that, with no idea how to proceed.

The summer before, I had attended the first SMU Writers' Workshop outside Taos, New Mexico, and made a new set of friends from Dallas associated with Southern Methodist University—fiction writers, poets, grad students, and a reporter for the Dallas PBS station who encouraged me to consider broadcast journalism. I had gone there by chance, at the suggestion of my dad, who was then enrolled in a master's program at SMU in English. His advisor, Marshall Terry, the novelist and department chair, also ran the workshop and allowed me late admission even though I had no writing project to show him. I told him I was trying to write songs like the ones James Taylor and Cat Stevens were singing, and he said, fine, come out and write some songs. Which I did. The whole experience turned out to be the best summer camp for grown-ups you could imagine: three weeks in the cool mountain air of northern New Mexico, seventy-four hundred feet above sea level and a blessed distance from the terrible summer heat of Texas.

The facilities at Fort Burgwin, an abandoned nineteenth-century Army post owned by SMU, were rustic, and there was no electricity in the cabins. Reading and writing could only be done during the day, with nights given over to activities that required no lighting: drinking, music making, and other frivolity. This is where I met the writer David Searcy, who was not only a rising star as a prose stylist but a talented singer who could take the lead on "Duke of Earl" and "The Lion Sleeps Tonight" and, with enough whiskey, approximate the sound of a Delta bluesman. We had great fun singing and playing guitars into the night. I wanted to do more of that.

The Fort Burgwin experience was a big reason I decided to return to Dallas when my second year at Country Day was over. If I were going to try to break into the media, I reasoned it might as well be in Dallas, where I knew the names of the streets and some people as well. I had come to like Cincinnati but reading my first Larry McMurtry novel and seeing *The Last Picture Show* introduced the notion that maybe I was a Texan after all. The two dailies, the *Dallas Morning News* and *Times Herald*, seemed within reach and a good place to start. My youthful aspiration to be a sportswriter had been reshaped by my college experience and teaching English. I now wanted to write about the arts. When the time came, I gave notice to the new headmaster, and at semester's end headed back to North Texas, blissfully unaware of how difficult it was all going to be.

Part Two

CHAPTER TWENTY

Starting Over

S PRING BREAK THAT FINAL SEMESTER AT COUNTRY DAY, I HAD GONE TO DALLAS and met the second-string film critic at the *Times Herald*, Bob Porter, whose wife, Pat, worked with my dad at the museum. He generously allowed me to tag along with him as he covered the second USA Film Festival at SMU, which included a tribute to the famous director Frank Capra, the maker of *It's a Wonderful Life* and *Mr. Smith Goes to Washington*. Growing up, I had never paid much attention to the old movies that ran all day (with ample commercial breaks) on a local UHF channel, again showing the influence of my father, who routinely disparaged the golden age of Hollywood. But I was captivated by the new wave of American films like *Bonnie and Clyde*, *Five Easy Pieces*, and *Joe*, aimed at my generation. Given my training as an English major, measuring the world in term papers, I was drawn to film criticism to engage and examine an art form that was moving rapidly into grittier and more honest stories. I wondered if the *Times Herald* or *Morning News* might be looking for someone younger than Bob Porter to write about what was happening now?

I went back to Cincinnati after the break and wrote what I'm sure was a pedantic—if heartfelt—essay about the different uses of violence in two recent films, Stanley Kubrick's *A Clockwork Orange* and Sam Peckinpah's *Straw Dogs*. I sent it to the entertainment editor at the *Times Herald*, a man named Don Safran. He did not favor me with a reply.

That was as far as I had progressed toward getting on at the *Times Herald* or the *Morning News* when I landed back in Dallas in the summer of 1972. My return began with an unpleasant surprise. I was staying with my parents on Eric Lane and waiting for the Allied Van Lines eighteen-wheeler to show up with my belongings. The truck was late. One afternoon the doorbell rang, and it was the driver, standing there at the door oddly holding the cheap metal bed frame I had bought at Sears. Behind him, parked at the curb was the enormous orange and black truck I recognized from the load-out in Cincinnati.

"Did the office call you?" he said.

The office had not called me.

"They were supposed to tell you that the van broke down in Tennessee, and looters got to it before we could get it fixed."

Bottom line: Everything I owned was gone, save for the bed frame.

Angry and suspicious, I immediately called Allied and learned that there was really nothing I could do and that the standard moving company insurance was pennies on the dollar. I made myself a Scotch and in frustration stupidly kicked the nearest door.

Next, I discovered that the welcome mat I was expecting to find at the newspapers was nowhere in sight. "Have you ever had any professional newsgathering experience?" a gruff assistant managing editor at the *Times Herald* asked me, glancing at my youthful résumé. "Newsgathering," the term was new to me and sounded simple-minded, but the answer, I had to admit, was no. I was surprised and annoyed that my English degree from Brown seemed to count for so little. I had a similar interview at the *Morning News*, where a friendlier inquisitor told me the *News* did not hire anyone without at least two years of experience and suggested I call an editor he knew at the *Corpus Christi Caller-Times*, a smaller paper on the Texas Gulf Coast.

Which I probably should have done. But I was hampered by the presumption I deserved to start somewhere higher than Corpus Christi, especially since I was aiming for the arts and culture pages. I might not have any "newsgathering" experience, but I read the local papers and believed I could do as well, maybe better. The only journalist I knew was Mike Ritchey, the guy from Fort Burgwin—a former newspaperman who had become a reporter for *Newsroom*, an experimental nightly news show on KERA, the local PBS station, funded by the Ford Foundation and hosted by future PBS star Jim Lehrer. Mike, who was only a few years older, invited me down to see the show in production and tempted me with the idea I could become a broadcast journalist like him. I had a prejudice against television news, which seemed inherently shallow, but *Newsroom* looked like an exception. Mike was becoming a star himself, part Dan Rather, part Don Meredith. "You can't beat television," he told me. "The money's better, the lights are brighter, and the girls are prettier." I had to admit feeling an excitement in the studio as the red light came on, and the program went live, with Lehrer interviewing the reporters circled around him like the city editor he once was.

But how was I going to leap right into that? Mike did introduce me to the managing director of KERA, a man named Bob Wilson who was then laying the groundwork for an NPR affiliate in Dallas. Wilson, a former adman whose sons Owen and Luke would one day become Hollywood players, had gone to Dartmouth, and seemed mildly interested in me. We played tennis a few times, and he asked me to write down my thoughts about what a public radio station in Dallas might look like. NPR was in its infancy, so I didn't have a lot to go on. I did some research, read a *New York Times Magazine* story about WBAI, the lefty Pacifica station in New York, and turned in a ten-page prospectus. Weeks went by as I waited anxiously for a response. In the end, nothing came of my proposal, and Wilson backed away. I'm sure my mentioning WBAI was a mistake, but Wilson and I didn't really connect.

I tried other doors, approaching station producers and administrators, hoping for any kind of job doing anything inside the walls of public broadcasting—and got nowhere. Ritchey even suggested that once the radio station was up and running, the two of us might do a show together. A tantalizing prospect, but meanwhile I was jobless and living at home with Gene and Lu. And when autumn arrived, Mike was off to Harvard for a year on a Neiman Fellowship.

I had spent the rest of the summer trying to locate jobs in the arts and communications and even looked into becoming a librarian, remembering my job at "the Rock" in college. (I knew the great Argentine writer Jorge Louis Borges had been a librarian.) I began to wonder if I was spinning my wheels in Dallas. On the remote chance I might yet get into public radio, I set about educating myself in classical music and jazz, about which

I knew too little. I read books; I bought LPs. On occasion I joined David Searcy and some of the Ft. Burgwin crew to rekindle our camaraderie in someone's living room, singing and playing into the night. I went to see *The Last Picture Show* again.

I had a lot of time to brood about my present and future existence. Influenced by Henry David Thoreau's journals that I had read at Brown and assigned to students at Country Day, I kept a diary chronicling my daily activities, readings, and insights, especially regarding the creative process. I went to hear the poet Howard Nemerov give a reading at SMU and jotted down something he said: "Poets are not the experts in the mysteries of life, only on the words of which they're made."

My writer's impulse kept surfacing. I wrote a long letter published in the *Texas Observer* defending Bud Shrake's novel *Strange Peaches*, about JFK-era Dallas, that a critic had trashed. My dad had been reviewing books for the *Dallas Morning News* and introduced me to the book editor, Allen Maxwell, who let me break into print reviewing a title about Grateful Dead guitarist Jerry Garcia and a critical assessment of J.R.R. Tolkien. The pay was only the book itself and a byline, but, given my blank literary portfolio, it was something.

As summer's end approached, I wrote in my journal: *I miss the kids in Cincinnati but hold on—this is the right course. I've got to do these things.*

ALAN FEDMAN WAS NOW IN LAW SCHOOL AT THE UNIVERSITY OF OKLAHOMA IN NORMAN, and I made the two-and-a-half-hour drive north in my Fiat to spend a weekend with him. Alan's other obsession besides the Beatles was OU football, and he took me to see the Sooners defeat Oregon 68–3. But more significant was an evening we sat in his apartment, smoking dope and discussing his newfound interest in Eastern religion. Alan, who was Jewish, had been influenced by the metaphysical book *Be Here Now*, by Ram Das (né Dr. Richard Alpert, PhD, cohort of Timothy Leary at Harvard), and even as he was studying to become a lawyer, was immersing himself in the teachings of Zen and its anti-materialist philosophy. He listened to my professional frustrations and suggested I had been misled by my ego into "trying to be Norman Mailer in a place where they don't understand Norman Mailer." It made me think. He offered up other ideas I had not given much consideration but could no longer ignore, coming from such a close friend. The notion that serenity and peace lay in accepting the world as it was and not trying to remake it threw me at first. It was a tempting thought, but it also seemed to challenge my restless creative impulses, my very reason for being. And so, it scared me.

When I returned home, I wrote in my journal that the weekend in Norman had been a *mindblower*. Alan mentioned reading the British writer and philosopher Alan Watts, and I went to a bookstore and bought a copy of Watts's *This Is It* to get an introduction to Zen Buddhism.

I asked Dad what he thought about Eastern religion, given that he was not very religious in the conventional sense and often mocked the fake piety of alleged Christians. He said his agnosticism extended to Zen, which he was too old and too Western to bother with. I wondered if that might be true for me as well.

Then came the presidential election. My journal entry for Tuesday, November 7, 1972, probably written under the influence of Hunter S. Thompson, the father of gonzo journalism, reads: *Nixon wins landslide as clayheads turn out in record numbers. Dallas County goes 75 percent for Tricky... McGovern has carried only Massachusetts and the District of Columbia. Nixon will win the greatest electoral and popular majority in American history. The reasons are still not clear. It will have to be attributed to madness...*

I wondered if the Republican supermajority in Dallas offered more evidence that I was misplaced here? I also noted that the local liquor option in Farmers Branch was defeated and that the students at its R. L. Turner High School, in a straw vote, had gone for Nixon five to one.

At the end of November, I had been back in my hometown for six months, unable to make anything happen—a turn of events I was struggling to accept. It had become uncomfortable living again under the same roof with my parents, as if I were back in high school. As I thrashed about in my journal, I was also writing more songs on the guitar and trying them out for my Fort Burgwin friends and others. It was tempting to think maybe *that* is what I was really meant to do, as someone remarked after hearing one of my songs at a party. I doubted my abilities as a singer, but I took encouragement from the examples of Leonard Cohen, Randy Newman, Loudon Wainright III, and other songwriters with modest vocal range who managed to deliver

Performing at the art museum

their own material with a winning authenticity. I was also taken with the idea that songwriting might represent a reconciliation of my parents' divergent literary and musical talents, a fusion that would make sense of the three of us.

The impracticality of joining the horde of young troubadours inspired by James Taylor and Carole King was overshadowed by the romance of it. You only needed to hear a stray compliment here or there to give you confidence against all reason.

My mother booked time for me at a local recording studio, and, with the help of a sympathetic engineer, I laid down three originals. Optimistically I took the reel-to-reel tape to a local FM radio jock who was nice enough but probably never listened to it. What was I expecting anyway?

My flirtation with songwriting and performing pushed me closer to Mom, who had given me a backstage pass from a young age. The summer at Fort Burgwin, she managed to get a booking in the nearby resort town of Red River, New Mexico, opening at a club for Three Faces West, a folk-rock trio that included future progressive country hero Ray Wylie Hubbard. She asked me to come along and provide some additional guitar, and I remember thinking, this was cool, being on the same stage as these guys.

In December Mom got me on the bill for the Folk Music Society's Christmas concert at the art museum—another chance to perform and feel my songs being accepted by an audience. *When you're doing that, you think nothing else could be as much fun.*

SMU professor and Fort Burgwin faculty member Charles Oliver asked me to play guitar behind a reading of one of his short stories, with additional interpretation from two SMU dance students. I drove with Charles and the dancers to Northeast State University in Tahlequah, Oklahoma, where we performed "White Butterflies" in an auditorium full of undergraduates. More fun. Another worthwhile, unpaid use of my time.

One of those dancers, Cerelle Woods, and I began spending time together after the trip, but meanwhile I had to find a job. I was giving up on Dallas and thinking maybe New York would be a better fit. Dad thought so and called my attention to a column in *Newsweek* making the case that the East Coast was still preeminent in publishing, journalism, and the arts. Bob Barnes, the guy who had "tripped" with me through London, was working as a copywriter at an ad agency in Manhattan and encouraged me to come up and consider the opportunities on Madison Avenue. I was skeptical, but I was also at a loss. I decided to take him up on his offer to stay at his apartment in Greenwich Village but to wait until after the holidays. I had one more option to check out in Texas first.

Texas Monthly, a glossy new magazine modeled after *New York Magazine*, was just getting started in Austin and looked promising. The editor and managing editor were young Rice University graduates. I knew the founder and publisher, Mike Levy, who had been a couple classes ahead of me at St. Mark's and worked in student publications. I called him, and he told me he would introduce me to the editor, William Broyles Jr. if I were ever in Austin. I made immediate plans to visit.

Another Fort Burgwin alumnus, Dan Cotter, a Vietnam veteran whose experience there had left him emotionally damaged, told me he had a friend from Vietnam he wanted to see in Austin. So, we made plans to drive down together in late January.

The first night we went to the home of Dan's friend, who told me that when he reported to his Duster anti-aircraft tank unit in Vietnam, he discovered that his fellow crew members were all on heroin and had nothing much to do all day but clean their weapons. I thought back to my discussions about the war with the Country Day football coach.

I went by the *Texas Monthly* offices and briefly met the editor, Bill Broyles, who was busy getting out the second issue. In the five minutes he gave me, I floated the idea of "A Texan in New York" column, but I had little to show him in the way of writing samples. I got more time with Levy, who tried to interest me in selling advertising, but that was the furthest thing from my mind. I left their offices feeling I had caught a blast of the fast talk and hustle of major commercial media and wondered if that's what my future held?

While I was at *Texas Monthly*, President Lyndon Baines Johnson, the former commander in chief of the still-unended war, died of a heart attack at his ranch in the nearby Hill Country. He was sixty-four. As Dan and I started our drive back to Dallas the next afternoon, we passed the long line of people standing outside the LBJ Library in a cold darkness, waiting to view the thirty-sixth president lying in state. Dan said, "I wouldn't stand in line to see him alive, let alone dead." I had nothing to add to that.

CHAPTER TWENTY-ONE

Go East (Again), Young Man

THE DAY AFTER MY TWENTY-FIFTH BIRTHDAY, at the end of January 1973, I took off in the Fiat with my Martin D-28, Smith Corona portable, and assorted belongings, headed for New York City. The weather was perfect: cold and sunny. I put the top down and turned the heater on, as I liked to do. John Denver was on the radio singing "Rocky Mountain High." *Departed Dallas at 8 a.m., was able to cruise at 90 through east Texas, 80 through Arkansas, reached Little Rock by 12:30, Memphis by 3, Nashville by 5:30.* I stopped overnight in Nashville to see Dawson Nesbitt, a member of the gin-and-tonic-and-Fitzgerald fan club at St. Mark's. Dawson had gone to Vanderbilt and stayed. He was now into yoga and health food, which I described as "dreadful" in my journal. After a brief tour of the Grand Old Opry and Music Row, I was off to DC, where I planned to leave my car in a garage belonging to the sister of my former roommate, Bill "Burundi" Barringer, now studying at Georgetown Law School, as was my cousin Monica. *Spent a day at Georgetown Law rapping with Monica and Bill re: futures.* Bill's future would include joining a law firm in DC specializing in international trade; Monica would go to work for HUD and later the City of New York in its housing department.

I took the train up to Penn Station the next day and found my way to Bob Barnes's apartment on Perry Street in Greenwich Village. Bob was in the same fraternity as Bob Rozelle, which is how I met him. We had literary ambition in common and both of us helped organize an independent study seminar in the modern American novel senior year. And we had explored London together on that spring break trip. He was employed as an advertising copywriter and reminded me that Joseph Heller had worked in advertising before writing *Catch-22*.

Bob had chiseled features that drew comparisons to Paul Newman. Women found him attractive, and I remember him dating some Pembrokers. But not long after I arrived at his place on this night, he earnestly broke the news to me that he was gay. Whoa. While some guys at Brown seemed "different" or uninterested in women, Bob was not one of them, and nobody was "out" during those years—at least no one that I knew. "Gay" was not yet even a widely used term.

Bob made it clear to me that he didn't want this to affect our friendship and that I could relax around him but that his circle of friends in New York were largely gay men, including some members of our Brown class. In the week I stayed with him, going out to dinner and to bars, meeting his friends, I got a glimpse of a world I knew nothing about. This was my postgrad introduction to New York.

I had other contacts and acquaintances to look up in Manhattan, among them the divorced mother of one of my students from Cincinnati who had recently moved to New York to pursue an acting career. Her name was Dorothy Schott. She had money and was living with her teenage daughter in a large penthouse apartment on West Fifty-seventh Street. She generously offered me the guest bedroom while I looked for work. A godsend. But as I began to hit the streets, I couldn't help noticing an alarming lack of interest in my value as a future member of the media. I don't recall hearing the term "networking" at Brown, but I could have used some, along with a mentor, as I crashed my way into perfunctory interviews at the *New York Times, Wall St. Journal, TIME, Newsweek, Rolling Stone*, Voice of America, the TV networks, ad agencies, PR firms, and publishing houses, exhausting whatever contacts I had—to no avail. It was a hiring guy at the Associated Press who gave me some sensible advice, telling me to get out of New York and try someplace like North Carolina. I ignored him. It was Corpus Christi all over again.

The thing was, amid the daunting job search, I was thrilled by New York—the pulsing rhythm of the streets, the subways, the boldface names you might encounter, the Russian Tea Room, Sardi's, Broadway, Washington Square, the enticing self-importance of it all. I wanted to be here and could see my future here. I went with Dorothy, my hostess, and her daughter to see plays and shows, including the off-Broadway debuts of Lanford Wilson's *The Hot L Baltimore*, with Judd Hirsch and Trish Hawkins, and *Lemmings*, the National Lampoon's wicked satire of rock and roll featuring future *Saturday Night Live* cast members John Belushi, Chevy Chase, and Christopher Guest.

Various theatre and film folk came to visit Dorothy, offering me a glimpse of the innards of show business: fellow actors who were auditioning for commercials and complaining about their agents, a producer without portfolio, an obscure stand-up comedian who assured me he was "big." While working as an extra on *The Exorcist*, then filming in Manhattan, Dorothy brought back news that director William Friedkin had invited her to dinner and promised her a larger role if she would sleep with him. She declined. (So, it's true what they say about Hollywood, I thought.) She got another gig as an extra in an ABC TV movie filming at the Wollman ice-skating rink in Central Park and told me they needed more skaters. Did I want to join her and make $65? Of course, I did and spent an afternoon skating with Dorothy in the crowd somewhere behind the focus on star Karen Valentine. I got paid, but I never saw the movie.

I started an article about being an extra in a TV movie but didn't get very far. After reading an album review in *Rolling Stone* that bashed "American Pie" songwriter Don McLean as "Nixon's Dylan," I sent off an angry defense of McLean both to *Rolling Stone* and *Texas Monthly* (as a writing sample). An editor at *Texas Monthly* took the trouble to write back, judging my prose to be OK except for its strong academic aroma. Not what I wanted to hear.

Publishers Weekly offered me books to review freelance for a pittance. Again, it was something. I managed to get an interview for a copy-editing job at the new *Country Music* magazine, which had a British editor in chief and a publisher from Yale. Country music I wasn't sure about, but when they asked me back for a second interview, I warmed at the prospect and tried to conceal my preference for Fairport Convention and folk rock to Tammy Wynette and George Jones. They were probably looking for someone who'd heard of Willie Nelson, but I was sorely disappointed when I didn't get the job and felt like I had hit the wall. What was it going to take? Not for the first or last time, I thought, if I had known how hard it was going to be to get into journalism, I might not have left teaching. It took me a while to recognize that I had been spoiled to this point in my life, getting into St. Mark's, getting into Brown, getting the first teaching job I interviewed for. I wasn't prepared for the world to be giving me the cold shoulder, and it threw me.

Gene and Lu had been so supportive, but I think they, too, were perplexed at my inability to get a foothold anywhere in the media. After I didn't get the *Country Music* job, I sat down at my Smith Corona one night and banged out a tedious soul-baring letter examining my life and shortcomings, to explain my sorry state of thwarted ambition. I shared the conclusion that I should have been more focused all along, worked on the *Brown Daily Herald* instead of playing soccer, not allowed literature and creative writing to distract me from the more practical path of journalism. Ditto the two years I spent teaching, not to mention fooling around with songwriting and the guitar. Selfishly, I took a few shots at Dad, blaming him for (1) the imperious authority he exerted during my childhood, blunting my own self-confidence (*Could I ever live up to him? Could I ever be as good?*) and (2) his contributing to my reservations about newspapers *because of the constant bad-mouthing they received from the reigning intellect in my home.* I also faulted the influence of Thoreau, who in his journals denounced the members of the press as mindless, scandal-pandering nitwits. My problem was, regardless of Thoreau and my father's well-founded rants about newspapers and the TV networks, I had decided I wanted to be a journalist—or at least a *new* journalist. And I was desperate to identify reasons I was failing to get in the door after nearly a year of trying.

Dad didn't deserve my flailing criticism, and I soon tried to make amends in a painful phone call that only revealed how much my screed had drawn blood. In a voice both angry and defensive, he muttered that he hadn't realized what a "ranting bore" he was. Now it was me who felt wounded. What had I done? Mom was listening on the other phone but didn't say much.

I followed up with a conciliatory letter in which I tried to explain away my complaints as *an exercise in inexcusable self-pity* that I tried to excuse nonetheless by noting that our confrontation was brought on by obstacles beyond our control, and that we shouldn't let the world get between us.

One thing I had not learned at home or at school was how to deal with adversity, failure, and rejection. As an only child I had been favored with my parent's undivided attention. Gene and Lu lacked the disposable income to spoil me with material things but nevertheless had cast me in a starring role in the family I didn't have to audition for. I took it for granted that my welfare and advancement were priorities. Which is surely preferable to being neglected, but now I questioned whether being the center of attention had been a good thing. I was searching for my fatal flaw. There had to be one.

CHAPTER TWENTY-TWO

Washington

READY FOR A BREAK, I HEADED BACK TO DC, where I knew Barringer had room at the aging Capitol Hill row house his dad had bought for him. Jim Lehrer had moved from Channel 13 in Dallas to DC to become a correspondent for PBS, and I was acquainted slightly with two women from Texas who were on his staff. They vowed to alert me to any possibilities at the Corporation for Public Broadcasting. I also sought interviews at the nascent National Public Radio, already struggling financially and taking fire from the Nixon White House. Someone there showed me the studio where an early edition of *All Things Considered* was in progress.

Somehow, I learned that the deputy features editor of the *Washington Star-News* was the mother of a Pembroker I had met once, briefly, Stephanie Crutcher. The *Star-News* was an endangered species, an afternoon paper, losing its circulation battle with the dominant *Washington Post*, but it still had a few stars like columnists Mary McGrory and Tom Donnelly. It was a long shot, but I contacted Anne Crutcher and got a meeting, mailing her my book reviews in advance. When I arrived at her office, I found a woman in her fifties with a kind face and welcoming manner, her light brown hair drawn back American Gothic style, her voice full of education and ideas. She was complimentary about my writing samples but made it clear there were no staff positions available. All she could do was keep me in mind for freelance work.

That's where we left it, and after a couple weeks I was resigned to go back to New York and resume my job search, but minutes before I was to leave for Union Station, the phone at Barringer's rang. It was for me, one of Bill's roommates said. "A woman named Crutcher." She asked if I would be interested in interviewing Reed Whittemore, the poet and literary editor of the *New Republic* who was kicking off a new poetry series at the Textile Museum? I didn't have to think before answering.

I did the Whittemore piece, my first article for a newspaper other than book reviews. This was before computers, and I had to go into the *Star-News* following his reading and bang out the story in ninety minutes on a manual typewriter, on deadline, an unfamiliar and challenging task. Anne seemed pleased with the result, an indication I knew what I was doing when in fact I was just winging it. I hadn't studied journalism formally, but I had a sense of how it was done. This began a series of regular assignments for the features section. Here was my chance at last, however meager and low paying. I decided to stay in Washington.

Barringer gave me a room at the townhouse for seventy dollars a month. A freelance story for the *Star-News* brought the princely sum of fifty dollars, so I had to find other work to support my budding newspaper career. Michael Hahn, the beret-wearing keyboardist from Sigma Nu, was living at Barringer's while attending grad school at Georgetown in international relations and had a side gig painting houses for Georgetown faculty. He let me in on that and while painting, we listened to FM radio and talked about music all day. Through an acquaintance, I found a job as a part-time assistant bartender at a restaurant downtown but got fired the first week for mixing a Manhattan incorrectly. In the classifieds I located another bartending job in the suburb of Rockville, Maryland, at the restaurant where it was later revealed that Watergate conspirator James McCord received his orders (in a parking lot phone booth) to burglarize the headquarters of the Democratic National Committee.

The history-making break-in had occurred the year before, but in the summer of 1973, as I learned to navigate L'Enfant's four quadrants of Washington, the truth of what had happened and the illegality of it all was catching up with the Nixon White House. "Watergate" was in the news daily as the Senate began its televised hearings into the scandal that would eventually force Richard Nixon to resign his second term as president.

The features section was some distance from the political storm, but Anne sent me to cover embassy parties and social events where I learned to approach congressmen and other political figures for quotes. I went to a fundraising party at Sargent Shriver's house and to a speech by former LBJ secretary of state Dean Rusk. I did a story about T-shirts being marketed with the likeness of Dixiecrat Senator Sam Ervin of North Carolina whose colorful declarations as chairman of the Senate Watergate Committee had turned him into a folk hero.

Mainly I was given arts assignments: a scene piece about a Grateful Dead-Allman Bros. concert at RFK Stadium, high-profile poetry readings at the Library of Congress, the Smithsonian Folklife Festival on the Mall, interviewing the makeup artist from the *Planet of the Apes* movie franchise and Count Basie performing at an Arlington, Virginia, high school. I talked my way backstage at a Kris Kristofferson-Rita Coolidge concert at the Kennedy Center and ended up riding with the two of them in a limo to a party at, yes, the Watergate Hotel. I got an article out of it. I also interviewed the distinguished Harlem Renaissance poet Sterling Brown, who lived in DC. He took a phone call during our conversation in which he told the caller he was "talking to a newspaperman." It was the first time I heard myself so described.

Anne was an instructive editor who showed me how to shed my formal academic tendencies in favor of a more plainspoken style. She made me see that the *Texas Monthly* editor had been right. It all happened in a short space of time.

She sent me to New York for another scene piece, this one a concert at Carnegie Hall given by Josephine Baker, the glamorous Black expatriate and darling of the Jazz Age making her first American appearance in ten years. Grace Slick was my

Anne Crutcher with Lu at Nathan reception in New York
AUTHOR COLLECTION

idea of an exotic chanteuse, and I knew nothing about Josephine Baker, but I ran to the library before jumping on the train to New York. In the Carnegie Hall lobby, I noticed a man in an immaculate pin-striped suit that I believed to be Truman Capote. I should have tried to talk to him and get a quote, but I was too shy, a drawback in my new line of work. When the concert and party were over, I had to dictate my story over the phone from the lobby of the Plaza Hotel to an editor back in DC, another new experience.

For the Sunday section I wrote an essay—with some reporting—about *Rolling Stone* magazine, pegged to my perception that it was betraying its counterculture roots and ideals by locking arms with the record industry. Harking back to my training in English Lit, I chose to begin with a scholarly conceit, tracing the magazine's genealogy to the antiestablishment Beat poets of the 1950s, specifically to a night in New York City when Columbia University poet Louis Simpson lent his copy of Henry Miller's *Tropic of Cancer* to friend Jack Kerouac, who found in Miller the voice to write his stream-of-consciousness classic *On the Road. Which would inspire a generation of hipsters, some of whom settled in San Francisco and laid the mystical, anti-materialist foundation for the counterculture that spawned the nontraditional journalism of Rolling Stone* ... It was a fanciful lede but intended to mirror the cosmically inclined prose the magazine had made fashionable. And the facts were real, drawn from Simpson's autobiography that I had reviewed for the *Morning News*.

I did some additional freelancing for a Washington entertainment weekly and got assigned a profile of Bill Danoff and Taffy Nivert, a local duo who had written the hit song "Take Me Home, Country Roads" for John Denver. I loved the song and others Bill and Taffy had recorded on two albums for RCA that got played on Washington radio stations, including "Flying Home to Nashville," composed (but not used) for Robert Altman's 1975 film *Nashville,* and "Boulder to Birmingham" that Bill had coauthored with Emmylou Harris about the death of her singing partner Gram Parsons.

During a week Bill and Taffy were booked at the Cellar Door, a prime venue in Georgetown, I got to hang out with them between sets in the green room and taped a long interview for an article that ran in a tabloid called *Washington Scene.* I was drawn to their touching and clever songs for acoustic guitar and two-part harmony—high-level examples of the music I had grown up with. Robert Altman, they told me, had flown them to Los Angeles as he was developing his movie about Nashville, filling their heads with thoughts of how *The Graduate* had made Simon & Garfunkel famous. In LA they were wined and dined and told "these are the 'B people' you're meeting," Taffy recalled ruefully about a party they attended. After returning to DC, they never heard from Altman again. He ultimately decided not to use them, but they only learned this inadvertently from the film's screenwriter, Joan Tewkesbury.

This was my first experience up close and personal with the composers of a hit song, getting to ask them anything I wanted and then

Larry McMurtry listened to my song
COURTESY OF ANDY HANSON,
DALLAS TIMES HERALD

shaping a narrative to tell their story, with digressions and insights into the music (and movie) business. Cool. I could do this. And I found it interesting.

I was still writing my own songs, not sure where that was going, but one of my favorites was inspired by Larry McMurtry's novel *All My Friends Are Going to Be Strangers*. I entertained the youthful notion that my song might be used when the movie of the book was made (and unaware McMurtry had borrowed the title from a line in a song by Merle Haggard, not to mention the book was uncinematic).

I knew that McMurtry had recently moved to DC from Texas and opened a used bookstore in Georgetown. Betraying none of the shyness that kept me from approaching Truman Capote, I drove to Booked Up with my guitar one afternoon, found McMurtry inside and straightaway asked if I could play the song for him. Famously unsocial, he said, OK, kid, go ahead. We were the only two people in the store. I sat on a stool, performed "All My Friends," and he listened politely without showing any particular interest or enthusiasm. I hastily apologized for changing Danny Deck's car from a Chevy to a Dodge because I needed the syllable, and he immediately sympathized. "You always have to change things," he said and preempted further discussion by assuring me he would mention my song to the director if a film version ever went into development. I chose to take this as encouragement rather than the more likely truth he was hoping I would just walk out the way I had walked in.

The *Star-News* assignments (and more book reviews) continued into the fall, by which time I had moved in with a girlfriend I met on the poetry circuit. She was not a poet but the friend of the wife of a poet and worked as an office manager for the City of New York's office in the District. Born in Germany, she was six years older than me and divorced, with two young sons who lived mostly with their father. Her passing resemblance to Ingrid Bergman was a problem in that she attracted men left and right and did not always discourage their advances. Eventually I moved out and stayed with another friend while assessing my precarious situation. The Newspaper Guild was complaining to management about the number of "Special to the *Star-News*" freelancers like me the paper was using as substitutes for full-time staffers (a tell-tale sign of its financial decline).

The dicey reality of the *Star-News* was complicated by the affection I had developed for Washington, which now seemed like the perfect place for me, being an intersection of the North and South combined with the import of being the nation's capital.

With Christmas approaching, Anne, my champion, confided that she might not be able to use me as much as previously. I had been working nights at yet another bar, on Connecticut Avenue near the zoo, where the clientele included limo drivers who would come in after their shifts and get hammered. As I was not drinking on the job, standing behind the bar and watching these guys in tuxedoes gulp Galliano till their eyes glassed over was not fun. In Rockville, I had made drinks for the waitresses to carry out to the tables, but here I was face-to-face with the customers, which I learned took a certain talent. Limo drivers and most people who sit alone with a glass of whiskey or beer expect the bartender to keep them company, and I was not doing that, as Wally, my girlfriend, pointed out one night when she dropped in. The customers were taking their tips back, she noticed. Coins and bills placed on the bar earlier were now missing, a judgement on my lack of schmooze. After that I tried to be more like Ted Danson on *Cheers*, but it wasn't me. I wanted out. I wanted a real job. I decided to drive back to Dallas for the holidays and rethink everything.

CHAPTER TWENTY-THREE

Sitting in Limbo

T HIS BRINGS US TO THE POINT WHERE I STUMBLED INTO THE JOB AT THE *ICONOCLAST*. I neglected to mention earlier that my original link to the *Iconoclast* was Christie Seltzer, my former LRY confrere who was back in Dallas after Oberlin and, like me, investigating journalism. She'd been working with Jay Milner (the editor I never met) and told him about my Kristofferson story. I'm not sure if Milner's departure occasioned her own, but I had lost touch with her by the time I went down to the office to get that check.

My appreciation for the wild, sleep-deprived sojourn at the *Iconoclast* would grow over time, but in the immediate aftermath I worried that by taking that job I had burned any bridges to more mainstream media, where one could take home paychecks that didn't bounce. I made another pass at the *Herald* and the *News*, figuring my underground newspaper stint was problematic, but I also had my Washington *Star-News* clips. None of it mattered. The old guard was still in charge at both papers, and they were not scouting for alumni of *Iconoclast* or Brown. I pursued some freelance ideas, selling a spec piece to the *Nation* about the DuPont plant in Corpus Christi that was manufacturing the chemicals burning a hole in the ozone layer— and another to the *Texas Observer* about Dallas Black activist Al Lipscomb's run for city council. I took pride in being published in two of the liberal magazines Dad had read and quoted when I was growing up, but the fees were little more than honorariums. I needed real money to buy groceries and pay the rent.

Charles Oliver, the SMU professor I had traveled with to Oklahoma for his reading of "White Butterflies," notified me of a job overseeing the student publications at SMU. He was on the selection committee and told me I would be his candidate. I applied, made the first cut, and went through rounds of interviews before being told I was not the committee's final choice. When Charles phoned me with the news, he added unexpectedly that he had not voted for me. Which seemed weird but not as weird as learning a few months later that Charles had jumped to his death off an SMU-adjacent bridge spanning Central Expressway into the traffic below. A stark reminder that writers often struggled with mental health.

I wrote some other spec pieces that went unpublished and a few book reviews for the *Star-News*. Anne had not forgotten me. But I needed help from my parents to keep a roof over my head. Holed up in my starving artist apartment on McFarlin, I did a lot of reading and played the guitar, under the spell of Dylan's latest, *Blood on the Tracks*, and Jackson Browne's *Late for the Sky*. The sway of rock and pop music was producing a new literature of rock criticism that I devoured and wanted to try myself. I subscribed to the *Village Voice* and read an anthology of the New Journalism edited by Tom Wolfe, who had become a hero. I wrote Wolfe a fan letter and included one of the spec pieces I had been unable to place. He wrote back by hand, offering encouragement in an eye-catching calligraphic script. I framed his letter, and it kept me going for a while, but all of this seemed irrelevant to the dull and dreary Dallas dailies I was trying to crack.

I hadn't abandoned the idea of writing fiction, and with memo-

The poster for the radio production of Dad's play Menelaus
AUTHOR COLLECTION

ries of R. V. Cassill in my head, fumbled my way through some short stories that I sent out to *Esquire* and *Redbook*. Unsurprisingly, no responses came back.

Teaching reentered my mind. Not Country Day, but college. Maybe I could afford to get a PhD in English at the University of Texas. I tried to imagine myself as a guitar-strumming professor in Austin. But did I really want to do that? I had already weaned myself from academic writing, which I now saw could be stilted in its reliance on scholarly syntax and big words. Greg was finishing up a PhD in history at Michigan; Bob was teaching at a private school in Tacoma; Dick Wincorn had shelved plans to become an architect and apprenticed himself to a furniture maker in Santa Fe; Eric was now an intelligence officer and lieutenant in the Navy. We were heading into our late twenties, us class of '66ers. We weren't kids anymore.

After reading a magazine piece about the making of the movie *Lenny*, starring Dustin Hoffman as Lenny Bruce, I noted in my journal that Hoffman was twenty-nine when he got his breakout role in *The Graduate*, and that he still remembered how people treated him before that, "how nobody would give me a job."

When I heard a song on the radio by the great Jamaican reggae musician Jimmy Cliff, the lyrics took on new meaning: *Yeah, now, sitting here in limbo / Got some time to search my soul / Well, they're putting up a resistance / But I know that my faith will lead me on.*

My faith was being tested, for sure.

One thing I figured I could do during my own stretch of unemployment was help Dad find a publisher for the novel he had written about the museum for his master's thesis. He had also written a full-length play, *Menelaus*, a comedic reworking of the Helen of Troy legend, with an anti-war theme. Unlike Mom, Dad was shy and reluctant to promote himself. So, I decided to act as his agent, reaching out earnestly to book critics and publishers; I also arranged meetings with all the local theaters. These efforts led nowhere except to persuade the new public access radio station, KCHU-FM, to let us produce a live version of *Menelaus*, using actors drawn from Fort Burgwin, the museum staff, St. Mark's faculty, and friends of friends. It was a family affair; I was the producer and director, and Mom handled the sound effects and music cues. David Searcy played Odysseus. Michael Bennett, a young St. Mark's Latin teacher with more theatre in his future, played the title role. Novices in the studio, we guessed at the mic levels and other technical stuff. It might not have been BBC quality, but it was good enough to qualify as a long-overdue triumph for Dad, which gave me immense pleasure. At the cast party afterward at the Stoneleigh P bar, I took in the scene of family and friends, reflected on what I had done to make this happen and thought, maybe I did belong in Dallas. But how was I going to earn a living?

The Times Mirror company that owned the *Los Angeles Times* had bought the *Times Herald* in 1970 but waited five years before hiring new editors from the East Coast and overhauling the staff. I was aware of this development, but the smug likeness of Don Safran was still staring at me from the top of the Living Section, above his column surveying all manner of entertainment. The arts and features section was always the last concern for guys running newspapers, and the *Times Herald* was no exception. Eventually they did hire a new features editor from California, and I managed to get in to see him, introduced by a young reporter I had met, Greg Graze. His name was Ted Warmbold; he was a couple years older, with a buoyant manner, *Gentleman's Quarterly* attire, and the short blond curls of a perm fashionably crowning his head. He didn't conceal his low regard for Safran and the room of outdated scriveners visible through the glass wall of his office. The times were a' changin', he said. He hoped to hire me.

But it wasn't that easy. I had to be vetted by other editors above him, and scheduling those appointments dragged on for months, leaving me blue and angry. The new *Times Herald* was snobbishly hiring reporters only from established papers like the *Chicago Tribune*, the *Detroit Free Press*, and *Miami Herald*. More than three years had passed since my first attempts to get a newspaper job, and I had paid some dues. But I still lacked the standard industry pedigree of working full-time at a "major metro."

Though Warmbold stayed in touch, assuring me I would eventually get an interview with the managing editor, by the time October turned to November, I wasn't sure I even wanted to meet the guy. Enough was enough. If I put my mind to it, I thought I might be able to make a living as a musician, join the union, maybe play bass in a blues or country band—and write fiction about it later. It was a pipe dream, but I was again out of options. I began studying jazz and rock guitar, with two different teachers. David Searcy and I continued to jam at parties; by now we were often joined by a slide guitar player, Martin Delabano, the son of a well-known painter who had worked with Dad at the museum. Martin himself was an artist. One night, in someone's living room, we found ourselves backing a young female singer who could wail and said she was looking for a band. I was intrigued, but David less so, and we never saw her again.

Mom remained supportive of my musical endeavors and said she hoped I got in a band and went on tour and all that. Dad was quietly despondent.

"IS THIS SEAN MITCHELL?"

I answered the phone at my apartment one morning, and it was a secretary at the *Times Herald* calling to schedule an interview with managing editor Will Jarrett. Christmas had come and gone, and the wind had changed. I agreed to come in and meet Jarrett, and, then on subsequent days the city editor and editor in chief Ken Johnson. I wasn't sure if I was giving the right answers or asking the right questions. I remember telling Johnson, a tough-talking corporate executive, how important I thought the book section was because books were sometimes news. Not the right thing to say to a macho man like him, but maybe I didn't care at that point. In truth, my objectives had changed in the year following my *Iconoclast* experience. Having gained a greater appreciation for all manner of reporting, I now wanted to start not in the arts section but the place most big city daily reporters started, on the police beat. But the choice was made for me. Warmbold called the next day and offered me $225 a week to be a feature writer in the Living Section and also serve as the paper's first rock critic. I accepted.

My first day on the fourth floor, the anodyne city columnist Dick Hitt, whom I had frequently mocked privately, walked over and said, "Welcome aboard, Sean." What a stand-up guy. Things looked different on the inside, where I now had a desk and a typewriter—at last.

CHAPTER TWENTY-FOUR

Staff Writer

I HAD ONLY JUST STARTED WHEN WARMBOLD TOLD ME TO GET ON A PLANE TO HOUSTON, where Bob Dylan (him again) was hosting a benefit concert at the Astrodome for imprisoned boxer Rubin "Hurricane" Carter. When I asked how I was supposed to pay for the flight, Warmbold looked surprised and said to put it on a credit card and they would reimburse me. Credit cards were not yet ubiquitous, and—except for Gulf Oil—I didn't have one, but I worked out some arrangement and later signed up with American Express. After attending the concert that night with a press pass and hearing Stephen Stills, Carlos Santana, Cat Stevens, and Kinky Friedman, along with Dylan, I retreated to my motel room, dashed off thirty inches, called a cab and took the copy to Western Union, where it was wired to the *Times Herald* overnight. When I landed at Love Field the next day, I rushed to a newsstand in the terminal and grabbed the paper. There was my story, leading the Living section, dateline Houston, with a wire photo of Dylan, my byline, and the words "Staff Writer" underneath.

When I got my first paycheck, I went to the Varsity Shop on Hillcrest, around the corner from my apartment, and charged two three-piece suits. This was the fashion being modeled by Warmbold and the top editors—impractical for Dallas in the sweaty summers but an outward sign of the gentrification underway at the city's former blue-collar afternoon newspaper.

Times Mirror saw death coming for afternoon papers and introduced a morning edition, making the *Times Herald* an "all-day" newspaper. The multiple editions and overhaul of the staff were paying dividends in increased circulation and prestige. *TIME* magazine, in a cover story about the New South, keyed to Georgian Jimmy Carter's bid for the White House, named the *Times Herald* one of the five best newspapers in the region, implicitly slighting the *Morning News*, which historically had been the paper of record. It was an exciting time, and I put my reservations about the trade aside as I made a place for myself at the paper, turning out several articles and reviews a week.

Warmbold encouraged irreverence, as if to make it clear this was not the old *Times Herald*, and assigned me to interview the self-important advice columnist Ann Landers when she came to town. He'd had some experience with her and suspected I might not pay Ann the deference she was accustomed to at newspapers that carried her column. He was right, and after I noted in my story her conspicuous self-regard ("Let's face it, for a woman who's going to be sixty in two years, I'm in pretty incredible shape"), I got my first taste of a famous person complaining to my bosses about a story I had done. Warmbold loved it.

I dropped my guitar lessons and stopped writing in my journal. I was too busy with the task at hand. I clung to the thought that feature writing was more creative than straight news reporting, but I also knew it wasn't poetry. It was the best I could do, for now. And it was fun, sometimes. I took my company-issue 8x4 inch reporter's notebook to concerts and clubs and learned to scribble in complete darkness my initial reactions and impressions. I also used the back of envelopes, which were easier to stash in a breast pocket. I now had a backstage pass and grabbed quick interviews with Bob Seger, Lionel Ritchie, and Tom Jans, among others, using my own form of shorthand to jot down their answers to questions.

Linda Ronstadt wasn't giving interviews while rehearsing in Dallas for a national tour, but her manager, the former British pop star Peter Asher, agreed to talk to me. I found him in his hotel room at the Fairmont addressing a technical problem with the test pressing for Ronstadt's new album, *Hasten Down the Wind*, which was waiting to be released to radio stations and record stores across the country.

"Look, I've listened to it, and it sounds fine to me," Asher said over the phone to a recording engineer in California as I looked on. "Let's get it out." A live peek behind the scenes of big-time rock and roll for the readers of the *Times Herald*, I thought.

Having the designation as the rock critic at a major metropolitan daily meant I was deluged with attention from record companies and club owners. New LPs arrived daily, addressed to me, along with phone calls from purring publicists stoking my interest in bands coming to town. I was now in the data base, a member of the media. There was the literary problem that music defied description, but I tried to offer a sense of my delights and disappointments in listening to it, aware that my opinions were subjective. When Paul McCartney returned to America for the first time since the breakup of the Beatles, opening his 1976 US tour with Wings in Fort Worth (because the band's light and sound company was based here), I got a call at my desk from the Chicago radio giant WLS, asking me to share my experience of the concert. Before I could gather my thoughts, I heard the DJ shout, "Welcome to Chicago, Sean!" and realized I was on the air, offering my half-baked critique of Linda McCartney to thousands of listeners across the Midwest.

I was smitten with the newsroom—the clatter and hum of typewriters and voices, editors and reporters trying to make sense of Dallas and the world every day, explaining how and why things happened and mattered, including in sports and entertainment. The atmosphere was electric and produced a camaraderie among like-minded souls drawn to the vibe. Each morning a copyboy passed through the room with an armful of the latest edition, fresh from the presses below, and plopped one on your desk, the ink barely dry. A cheap thrill, especially if the newsprint carried words you had typed the night before, now staring back at you under a headline someone else had written.

I was not a fast writer, but I did the best I could. "You just have to be faster than anyone better and better than anyone faster" was the adage given me by a young editor my age, Kerry Slagle, who looked a little like the comedic actor Gene Wilder and had already worked at several papers. The deadline pressure was relentless and addictive, requiring adrenaline to get the copy in, followed by a letdown after it passed muster. And then the cycle started all over again. No wonder a lot of reporters drank. And everybody smoked, or almost everybody. Cigarettes seemed essential to the very process of writing under pressure, and the newsroom was cloaked in a tobacco haze. I was a light smoker before joining the *Times Herald* but upped my usage as needed. I promised myself I would quit before I was thirty, and though I kept that promise, when I did quit, I worried that I would not be able to write without smoking and would have to quit newspapers as well.

By now I had accepted the identity of being a journalist and newspaperman, which carried with it a sense of belonging to a caste apart from the rest of society, bound by its own codes and obligation to report the "truth," however inconvenient or unfiltered. I had learned that being a journalist made you popular with some people, including newsmakers, because your friendship offered them proximity to publicity. Others eyed you warily as an intruder who, allowed backstage or into a party, might see or hear something embarrassing that could end up in the paper.

People always tell you more than they want to. Every reporter knew this. It was knowledge gained quickly on the job and not often discussed because it advertised a journalist's eagerness to take advantage of human frailty—albeit to gain information that might improve a story.

I had returned to my journal, now and then.

I NO LONGER FELT AT ODDS WITH DALLAS. I had a job that seemed to suit me in a city that was bristling with the promise of the Sun Belt, a new term (pre–global warming) that said the energy of America, more than ever, had shifted south and west. Just look at the new highways, the shiny glass high-rises everywhere, the expanding art museums, the sudden vitality of regional music and culture, the new media like *Texas Monthly, D Magazine*, and the *Times Herald* itself.

One morning in those early months I arrived at the office, got a cup of black coffee, which was breakfast, and sat down at my desk with the first edition, ready to consider all that was now right with my life. Suddenly a strange foreboding came over me, a sensation I hadn't experienced before. It scared me, and without speaking to anyone, I got up from my desk, took the elevator to the first floor and walked out on to Pacific Avenue to get some air. It was warm, I loosened my tie and walked east through downtown, not sure where I was headed, this mysterious demon pursuing me. Eventually I entered a building with a lunch counter, found my way to a second-floor men's room and into a stall where I threw up. I feared I was having some kind of breakdown—at 10 a.m. on a Wednesday. But why? I finally had the job I had been seeking for so long. I had a girlfriend, Wanda McDaniel, the paper's young society editor, who had a Fiat Spider just like mine. For the first time I sought out a therapist, who guided me eventually to the insight that, on a subconscious level, I worried that I was cutting in line ahead of Dad, whom I wanted so badly to get his due as a writer.

Whether that was the entire reason for the anxiety attacks that persisted for a year, I'm not sure, but it made some sense to me. It was a measure of how much I had absorbed the unfairness of his life. There might have been other factors, including the sort of chemical imbalance that psychotherapists later came to believe was a common source of anxiety and depression—and treated with antidepressants. This also would have explained my father's black moods, which I suspected I might have inherited.

I continued to see the therapist, Don Giller, once a week for a couple years, without the benefit of insurance. The *Times Herald* health plan did not yet cover psychotherapy. Giller, who was a member of the First Unitarian Church, let me pay what I could afford, with the understanding that I would make it up to him when I was able. Thank God (or whomever) for Unitarians. I looked forward to our fifty minutes together each week and would usually leave his office feeling energized and reassured that I was OK. Once, I told him I had read a *New York Times Magazine* story about psychotherapy in which an analyst said many of his patients hated themselves. I did not hate myself, I said. It was something else bothering me. He agreed.

CHAPTER TWENTY-FIVE

Long Form

ALTHOUGH PRAISED BY *TIME* MAGAZINE AS BEING IN THE SOUTH'S TOP FIVE, the revamped *Times Herald* was still young enough and small enough that its organizational chart was sketchy. This worked to my benefit, allowing me to cover rock music but also write other features and take longer assignments for the Sunday magazine on a range of topics. This would not have happened at a bigger paper, where beats were more rigid and narrowly defined. I enjoyed the mix and continued to document the adventures of Willie Nelson and Ray Wylie Hubbard, review the Eagles and the O'Jays when they came to town, and, for the magazine, take a week here or there to visit an oil rig in the Gulf of Mexico, profile a new congressman, and examine why it took so long to integrate the football teams of the Southwest Conference. Apart from the rich experiences these stories offered, they forced me to learn how to write longer pieces, which was invaluable. Slagle, the magazine's editor, gave me the opportunity, if not much direction. As with my first year of teaching, it was on the job training.

He sent me and a photographer, Skeeter Hagler (who would one day win a Pulitzer) to Alaska with two long-haul truckers to report on the lives of the men who had become folk heroes even as their eighteen-wheelers clogged the interstates. The trip took ten days and nights and included dicey encounters with other trucks and cars at high speeds, plus the ordeal of the rugged Alcan Highway itself, some of it only dirt and mud on the way from British Columbia to Fairbanks. The result was an edgy, not-suitable-for-PR profile of the two ornery drivers and their unforgiving occupation. The whole experience was a test of nerves. The driver I was riding with at one point brandished a sawed-off shotgun at a Canadian rival, instructing me to roll down the passenger window to give him a clear shot from the driver's seat. Which, when the stand-off was concluded without bloodshed, sent me in search of some Valium I had brought along for the ride. The article was a runner-up for a prize in a national Sunday magazine competition, so I concluded it was worth it and that maybe I had found my calling.

I played center field for the *Times Herald* softball team, but I missed the deeper male bonding that took place at Joe Miller's bar and weekly poker games. You'd think the schools I attended would have prepared me for such macho activities, but I was a minor leaguer when it came to hard liquor, and I wasn't drawn to card games and gambling. My loss, I feared, suspecting that Scotch and smoke-filled bars were essential to a newsman's life.

If I had gone more often to Joe Miller's, I might have gotten to know Blackie Sherrod, the sports columnist hero of my youth who, a dozen years later, looked a little less heroic standing on the other side of the generation gap, where sportswriters who had fought in World War II were reluctant to call the former Cassius Clay by his newly adopted name, Mohammed Ali. In response to my magazine story about the belated integration of the Southwest Conference, Blackie wrote a column pushing back with a defense of the conference's segregation as simply a reflection of the state's sociology and not that far behind the rest of the country. This was in my first year at the paper, and while I took his public reproach as a badge of honor, unfortunately it probably kept me from ever getting to hear him retell the story of how, the night of the Kennedy assassination, he, the sports editor, had taken charge of the chaotic newsroom and coordinated the *Times Herald*'s coverage. It was one of those legends you only got to hear told firsthand after enough Scotch, in trusted company. I missed the cut there.

One night in my early years at the *Times Herald*, I stopped on the way home to pick up a bucket of Colonel Sanders fried chicken, and after consuming my greasy, overpriced dinner back at McFarlin, it occurred to me I had done this too many times. I was a captive of fast food. I wanted my freedom and was going to have to learn how to cook. I had never paid much attention to the food sections of newspapers, but I started reading them, along with the James Beard primer *Theory and Practice of Good Cooking* that I saw reviewed favorably in those same pages. Methodically, I made my way through the book and its recipes, finding that cooking could be pleasurable and therapeutic, working with your hands after working with your head all day. And it connected to the idea of self-reliance that I had learned from Thoreau and Emerson.

Newspapers were always in flux, I discovered, editors coming and going, beats changing, the ground constantly shifting under your desk. Warmbold soon left to edit the city magazine, *D*, and was replaced by a woman from the *Chicago Tribune*, Sue Smith. Sue was a UT grad from the small Texas town of Lockhart and had spent a decade in Chicago stretching her mind and imagination at the *Tribune*. (Her ex-husband ghosted a column for the Reverend Jesse Jackson.) She had a gift for nurturing writers and showed me the value of an article being "a good read" without having to answer any existential questions. She hired more literary talent, including the Texas-born novelist C. W. Smith to be the film critic.

The Living Section was crowded with good writers, and everyone was influencing everyone. We were young and unattached, many of us, and we had all the time in the world to devote to the project of making ourselves and the features section worthy of notice. We stayed late at the office working on stories and talking about writing, from the novelists we admired to journalists like A. J. Liebling, Mike Royko, Hunter Thompson, and Tom Wolfe. Were we ever going to write anything that good?

Given the *Times Herald*'s limited staff, I still covered the occasional rock concert and interviewed songwriters like Steve Goodman and Jimmy

With Times Herald *photographer Skeeter Hagler after returning from Alaska*
AUTHOR COLLECTION

Buffett if they were in town. For the five-city Texas leg of Jackson Browne's *Running on Empty* tour, I rode in an equipment truck with the stage crew to profile the Dallas company SHOWCO that also provided lights and sound for Paul McCartney, Linda Ronstadt, the Bee Gees, and the biggest bands in the business. The story gave me some insight into how physically punishing a rock tour can be, offset by the recurring elixir of live performance. At a soundcheck before the show in Austin, I walked to the front of the stage and gazed out at the empty auditorium, imagining the perspective of the musicians who would be standing in this spot in a few hours when the seats were full, the lights went down, and Jackson Browne stepped forward to strum that first electric chord, followed by the words *Well, I've been running down the road tryin' to loosen my load / Seven women on my mind ...*

Show business. I wasn't in it, but I felt an attraction.

When a New York publicity firm, hired by the long-bearded Texas boogie-rock trio ZZ Top, invited the *News* and *Times Herald* to preview the band's new show in Washington, DC, I made plans to go. Michael Hahn was still in DC, and I asked him if he wanted to attend the concert with me. We ended up riding in a limo provided by the PR firm and were driven in unaccustomed style to Maryland's Capitol Centre, where the limousine was waved down a ramp in the rear, entering the arena on a subterranean level and rolling to a stop on a polished concrete platform backstage. As a reporter I had been in limousines with celebrities before, but this was different and more fun—just Michael and me, former house painters and fraternity lounge musicians, pulling into a big venue in a stretch, past waving fans and security, getting a glimpse through the tinted windows of what it would have been like to be rock stars.

When I got home to write the story, I decided to try something new and frame it around the New York PR guy who was being paid by the band to buff up their image and had arranged the trip. He was selling me (and I'm sure the critic for the *News*) the power and glory of ZZ Top as adamantly and methodically as Ford sold trucks and McDonald's sold hamburgers. I made him a lead character in the story of ZZ Top "conquering" DC, identifying him only by the initial of his last name. This was chancy and unconventional, but the whole experience had given me a close-up view of the marketing machine behind the big business rock and roll had become, and I wanted to share that with readers. I was relieved when Sue, my new editor, said she liked it and didn't ask for any major changes.

The first computers arrived around this time, transforming the newsroom in ways that could be challenging. It was an adjustment to give up electric typewriters and switch to digital screens with glowing green characters set against a dark background. The novelty and utility were intriguing, but the initial system was temperamental, subject to crashing without notice and erasing the last two paragraphs you had just produced.

It occurred to me later that I spanned the modern history of a newspaperman's modus operandi: arriving at the end of the manual typewriters era at the *Star-News*, adapting to the chunky Olivetti electrics with special-margined carbons at the *Times Herald*, and then finally to the various stages of computer systems at the *Times Herald* and beyond. Behind the scenes and on another floor, pressmen were being eliminated by these technological changes.

THAT FLUX THING AGAIN. Slagle left to become sports editor of the *Chicago Sun-Times*, ending our fruitful working relationship. The stories I had done for him at the magazine led me to see the benefits of being a generalist—someone entrusted with long profiles and in-depth pieces about different subjects. Slagle thought that suited me and confided that I might be asked to join a new unit in the A Section assigned big "take-outs" on major stories. I was intrigued, but that never happened, and when he left for Chicago, my status remained fixed in features, considered the back of the bus to the hard news guys sitting up front. When the city editor chose to advertise a story of mine on the front page with a teaser that read "Rock writer Sean Mitchell goes backstage" with whoever, instead of being flattered, I was dismayed at being defined as the "rock writer."

Rock music in the late 1970s was losing some of its appeal to me as a subject. Circus acts like KISS and Alice Cooper were selling out arenas, hiding their meager musical talent behind cheesy stagecraft, deafening decibels, and clouds of dry ice. *I have been closer to music listening to a 747 take off*, I wrote after attending a KISS concert. At the same time, esteemed critics were becoming enamored of the grungy minimalism of punk that was allegedly restoring authenticity to a genre that had become overproduced and studio centric. I didn't hear it and felt increasingly out of place on the beat.

In the Safran years, the *Times Herald* did not have a theatre critic or a rock critic, and now it had both, with the precocious John Bloom deciding to take up the theatre beat when no one was looking. Bloom was a young star from Arkansas and Vanderbilt who would soon transform himself into the popular and politically incorrect "drive-in movie critic" Joe Bob Briggs, an ironic redneck alter ego that got him in trouble with the bosses at the *Times Herald* but led to a lucrative career and cult status on cable television introducing B movies.

Before he disappeared into the persona of Joe Bob Briggs, Bloom managed briefly to introduce the notion of theatre in Dallas as being worth the attention of a top writer. When he moved on, I saw the chance to do something interesting.

CHAPTER TWENTY-SIX

Two on the Aisle

T HE THEATRE CRITIC POSITION CAME OPEN midway
through my second year at the *Times Herald*, and I asked for the job.
The bosses were not ready to hire another rock critic yet, but I was
given the OK to start reviewing plays so long as I didn't ignore pop music
altogether. I still wanted to be a generalist, but with Slagle gone and the way
the paper was structured, I didn't see how to make that happen.

After tiring of the star-making machinery of rock (to quote a Joni
Mitchell lyric), I saw in the theatre the prospect of a wider world to write
about, involving stories and ideas, history, and politics and songs with lyrics
meant to be understood. I admired the ancient art form itself and thought
back fondly to my time in the Harlequin Players, regretting that I never got
into the theatre at Brown. Plus, I knew nothing would please Dad more than
for me to become the theatre critic. What I knew about the theatre I had
learned mainly from him, with additional contributions from Tony Vintcent.

I was taken with the idea of treating the theatre as a subject worthy of
the same scrutiny directed at city hall and sports, not to mention classical
music and restaurants. "There is no theatre in Dallas," Don Safran had said
to me once, meaning no major professional companies to compare with the
Dallas Symphony and Opera. While that was somewhat true at the time, I
sensed a fresh excitement going on in regional theatre across the country,
making Broadway less primary. I found that appealing and knew Dallas had

been a player in the regional theatre movement early on, dating to the 1940s, when director Margo Jones, a Texan, had invited the young Tennessee Williams to work on new plays at her revolutionary theatre-in-the-round in Fair Park. I was curious about that history and why it had been plowed under, leaving Dallas on the outskirts of what the American theatre had since become. I saw it as a project that might last three or four years before I moved on to something else.

But even as I was motivated to begin, I felt nervous about my qualifications and expertise. Unlike movies and rock music, theatre was a niche art form, drawing a smaller but more discerning audience. It was also much older and represented a vast store of knowledge not readily acquired. Many film and rock critics were young and brash, suitable for sounding off on pop culture, but the image of a theatre critic (or the image I had) was of a seasoned boulevardier who had seen at least ten *Hamlets*, including Laurence Olivier's, plus big-time productions of *Oklahoma!* and *Waiting for Godot*. I was not that person.

Journalists often must be quick studies, and before becoming a rock critic, I had read collections of reviews by Robert Christgau and Jon Landau to prepare. Now, I surveyed collections by Walter Kerr, John Simon, Harold Clurman, and Kenneth Tynan, just looking to see what they chose to praise or complain about and how they did it. Reprinted between hard covers, their descriptions of long-ago productions in New York and London carried an abstract authority that was both humbling and inspiring. I took pleasure in their prose and set out to find a way of doing something similar in my own voice.

The main institution under my purview was the Dallas Theater Center, by virtue of its budget and building. The only theater ever designed by Frank Lloyd Wright, the hulking white edifice hid behind a wall of foliage on a Turtle Creek hillside, not far from the city's wealthiest neighborhoods. Built in 1959, four years after Margo Jones's death (at forty-three), the Theater Center was led by a man named Paul Baker, who had attracted attention as head of the drama department at conservative Baylor University in Waco by staging an experimental version of *Hamlet* with three actors playing different aspects of the prince. He later moved to Trinity University in San Antonio and brought that affiliation with him north to Dallas when he founded the

Theater Center, whose company members and students were credentialed by Trinity, 274 miles away.

It was an unorthodox arrangement that notably excluded Actors Equity, the national stage actors' union, and explained why actors from outside the company were rarely seen on its stages. I soon came to view the Theater Center as a cloistered operation that revolved around Baker and his musty reputation. I hadn't seen the three *Hamlets* in Waco, but I had seen Baker's ill-conceived attempt in 1974 to reckon with the Kennedy assassination, *Jack Ruby, All-American Boy*, a shallow, titillating spectacle he directed about the low-life strip club owner who murdered Lee Harvey Oswald. To my eye what Baker was producing now was not on a par with shows I had seen at the Guthrie in Minneapolis, the Goodman in Chicago, the Actors Theatre of Louisville, and The Alley in Houston.

The Theater Center did have a few good actors who stood out in chestnuts like *The Royal Family* and *Three Men on a Horse*, but the other professional company, Theatre Three, using an arena stage, exhibited a more modern sensibility and had one guy, Larry O'Dwyer, who gave state-of-the-art performances in everything from Molière to Simon Gray. O'Dwyer had his Equity card and could have acted anywhere but for whatever reason stayed close to Dallas and Theatre Three.

The city also had the summer Shakespeare Festival that brought in actors from New York like Morgan Freeman and Sigourney Weaver (before they were famous) to the sweltering Fair Park bandshell, Broadway road shows at the Music Hall, two dinner theaters, and a handful of amateur groups and college productions—notably those at SMU, whose undergraduate program had produced actors Kathy Bates and Powers Boothe, playwrights Beth Henley, Jack Heifner, and James McClure, and the Broadway set designer John Arnone. It was a beat if you wanted to make it one. I was determined.

Unlike covering a sports team or City Hall, being the theatre critic was a lonely pursuit, with only your counterpart at the *Morning News* to compare notes with on occasion. If you reviewed movies or television, you could expect editors and others at the office to be familiar with the things you wrote about. The theatre not so much. And you couldn't get close to theatre people themselves for risk of conflict of interest. Most of the time you were soloing on the trail as you were building it, trying to create a sense that the shows and what

O'Neill critics, 1978: Dan Sullivan, kneeling lower left; Ernie Schier standing far right; I'm seated in the middle, wearing aviator shades, Larry DeVine behind me.

AUTHOR COLLECTION

you said about them mattered—as if this were New York and not Dallas, as if the city and its fragile theatre community were anxiously awaiting word of what happened at a store-front opening night that attracted an audience of sixty-five. You carried the report in your head, ready to be shaped and shared.

We generally ran reviews a day later, allowing me to come into the office at nine or ten the morning after an opening night and have a few hours to knock out the review before the 2 p.m. copy deadline. That gave me a night to sleep on the experience before rushing to judgement as Brooks Atkinson and the first-nighters of old had done, sprinting to their newsrooms to issue instant verdicts on the latest Broadway openings.

I came to agree with Joan Didion, who once said, "I don't know what I think until I write it down." When a play or musical was terrific or awful, it was easy enough to register an opinion, but when the experience was somewhere in between—which was most of the time—fashioning a response took some deliberation as you added up the sum of the parts while trying not to forget what you felt in your gut as you left the theater.

After my first year of doing this, in the summer of 1978, the bosses at the *Times Herald* allowed me to attend the National Critics Institute at the Eugene O'Neill Theater Center in Connecticut—a monthlong workshop attached to the National Playwrights Conference, designed to nurture and groom young critics. This proved to be culture shock of the best kind: escaping the isolated scene in Dallas to mingle and work with top New York actors and directors, as well as other critics, led by veterans Ernie Schier of the *Philadelphia Bulletin*, Dan Sullivan of the *Los Angeles Times*, and Julius Novick of the *Village Voice*.

I went eagerly but with some trepidation. The place was named for Eugene O'Neill, after all, the offices located in a house on the coast that was the model for *Moon for the Misbegotten*. The stages were outdoors, Long Island Sound was in the background, meals were taken communally, and a serious informality prevailed. East Coast theatre folk called it Camp Eugene.

Not long after I arrived and found my dorm room at nearby Connecticut College and unpacked, I went out exploring the grounds and ran into Chris Sarandon, the actor—then married to Susan—who had just arrived from New York. He was friendly, asked if I was an actor, and did not recoil when I said I was a critic. I had seen him in the films *Dog Day Afternoon* and *Lipstick* and thought, OK, this is the big leagues. I hope I can fit in.

At the opening seminar on "The Art of Criticism," Ernie Schier, the director, looked out at the dozen young critics before him and issued the stern warning that he didn't want to read in a review whether a play "worked" or not. Ernie also did not like the word "rather." I felt a twitch in my stomach, thinking that I had used both those words many times, and did this mean I would not be up to the standards here? It came as a relief a few hours later, to hear Lloyd Richards, the director of the Yale Rep and head of the Playwrights Conference, use the term "works" repeatedly in his welcoming remarks to us. It was proof of playwright Lillian Hellman's famous observation that "almost everything in the theatre contradicts something else."

Ernie had a gruff, East Coast demeanor but turned out to be a sympathetic mentor, instructing us to "write what you see," as opposed to checklist reviewing, that ticked off all the elements of a production while avoiding the defining one. "You might want to write about one performance if it dominated the play," he said. I took this to heart, even as it contradicted Edith Oliver, the circumspect off-Broadway critic for the *New Yorker*, who stated the opposite during a visit with us, endorsing the "tip of the hat" acknowledgements to lighting, sets, and costumes that filled her reviews. More proof of Lillian Hellman's dictum.

The new plays were staged every few days under workshop conditions with the actors still holding their scripts, and we wrote overnight reviews that were discussed and critiqued in our own group sessions led by the senior critics. Over the course of the month, each of us served as a dramaturge, or literary advisor, to one of the productions during its week of rehearsals, providing feedback to the playwright and director. The play I worked on was not destined to join the list of illustrious titles birthed at the O'Neill, like John Guare's *House of Blue Leaves*, Wendy Wasserstein's *Uncommon Women and Others*, or August Wilson's *Ma Rainey's Black Bottom*, but the experience gave me a chance to see how things looked from the other side of the footlights when mounting new work.

This was heady stuff, but the workshops and tutorials also gave me confidence in what I was doing—and renewed purpose. The encouragement I received from Ernie, Lawrence DeVine of the *Detroit Free Press*, and others made me sorry to see the month come to an end. I knew there would be no such camaraderie back home and no theatre community like this one.

On the bus carrying campers back to New York City, I grabbed a seat next to actor Dominic Chianese, who would later be known as "Junior" Soprano on *The Sopranos*. I had gotten to know Chianese casually at the O'Neill and found him to be open and likable. He had a guitar with him, and as the bus rolled down I-95 toward Manhattan, he strummed and sang, asking for others to join him. I didn't know that he once hosted open mic night at Gerdes Folk City in the Village and had done musical theatre or I might not have said yes when he asked me if I played. He handed me the guitar, and I picked out the song "Border Affair" I had learned recently off a Lee Clayton album. He listened graciously and sang along on the chorus, adding to my sudden romantic desire to stay in New York and not have to say goodbye to these people.

CHAPTER TWENTY-SEVEN

Nothing If
Not Personal

W HEN I RETURNED TO DALLAS, I FELT CHANGED. I now had more context and comparison for making judgments and gauging my reactions and opinions. I was reassured that criticism is nothing if not personal, and that it should reflect as much as possible my own taste and predilections if I were going to make my reviews and stories as readable as the sports columns in the *Times Herald* that I admired.

Sportswriters were often regarded as the literary stars of newspapers, with arts writers overlooked entirely. Why was that? I think it had to do with the "back of the bus" prejudice endemic to newspaper management, but also arts reviews tended to be aimed at an audience of the initiated, resisting connection to average readers and the wider world. Which I thought was a mistake. The number of readers interested in the theatre was never going to match the number interested in football and baseball, but if you were going to put something in the newspaper, wasn't the object to get people to read it?

I sometimes thought I should be writing a column called "Theatre and Popular Music," reflecting my own interests in two branches of the performing arts that I loved but that had been separated for decades by changes in the cultures of both. For whatever reason *HAIR* had not launched a new era on Broadway, and most musicals sounded stale and effete to me. Meanwhile, the smart, contemporary songs of Randy Newman, Paul Simon, and others

Johnny Simons and Julie McMahan in Hip Pocket's Tommy

from the world of literate rock were crying out to be adapted for the stage. I thought I might have heard the future, briefly, at the Actors Theater of Louisville one night, when, at the conclusion of Jane Martin's *Talking With*, a lively evening of female monologues, the recorded sound of Linda Ronstadt tearing into Warren Zevon's "Poor, Poor Pitiful Me" filled the house as a coda. Perfect.

Back in Dallas—or Fort Worth, to be precise—there was a fringe theater staging musicals with rollicking original songs that sounded to my ears better than most coming from Broadway. It went by the name The Hip Pocket Theatre, and I was drawn to their moxie and countercultural imagination. The founders, director Johnny Simons, his wife Diane, and composer Douglas Balentine, were refugees from Casa Manana, Fort Worth's uninspiring institutional theater. At a roughhewn outdoor summer space on the banks of Lake Worth, Simons and Balentine staged fanciful shows of music and dance based on local folklore and malleable pop classics like *Peter Pan* and *Tarzan*. The actors were mostly amateurs, but the scripts and music were sometimes magical. It was fun just to go there.

A few of the Hip Pocket's shows, including a surprisingly successful adaptation of The Who's rock opera *Tommy*, were highlights of my years on the theatre beat, along with, improbably, a Dallas dinner theatre production of *Last of the Red-Hot Lovers* starring Sid Caesar. Sid Caesar doing dinner theatre sounded strange and maybe a little sad, but he was as funny as ever, adding his instincts and mannerisms to a sturdy Broadway comedy written by his former *Show of Shows* colleague Neil Simon. One of my earliest memories of television was watching *Your Show of Shows* (the original *Saturday Night Live*) with Gene and Lu in the den on Holbrook, so I was excited when Caesar agreed to an interview. He was the first star from my youth that I met, and he didn't disappoint. Over lunch somewhere in Oak Lawn he was funny just being himself, but he also held nothing back about the burnout pace of his early years at NBC.

"We did ninety minutes live every week—for thirty-nine weeks, not twenty. You do that for eighteen years . . ." He blinked and smiled faintly. As for slipping out of sight for two decades, he said, with some bitterness, "People from your past don't want to know you." He groused that *Saturday Night Live* would never use him as guest host, and I sent my article, circling that quote, to the show's headquarters in New York. Whether it ever reached the desk of producer Lorne Michaels I have no idea, but I was pleased a few years later to notice Sid Caesar hosting "SNL."

THE THEATER CENTER'S MAIN TRIUMPH DURING THESE YEARS was unearthing a homegrown playwright, Preston Jones, who was briefly national news after the *Saturday Review* put his picture on its cover, with the headline "Has the Southwest Spawned a New O'Neill?" Jones had written three connected full-length plays about the outmoded and unhappy denizens of a fictional west Texas town abandoned by its young and bypassed by the new highway. First produced at the Theater Center, Jones's *Texas Trilogy* was next done successfully at the Kennedy Center in Washington before an ill-fated transfer of all three plays in the fall of 1976 to Broadway, where they lasted but a few weeks. Jones told me later, with some justification, that the New York critics were laying for him. The unlikely comparison to O'Neill, before anyone in New York had seen his work, did not help.

Jones died three years later at the untimely age of forty-three (same as Margo Jones) after undergoing abdominal surgery. His trilogy had been re-staged to popular success at the Theater Center, and not long after his death, one of the plays, *The Oldest Living Graduate*, would be performed live on national television from Dallas, with Henry Fonda in the leading role of Colonel J. C. Kinkaid, a shell-shocked veteran of World War I. The play was not broadcast from the Theater Center as originally planned but instead from the Bob Hope Theater at SMU, where the network detoured after Baker insisted the production use Theater Center actors. It became a newsworthy controversy, full of legal issues, egos, and artistic principles that I covered like a court reporter. NBC wanted to cast the play in Los Angeles and found an illustrious group that included, besides Fonda, Cloris Leachman, Harry Dean Stanton, George Grizzard, John Lithgow, Penelope Milford, and Timothy Hutton—surely the most acting talent ever gathered onstage at the Bob Hope Theater in one night.

On the evening of April 8, 1980, the national spotlight in the theatre was on Dallas for a change as the first live drama for television in eighteen years went off without a hitch. It was to be the first in a regular series of broadcasts from the nation's regional theaters, but despite the high quality of *The Oldest Living Graduate*, NBC only aired one more of these before dropping the idea. That's network television for you.

The other big local theatre story that year also involved the Theater Center and D. L. Coburn, a local author whose first play, *The Gin Game*, was a Broadway hit starring Hume Cronyn and Jessica Tandy, winning the 1977 Pulitzer Prize. After the Broadway run, Coburn decided to go public with his decision to deny the Theater Center the rights to produce *The Gin Game* in Dallas, based on his low regard for Baker and the company. Coburn had become a friend and gave me the scoop, which led the arts section on a Sunday. His celebrity status as Dallas's only Pulitzer Prize-winning playwright added credibility to the criticism I had been leveling at the theatre for years. Together, in a sense, we had made the case that Dallas deserved better. The board finally agreed and ousted Baker in 1982.

Years before that, Baker had made a trip downtown to complain about me to the top editors, who, I was pleased to learn, were not swayed by his self-serving vitriol. The guys running the *Times Herald* no longer scurried to appease local honchos and special interests when they objected to unfriendly coverage in the paper. But Baker was stuck in the past when the Dallas press had accepted him at face value.

CHAPTER TWENTY-EIGHT

Prize at the End of the Line

FTER FOUR YEARS OF GOING TO OPENING NIGHTS at the Theater Center, Theatre Three, Broadway, and regional theaters, I had begun to think I might be coming to the end of my project. I wanted to do other kinds of writing and even thought about becoming a copy editor, allowing me the mental space away from the office to write fiction or even try a play. I'd found I couldn't do that as a critic, which took all my attention and mental energy. I knew some critics made a career of it, cranking out reviews of plays or movies or books for decades. I was amazed how they did that. I worried about repeating myself, plus I wasn't always comfortable making the harsh public judgments the job required.

In early December of that year, I got a visit from my college buddy Alan Fedman, now an attorney with the Department of Energy's office in Tulsa. He had a business meeting in Dallas, and it happened to be on the day after John Lennon was shot and killed by a psychotic fan in New York City, his death announced by ABC sportscaster Howard Cosell toward the end of a *Monday Night Football* game. Alan, who had introduced me to eastern religion during that weekend in Norman when I was flailing in my attempts to get into the media, was newly married and someone I admired as a keeper of the faith, someone helping to regulate the powerful fossil fuel industry. It was fitting that Alan and I could be together to reckon with Lennon's untimely passing at the age of forty, harking back to what the Beatles had meant to us in college and the night we listened to *The White Album* driving to Wheaton.

After dinner, we drove by a vigil being held at Oak Lawn's Lee Park, the childhood playground I had roamed with Eric Nye that had since become a gathering place for political and other assemblies. The Beatles would never be getting back together now was the thought we shared with all the dee-jays blanketing the airwaves that night with elegiac tributes to John, Paul, George, and Ringo. We were ten years out of Brown and already assessing the retreat from the social revolution we thought might follow us through the Van Wickle Gates. Lennon's death seemed to be another mile marker on the road out of Eden.

I ONCE WROTE A SONG in the vein of Paul Simon called "Prize at the End of the Line," questioning society's markers of success (*I've got my diploma, my sheepskin aroma / People say I smell just fine*), and, as things turned out, that forgotten title was about to take on a new meaning for me. Not long after Lennon's murder and Alan's visit, I answered the phone at my desk one afternoon in December, and on the other end was a woman named Dorothy calling from Manufacturers Hanover Trust Bank in New York.

"I have an early Christmas present for you," she said.

I had no idea who Dorothy was and hadn't yet connected the dots in my head when she added, "You are the winner of this year's George Jean Nathan Award."

Good grief! I must have said "thank you" or "nice of you to call." I don't remember, only that I was stunned. The George Jean Nathan Award was the top honor in the field, named for the eminent New York theatre critic of the 1920s, '30s, and '40s who had endowed it, arranging for the recipient to be designated by the heads of the English departments of Princeton, Yale, and Cornell (Nathan's alma mater). Previous winners included the men whose reviews I had studied—Walter Kerr, John Simon, and Harold Clurman, which is why I was reluctant to even submit my work to the committee. But Sue Smith had insisted I do so.

I was exhilarated by this news but also wary that someone might be pranking me—as had occurred a year earlier when a member of a garage band in Dallas had called, impersonating an editor from *Rolling Stone* and directing me to check them out. I knew that Manufacturers Hanover Trust administered the award, so I called the bank and asked to be connected to the woman who had called me. It was no prank.

I told Sue ("You're not going to believe this . . . "), called Dad and then Mom. As word spread in the newsroom, Susan Stewart, a leading feature writer, came over and said to me, "You know your life is never going to be the same, don't you?"

I did not know that. All I could think of was, what was I going to do now? I wouldn't be able to quit being the theatre critic! Fate had intervened. But maybe I would get more trips to New York and a raise. I accepted congratulations from my colleagues in the Living Section and tried not to show the elation I was feeling inside.

When I figured Dad was home from the museum, I drove out to Farmers Branch, stopping at a liquor store to buy a fifth of Jack Daniel's. Mom was attending a class at Richland College, where she was now studying to get her associates degree. Once in the house, I immediately saw the joy in Dad's eyes and hugged him without saying a word. It was as if, together, we had accomplished this. I thought back to the embarrassing letter I had once written him from New York, blaming him for my inability to get a job. That was behind us now. I went to the kitchen, found two glasses and filled them with ice cubes. I cracked open the plastic seal on the bottle and poured the Tennessee whiskey. We clinked glasses and offered a toast to George Jean Nathan, whose name meant much more to Dad than to me. I thought he deserved the award more than I did.

The *New York Times* noted the geographical anomaly of a critic from the Dallas *Times Herald* winning the Nathan when it

Congratulations from Editor Ken Johnson; Will Jarrett is behind him
COURTESY OF ANDY HANSON, *DALLAS TIMES HERALD*

included me in its People column under the subhead, "Texan Wins George Jean Nathan Award."

In February I went to New York for the official presentation and a reception at the headquarters of Manufacturers Hanover Trust on Park Avenue. Sue came with me, as did Gene and Lu. At a lunch, a vice president from the bank handed me a check for ten thousand. Mercifully, I did not have to give a speech, but I was interviewed by NPR and the Voice of America, two outlets where I had once sought employment. There was some novelty attached to my being from Texas, still regarded by many on the East Coast as a cultural desert, and I suspect my not having a Texas accent came as a disappointment to my interviewers.

The best part about the evening was seeing all the newspaper people, writers, and friends who turned out, foremost among them Anne Crutcher, who came up from DC, as did Larry L. King, the irreverent Texas author and playwright who had become a friend. Tom Hartmann, my first St. Mark's headmaster, came, as did Julius Novick from the *Village Voice* and the O'Neill; Sarah Riggs, a columnist from the *Iconoclast* now living in New York; Gary Pearle from the Harlequin Players, now a director in New York; and my cousin Monica and her husband Michael Smith. The whole thing felt a little like that old TV show *This Is Your Life*. I was lucky to have won such a prize, but I was not at the end of the line. I was thirty-three.

CHAPTER TWENTY-NINE

Upheaval

S OME PEOPLE WHO KNEW ME ASSUMED I WOULD
SOON BE GONE FROM DALLAS, lured by opportunities else-
where. But that didn't happen, not right away. Even as I imagined the
benefits of living and working in a bigger and more cultured city, I was wary
of leaving the fraternity of the *Times Herald*, especially my colleagues in the
features section—Drew Jubera, Jeff Unger, Susan Stewart, Thom Marshall,
Chris Wohlwend, Marcia Smith, John Clark, and others who were not only
fine journalists but made up a circle of friends that gathered for dinner parties and holidays. By now, I had come to think of myself as a Texan, accidental or not. I had assimilated the new wave of country music based in Austin,
enjoyed the native cuisine called Tex-Mex, drank Lone Star beer in longneck
bottles, and came to see that all of this made Dallas feel like home, no matter
its Bible Belt background and infernal summers. I was forever torn.

Another inducement to stay was the promotion the editors gave me
to the position of critic-at-large, with the idea that I travel extensively as a
national cultural correspondent. I wanted to believe the *Times Herald* was on
its way to becoming an important paper, the best in Texas, with a budding
national profile. The last part was a stretch.

I decided to buy a house, using part of my ten-thousand-dollar
George Jean Nathan check for a down payment. After being outbid on an
older home in Oak Cliff and another in Old East Dallas, I found a newly con-

structed townhouse in Casa View, a lesser-known neighborhood on the east side. I built my own brick patio for its tiny backyard following directions in a *Sunset* magazine book and discovered that I enjoyed working with my hands. On most Sunday nights, I still drove out to Eric Lane to have dinner with Gene and Lu.

In print I continued to advocate for theatre against the competition of mass market entertainment. *Theatre remains a handcrafted form in an assembly line culture, as it remains the seed of all the other dramatic arts.*

I was invited to serve on the Pulitzer jury in drama, which then consisted of only three critics, the other two that year being Frank Rich of the *New York Times* and Jack Kroll of *Newsweek*. They both wanted Marsha Norman's *'night Mother*, a play about suicide that I found grim and uninvolving; I nominated instead Sam Shepard's *True West*, a dark farce about two brothers with opposite personalities locked in an existential wrestling match in their mother's kitchen on the scrubby outskirts of Los Angeles. Shepard had already won a Pulitzer for *Buried Child*, but I thought *True West* was better— more vivid and explosively funny. The production, which began at Steppenwolf Theater in Chicago, marked the New York stage debut of John Malkovich as the violent anarchist brother Lee; Gary Sinise played his smooth and successful screenwriter sibling. By a vote of two to one, *'night Mother* was awarded the Pulitzer, but I filed the minority report for *True West*, lending it the status of being a finalist.

The title critic-at-large was rich in promise and possibility but lacked an operating manual or clear agenda. There were no role models at other papers to follow, and, without much guidance, a lot of what I did was travel to New York more often and to regional theaters and festivals. I wanted to think I illustrated the job's potential when I went to New York in October for the much-anticipated Broadway opening of the eight-and-a-half-hour British adaptation of Charles Dickens's *Nicholas Nickleby* and after filing my review, flew across the country the next day to catch the Rolling Stones perform at Jac Murphy Stadium in San Diego. For a newspaper in Dallas, this was ambitious.

I traveled to St. Paul to see a live outdoor performance of *A Prairie Home Companion* and get my first look at the not-yet-world-famous Garrison Keillor. I was enamored of what public radio had become and this show in particular.

On a trip to Washington, DC, I managed to have breakfast with Frank Mankiewicz, the former Democratic Party operative and now president of National Public Radio whose political savvy had saved NPR from the Reagan administration's plan to defund it out of existence. And yet Mankiewicz's East Coast parochialism prevented him from seeing the appeal of Keillor, whose endearingly folksy Saturday evening celebration of heartland music and humor would become a national phenomenon distributed not by NPR but by an emerging rival, American Public Radio, based in Minnesota.

One of the staffers at the paper who shared my appreciation for Keillor was Thom Marshall, an earthy Texan from the Panhandle and gifted feature writer who invited me to accompany him and another *Herald* colleague on a rafting expedition along the Rio Grande through the canyons of the Big Bend country in the fall. I had never seen the Big Bend, which is a day's drive from Dallas, in a remote part of the state, stunning in its austere beauty and profound quiet, miles from nowhere. The trip turned into an adventure—or misadventure. We were only on the river half a day before a violent thunderstorm forced us to seek cover on a narrow sand bar at the bottom of a towering canyon wall. We stashed the inflatable pontoon raft around a corner and waited out the storm. It wasn't long before we noticed a roaring sound and, peeking around the corner, discovered a raging stream pouring into the river. Which told us that a flash flood had been unleashed by heavier rain somewhere above us. The raft was gone.

Realizing our planned three-day excursion on the Rio Grande had ended prematurely, we hiked to safety up a rocky hillside and finally to the river road, where we flagged down a flatbed truck. The driver directed us to hop on the back, and he took us back down the two-lane highway we had traveled in the other direction the day before. At some point, the truck stopped suddenly, and we looked over the cab to see a yawning space where yesterday had stood a concrete bridge spanning a deep arroyo. The bridge had been washed away by the incalculable force of the torrent. If the driver had not been alert, he could have plunged us all over the edge into oblivion. There was no way now to get to the other side, so he turned the truck around and began a tedious hours-long detour to return us to where we had left our car.

Through it all, I remained enchanted by the ethereal tranquility of this sprawling desert refuge and tried to imagine what it would be like to live here, far from the theatre and the urban excitement of Broadway I was experiencing more frequently now.

Back at work, the *Times Herald* was suddenly reneging on its promise to become the sort of place you wouldn't want to leave, self-destructing because of the ego battles that afflicted businesses of all kinds. And Times Mirror just let it happen. The hard-drinking executive editor, Ken Johnson, was directed to rehab, and while he was gone, competing factions vied for control of the paper, split between those aligned with a smart young caretaker editor imported from Baltimore and a canny rear guard loyal to Johnson. The uncertainty was all.

Kerry Slagle had returned to take a new job as assistant managing editor for Features, placing him over Sue Smith, who was no longer my editor but remained my girlfriend and was in the way of Slagle consolidating his new power. Kerry was in Johnson's camp while Sue had bet on the new guy. Many believed Johnson would never come back. But he did come back, and overnight the new guy was gone. Slagle then made his move, forcing Sue out.

It happened late one weekday afternoon. Sue called me from her office across the room, and I could see her through the partition glass, holding the phone as she looked my way. "Kerry just asked me to look for another job," she said quickly, blocking any emotion from her voice. "I thought you should know." In that instant I knew I would not be able to stay at the *Times Herald*. Slagle had been my close friend and advocate during his first stint at the paper, but now, returned as the rising organization man, he had allied himself with the mucky mucks we once disparaged. As if to drive me away, he hired as the new features editor a business editor from Buffalo who knew or cared little about the arts and questioned why I was sometimes reporting from Boston or Seattle.

That fella stood out to me as an example of how newspapers confoundingly hired and promoted mediocrities. It defied reason. And he was just one example. There was a ranking copy editor whose limited journalistic skills were evident each time he wrote a headline for one of my reviews—terrible headlines that were misleading and sometimes unnecessarily cruel, like the one that ran over the review of a play called *A Disposable Woman* and read, "'A Disposable Woman' Should Be Disposed Of." I wanted to call the playwright and apologize, explaining that the writers did not write the headlines.

The time had come to move on. Much as I abhorred the way the brass had treated Sue and believed she deserved credit for transforming the Living Section into an exemplar of arts and features coverage, I also knew that she and I were not bound to stay together. A former *Iconoclast* reporter I had dated, Deborah Goodall, once told me that she imagined me as someone who would always be single. I said I hoped that was not a curse she was issuing upon me.

The *Philadelphia Inquirer* and *Boston Globe* had each expressed interest, but I wasn't sure I wanted to live in those cities or take the jobs being offered. I contacted National Public Radio, but they were struggling to survive Ronald Reagan's renewed attempts to eliminate them entirely. "Come back and see us later if we're still around" was the message I got from NPR.

The New York newspapers seemed out of reach, but I had not forgotten the glorious summer in San Francisco during college, and I'd been intrigued by Los Angeles ever since going out to do a location piece about the movie *FM* in 1977. I returned two years later, on my own time, to look around, staying with Taffy Cannon, my *Iconoclast* compatriot, and her lawyer husband, Bill Kamenjarin. (Not to be confused with the Bill and Taffy who wrote "Take Me Home, Country Roads.") They were good friends who had moved there after Dallas, loved it, and urged me to join them. With its coastal climate, swaying palms, Spanish history, and movieland aura, Los Angeles seemed exotic to me, so different from the staid and conservative Dallas that I had made peace with. I was tempted by the prospect of living there and, despite my affinity for the theatre, I was curious about Hollywood and how it worked, given its outsized influence on our culture and the world. Another project perhaps.

I'd recently read a conversation in *Esquire* between the novelist and screenwriter John Gregory Dunne and filmmaker Paul Schrader attacking movie criticism as a profession that people like the *New Yorker*'s Pauline Kael "settled" for after failing at filmmaking or other creative endeavors. The article struck me as unfair but touched a nerve. I was still ambivalent about being a critic and preferred to think of myself as a reporter with a point of view. Theatre reviews—all reviews—were essentially little essays, and I'd been practicing that form since middle school. Which was all well and good, but I was increasingly interested in the different narrative techniques required to write longer pieces and profiles. I liked the idea of possibly exploring Hollywood not as a critic but by writing *about* the people in film, theatre, television, and radio who produced all that entertainment. As it happened, the *Los Angeles Herald Examiner* was looking for just such a person.

CHAPTER THIRTY

That *Under* Milk Wood Guy

T HERE SEEMED TO BE AN UNWRITTEN POLICY barring the parent *LA Times* from poaching anyone from the *Times Herald*. But the *Herald Examiner* was another story. The editor, Mary Anne Dolan, the first female editor of a major metro and a former feature writer at the Washington *Star-News*, remembered me. I had done a few stories for the *Herald Examiner* from Texas, including one, in the summer of 1980—the summer before Reagan knocked Jimmy Carter out of the White House—that offered me a crash course in moviemaking and Hollywood celebrity. It involved traveling to the Rio Grande Valley in a heat wave and spending five days on the set of an ill-fated movie called *Back Roads* to write a Sunday magazine profile of my old St. Mark's schoolmate Tommy Lee Jones. Jones was costarring in the film with recent Oscar-winner Sally Field under the direction of the distinguished Martin Ritt. The *Times Herald* allowed me to do it, with the proviso they could have the story also.

Dolan and the *Herald Examiner* editors didn't know that I knew Jones from St. Mark's, but they were pleased to learn this because Jones already had a reputation in LA as a testy and press-averse young actor who saw no reason to cooperate with the media. He had given a bracingly authentic performance as Loretta Lynn's Butcher Holler husband, Mooney, in *Coal Miner's Daughter*, released that spring and was a rising star in Hollywood. But he kept a low profile.

I must have been the only reporter in America who had played on a high school team with Jones and seen him onstage in his first roles as a teenager. I was also a fan, especially after seeing him in *Coal Miner's Daughter*. When I came out of the theater, I wanted to shout, "I know that guy!"

But did anyone really know him? Even at St. Mark's he was an enigma, self-possessed and aloof. He was a year ahead of me, and we weren't close but shared certain interests and activities. He arrived sophomore year straight out of West Texas, a fearsome football player with a flattop, a cowboy drawl, and physical skills that would get him named to the all-metro Dallas first team as a pulling guard—an uncommon achievement at St. Mark's. He joined the drama club right away and in the winter took up what was then the novel sport of soccer. We played alongside one another in that men's Sunday league; he was captain one year, I the next. We both worked on the literary magazine and acted for Tony Vintcent. I had not forgotten his virtuoso turn in *Under Milk Wood* that presaged his future.

He went on to Harvard and I saw him once during college, after the Brown-Harvard football game in Providence my sophomore year. I went down to the field to say hi, and he greeted me with an affront: "I can't imagine why anybody would want to go to college in Providence, Rhode Island." An indication he had become that rare thing: a redneck snob. The week after graduation, he got a small part in a Broadway play in New York, turning pro immediately. When he showed up on the daytime soap opera, *One Life to Live*, I watched it occasionally since I knew the guy playing Dr. Mark Toland. I followed his rise from soap opera actor to caustic leading man, rooting for him as a former teammate and fellow prep school literary acolyte. I guess I had forgotten the times he mocked me for quitting football and dissed Brown as a Harvard man.

In my seat aboard a Braniff 727, flying south to Brownsville, at the southern tip of Texas near the end of June, I tried to imagine the reunion. I had not spoken to Jones in more than ten years. From published reports I knew that he had married into the literary Lardner family of New York, divorced, then lived with high fashion model Lisa Taylor in Marilyn Monroe's old house in Los Angeles. He was rich and at least semi-famous. He played polo on weekends.

I checked into the Holiday Inn where the company was headquartered and at midday drove out to the location, down a lonely two-lane highway to a spot where a cluster of beige RVs signaled *movie set*. The honky-tonk being used for that night's scene was not far away. Escorted by a film company factotum to Jones's mobile home dressing room, I climbed the metal steps and knocked. The door opened, and there he was, in jeans and a baseball sweatshirt stretched over the sinew and muscle of the running back he never got to be. That familiar unforgiving face yet bore the scars of teenage acne, a vexation we had shared. "Sean Mitchell, you're an old man" were the first words out of his mouth, a reminder of his disarming personality. We were both in our early thirties, and he was a year-and-a-half older. We started talking about soccer and Boz Scaggs, who had also once been captain of the team—what the three of us had in common. His father, Clyde, a former oil-field roughneck, was there, as was a mangy black dog named Faye.

The interview had been arranged through the film company's publicist—the way these things were done—so I had not yet had a chance to speak to him about the scope of my assignment and what was involved in an in-depth profile. I wanted to be sure he understood this was not a social call.

"Aw, it's just journalism," he said when I brought this up.

He warmed up slightly and then went off to get into makeup. On that first day, as I began to mingle with the crew, I realized I had a problem. After eight weeks, Jones had alienated much of the company with his surliness. "So, you know him?" people on the set would ask me. "Was he like this in high school?" My first instinct was fraternal and protective, but I was here as a reporter, not as his friend. I didn't know what to say. Yes, no, maybe. A little. The film's production designer referred to him facetiously as "Mr. Charm." A wardrobe person said worse. I hadn't come prepared for this.

I also had a problem with Jones himself. He had once signed my yearbook generously ("You have

Jones yearbook photo, with an encouraging note to me
AUTHOR COLLECTION

Jones with coaches John Hoffman and Lud North
AUTHOR COLLECTION

consistent quality, and that's what's needed to achieve . . . ") and he had agreed to the story. But I soon realized he had as much interest in talking to me about his craft and career as preparing for a colonoscopy. He acknowledged our schoolboy tie by allowing me to watch him filming scenes with Field one night while banishing a reporter from *TIME* magazine. But he remained elusive. Admittedly busy with his role as a washed-up prizefighter hitchhiking to California with a kindly prostitute, he would agree to a meeting and then disappear, repeatedly, never explaining his absence.

My days and nights on the set were spent catching a few minutes with him here, a chance meeting there, otherwise waiting in his trailer with Clyde, Faye, assorted hangers-on, and Gary DeVore, the film's screenwriter. It became apparent that Jones was the center of a universe spinning around him. I wondered what that felt like and if I would have a chance to ask him?

We had not had the one sit-down interview I knew I needed for the piece. He kept saying sure, sure, and he kept disappearing. At a wardrobe fitting, I noticed when a young costumer showed him a pair of jeans he would be wearing for a scene and asked him if thirty-two inches was the right waist measurement? He said it was, but how was that possible? He was six foot-one.

The aura of mystery he flung over himself grew larger one afternoon when he invited me to come riding with him at the farm he owned in nearby La Feria. He kept his polo ponies there among stands of orange and grapefruit trees. Jones knew I was a city boy who'd had little experience with horses, nevertheless he found a mount for me, and for an hour we crisscrossed the fields on horseback, exercising the animals if not our mouths. We had barely spoken when he was summoned to the house for a message. When he returned, he dramatically thrust forward a slip of paper, bearing only a local phone number.

"This is for you," he said, and rode away, grim-faced.

Which made no sense and left me feeling fearful as I rode back to the house to use the phone. Something bad must have happened back home. Why would anyone try to contact me here? I rushed inside and dialed the number. The voice on the other end was unfamiliar, that of a woman who oddly didn't know why I was calling. Gradually we established that she had been one of the people hanging out in Jones's trailer on the set. It was Jones she wanted, not me.

When informed of this, he said nothing, then began to demonstrate the proper use of a polo mallet by cracking a hard wooden ball at me from ten yards away. I leapt aside to avoid a direct hit to my shins. He moved on to another ball without looking up.

I was tempted to shout, "Hey, I know you're a tough guy—you don't have to prove it to me. I remember what you did to that goalie!"

No matter what anybody said about the difference between acting and real life, some years later when the miniseries based on Larry McMurtry's *Lonesome Dove* debuted on television, it was apparent to many that Jones was born to play Woodrow Call, the pitiless former Texas Ranger driving cattle to Montana with a partner played by Robert Duvall. Or put another way, had he been born a century earlier, Jones could have *been* Woodrow Call.

Sally Field would not talk to me about him. Martin Ritt, who had directed Field to her Oscar in *Norma Rae*, did talk to me briefly and offered a description of his male lead that found its way into the headline in the *Times Herald*: "I did feel in Tommy a certain violence and a great sweetness, which I knew I needed in this part."

Gary DeVore, the screenwriter, said to me, "He's eaten everybody on this film alive."

Over the five days of shooting, I did manage to snag a few Q&As with Jones on the fly, interviews that I tape-recorded or documented with notes. His contrarian musings, candor, and poetic asides gave me a lot to work with despite his recalcitrance. I admired his irreverence and nonconformity, his willingness to acknowledge the insincerity of Hollywood.

"I know people in the movie business that smile and smile and smile and yet remain villains."

I felt a kinship in hearing a statement like that. We came from disparate backgrounds (Jones could trace his ancestors in Texas back six generations), but I tried to see what we had in common: both of us only children who attended St. Mark's on scholarship, both transformed by the experience, both gone east to college and drawn to the orbit of the theatre. I had to marvel at the role he had fashioned for himself as a Harvard-educated rustic philosopher, declaiming wisdom and verse for the common man at every opportunity.

"The next thing I'll do with my money is buy some real estate here in Texas, out in the country choked up with mesquite, jackrabbits, the wells down, the fences down, the man is too old, and the kids all gone. I'll put it back the way it ought to be. I couldn't think of nothin' else better to do. Except maybe go to Beverly Hills and throw it all up my nose. But that ain't no way. I can't do it like that."

At some point, I remarked on the oppressive heat bearing down on us in this record-breaking Texas summer, and he responded philosophically, in Spanish: *No hace mas calor que quiere dios en el cielo.* It's not hotter than God wants it to be.

When I got home, I had more to do. I called scores of people from his past, including a former brother-in-law, a Harvard theatre director, soap opera actors, Sissy Spacek, movie producers, St. Mark's students who had lived with him in a teacher's boarding house, and others. I called his mother in Midland.

"Why are you calling my mother?" he said sharply to me in a tense phone call after the film wrapped. In pursuit of a woman, he had taken up temporary residence in Dallas and at last was interested in the story I was writing. Again, I tried to explain that this was routine for a major profile. He didn't seem to understand and asked if he could see the story before I turned it in. When I explained that was against protocol and could get me fired, he bristled and wanted to know the angle I was pursuing. I said I didn't think in terms of angles but was trying to sketch an honest portrait of him as best I could. Pete Hamill, the New York City newspaper columnist, once told me that he saw himself as a sketch artist, "a good sketch artist, like Daumier for example." That seemed like a fine ambition.

It wasn't easy. Staring me in the face was the simple truth that the qualities that made Jones so good as an actor were the same things that made him so difficult as a human being. If he were a nice guy, he wouldn't have become a movie star.

When it was completed, the profile ran to nine thousand words in the *Times Herald*, an anomalous length resulting from it being chosen as the cover story in a new, expanded version of the Sunday magazine with extra space to fill. Lots of photos of him in various film and television roles. Foolishly, I thought Jones might like the article. It offered ample evidence of his gifts and achievements while quoting him at length on a wide range of topics from farming to football to fame.

"It's not going to read like a studio bio," I had told him in that phone call. And his response was to chuckle, as if acknowledging the laughable superficiality of most Hollywood publicity. I allowed myself to imagine we were on the same page. Tommy Lee Jones, well-read, bullshit-banning actor and iconoclast, would want a fellow Marksman to tell it like it is, would he not?

As it turned out, no. I overestimated his self-knowledge and willingness to share it. He didn't call me after the story was published. In fact, he never spoke to me again and didn't give another interview of any length to anyone for the next ten years. While filming *The Executioner's Song*, his next project, in which he played convicted killer Gary Gilmore, he was quoted in the *Dallas Morning News* calling my profile "a betrayal."

That hurt, but I was proud of the story and the length of the narrative I was able to construct based on knowing him in high school, the recollections of people from his past, and watching him in action in Brownsville. It was my first and only chance to draw a portrait of someone from my youth who climbed to the top of the movie business, was anointed with fame, and entered the halls of American popular culture. In many ways, it was an introduction to Hollywood before I got there.

No one in the St. Mark's community expressed any displeasure or disagreement about the profile to me. Tony Vintcent, writing from Montreal, issued his approval. On a visit to the campus, I ran into Mr. Connolly, my old Latin teacher, who said, "I give you an A+ for that story." I didn't remember ever getting an A from Mr. Connolly.

Jones and I would not cross paths again for another decade, not until I visited the set of a now forgotten movie he was making in North Carolina with Kathleen Turner. I was there to do a story about Turner for *USA Today*, but as arrangements were being made, I told the publicist he should inform Jones I was coming, given our history and the possibility he might not be thrilled to see me. The publicist assured me that "Tommy had changed" and would love to talk to me.

Really? Stories I'd heard from other journalists through the years did not indicate he had changed. But again I was tempted to imagine otherwise—that we might even share a whiskey-fueled reconciliation and reexamination of what I got wrong and what I got right about him in my profile. Pure delusion on my part.

When I arrived in Greensboro and drove to the set, in a wooded area outside of town, the publicist was there to greet me with a requisite professional smile. And he had a new message for me. "Tommy hasn't changed," he said, his tone all business and markedly different from our earlier phone conversation. He was admitting that he had lied. (Hey, this was Hollywood.) Then he warned me not to approach Jones or try to speak to him. "Stay out of his face," he said. Stay out of his face? What would Tony Vintcent or J. J. Connolly have to say about that? I could only wonder.

Part Three

CHAPTER THIRTY-ONE

Westward

S IX MONTHS AFTER THE JONES STORY, the *Herald Examiner* offered me a job, but I didn't take it. I didn't leave the *Times Herald* for another two years, not until Sue got axed and the business editor from Buffalo replaced her. When that happened, I called Gary Spiecker, the features editor at the *Herald Examiner* and asked if they still wanted me. I was newly interested in Hollywood now that Reagan, one of its own, was president. Celebrity had overtaken American culture, and Hollywood was its wellspring. After some negotiation over salary and moving expenses, I rented out my townhouse and left for LA in May of 1983.

Sue accompanied me on the two-and-a-half-day drive, as if blessing my decision to go my own way. Fleetwood Mac songs were surely in our heads as we traversed the Southwestern desert in my Mercury Capri, neither of us mentioning the conspicuous ending and beginning the journey signified. Approaching LA on a Saturday night on the I-10, we came over the rise around West Covina that affords a first panoramic view of the glittering megalopolis beyond. This was it. Who knew what life-changing events waited down there among all those twinkling lights?

Many journalists had been drawn to Hollywood by the lore and legends of its golden age, but I had never been an old movie buff. When Lauren Bacall came to Dallas to promote her autobiography, I went to the interview lacking an appreciation for the big screen roles that had made her such a star in the 1940s. I focused instead on the diva-like behavior she exhibited toward me and her entourage. I had read the Hollywood novels *The Deer Park* by Norman Mailer and *Day of the Locust* by Nathanael West, but I was at least as intrigued by the genre-blending folk-rock music that emerged from LA's misty canyons in the 1960s and '70s. The Mamas and Papas, The Byrds, Joni Mitchell, Crosby, Stills & Nash, Carole King, Neil Young, Jackson Browne, Linda Ronstadt, and The Eagles had provided the soundtrack of my young adulthood. All that music was made in Southern California.

I had written favorably of The Eagles and interviewed Don Henley over a room service meal at the Fairmont Hotel before their "Hotel California" concert in Fort Worth in the fall of 1976. The title song, with its evocative lyrics about a mysterious place in the desert too beautiful to resist and impossible to leave only added to LA's allure.

But by the time I got there, The Eagles were no more, and most of the others were gone, too. Pop music had moved on to new sensations like Giorgio Moroder's synthesized disco score for *Flashdance* and feel-good bouncy tunes suitable for aerobics workouts. The famous Troubadour nightclub on Santa Monica Boulevard, where Buffalo Springfield, Carole King, James Taylor, Randy Newman, and Elton John had made history, was now a showcase for glam metal bands.

Just off Sunset: first place in LA
AUTHOR COLLECTION

I found a two-bedroom duplex to rent on a street above Sunset Boulevard in the grittier part of Silver Lake for $650 a month. It was a funky pink Spanish stucco place, not far from downtown (where the *Herald* was) and roomy enough, with a sun porch where I sat and read the *LA Times* in the morning. It had no garage, and I had to park on the street. Both my car and the apartment were burglarized within the first month, prompting me to reassess the neighborhood I had picked out.

The *Herald Examiner* itself was hard to peg—surely one of the stranger newspapers in America. Behind its big black headlines (geared to newsstand sales) was a feisty band of young journalists charged with reviving the corpse of William Randolph Hearst's once paunchy conservative presence in Los Angeles. Formerly the largest circulation afternoon daily in America, it had been hollowed out by a spiteful, self-destructive ten-year strike initiated by management that ended in 1977, by which time the *Los Angeles Times* had complete dominion over Southern California.

Since then, the New York–based Hearst Corporation had hired a series of talented editors and columnists in a quixotic effort to compete with the *Times* and regain a stake in the Los Angeles market. Nothing had worked. It was too late. The damage done by the strike was still visible on the historic building's adulterated street level facade, where architect Julia Morgan's original 1923 line of repeating Spanish Colonial windowed arches had been filled in protectively with plain stucco, leaving the paper with the face of an abandoned fort.

The interior had a spectral quality about it. Dimly lit, with a dark linoleum floor, gray metal desks gathering dust and a computer system that belonged in a museum, it looked like the movie set for a newspaper unearthed by archeologists. Its meager resources were made apparent to me the first week on the job when I learned that if I worked late, I had to pick up my car keys at the ticket window of an X-rated movie house nearby with titles on the marquee like *Anal Alley* and *Here Cums John*. This was different.

Louella Parsons, the fabled Hollywood gossip columnist, had worked here for decades beginning in the twenties, burnishing the image of Hearst's movie star mistress, Marion Davies. Columnist James Bacon, a white-haired, glad-handing holdover from an earlier era when reporters partied with the stars, was still around on occasion, one of the few who came to the office in a coat and tie, brandishing an 8x10 glossy smile. He seemed to be ignored by the editors, and so I ignored him, too, which I later regretted. He was a link to the past and no doubt had stories to tell. In one of his books, he claimed to have slept with Marilyn Monroe, likening her breasts to "two satin pillows fluffed and warmed by room service." This was different.

People in LA were not as open and friendly as they were in Texas, and that was certainly true at the *Herald Examiner,* where the staffers in the Style section shuffled back and forth, heads down, often too distracted to say hello, even in the morning. They were serious, well-read, and, I gathered, preoccupied with their careers.

I was introduced to a Jane Austen–quoting feature writer from Yale who heard I would be interviewing movie stars and said to me sarcastically, "Do you think these people have anything to say?" Quite a contrast from the "welcome aboard" greeting I got from Dick Hitt that first day at the *Times Herald.* It was different here.

At a Style section staff meeting to discuss how the paper was going to cover *Return of the Jedi,* the final installment of the George Lucas *Star Wars* trilogy then packing the theaters, an editor proposed assigning a Jungian analysis of the three pictures. Which was a measure of how the place I was now working existed in a galaxy light years removed from Joe Bob Briggs.

The *Herald Examiner* had two film critics, Peter Rainer and David Chute, both nimble writers who had seen everything and were not easily entertained; I was given a desk between them and the early insight that I was, by comparison, a pushover as a critic. Also in the room was the theatre critic, Jack Viertel, a Harvard graduate who had played steel guitar on an early Bonnie Raitt album; the art critic, Christopher Knight, who would win a Pulitzer years later at the *Times*; the classical music critic, Mark Swed, who had an agent (the classical critic had an agent?) and was busy writing a biography of someone. The pop critic, Mikal Gilmore, was the brother of the infamous murderer Gary Gilmore and notable for the fact that Bob Dylan thought enough of him to show up at his apartment for an interview. One of the editors, David Gritten, was from England and another, Chris Hodenfield, had once been the London bureau chief of *Rolling Stone.*

This group was less like my newspaper colleagues back in Dallas and more like a department of scholars devoted to popular culture. Which made sense given that Los Angeles was a cultural capital, and movies were more than mere entertainment here; they were serious business, the hometown industry, with gaudy billboards on Sunset Boulevard to remind everyone of the new product line. Even the editors at the paper attended screenings of the latest offerings from the studios.

I wasn't sure where I fit into this scrum of cineastes and hipsters, whose knowledge of Texas was slim to none, sometimes laughably so. I went to a backyard party wearing a T-shirt bearing the logo of Dallas's oldest honky-tonk, the Longhorn Ballroom, and one of the guests asked me if that was a gay bar. But soon enough I became a regular in the crowd gathered two or three times a week in the screening rooms of Paramount, MGM, Warner Bros., and the rest. Even if the pictures were not great, the atmosphere was seductive, feeding the notion that we were insiders, getting a first look at the movies America would soon be talking about.

In the evenings when there were no screenings to attend, I would often leave the paper at five or six and just drive around LA, acquainting myself with its myriad neighborhoods, seeking out vistas in the Hollywood Hills, breathing in the scents of eucalyptus and orange blossoms that traveled on the night air. At night the hills sparkled with lights, creating a romantic tableau unavailable in flatland Dallas. An ocean lapped against the city's western flank, and the marine layer of atmosphere it created made even summer evenings cool—unthinkable in Texas.

I drove around the wreck of the old Hollywood district itself, trying to imagine what it must have looked like in the '30s and '40s, when Fitzgerald and Nathanael West were here, before the big studios moved out, leaving it to become a slum. On Western Avenue for blocks there were sad-looking used furniture stores, one after another. They were open late, and I would browse the crowded isles perusing what I took to be a repository of continental detritus—all the coffee tables, armoires, bed frames, and couches that had traveled further and further west, in vans and pick-ups and U-Haul trailers, changing hands state after state until they ended up here on Western Avenue, gathering dust on the fraying edge of Hollywood. I hoped the same could not be said about me.

CHAPTER THIRTY-TWO

Welcome to Starland

I FELT LIKE A REPORTER POSTED TO A NEW COUNTRY, learning the language and local customs, adjusting to a city where the names of the men running the studios were better known than members of the city council. It was a whole new deal here, and I was figuring it out as quickly as I could, starting over again at the age of thirty-five after foregoing the perks of the career I had made for myself in Dallas.

In an early interview with the actor Cliff Robertson, when I mentioned that I was new to town, he brightened and encouraged me to take notes. "It's only your first year once," he said to me over lunch at a barbecue place in the Valley. I deduced that he might have done the same when he arrived from New York City to work in television in the 1950s.

Los Angeles was indeed another world. In my Silver Lake neighborhood, nighttime often brought the menacing sound of helicopters overhead, indicating crime nearby. A weathered and well-worn strip of Sunset Boulevard was just down the hill, offering a stark contrast to the clean concrete avenues I'd left behind in North Texas. Yet no matter the look and feel of hard use and neglect all around, in the light of day vanity prevailed. Stopped in traffic, men spent as much time primping in their rearview mirrors as women did back in Dallas—possibly because they were on their way to an audition somewhere. It was not uncommon to see the bumper sticker "I'd Rather Be Acting" and custom license plates like "IMADEIT." Sunglasses were very important—the style and brand evidently said a lot about you.

Even in LA's ruined neighborhoods, the hint of glamour was seldom far away. On the tattered fringe of downtown, on a graffiti-tagged stretch of Olympic Boulevard, there was a crummy car wash with a marquee that read, "Car Wash Movie Filmed Here." No doubt.

On the West Side, the locus of the entertainment industry, people I met seemed both wary and wan. In the city that lived on stories, they had heard and seen them all. At my first haircut, in a West Hollywood salon recommended by one of my new colleagues at the paper, I sat down in the chair and noticed a plexiglass sign that read, "Thank you for not talking during your haircut." Bubba say what?

In a department store, a clerk asked me what I did for a living.

"I'm a writer."

"TV or film?"

I went for a run around the track at nearby John Marshall High School (its facade familiar from *Happy Days*) and encountered another runner who, while jogging, told me he wanted "to be to the screenplay what Hemingway and Fitzgerald were to the novel."

I was far from home, hearing strange voices and wondering: Was I going to be impressed by movie stars? I wanted to think not, as if to admit as much would be a sign of weakness and immaturity for anyone who had studied "The Wasteland," Chaucer, and the origins of the French Revolution. Yet I had to admit there was something about movie stars that was alluring and intriguing and possibly made them worth writing about, no matter what the feature writer from Yale had said.

True, there was often a lot of nonsense blocking the view. Sitting at my gray metal desk in the dusty second-floor newsroom of the *Herald Examiner* one morning, I was reading the *Hollywood Reporter*, an important trade publication, when I happened upon a column item that caught my eye. Lauren Bacall, it said, "is very happy with the promptness of room service at the Westwood Marquis Hotel," where she was staying during the local run of the play *Woman of the Year*. Is this what constituted news on my new beat? I couldn't help but remember the time I interviewed Bacall in Dallas, when she had insisted I ask my questions through a bathroom door at the Fairmont Hotel while she was having her hair done.

In thinking about the stars and their lives, I had begun to realize that their happiness was a major concern to many entertainment publications and their headline writers. "Cher Has a New Man, a New Life, Happier Than Ever." It was not enough to report on their films and other projects; it was also newsworthy to note their state of contentment, perhaps because Hollywood stars were living, on some level, so many people's dreams. Who knew what was truly in their hearts, but if they said they were happy with a new movie, new diet, new guru, new boyfriend—room service—then presumably we could be happy that they were happy. And if we weren't ourselves happy, they could be happy for us. The illusion would hold, the ritual observed.

I hoped to avoid such bunkum. I knew that Truman Capote had once derided the movie star interview as "the lowest level of journalistic art, the most difficult to turn from a sow's ear into a silk purse," before disproving his dictum in the profile of Marlon Brando he wrote for the *New Yorker*. But then he was Truman Capote, writing for the *New Yorker*, a world apart from the ink-stained wretches working for a paycheck at newspapers. I was keenly aware of this class distinction and resented it. The lefty essayist Gore Vidal, whom I otherwise admired, was another offender, using the term "newspaperman" almost as an epithet.

I tried to ignore Vidal's outmoded snobbery as I set about the task of bringing Hollywood people to life in the pages of the *Herald Examiner*. In Dallas, reporters who covered the arts were often relegated to a secondary status (below those assigned to crime and the courts, politics, and sports). While that was less true in Los Angeles, entertainment reporters were sometimes belittled in the trade as either lazy purveyors of puff or preening peddlers of snark. The term "puff" derived from "puff piece," describing the cotton candy profiles that once filled the fan magazines—the journalistic equivalent of baseball cards. More recently, an opposite attention-getting genre had emerged, based on the notion that all Hollywood elites qualified for mockery and derision, regardless of their talent and accomplishments. Snark, in other words. Puff or snark, were those the only choices?

Not that reporting here was easy. I knew you couldn't just call up Meryl Streep and ask for an interview. Hollywood had its own rules. Unlike professional athletes and politicians, who traveled in the company of reporters for months at a time, Hollywood stars were usually only available to the press when they had a new movie or show to promote. I was not going to have the kind of time and access I did with Tommy Lee Jones, but neither was I going to be writing at such length. Depending on whether it was a daily or Sunday piece, the word count was more like fifteen hundred to two thousand—thirty to forty column inches typeset. The usual time allotted for the interview by the studios was forty-five minutes to an hour, in an office on the lot or in a restaurant over lunch, occasionally at a residence.

The first home I got to visit belonged to Karen Black, the sensual offbeat siren I'd seen in *Easy Rider* and *Five Easy Pieces*, two seminal films of Hollywood's New Wave—as well as in Altman's *Nashville* and John Schlesinger's *Day of the Locust*, prominent pictures all. Karen Black had been a big deal. She'd been onscreen with Jack Nicholson, Robert Redford, Bruce Dern, Dennis Hopper, and Peter Fonda. But she was now forty-one and making pictures with a director named Henry Jaglom.

When I found the address, it was an ordinary-looking frame house on a flat block north of Sunset, far enough east to qualify as "You've got to be kidding" in terms of movie star real estate. One could surmise that she had arrived in Hollywood before the big money—or else had given it all to the Church of Scientology, that she would tell me was more important to her than classes she had taken with Lee Strasberg in New York.

A guy in casual designer threads, her publicist, greeted me at the front door and said Miss Black was running late and was somewhere in back getting ready for the ordeal of being photographed. "Come on in, have a seat. Can I get you anything? She likes a lot of front lighting and favors her left side."

The small living room had lace curtains, an overstuffed Victorian couch, and shelves full of faded movie magazines from the '40s and '50s—a retrospective of beauty and stardom and hairstyles from those who had gone before. Suddenly, into the room came, not Karen Black, but a line of little people—several girls and a boy, all under the age of eight. The girls were the children of actor friends, and the boy, Hunter, was Black's son with screenwriter Kit Carson, with whom she was no longer keeping company. The girls were costumed in Black's dresses, soft and silky things, draped over their small frames. They wore lipstick and makeup and plodded childlike in her high heels. Suddenly they were performing a scene of their own improvisation, pretending to be Sunset Strip hookers while Hunter arrested them, waving a plastic .45 automatic under their noses.

"I like children," Black announced as she made her entrance. "Do you?"

She was not beautiful but striking, with large, teardrop-shaped blue eyes that seemed to be sliding toward one another, a wide, seductive mouth and wavy red hair. You could see why she got cast in a lot of movies. She was something to look at, something wild and provocative.

"He didn't say much," she said about working with Altman, whom she recalled telling her again and again that she was "great" and "wonderful." Same for Bob Rafelson, who directed her to breakthrough success in *Five Easy Pieces*. "But you know, directors don't say much. It's they're being there. They make it safe. Their job isn't to tell you how to do it. That's your job."

Before she got up to begin the photo session, from her seated position, she unexpectedly stretched her long arms over the back of the couch until her head of red, wavy hair had disappeared from view, leaving only her estimable torso. Strong and athletic, she arched it upward, thrusting her chest out. Had Jack Nicholson seen this? When she recoiled and popped up again, her face was clean of worry and shadows. The light had come back into her eyes. She shot me a glance and headed for the camera. The realization hit me that this job was going to be different from interviewing actors and theatre people back in Dallas.

CHAPTER THIRTY-THREE

One-on-One

NOTHER EARLY ASSIGNMENT INVOLVED THE MAY-
HEM-DRIVEN ACTION THRILLER *BLUE THUNDER*,
about heavily armed police helicopters sky-rocketing across the
LA basin to blow up bad guys. The director was *Saturday Night Fever*'s John
Badham, and if I wanted to talk to him I had to call up the Columbia Pictures
publicist, who turned out to be none other than . . . Don Safran! The one and
only. I'd lost track of Safran since he disappeared from the *Times Herald*, but
he'd made his way to Hollywood and was now handling press relations for
mega producer Ray Stark. Which seemed kind of perfect. It was his job now
to help me gather information for a story, and I let the irony speak for itself.
I don't think I encountered him again.

In my new position at the *Herald Examiner*, my plan was to bring along
a critic's sensibility even if I was no longer officially a critic. But the cadre of
publicists in Hollywood, I discovered, regarded such honesty and opinion
in a reporter as dangerous and disqualifying. The Hollywood press was for
promotion, not inquiry or skepticism.

When I asked Mel Gibson and Danny Glover, in a joint interview, if
they saw any redeeming qualities in the violent melodrama *Lethal Weapon*
in which they costarred, I was thinking of the terrific performances each
had given prior to this—Gibson in the Peter Weir film *Gallipoli* and Glover in
Athol Fugard's play *Master Harold and the Boys* on Broadway. But the Warner

Bros. flack sitting in on the interview of course was not thinking of those performances and nearly called security. Such impolite questions, I learned, would not be tolerated in the red-carpet world of movie publicity.

"If you didn't like the picture, why didn't they send someone else?" the flack asked me, clearly annoyed and angry.

It didn't take much to be perceived as unfriendly.

The second house I got to see was the home of Ann-Margret, who brought to mind not the New Wave, but Elvis movies, Las Vegas, and photo spreads in *Playboy*. Roughly the same age as Karen Black—and, like her, a Northwestern University dropout—Ann-Margret, in fact, had been nominated for two supporting actress Academy Awards, for *Carnal Knowledge* and *Tommy*, and her success as a more traditional Hollywood vixen had earned her a house at the top of Benedict Canyon that once belonged to Humphrey Bogart and, yes, Lauren Bacall (when they were married). It was a hundred yards from the main road, reached only after passing through an electrically powered iron gate that opened after I recited my credentials into a speaker box. She lived here with her husband and manager, the *77 Sunset Strip* actor Roger Smith, and allowed me in one afternoon to discuss an upcoming network television production of *A Streetcar Named Desire* in which she played Blanche DuBois.

At forty-two, she was pushing the Hollywood age limit for voluptuous babes, and maybe that's why she was playing Tennessee Williams's delusional spinster. She still looked great, was pleasant, and spoke freely but never in answer to anything I asked her. That thing I learned in Dallas about people telling you more than they wanted to did not apply in Hollywood, where actors, like politicians, were programmed ahead of time with talking points they followed carefully to present whatever case they wanted to make about whatever project they were promoting.

Describing the rape scene in which the brutish Stanley Kowalski (Treat Williams) manhandles Blanche, his fragile sister-in-law, the actress said angrily, "We did it as the vulgar, cruel, criminal violation that it is." Which might have been sincere but also sounded like a money quote if you remembered Ann-Margret from those layouts in *Playboy*.

As a journalist, you tried to scoot around such marketing soundbites, hoping to elicit something real or revelatory. I don't think I succeeded with Ann-Margret. But I did get to see her swimming pool. From its edge, you could look down into the city far below and know that very few people in LA or America had a view like that.

Sam Peckinpah, meanwhile, was sleeping in a trailer, even though it was a trailer parked at Paradise Cove in Malibu. In a room at the Bevely Hilton Hotel the famous director told me he was broke and "living on handouts, depending on the kindness of strangers," to quote Blanche DuBois, which he was doing with a tight smile when I spoke to him—another A-lister I was catching on his last lap. Never gregarious or welcoming to reporters, Peckinpah had been known to part with words as carefully as gallstones. He had a pitiless stare and, at fifty-seven, the weathered face of a cowboy, only an expensive shirt jacket and dangling pair of sunglasses suggesting a different occupation. It was probably in his contract that he had to do some press to promote the picture, a ramshackle thriller called *The Osterman Weekend*, adapted from a Robert Ludlum novel about CIA thuggery.

But he was still Sam Peckinpah, a legendary badass who had won the heart and mind of Pauline Kael and other critics for his realistic (some would say voyeuristic) depictions of violence onscreen in *The Wild Bunch, Straw Dogs*, and *Bring Me the Head of Alfredo Garcia*. I was reminded of the academic, unpublished essay I had written a decade earlier for Don Safran, questioning Peckinpah's machismo. Now I was talking to him.

He turned out to be a prickly interview, perversely disavowing his reputation for depicting slow-motion bodily harm while very nearly disavowing this work-for-hire he had just done. "It's my first exploitation film, and I don't feel too bad about it," he offered with a straight face.

As he continued to insist that he had toned down the violence in *The Osterman Weekend* from what the producers originally wanted, I asked him if he felt he was misunderstood.

"By what? By whom?" he shot back, his hard brown eyes getting harder.

Maybe indicating that he was at least a little sadistic, he asked me directly if I enjoyed it, surely knowing *The Osterman Weekend* was about to be pilloried by critics and ignored by audiences. I don't remember how I responded, but I would not forget the next thing he said: that he could write a film script but not a letter. The idea confounded me at the time, but later I saw this was not so uncommon in Los Angeles, where Edmund Wilson would have had to wait tables to earn a living.

Whatever the experience of sitting down to a one-on-one (as they were called) interview with Sam Peckinpah, it was not something that would have happened in Dallas. Which is why I had come to LA presumably, to one of the strangest newspapers in America.

Despite the interference of the publicists, in that first year I couldn't help noticing what it meant to have a backstage pass in Los Angeles. For a story about the young playwright Ernest Thompson, the author of the hit play and movie *On Golden Pond*, I was invited one morning to a nondescript building across the street from the Music Center downtown to watch Jack Lemmon and Estelle Parsons rehearse a scene from Thompson's new play *A Sense of Humor*. Once inside the door, there was Jack Lemmon, right in front of me, learning his lines.

Back home I would not have been able to visit Clint Eastwood in his bungalow office on the Warner Bros. lot in Burbank and hear him address me by my first name. And I would not have expected that hearing Clint Eastwood merely say "Sean" would sound so odd and pleasant, proof of the spell Hollywood cast over all of us, even those vowing not to be impressed by movie stars—and knowing it was not personal but the practiced art of ingratiation.

I once held Eastwood in low regard, seeing him as a prime example of a screenland personality whose cold, impassive face did all the acting required for a medium based on the camera. Plus, the box office triumph of his *Dirty Harry* movies was a measure of the public preference for simple-minded revenge over more complicated drama.

But my relocation to the film colony had softened my bias against acting for the camera and given me an appreciation for the subtleties of saying little onscreen and making it count, as Eastwood did. And now, it was a revelation just watching him walk in long strides across the deep pile carpeting of his office in jeans and running shoes to greet a journalist who had brought with him only the threat of questions about how he did what he did, most recently in a thriller called *Tightrope* set in New Orleans.

I had already been vetted and frisked the day before, over the phone, by a man whom Eastwood and Warner Bros. employed for such purposes.

"Sean, I don't know if I do it consciously or not," Eastwood said about the facial tick that frequently signaled the temperature rising in his weary cop's brain as he leveled a .44 Magnum revolver at the bad guy and uttered a quiet line like "Make my day" or "Feel lucky?" "I think most of the time something like that comes out of what your inner feelings are at the moment."

He spoke with just enough force to get the words past his lips, on-screen and off, but that was his manner, traceable to the dust-covered trail-hand Rowdy Yates he once played on the series *Rawhide* I had watched every week as a kid in the TV room on Eric Lane. The less said, the more left to the imagination, he once explained about the method of his screen presence. Talking to him in the warmth of a sunny midmorning in Burbank, it occurred to me that his name should have been Westwood, not Eastwood, as he looked every inch the lean and healthy Californian, a bright yellow T-shirt covering the inverted pyramid of his still-trim torso. He was fifty-four.

Until you met him, it was hard not to be a little cowed by the fearsome image he created as an unshaven bounty hunter in Sergio Leone's "Spaghetti Westerns," the violent enforcer in *High Plains Drifter* and the rogue cop Harry Callahan meting out vigilante justice to low-lifes in San Francisco. He had played a variety of roles, but it was the violent ones that stuck to him and most connected with the public. His taut and determined face had been up there on all those movie billboards for years promising the vengeance of Yahweh.

Maybe because he didn't say much onscreen, the possibilities of who he might be in person were broader and more troubling—if you chose to think of the body counts. Might he carry some of that menace with him yet and direct it at a reporter?

Not today. When you heard Eastwood carry on a regular conversation, it was a stark reminder of the powers of make-believe. I knew about this in the abstract, of course, but seeing it up close—seeing *him* up close—was another matter.

"I'm not a cowboy or a detective," he said. "There are some elements in your soul that make you portray 'em."

Some years later, I was doing a story about Eastwood's adaptation of the popular novel *The Bridges of Madison County*, in which he played a very different kind of character (a romantic photographer) opposite Meryl Streep. Coproducer Steven Spielberg called me from his car one morning to testify why he believed Eastwood was right for the role. "It's because I know Clint personally. The part of Clint that friends of his know well but have never seen acted is what Clint has brought to *The Bridges of Madison County.*"

By then, even I could see how this was true.

CHAPTER THIRTY-FOUR

Love and Happiness

L A, I DISCOVERED SOON ENOUGH, DID NOT DESERVE
ITS CLICHÉD IMAGE as "the place where all the fruits and nuts
had rolled," as Bob's real estate brother in Houston joked when he
heard I had moved. Yes, New Age punditry abounded, along with faddish
seekers of cosmic truth, but I encountered a lot of smart people, drawn to
the worldwide platform of the movie business, several great universities,
high art and low, everything. You felt more creative just being here.

The size of the "Southland," as the TV weathermen referred to the LA
basin, stretching from the encircling San Gabriel Mountains to the sea, was
overwhelming. It included countless microclimates, plus Orange County to
the south, home to Disneyland, the American League baseball team, defense
contractors and more beaches. After my first trip "behind the Orange Curtain," to see a Sunday matinee at the impressive South Coast Repertory in
Costa Mesa, I drove back on PCH, the Pacific Coast Highway, and was struck
by the view of what made Southern California such a national brand: youthful joggers on paths near the ocean, their shoes and outfits plucked from
magazine layouts as they trotted past new wood-shingled townhomes and
condos, sprinkler-green lawns and fresh imported palms, neat rows of fast
food franchises and ATMs huddled under red-tiled roofs, a cleansing mist in
the air. If you came here from the Midwest or the plains, this tableau offered
a promise of sweet reinvention: health, exercise, beauty.

That wasn't what I came looking for, was it? I could see the appeal, but what did all these beautiful people do for a living?

Proximity to the ocean was a major factor in the price of real estate, I learned, and that went for rentals as well. After nine months in Silver Lake, I wanted to move to Santa Monica or Venice but could find nothing affordable. I settled on a one-bedroom in what must have been the cheapest block of Beverly Hills, in the flats off Wilshire and San Vicente. Five miles from the ocean but fewer helicopters at night. It was a cream-colored two-story vaguely Art Deco building with two entries and eight apartments in all, birds-of-paradise blooming next to the windows and a garage space for my car.

At my new address, I worked out a jogging course through the neighborhood that took me south to Olympic and back up San Vicente, about three miles. I hadn't learned to jog until I got to LA. Before then, when I wanted to exercise, I would run a mile at full speed, often around a track, a holdover from soccer training. A woman friend took me up to the Hollywood Reservoir in the hills one afternoon and showed me how to run as slowly as possible around its 3.1-mile circumference. I was hooked and became a jogger for the next thirty years.

My social life had gotten off to a slow start. The Yale feature writer agreed to attend a party with me, but it became clear before the night was through that she wasn't interested. I asked one of the freelance dance critics at the paper to a play and when we went for a drink afterward, she ordered a cup of hot water. No teabag, just a cup of hot water. Not a sign of future festivity, I inferred. Many of the women I met that first year in LA were invariably in thrall to the "industry," sifting potential partners for evidence of what kind of clout you had and what you could do for them. Journalists—and certainly anyone who worked for the underdog *Herald Examiner*—had little to offer in this regard.

Journalists were not top catches in a society devoted to money, and in LA they were further marginalized by the status and income potential of the thousands who wrote for film and television. Plus, every checkout clerk and valet parker had a script in their back pocket. Like Sam Peckinpah, they might not be able to write a good sentence or paragraph, but it didn't matter; if they sold that script, who knew what riches awaited them? That was the myth anyway, and journalists were not part of the myth. I began to wonder if this was a city conducive to a search for love and happiness.

Sunday nights I had a standing invitation for dinner at Bill and Taffy's place in Venice. Taffy was writing a novel about the Sixties (that would be published by William Morrow) and trying to get into TV, and Bill was trying entertainment law. They were renting a small, two-bedroom house a couple blocks from the Pacific where for years they had hosted a Sunday night potluck barbecue following a co-ed beach volleyball game for entry-level Hollywood boomers. But that had come to an end, and now they were just hosting me. On the drive over, often wearing my jean jacket with the collar turned up and the sunroof open as I headed toward the ocean, I felt glad I had made it to California.

Bill and Taffy were the only people I knew when I arrived, but they introduced me to friends who became my friends as well, in particular Walter Impert, a painter, and Paul Most, a writer who, like Taffy, was trying to get into TV and had also coauthored an ESL textbook. Walter and Paul were from the East and had gone to Exeter together. Paul introduced me to Trader Joe's, the distinctive low-budget food and wine store, and Walter introduced me to the LA art scene.

I started to look up other acquaintances I'd heard might be out here. Louis Blumberg, who played bass in The Bountymen and went to UC Santa Barbara, was about to leave for graduate school in urban planning, but for now was playing drums in the house band that warmed up the audience for *The Bob Newhart Show*. I asked him to give me a drum lesson, and he showed me how to alternate the bass and snare on the first bars of "Get Off My Cloud," by the Rolling Stones. We spent a day in Santa Monica playing tennis and catching up. Tom Herod, a stage director in Dallas and a UT film school grad about my age, introduced me to Thai restaurants and tried to explain why he was shopping a script he'd written called *Vampire Truckers*. "It's a way in," he told me, and no doubt he was right, but I was too green yet to understand and just thought it strange.

I reconnected with David Schmoeller, a soccer teammate from St. Mark's who had written and directed a soft-core studio film starring Dallas-born sex kitten Morgan Fairchild. David had made it to the big time with *The Seduction*, but, like so many strivers in Hollywood, was struggling to sell his next script while earning a living in the lower depths, directing B movies aimed at the home video market. One of them, a horror thriller called *Crawlspace*, starred the notoriously difficult German actor Klaus Kinski (Natasha's father) as a sadistic landlord who spied on young female tenants before murdering them. One night at a restaurant on Sunset across from the Chateau Marmont, David shared tales of working (or trying to work) with the impossible Kinksi and a wealthy producer who kept hiring him to make dreck like this. I respected and enjoyed David and appreciated the chance to learn from him about the parts of Hollywood not covered by *Entertainment Tonight* and the *Times*.

I knew that Wanda McDaniel, the former society editor of the *Times Herald*, whom I once escorted around Dallas, had moved to LA but I did not expect to see her. She had left the realm of ordinary people, married the producer of *The Godfather* and would soon be working for Gorgio Armani as his ambassador to Hollywood. To think that she had once gone out with me.

In search of female companionship, I did something I had never done before. I answered a personals ad in the *New York Review of Books*, which read, "Novelist, SWF [Single White Female], very attractive, university professor in the Los Angeles area, seeks literate, lively smart man for fun and seriousness."

I mailed in my own profile to the box number, and one evening my phone rang. It was her. We arranged to meet at Molly Malone, an Irish pub on Fairfax. The first thing I noticed when I arrived and found her seated in a booth was that "very attractive" was subjective. Not sure what she thought of me, but I hadn't lied about my height and weight. There was a live band playing, which made conversation difficult, but I'm not sure we had that much to talk about. I hung in for ninety minutes, learning that in addition to teaching creative writing, she wrote for women's magazines and had interviewed the actor Matt Dillon for *Playgirl*, a magazine that featured handsome, muscled young men in states of undress—a counterpart to *Playboy*. Which might have been provocative on another night in another bar—with another woman. I did not answer any more personal ads.

A FEW WEEKS BEFORE I LEFT FOR CALIFORNIA, I attended a benefit dinner for the Dallas Shakespeare Festival and was seated at a table of eight that included the English actor Michael York, who had starred in the popular film *Cabaret*. At the time, York was quite the catch for a Dallas charity event, and after chatting with him amiably I remember thinking, here was somebody else I could look up when I got to Los Angeles. Ha. In fact, I did spot York in his tuxedo at some film premiere in Century City a year or so later, but by then I realized he would not have remembered me and what did we have to talk about anyway? Hollywood people and the press were members of different castes and rarely crossed paths except when brought together by the promotional interviews. It was one of the first things you learned. Yet the job was constantly throwing you into situations that seemed friendly, tempting you to think this person from the other caste earning untold multiples of your humble paycheck was relating to you as a human being and not as a reporter. Which was largely an illusion. And yet I still asked Alice Krige out to dinner and a play. What was I thinking?

I knew or had heard that the caste lines were sometimes crossed. Well, there was James Bacon. But also, Joe Hyams, the *New York Herald Tribune* correspondent who in the 1960s married the marquee actress Elke Sommer (and later became a studio publicist). How did that work? There were rumors of this journalist or that crossing the line, and I'd heard women reporters recount tales of famous actors coming on to them during interviews. I knew that Clint Eastwood occasionally played golf with a movie columnist. But these were exceptions to the code.

In my case, I wasn't thinking. I was infatuated, against all professional protocol. Alice Krige was a young South African actress who had worked in London's Royal Shakespeare Company and was beautiful enough to be cast as Bathsheba, the woman Richard Gere takes as his wife in *King David*, a ponderous biblical epic directed by Bruce Beresford. She was also just then starring with Richard Chamberlain in a television movie about a Swedish diplomat who saved thousands of Jews from the Nazis. I had lunch with her at an outdoor café in Beverly Hills for a short profile, all in a day's work, but afterward I could not get her out of my head and my heart. Was I going to be impressed by movie stars? I was by this one.

Because she did not live in Los Angeles and was in town briefly from London, I thought she might be curious about theatre in Los Angeles and, by the way, I had press tickets for a production of Jonathan Reynolds's *Geniuses*, a satire of the making of *Apocalypse Now*. A perfect play to see in LA if you were a theatre actor visiting from London. She seemed genuinely interested and agreed to accompany me to *Geniuses* and afterward to dinner at Joe Allen, the West Hollywood show biz eatery. So, I took Alice Krige to her first play in LA, *chatted over wine and dinner about some of the big questions*, as I noted in my journal, thoroughly enjoyed the evening, and kissed her goodnight but knew I was unlikely ever to see her again. How could I? This was her world, this was Michael York's world, and when all was said and done, I was a visitor, a journalist.

CHAPTER THIRTY-FIVE

Transcribing Fame

UNSPOKEN BUT ALWAYS PRESENT on the Hollywood beat was the voyeurism of imagining fame. What was it like to be as famous as Jack Nicholson or even his Mulholland Drive neighbor, Harry Dean Stanton? Most of us would never know, and the subject was avoided head-on, yet the scent of fame was always in the air around these interviews. As a reporter you might pretend to be too cool to notice it, but I would never forget walking through a hotel in LA with Kris Kristofferson once, following a joint interview I did with him and Willie Nelson for the underappreciated movie *Songwriter.* As he and I passed through the expansive atrium lobby, you could feel heads swiveling from a distance, eyes trained on him, whispers, conversations stopping—some maybe wondering who was the guy with him? For a moment I got a sense of what it must be like to be Kris Kristofferson.

The public fascination with actors no doubt had to do with the emotional power they wielded over all of us in the stories they brought to the big and small screen, transforming fictional characters into people we loved and hated. As such, they became royalty in a nation that eschewed royalty. The power of their fame grew in part from the enigma of acting itself. There were countless methods, classes, books, and theories about acting—and in Los Angeles, endless talk about it in delis and laundromats—but in the end, most agreed that getting into someone else's skin on stage or in front of a camera required some incalculable combination of the actor's own personality with that of the character.

I'm not a cowboy or a detective. There are some elements in your soul that make you portray 'em.

Actors were often being asked to show us where the line was drawn. You would never catch a magician revealing such secrets in public, but actors were expected to do this regularly, on talk shows and in interviews with people like me. There was a downside to this, as the brainy John Lithgow pointed out in one of my first stories for the *Herald Examiner.* Lithgow, a Harvard-educated theatre actor who had recently moved from New York to "Cloud Cuckooland," as he referred to LA, had a part in *Twilight Zone: The Movie*, which he was then helping to promote.

"It seems to me that a very important part of acting is mystery," he said. "People not quite knowing what's behind the character. Of course, the whole nature of doing promotion is saying, 'Well, this is who I am! Let me tell ya all about myself!' So, there is a kind of contradiction there."

It became hard, Lithgow reasoned, to separate someone like Jane Fonda or Robert Redford from what you knew about them outside the roles they played. True enough, and I had to admit I was now actively involved in this great unmasking—if you wanted to think of it that way. Yet I believed there was something worthwhile in talking to thespians like Anthony Hopkins and Judy Davis, hoping to gain some insight into their artistry and who they were as human beings. It was natural to be curious about performers who were that good, and I was a proxy for thousands of readers who would never get the chance to meet them.

Whenever possible, I tape-recorded the interviews—very much de rigueur in Hollywood—but it was tedious and time-consuming to transcribe them, and I had second thoughts about whether the process produced the best stories. Nicholas Roeg, the English director (*Don't Look Now*), once said to me, "I know journalists all use tape recorders now, but I actually, years ago, preferred it when they would just make it up afterward. They would think more about who they were talking to."

While seemingly provocative and playful, Roeg's statement got me thinking about the downside of tape-recorder journalism. Long, uninterrupted quotes might or might not be interesting, depending on who was being quoted, but they were sometimes a lazy substitute for reportorial engagement and analysis. Print journalism, one hoped, was not just a transcription service for the stars, a record of what Hollywood players said when someone turned on a mic in front of them. Some stories, many in the *Times*' entertainment section, read like that.

I worried that I was falling into the same trap and took steps to avoid it. When I returned to the office after an interview, before I began transcribing the tape, I would review my impressions of the person I had just talked to, think about their manner and defining details, look at any notes I had jotted down, and then compose a lead paragraph. I might or might not keep it after I listened to the tape, but it gave me a start independent of the verbiage that had been recorded.

Not surprisingly, it would be Tom Stoppard, the intellectually dexterous playwright, who, during an interview with me at the Biltmore Hotel, would blow up the idea of the interview itself, blaming misbegotten notions about him on the flaws of journalism and its conventions. After the *New Yorker* profiled him once while playing cricket in London, he was thereafter described in print as an obsessive cricket player.

"That damned article. It seems to be the one thing on earth that everybody has read. I play a few times a year. But I've just accepted my role as an English cricketer. I've given up trying to dissuade people that I'm not. I get asked to write cricket books."

He went on. "Each interviewer breathes from the previous interviews, so the error is being reinforced each time. In the end, it's just been cemented into this person. I'm beginning to understand people who just simply never do any interviews of any kind."

Which was not something a reporter wanted to hear, yet he was Tom Stoppard, the best of the best and bearer of inconvenient truth. "The interview situation changes you," he continued, offering another provocative thought. "You're trying to oblige somebody by making more sense of things than you normally feel. So, you end up as somebody who has much more definitive positions on all kinds of topics because you somehow didn't realize you could sit there and say, 'Actually, I have no idea.'"

CHAPTER THIRTY-SIX

Third Time in a Second Place

W ITH ENOUGH WATER (SEE *CHINATOWN*), ALL MANNER OF FLORA GREW THROUGHOUT THE WINTER in semitropical Southern California. You could play tennis and golf year-round—not the reason I moved here, but I took advantage of it, finding three different tennis partners at the paper and playing almost every week. My main partner was Don Frederick, a political editor who had grown up in DC and worked in Santa Fe at the same time as two contemporaries of mine—Frank Clifford, a top reporter at the *Times Herald*, and Bill Hart, the astute upperclassman and jazz drummer from Sigma Nu who had become a journalist. Don was a good match for me on the court, and we found kinship in being newcomers to LA, as well as in discovering our six degrees of separation.

Tennis was booming in America in the 1980s, and public courts had to be reserved days in advance. We often played at the Rancho Park complex on the West Side and sometimes in Beverly Hills at night under the lights, in a clammy chill that accompanied the marine layer, even in the spring. Unlike Dallas, it was rarely too hot for tennis, but in the summer the unhealthful air of Los Angeles sometimes discouraged strenuous outdoor activity. You could feel the microbial pollutants in your throat and lungs by the third set.

The smog was visible, a lowering cloud of off-white gunk obscuring the mountains and muting the colors in the landscape. Even before auto emissions, the Indigenous people here referred to the LA basin as "the valley of smoke." *This city is truly protean in the ways the atmosphere changes its appearance,* I wrote in a letter to Jeff Unger. *On a good day it can look and feel like paradise, on a bad day like the set for a gloomy futuristic movie that takes place after the bomb.*

September, I would learn, was sometimes the hottest month, ruining the semblance of seasonal change for anyone who remembered it. Local TV weathermen did not seem to remember it or care. They were bringers of jollity and ambassadors of sunshine who anguished if they were not able to send viewers to the beach every day of the year. Only grudgingly did they acknowledge the chance of rain, even in a drought. I found this weird, though I had to admit that having an ocean nearby was a glorious novelty coming from North Texas. I often went to the beach at Santa Monica on weekends to jog the bike path and inhale the sea air.

One Sunday evening there, the crowd thinning out, I jogged past a guy of indeterminate age with long stringy hair, in tank top and shorts, standing in a beachside parking lot, his face obscured by the megaphone held to his mouth as he brayed the nightmarish lyrics to the Doors' "The End" in the direction of the ocean. It became a scene from the movie of Los Angeles I was filming in my head.

PREJUDICED BY MY OWN AFFILIATION, I had come to view the arts and entertainment staff at the *Times* as mostly lackluster—fat and happy and oblivious to any outbursts of style or enterprise at the Hearst paper ten blocks away. Massive and prosperous, with no real competition on the West Coast, the *Times* was referred to in the trade as "the velvet coffin" because it was so comfortable and high-paying that no one ever wanted to leave, resigned to a cushy second city existence far from journalism's main events on the other side of the country.

The *Times'* drama critic Dan Sullivan, who had been one of my instructors at the O'Neill, finally did invite me to lunch with him and Sylvie Drake, the deputy theatre critic. It was an awkward situation because, it could be argued, winning the Nathan had positioned me for the next opening on the *Times* drama desk, but neither of them was going anywhere and, well, that's just the way it was. How inconvenient of me to have shown up in Los Angeles, at that other paper. I tried to be respectful and gracious, yet I couldn't help noticing that neither of them seemed to have read anything I had done for the *Herald Examiner.*

The *Herald* was the third second-place newspaper I had worked for, so I was accustomed to being outflanked and underrated, but the *LA Times'* grandiosity engendered a particular animus from the guerrilla band gathered inside Julia Morgan's Moroccan fort at the other end of downtown. There was more leeway for writers at the *Herald*—and presumably room to have more "fun"—but we had to put up with the *Times'* bullying tactics of demanding exclusives, sometimes at the last minute, with the result that a scheduled interview with a star would be withdrawn. I wondered if actors like Geraldine Page (one example I can think of) had anything to say about this? Or cared? In its Hollywood gossip column, the *Herald* sometimes impishly tweaked the sovereignty of the *Times*, which it dubbed "the Whale." The column once carried an item mocking the bulk of the Sunday edition, which had grown so large, the story went, a hefty copy hurled by a paper boy had landed on a small dog belonging to *Mission Impossible* actress Barbara Bain and killed it.

The features editor who hired me, Gary Spiecker, got a promotion to a higher position—that flux thing again—but he and I were able to continue working together for a time as part of a unit of editors and writers selected from different sections of the paper to brainstorm ambitious stories. It was called the Senior Writers Group, and my first contribution was an examination of the media mergers then rocking Hollywood, portending a further consolidation of power among the top studios and networks. Spurred by rules changes at the Reagan administration's deregulation-minded FCC, the mergers included CNN buying MGM, a little-known media conglomerate buying ABC, and the low-brow Australian press lord Rupert Murdoch snapping up Twentieth Century Fox, along with a group of TV stations, enabling him to launch a fourth TV network brimming with trash. All of this was news in the city that was home to the broadcast industry, but it so happened my "media merger mania" story was proposed during the summer of 1985 when the *Herald* was being overseen by an interim Hearst editor from the East Coast named Harry Rosenfeld, who did not think it was much of a story at all.

On loan from the mighty *Times Union* of Albany, New York, Rosenfeld carried with him the fame of having been Metro editor at the *Washington*

Post during Watergate, initially the editor in charge of Bob Woodward and Carl Bernstein. In *All the President's Men* he was played by Jack Warden, who was much more impressive on camera than Rosenfeld was in the flesh, his Brooks Brothers suits and bow ties doing little to improve the banalities he flaunted at the weekly meeting of the Senior Writers Group. At one meeting, he blithely threw cold water on the story Spiecker and I had been working on for weeks, offering his opinion that the media mergers were no big deal and that more power in fewer hands was not a threat to diversity in programming—even if the dean of the Berkeley graduate school of journalism, Ben Bagdikian, had already said as much in his 1983 book *Media Monopoly*. Rosenfeld could have been the spokesman for Ronald Reagan's corporate-coddling Federal Communications Commission.

Eventually the story, somewhat knee-capped and neutered, ran in two long segments on a Monday and a Tuesday in October, starting at the bottom of page 1 on both days and tagged with the generic header "News Focus." I was not proud of it, regretted that Spiecker and I had let Rosenfeld bully us into submission, and wondered if maybe this guy's role at the *Washington Post* had been exaggerated in the movie?

One good thing came out of it. The afternoon Rosenfeld ambushed me at the story conference, I had failed to adequately defend the premise of the story, a result of my innate shyness and fear of public speaking. This was not the first time something like this had happened, and I resolved, at last, to do something about it. Perusing a brochure of UCLA extension courses, I saw the title "Acting for Non-Actors." I signed up.

The class, which included some Hollywood development types and a few young actors new to town, met once a week at the home of the instructor, an actress named Valerie Mamches, who had been in a couple obscure movies and once acted at Washington's Arena Stage. She was serious but friendly and accepting, and I looked forward to attending class each week. At the first meeting, each of us had to explain why we were here, and without revealing my primary motivation, I said that I wanted to gain some insight into the actor's process since I was often writing about actors for the *Herald Examiner*. Not untrue.

The course involved exercises and discussion, with each of us expected to perform two monologues of our choosing. We also had to mime a scene of our own creation, with no props, to see if the class could make sense of it. I conceived a tantrum thrown by a major league pitcher after being lifted for a reliever and slinking off to the locker room. Alas, no one was able to figure out what the hell I was doing (maybe proof that baseball was no longer the national pastime).

Still, overall, the class succeeded in helping me become less fearful of public speaking and allowed me to understand why a lot of people in Los Angeles studied acting for years without ever going onstage or in front of a camera. "I'd Rather Be Acting" indeed. It was a form of generalized therapy, plus a way to embrace the zeitgeist of Southern California. I was glad I did it.

CHAPTER THIRTY-SEVEN

Getting Off
the Caravan

I STARTED THE JOB AT THE *HERALD EXAMINER* with the notion I would be picking and choosing people and subjects to write about based on my interests and assessments, rather than adhering strictly to what the studios wanted covered. This proved to be harder than I imagined. The studios, with their publicist-controlled access to the stars, had the power to set the agenda. The subservience of journalists was built into the system, and if you resisted, you found yourself on the outside looking in—not where your editors wanted you to be.

Caught up in the steady flow of new movies and shows, no matter how independent your spirit and inclination, you often felt conscripted into the corporate merchandising effort, marching in lockstep with everyone else in the caravan to the next star-gazing event. The challenge every week was to find a slightly different way to interview Michael Douglas or Michelle Pfeiffer without overstepping the bounds of decorum and becoming a liability to your publication.

To fill space in the paper, I had learned how to find stories in some of the questionable films that Hollywood sent to market. John Schlesinger, the honored British director, in town to promote an overcooked occult thriller called *The Believers*, gave me a lede not long after I arrived at the Chateau Marmont to meet him. He walked to the window of his bungalow, stared out at the grounds and said emphatically, "What I want to know is which one did Belushi die in?" Which seemed apropos as he was promoting a film that was technically a murder mystery. We progressed from there and talked a lot about *Midnight Cowboy*. He shot down the commonplace notion that the James Leo Herlihy novel was second-rate, which made it easier for him to reinvent as a great film. "I think *Midnight Cowboy* was a good novel. It made me want to do the film. I mean, that's the point. Does the novel make you want to do the film?"

When Universal stooped to manufacture and distribute *Psycho III*, hoping there were still bucks left in the old Hitchcock franchise about matricide, I dodged the studio's marketing campaign and found the original screenwriter of the 1960 movie, Joseph Stefano, living in Benedict Canyon. Stefano had not seen *Psycho III*, a campy sequel trading humorously on the legendary gore of the original. But he gave me a story about how the original Norman Bates, the troubled (and later iconic) homicidal son played by Tony Perkins was inspired by Stefano seeing Perkins on Broadway as Eugene Gant in an adaptation of Thomas Wolfe's autobiographical novel *Look Homeward, Angel*. "Because that's where I saw a tragic figure, which I don't think Norman was in the book [by Robert Bloch]. I got this touch of fragility, which I picked up from watching Perkins onstage and created the movie around it." So Hitchcock owed a debt to Thomas Wolfe for *Psycho*. Who knew?

I interviewed the great musician and arranger Quincy Jones, a producer and music supervisor for Spielberg's adaptation of *The Color Purple*. This one-on-one, apart from exploring his role in the movie, gave me a chance to ask Jones how difficult it was to pick the right key for forty-five of pop's biggest stars to record the song "We Are the World" (a benefit for famine relief in Africa), which he had recently orchestrated. I prefaced with, "This might sound like a stupid question, but . . . "

At downtown LA set of Rising Sun *with publicist Peter Haas before interviewing Sean Connery*
<small>Author Collection</small>

"It's not a stupid question," Jones answered immediately. "It's hard enough to get two or three people in the right key. The range we had to deal with was pretty wide there. Willie Nelson, Kenny Rogers . . . " The key he settled on was E major, and the result was the fastest-selling US pop single in history. "But I'll tell you," Jones said. "God was with us."

As an advance for a flag-waving TV movie about Navy pilot James Stockdale, imprisoned and tortured by the North Vietnamese, I interviewed the young producer Steve Tisch, who was my age and claimed to have been strongly antiwar when he was a student at Tufts in Boston. Stockdale had been one of the pilots in the sky over the US destroyer *Maddux* in the Tonkin Gulf in August 1964, when it was supposedly attacked by North Vietnamese gunboats, providing LBJ with a pretext for escalating the conflict into all-out war. But Stockdale, in the book the movie was based on, *In Love and War*, had written that the *Maddux* was never attacked that night. He rued that he had been used as a pawn by his government—a stark and history-altering admission the movie conspicuously left out. I asked Tisch about this.

"We wanted to make it more of a people story and less of a political story," Tisch said, in a memorable bit of spin-doctoring.

There was also the problem of some stories and profiles being too predictable and the stars too big for you to do much about it. When a reclusive diva like Barbra Streisand became available to promote her forgettable directorial debut in *Yentl*, you went knowing that your interview with her was one of scores she would be doing. In situations like this, you had reason to wonder whose eyes would glaze over first—hers or yours? Yes, I got to meet Barbra Streisand for a one-on-one, but the prospect of writing anything original or interesting about someone so famous after a brief audience with them was uninspiring, which was probably just fine with her steely PR representatives, who had vetted me as thoroughly as if I were being granted access to a head of state.

After the novelty of sitting down with people like Barbra Streisand, Mel Gibson, and David Letterman had worn off, I looked for ways to get off the caravan when possible and find stories about the quirky and less famous denizens of the film capital. To me it was more interesting to write about people who hadn't been interviewed thousands of times and grown inured to the mechanics of it.

At American Film Institute tribute to Elizabeth Taylor, with editor and future spouse Kelly Scott and critic Peter Rainer

A colleague in the Style section, Nancy Spiller, shared my aversion to the obvious, and the two of us often joked that we wanted to write stories about failure in Hollywood, since it was much more common than the recurring trope of the young director living in his car who maxed out his credit cards while writing a script that a Universal executive found in front of his gym locker and purchased for a gazillion dollars. But we were only joking because we knew that our editors were not interested in revealing the grim and gritty aspects of Hollywood so much as perpetuating its red-carpet celebrity myths and fantasies. Observing the status quo was the less risky course.

One way to stretch the status quo was to write about worthy "small" movies and the people who made them, but such enterprise was not always welcomed by bosses who were more comfortable swarming the blockbusters like everybody else. As it happened, the next two editors of the Style Section were not Americans but from Great Britain and Canada, adding a Commonwealth flavor to the pages that was different but on occasion led to conflicting views of how to cover movies with American themes. Case in point: the 1984 film *Country*, starring real-life partners Jessica Lange and Sam Shepard as midwestern family farmers struggling to survive hard times. The film was written by the notable Texan William Wittliff, with a rousing score by Charles Gross. I went to an early screening, was taken by it, and wanted to do a story. The plot was timely, reflecting the crises faced by small farmers up against the Reagan administration's agricultural policies and unforgiving banks, but when I expressed my interest the next day at the office to my English boss, he replied, "Let's wait and see how it does."

Let's wait and see how it does? This sounded more like a studio vice-president worried about box office potential than a journalist, plus I wondered if, as a Brit, he might be unaware of the political relevance of the film—or care. And I was reminded uncomfortably that my original job description granting me independence in what I covered had been lost in the various editorial shake-ups. I never got to write about *Country*, whose fate at the box office got no help from the *Herald Examiner*.

CHAPTER THIRTY-EIGHT

Theatre Under the Palms

I DID MANAGE TO GET AWAY from the Hollywood beat now and then with stories about the satirical advertising contrarian Stan Freberg; a long-running folk music show on the Pacifica public radio station; LA's Spanish language daily, *La Opinion*; and a late-night deejay who extolled and cued up the forgotten chanteuses of the big band era. And there was always the theatre, where I could retreat and find worthwhile subjects like Peter Shaffer, Sidney Kingsley, Ian McKellan, and Jason Robards. While overshadowed by Hollywood, the stage in LA still attracted some of the world's best.

I was able to do a dressing room interview with the brothers Randy and Dennis Quaid, who were performing *True West* at a small theater in Hollywood. I spoke to the great classical actor Ian McKellan about his one-man show devoted to William Shakespeare in his room at the Chateau Marmont with a view overlooking the city at dusk. Lauren Hutton, the high-fashion model, came west to try the stage for the first time, starring at the LA Public Theater as a woman fighting off a rapist in William Mastrosimone's rough-and-tumble play *Extremities*.

When you think of theatrical women scorned, of homicidal rage on the stage, of actresses who can scream like Medea, the name Lauren Hutton may not be one of the names that rushes to the tip of the tongue . . .

When we met, after a rehearsal, Hutton explained how this time of year (October) she was normally relaxing "at the end of Long Island, out past the Hamptons, where I have a place." This was before I had seen the Hamptons or the end of Long Island, but the way she said it, in her soft southern voice, I could picture her there, maybe in a Revlon ad at the beach, in contrast to what she was doing here, making her stage debut in a physically punishing role at the age of thirty-nine for $271 a week. (It turned out she was good, but I don't think she ever did another play.)

I visited the provocative Providence-born narcissist Spalding Gray at a rental house in Silver Lake to discuss his breakthrough autobiographical monologue, *Swimming to Cambodia*, that emerged from his experience acting in the film *The Killing Fields*. I had dinner with playwright Lanford Wilson in the Music Center's restaurant after a late rehearsal of *Burn This*—which dazzled me when it opened in a world premiere a few nights later (John Malkovich again, plus Joan Allen—unforgettable).

After seeing a terrific revue of Randy Newman songs called *Maybe I'm Doing It Wrong*, at the Roxy on Sunset, I wrote a piece about the young actor, Paul McCrane, who brought down the house with his interpretation of Newman's anti-Apartheid "Christmas in Capetown." I went to interview him at the Magic Hotel, famous as the no frills out-of-town actors' lodging in Hollywood, the same place Alice Krige would be staying the following year.

Theatre in Los Angeles attracted notable actors and writers who might be wary of the New York critics but were brave enough for Southern California—and were sometimes available for interviews. This was true for Lauren Hutton and also Buck Henry, the comedic screenwriter of *The Graduate*, who was starring in John Guare's inimitable *House of Blue Leaves* at the Pasadena Playhouse and sat for an interview in which he described the long-billed cap he was wearing as "the pro model of whatever it is," allowing him "to see every part of, say, an approaching woman up to her nose without her seeing what I'm looking at."

Even John Osborne came to LA. Osborne, the British playwright who wrote *Look Back in Anger*, the landmark 1956 work that gave birth to the term "angry young man," describing its protagonist Jimmy Porter and Osborne himself, was here to look in on a revival of his lesser drama *A Patriot for Me* at the Ahmanson, a Broadway-sized booking house at the Music Center. I was eight years old when *Look Back in Anger* rocked the world with its antiestablishment invective, and I had never seen a production, but just reading it in college was thrilling. Now I was having a cup of tea with its author.

He was staying with Tony Richardson, who had directed the original *Look Back in Anger* at London's Royal Court Theatre, then the film adaptation starring Richard Burton, and many more films, including *Tom Jones*, which Osborne adapted, winning an Oscar along with Richardson. Richardson had a house in the hills above Sunset, where so many Hollywood royalty lived, and I found my way there on an October afternoon warm enough to be the height of summer in England.

"It's a terrible albatross being a landmark," Osborne told me. "Like being a place on the map. But there's nothing one can do about that, I'm afraid. I can't say I relish it at all."

His uncalculated responses and general irreverence were not something a Hollywood reporter hears every day. The revival of the play, starring Alan Bates (whom I also interviewed for a separate profile) would be a bust, and if I had been a critic would have elicited from me a negative review. Better, I thought, to have a conversation with the man who meant so much to the modern theatre and turn that conversation into something more interesting to read than a bad notice. I think Bud Shrake would have approved.

"I don't understand these English actors who come out here and make these enormous sums, people like Michael Caine. What do they need it for? It's ridiculous. I live fairly well, and I don't make a lot of money at all."

Such was the sound of John Osborne, a man I would never have met if I had merely gone to review *A Patriot for Me*.

Los Angeles critics, while not as fearsome as their New York counterparts, could still halt a play's advance with tepid notices, as happened with *A Patriot for Me* and a major revival of Moss Hart's 1948 backstage comedy *Light up the Sky*, which nevertheless afforded me the chance to meet and write about its director, Ellis Rabb, a legendary theatre figure who, as an actor-manager, had headed Broadway's last repertory company in the 1960s. Rabb was directing a cast that included Peter Falk, Nancy Marchand, and Carrie Nye, the wife of Dick Cavett. I admired the show, but I remember Falk left the cast as soon as a TV job beckoned, which said something about the status of theatre in LA. Even when it was very good, it bowed to the eminence and lucre of Hollywood.

And Hollywood was never far away in Los Angeles, as you could hear if you were sitting in my row at the Ahmanson Theater on the opening night of *Light Up the Sky*. Just before the curtain, an older woman with a coif leaned over the back of her seat and said to the woman sitting next to me:

"Page, does Barbara Stanwyck have any family?"

"I don't know, I don't think so."

"I thought there might have been a son."

"I know she was married to Robert Taylor, but I don't know if they had any children."

"I just thought it would be nice to have somebody with her at the top of the horseshoe, like we did last year with John Huston."

"What about some of the men?"

"The young men?"

"No, the old men."

"Who's still alive?"

"What about Joel McCrae?"

"He'd be terrific. How is he?"

"Walter and I saw him about a year ago. He looks great."

"How old is he?"

"Joel? He must be eighty-one or eighty-two. But he looked great. Of course, this was a year ago. Didn't he look great, Walter?"

"Joel looked good, but she's the one you ought to see. Just remarkable. She has the figure of a twenty-three-year-old girl."

"They stay on the ranch. They don't come down much. You ought to see her. I mean, a figure to die for."

"How old is she?"

"She must be seventy-nine."

"Well, Joel's a great idea. Do you think he'll do it?"

"If he can wear boots."

ONE NIGHT, NOT WORKING AND FEELING MY TEXAS CON-NECTION, I ventured solo to a small theater in Santa Monica for the premiere of a strange play called *Two Idiots in Hollywood*. The author was Stephen Tobolowsky, an actor and a native of Dallas who had attended SMU with the future Pulitzer Prize–winning playwright Beth Henley (*Crimes of the Heart*). They were now a couple, living in LA and making forays into the movie business.

In the audience I gladly spotted Bill Hootkins, a St. Mark's classmate and former Harlequin who had become a professional actor, getting small roles in *Star Wars* and *Raiders of the Lost Ark*, among other films. He had also been onstage in London, where he fled rather than "go out to LA and sit around hoping to be a drug-crazed hippie on *Kojak*," he told me in Dallas when I did a story about him coming home to play the lead in *Deathtrap* at the Theater Center. Being in the business, he was invited to the cast party after the show at the home of Tobolowsky and Henley, in the Hollywood Hills, and he asked me to join him.

I'd never met Tobolowsky but during my *Iconoclast* year had seen him onstage at Theatre Three as Jesus in the musical *Godspell*. He could sing. After *Crimes* won the Pulitzer, Henley was arts page news in Dallas, and I had interviewed her once for the *Times Herald*. She was cold and difficult in my recollection, and I wondered on the drive over whether she would remember me—or want to? I needn't have worried. Once we arrived at the rambling ranch house and began to move among the guests and tables of food, it became clear that Henley and Tobolowsky were not here. Nor would they appear in the hour-and-a-half or so Bill and I stayed, enjoying Texas-style barbecue (rare in LA then) and catching up with each other. It seemed odd that the hosts were not around, but I inferred this was just another way of being cool in Hollywood.

CHAPTER THIRTY-NINE

Enough Already

A FRIEND IN DALLAS WHO HAD LIVED IN LOS ANGE-
LES and seemed knowledgeable about it once said it would take
me seven years to become a Californian, as if that were ordained
in Scripture. But after three years I wasn't sure I would be staying that long.
The enchanting vision encountered on the I-10 that Saturday night after
the drive west from Dallas was already in the rearview mirror. I had become a regular in the press corps and adjusted to the confounding sprawl
of the smoggy Southland, but the mystery of Hollywood that I had come
to unravel was by now unraveled. I had seen Jack Lemmon rehearsing his
lines; I had seen Clint Eastwood's office at Warner Bros. and Ann-Margret's
swimming pool. I had been in a production meeting for a new midday TV
show called *America* where a young female producer staring at a whiteboard full of drab ideas assured me that she had "never made a show to
please myself."

I had been on the San Fernando Valley set of a terrific drama about
minor league baseball called *Bay City Blues* that NBC yanked after a few episodes because of mediocre ratings (the network evidently forgetting that it
took *Cheers* a while to catch on). I had met Tom Hanks and Oliver Stone. I
had seen behind the curtain of Oz and wondered how much more there was
to learn about the place that writer Budd Schulberg had summed up so well
in his 1941 novel *What Makes Sammy Run?* about a self-promoting talent

agent named Sammy Glick who lived by the credo "Going through life with a conscience is like driving your car with the brakes on."

Nothing about Sammy's philosophy appeared dated or out of place in Hollywood forty-some years later. Fundamental insincerity remained an underlying character trait and one I that hoped not to acquire. I thought of trying to publish a collection of my pieces under the title "In the Garden of the Cheek-Kissing Savages."

From afar, Hollywood could be imagined as a small town where the stars worked, played, and dined together happily under that big, white-lettered sign on a hillside that symbolized movieland. This, of course, was a fiction on a par with all the backlot and sound stage make-believe manufactured here for more than half a century. Since the old studio system had collapsed in the 1950s, along with the rosters of contract players, the stars were often strangers to one another, and the movie business (including television) was just that—a business, cold and calculating, where art occasionally snuck in the back door. Entertainment was a product, like cars or corn flakes, and producers, in the main, were looking for titles built for profit; they commonly referred to a "property" they were developing as a "piece of shit" until it had attracted good notices or built lines at the box office, promising them "a chunk of change."

Chances are they had not read the script or source material. They were too busy being producers, raising or counting money, having lunch, scouting for more pieces of shit to option or buy. They paid underlings to read for them and submit summaries, called "coverage."

In a business devoted to ever refining the standards of physical attraction and aimed at the youth market, everyone in Hollywood, I had learned, lied about their age, including screenwriters and especially actresses. Given the prejudice and whims of studio executives, who thought nothing of ordering starlets to get breast implants, who could blame them? "If you were in my class at Brown, then you know how old I am!" Jobeth Williams exclaimed when I went to interview her for a film no one remembers called *American Dreamer.* The alarm in her voice was both ironic and real. Jobeth had played Cordelia in *King Lear* at Brown, made her brief big screen debut as Dustin Hoffman's sleepover girlfriend in *Kramer vs. Kramer* and was tapped for the ensemble of *The Big Chill,* but she had yet to find the role that would make all the difference.

And then there was screenwriting and the weird dichotomy that seemed to describe it: everyone acknowledged the preeminence of the script in movies and television, yet screenwriters had no real clout and were themselves often disdainful of the trade. The man who had written Steven Spielberg's first film, *Duel*, and more recently *Jaws 3-D*—his name was Richard Matheson—explained it all to me one hot afternoon at his comfortable home in the West Valley. He was dressed in a jumpsuit like the ones Pete Townsend of The Who wore onstage. For a story about *Jaws 3-D*, I had driven out to see him and discovered that, not only had Matheson not seen the finished film, but he had no intention of seeing it. Others had been called in to rework his original script, as was common practice, and the final credits would be submitted to the Writers Guild for arbitration, but the process, altogether normal, lowered his expectations. He wasn't upset, just resigned to the way things were done in the industry where he made a good living. Originally a novelist, he was lured into films for the money, and he regretted the "marvelous" scripts he had written that got adulterated and some that were never made at all. I would discover there was nothing unusual about Richard Matheson's career complaints. That's just the way it was.

THE *HERALD EXAMINER* WAS SAID TO BE LOSING $1 MILLION A MONTH, and raises were so small, I don't remember them. My salary was enough to pay for a decent apartment and to buy a new Mazda sedan, but there were days when I found myself walking the downtown streets of LA, avoiding the office and wondering, is this all there is? I had not forgotten Pete Hamill's example of Daumier, but how many more portraits of movie stars could one man sketch? I suffered from being too easily bored and dreaded doing the same thing over and over again, whether it be teaching the same book, reviewing plays, or writing profiles of the famous. I was ready for something different, but what was that going to be? I thought about trying to be a generalist again and maybe asking for a transfer to the city desk, but I noticed the editors on the city desk did not favor long stories.

The traditional path to career advancement and a bigger salary in newspapers was to become a section editor and climb from there, but the prospect didn't appeal to me. I preferred to stay on the front lines producing the words that readers bought the paper for. When Tim Kelly, a former assistant managing editor at the *Times Herald*, became editor of the *Los Angeles Daily News*, a third LA paper based in the San Fernando Valley, he asked me to lunch and offered me the job of *Daily News'* entertainment editor. There was my chance. But I told Tim thanks, I wasn't interested.

The *Herald Examiner* itself had been a learning experience, embedded as I was with a culturally sophisticated crew of critics and writers—California living up to its reputation as a cradle of new ideas and expansive thinking. Yet I missed the camaraderie of the relatively down-to-earth *Dallas Times Herald*, realizing I was not likely to find that again, the togetherness and friendship being a function of that time and place and our youth.

I can think of only one time I ever went for a drink after work with anyone from the Style Section, where the preferred beverage was Diet Coke, reflecting young executive behavior in Hollywood. Truth and candor were rare, camouflaged behind arch personae and nonstop irony. At a Style Section party, in conversation with another, younger reporter, I ventured the hardly original thought that I wasn't sure if we were part of the problem or part of the solution doing what we did, further enlarging the footprint of celebrities in our coverage of Hollywood. She offered nothing in response but an ambiguous smile, her eyes glossing over with incomprehension as she sidled away.

One low-ranking staffer, the handsome and aptly named Robert Palm, disappeared one day, leaving behind only the question of which network television show he had joined as a writer. This sort of thing happened now and again, fueling the envy of those left behind, maybe not blessed with the connections and/or talent to get to the real money available in "the industry."

By now, I had read lot about Hollywood and its history, including *New Yorker* writer Lillian Ross's famous profile of director John Huston that was published in 1951. In a preface to the collection that contained the piece, Ross warned, "If you are on the staff of a newspaper, and if what you want is to become a writer, don't stay on the staff for more than two or three years." Damn, I missed that memo! It might be pointed out that Lillian Ross, whatever her talent and source of income, was the mistress of William Shawn, the *New Yorker*'s longtime editor in chief. What about the rest of us who had to earn a living? And what determined the difference between a mere reporter and a "writer?" The snobbery was infuriating.

Nevertheless, she had a point. No matter what kind of writer you were, to be any good you had to develop a voice, and newspapers generally discouraged that. Newspaper copy editors, adhering to the formulaic and familiar, might remove or rearrange words that had been placed in a certain order to get a particular sound or effect. Some editors pooh-poohed such literary aspiration, arguing that writing for newspapers was little more than typing. Clearly, Lillian Ross wasn't just typing, nor was Joan Didion. But they were writing for the best magazines. How did one get in those doors?

As I was contemplating this in the summer of 1986, I got a call from Caroline Miller, the features editor at *New York Newsday*, a new venture launched by Times Mirror to take Long Island's tabloid *Newsday* into Manhattan and compete with the *Times*, the *Post*, and *Daily News*. They were building a separate Manhattan staff, and she wanted to talk to me about it. Jeremy Gerard, a loyal drama critic friend in New York, had shown her a story I'd done from New Mexico about Robert Altman adapting Sam Shepard's play of *Fool for Love*, with Shepard in the cast.

I flew to New York on their dime, my head turning eastward with thoughts this might be my chance to get back to Manhattan. I took a train out to Long Island to meet Caroline at the current *Newsday* headquarters in Melville, and we drove to dinner at a French place nearby. I liked her. She was about my age, from Seattle, and won me over immediately when she said that she was looking to hire the best writers she could find and then figure out where to put them. In the staid culture of American newspapers, I had never heard anyone say such a thing. It was an indication that Caroline was not just another department head but someone with smarts and imagination—someone who could make me better. I was ready for that.

The next day I met other members of the *New York Newsday* project, and they were not as enlightened as Caroline. Some were longtime vets on Long Island, and, while nice enough, were more conventional and less brainy. A woman who had the power—I forget her name and title—wanted me to consider the television news beat, where she was hoping to hire someone "who would kill for a story." That was not me, and maybe she could sense that. Covering television news not only did not appeal to me, but it also seemed a lesser job than the one I had at the *Herald*, roaming across Hollywood and the arts looking for interesting subjects. My ambivalence probably showed, and I flew home to LA with no offer but glad I'd held out for the kind of job I thought I'd earned by now. I wasn't sure where Caroline ranked in the hierarchy of *Newsday*, but I was not surprised to learn some years later that she had become the editor of *New York Magazine*.

CHAPTER FORTY

Screenwriter

THE TRUTH WAS, I HAD OTHER THINGS ON MY MIND and a reason not to care too much about the *Newsday* thing not working out. Like many a journalist in Los Angeles, I had become enchanted with the idea of writing a screenplay, the currency of the realm. When you see three movies a week, many of them bad, it's natural to think, "How hard can it be?" even suspecting it's harder than it looks and recalling the testimony of Richard Matheson and many others about the unsatisfactory nature of the whole enterprise.

This could be a second act, I thought, a substitute for the novels I had not produced like my sportswriter role models Bud Shrake and Dan Jenkins. Plus, screenwriting held its own appeal, fueled by the popular notion that the novel was passé and movies were the storytelling medium of our time, the place where a writer could have an impact on the culture while getting well paid for it.

So how did you do it? Since publishing the Valley View Athletic Association newsletter when I was twelve, I'd written only prose and some poems. I'd read a lot of plays, but screenplays were a different form, and at the time not many had been published or were readily available to study. There was a popular book out for beginners, *Screenplay: The Foundations of Screenwriting*, by a Southern California teacher named Syd Field. I bought it, read it, and began to watch movies in a new way, analyzing their structure and trying to identify the three acts Field said were present in all screenplays. The three-act structure was adopted essentially from the theatre and traceable to Greek drama. It made simple sense and could be restated as beginning, middle, and end, although that disguised the complexity of good storytelling. How each part was constructed was critical, as were the plot points dividing the acts and the major reversal required at the midway point.

Field had a local rival in the how-to-write-a-screenplay business—Robert McKee, a dour and magisterial figure who taught three-day sold-out seminars that included laborious frame-by-frame deconstructions of *Casablanca* and *Chinatown*. I signed up for a weekend with McKee and found myself in a lecture hall with more than a hundred fellow acolytes, all anxious to get the secret formula from the master. McKee, a former actor, put on such a show he had become a guru, like Werner Erhard or L. Ron Hubbard, dictating the rules of screenwriting as if unveiling the Ten Commandments. Hardly a hand was raised to question anything he said, and on the first day I felt out of place, as can happen to a journalist, trained to be skeptical.

If the appeal of Syd Field's book was the idea that anyone could write a screenplay (if they followed his advice), McKee's fierce pronouncements and elaborate whiteboard diagrams suggested the opposite: that anyone who thought they could write a screenplay might want to try something easier, like climbing K-2. It seemed worth noting that neither Field nor McKee had written any movies anyone had ever heard of, but I didn't want to hold that against them. Despite my reservations, I began to allow myself to see the importance of structure in storytelling, something I had never learned in school, even in R.V. Cassill's creative writing class.

It was humbling in my late thirties to admit that what I had been taught about literature at St. Mark's and Brown was incomplete as it applied to the nuts and bolts of storytelling. One learned at the best schools which authors were important and what critics had said about them, but not so much about how they engineered and built their plots and narratives—the basic stuff. And if you were a writer (as opposed to a scholar) that's what mattered more than anything.

Better late than never, I swallowed my pride and tried to apply these storytelling rules to the screenplay I was writing. Not only did I have to worry whether I was following the rules that Field and McKee laid down, I was also anxious about using the correct transitional grammar ("CUT TO," "Atkins' POV," "EXT-DAY") and whether to put the third brad in the middle hole of the conventional three-hole punch cover. It was said that the pros only used two brads, leaving the middle hole empty, and a novice script was easily identified and disregarded if a third brad was present. Really? This was the kind of dubious folklore and mythology a beginner had to sift as he tried to get into the game. Oh, and the script had to be 120 pages—not 119 or 121, but 120! Corresponding to one page equaling a minute of screen time and adding up to a standard two-hour length movie.

The script I was working on was technically an adaptation of an unfinished novel I had written with my father in the period between *Iconoclast* and the *Times Herald*. It was a whodunnit that was Dad's idea. He was a murder mystery buff and enlisted me as a partner in fashioning a plot based on the murder of a teacher at a private school like St. Mark's. I was to provide an insider's knowledge and details of the milieu. We alternated writing chapters, but the project stalled short of its denouement when a fiscal crisis at the museum demanded Dad's full attention.

Completing it now by translating the prose to screenplay form provided me with a story and plot, but there was a lot of work left to do. First, I had to overcome my resistance to some of the tenets of screenwriting, foremost among them that a movie was a story told in pictures, not words, and that dialogue was secondary and sometimes not needed at all. Coming from a newspaper background and carrying an affinity for the theatre, I found this a tough adjustment, even as I came to see the sense of it.

When I interviewed Brian DePalma, who had directed the Hitchcockian thriller *Body Double*, he defended the visceral impact of an erotic dancer being murdered with a giant electric drill, saying, "The point is that movies are a visual art form." His co-screenwriter, Robert Avrech, told another journalist that he and DePalma never talked about dialogue. "He left that completely to me," Avrech said. "Because he knows once he gets on the set, it depends on what the actors can do. Screenwriting isn't about dialogue anyway, it's only about structure."

Damn. I didn't want to hear that as I worked hard on the words coming out of the mouth of a Texas county sheriff sent to investigate the crossbow murder of an athletic young teacher at an elite boys' school that just happened to be in the sheriff's jurisdiction. This was Dad's idea and a good one, I thought. But it was just the start. I realized now we had neglected some storytelling essentials as I dutifully acted on the lessons learned from Field and McKee. I made sure the script had a three-act structure, with plot points in the right places, shorter dialogue scenes, more reversals and the stuff that makes a movie a movie. I was still at the *Herald*, getting up at 6 a.m. every morning to put in two hours on *All Boys in Mourning* before heading downtown to 1111 South Broadway to earn my paycheck as a newspaperman. Even though I figured Dan Jenkins must have kept a schedule like this to turn out his novels, I evidently didn't have the same constitution and drive, not to mention talent. I did it, but it made me crazy and depressed. For the first time since my sessions with Don Giller years before, I felt psychologically overwhelmed and asked my doctor for a referral to a shrink. Which, this time, didn't pan out; I only went once, not finding the connection I had with Don.

As I struggled to meet all the recommended criteria, working with two forms that were unfamiliar (the screenplay and a whodunnit), the script became an unnerving puzzle that I couldn't solve, no matter how hard I tried. I had invested so much time and ego into making it work, and I had failed. Or so I thought. No wonder I was depressed. This was supposed to be my second act. Now what?

I went back and forth in my head about the script and allowed myself to think maybe it wasn't all bad and that my hard work and study were not for naught. I had produced this 120-page thing—and only used two brads to bind it. It looked professional. I had enough connections by now in the business to get it read (or skimmed) by some development people, a young cinematographer looking for a project to direct, and a screenwriting instructor at UCLA Extension. No one got excited.

I screwed up my courage and got the script to Barry Corbin, the Texas-born actor I imagined as Sheriff Smiley Atkins. Corbin had played John Travolta's uncle in *Urban Cowboy*, and I met him during my first year in LA doing a story about *War Games*, in which he played an Air Force general. We hit it off and had stayed in touch. The Texas connection. Corbin read the script (or said he read it) and seemed genuinely grateful I had thought of him for the role but didn't express much enthusiasm about it. He said he thought it might make a TV movie, which I took to be a polite way of saying "I'm not interested." Fair enough.

At this point I had to take stock of my situation. I was ready to leave the *Herald* (like Robert Palm) and cross over into Hollywood itself, the world I had been writing about. This was an entirely unrealistic expectation based on a first script, but one I clung to, nonetheless. Despite the evidence that most screenplays, even the ones bought and paid for, written by people like Richard Matheson, never got made, I was still determined to be an exception. And I wanted to do something besides interview Johnny Depp again when he had a new movie to promote.

Naively I had thought that my résumé as a Brown grad, prize-winning critic, and long-form journalist would ease my way into screenwriting. But the truth was, my résumé meant next to nothing when it came to the business side of show business. All that mattered was, could you do this? Did you have a script that an agent or producer could recognize as cinematic while spotting evidence of the craft known to industry insiders?

I'm not sure how many drafts I'd done by now, but I wrote another and asked Terrel Seltzer if she would read it. Yes, my old LRY compadre, Christie's sister, the Terrel Seltzer who sang with The Bountymen and had since made her way to the West Coast, gotten into filmmaking in Berkeley and co-written (with the Chinese American director Wayne Wang) the low-budget noir comedy *Chan Is Missing*. The film was an art house oddity without national distribution until *New York Times* film critic Vincent Canby put it on his Ten Best List of 1981. The Ten Best list thing had changed Terrel's life, she explained during an interview I did with her on one of my critic-at-large trips to the Bay Area for the *Times Herald*.

Terrel's success resounded with me, not just because I knew her but because I had known her in high school, when she was a cheerleader, not a writer. After high school, she had headed off to the Kansas City Art Institute, intending to be a painter or sculptor. Which now, from my point of view, seemed proof that screenwriting was not a natural outgrowth of English lit or journalism but depended on an altogether different set of skills—storytelling skills, with a visual component, that Terrel had learned somehow. Self-taught, she had studied hundreds of movies and outlined them to analyze their structures. I had to give her credit. My own self-education was not as rigorous or fruitful.

When I interviewed Terrel in San Francisco following her *Chan Is Missing* breakthrough, she evinced a disdain for the commercialism of the movie industry and told me she would rather "reupholster chairs" than work in Hollywood. But four years later, here she was, writing a feature for Twentieth Century Fox about the increasingly daunting game of college admissions. We got together and discovered that her husband, a cookbook author named Isaac Cronin, and I were born on the same day in the same year. To acknowledge this coincidence, we threw a joint thirty-ninth birthday party brunch at my apartment in Beverly Hills, both of us inviting our separate lists of friends. One of Isaac and Terrel's friends who came was the screenwriter Nicholas Kazan, son of the man who directed *On the Waterfront*.

When Terrel finally got around to reading *All Boys in Mourning*, she gave me some notes that were useful but disheartening. She pointed out that any number of my early scenes contained behavior and bits of business that an audience (or reader) might presume would connect to something significant later on, but here had been abandoned without "paying off," as people in the industry liked to say. No doubt she was right, but again, I didn't allow myself to hear the criticism.

Impressed by what she had accomplished, I asked Terrel about her work habits. (Her future credits would include *One Fine Day*, starring George Clooney and Michelle Pfeiffer.) She told me that she got to her computer early each morning without fail. When I said I tried to do the same after first skimming the two LA papers, she looked puzzled and said she could never do that because reading a newspaper would be a distraction. Really? While I saw the good sense of such discipline, I also recognized that Terrel and I were different people. Newspapers were in my blood, never mind that I was trying to escape working for one. For me not to look at the front page each morning, scan the sports section, and check the columnists' topics would likely require a stay in rehab. I had a habit, which I accepted and hoped could somehow accommodate my new career as a screenwriter.

CHAPTER FORTY-ONE

Bethlehem Revisited

T HINGS AT THE *HERALD* WERE DETERIORATING. My Fleet Street editor had returned to London, replaced by a younger guy from New York who was even less simpatico and devoted to television. In what I remember as the nadir of my stretch at the paper, he sent me to cover an all-night *Cagney & Lacey* marathon at a multiplex in Burbank—twenty-two episodes of gals-as-buddy-cops melodramas back-to-back from a season just concluded. It was a promotional event staged by the show's producers to "pull the show closer to its constituency of upper economic strata females." This is the way people in TV talked. The fans present mostly had seen all these episodes before but were here to "get the large screen impact" and vote for the one they thought should be submitted for an Emmy Award, an Orion executive explained to me. By 4 a.m., when all the votes had been counted, the show's insomniac fans had picked the episode where Cagney's alcoholic father dies, and Cagney (Sharon Gless) discovers she's an alcoholic, too. Point taken.

One day the editor who had sent me to the multiplex in Burbank marched over to my desk and ordered me to chase a breaking TV business story—exactly the kind of thing I had declined at *New York Newsday*—and had heretofore been outside my duties at the *Herald*. My response was quick and uncalculating. "This is not what I was hired to do here," I said, realizing as I said it that I was drawing my line in the sand—or on the *Herald Examiner*'s dusty linoleum floor.

About fifteen minutes later, the editor returned, steam coming out of his ears and screamed at me, "DO NOT EVER, EVER, *EVER* TALK THAT WAY TO ME AGAIN!" Don't worry, I was thinking, wanting to ask him if he'd ever heard the Jimmy Webb song, "If You See Me Gettin' Smaller, I'm Leavin'"? Waylon Jennings had done an excellent version. I'd been at the *Herald* more than four years, which was plenty. (It would last only another two.) Now that I had my own personal computer, an early model Kaypro, I knew I was fine working from home and figured I could freelance. But what I really wanted to do was hone my script and then write another. I had some money saved.

Not long after the screaming incident, I informed the editor that I would, in fact, be leaving, but no hard feelings (right). I'm sure he was relieved, just as Chuck Yeiser, the new Cincinnati Country Day headmaster was relieved when I informed him that I would not be returning for a third year. (I might not have been every boss's idea of a model employee.) My good friend and coconspirator Nancy Spiller also happened to be leaving, and she invited me to cohost a going away party with her at the 1930s house in Glendale she shared with her husband, Tom Weitzel, a producer for *Entertainment Tonight*.

I had already planned to fly east at the end of August to meet my parents in Bethlehem, where Mom and her band were scheduled to perform at Musikfest, a new festival of folk and alt rock music intended to show off the city's tourist-worthy downtown now that the smoke and grit from Bethlehem Steel were gone.

During my four years in Providence, I had failed to get over to Bethlehem and had not been back since that summer trip when I was twelve. This would be my first time to see the city of my birth and family hometown as an adult. I wasn't going to miss it. Plus, I wanted to hear Mom's band of backup musicians that she'd given the name Catch-23.

She had taken early retirement from Kodak at fifty-nine, allowing her to pursue music full time, which brought unintended complications for Dad, who retired around the same time, at age sixty-five. For the first time in their long marriage, the two of them were together day in and day out, highlighting the differences obscured by decades of work schedules and making ends meet. Only their occasional collaborations on shows for the Unitarian Church—when Dad provided the text and Mom the music—bridged the gap. Now, the band was often at the house rehearsing, disturbing the peace and quiet Dad craved and reminding him that he had ceded the artistic right of way in the family to an activity he endured more than enjoyed.

The Sun Inn at Musikfest | AUTHOR COLLECTION

Twice he had escaped by flying out to spend a week with me in LA, attending Dodger games, the LA Philharmonic at the Hollywood Bowl, and once catching a show by the political comedian Mort Sahl at a comedy club on Sunset. I empathized with his predicament and presumed he had made peace with Mom's stepped-up career since he was accompanying her to Musikfest.

Musikfest took over Bethlehem for ten days, with multiple stages, large and small, spread across the city center and most acts, including Lu Mitchell, performing more than once. Members of the extended Reiser clan came out to support her, but not her father, Tony senior, who at eighty-three was almost blind. (He had always been deaf to his older daughter's talent.) Mom's brother, Tony, and his six kids—my first cousins whom I barely knew—all turned out for a show in the courtyard of the historic stone-walled Sun Inn, providing a rare semblance of family unity. Many of us went to hear headliner Joan Baez the night before and stood in the dewy grass of a big field waiting for "The Night They Drove Old Dixie Down" and other Joanie standards. Ireland's incomparable Clancy Brothers opened for her.

Dad had not been back in decades and couldn't get over the crowds filling the streets he had walked as a young man—ninety-four thousand on the opening Sunday, according to the Bethlehem *Globe-Times*. His brother Ron had driven up from northern Virginia with his wife, Jan, and one afternoon ferried us around the city, with him and Dad pointing out multiple residences the Mitchells had called home. Most were still standing: narrow, two-story wood-shingle and aluminum-sided row houses squeezed between others. The old brewery space that had been home to the Bethlehem Civic Theatre was gone but not the building that housed the cigar store where Dad

Lu onstage at Musikfest | AUTHOR COLLECTION

had swept the floor as a kid and updated the major league baseball scores with chalk on a blackboard.

I was reminded of the short story Dad had published in the *KERA* magazine, about braving icy predawn temperatures in the winter months of high school while delivering seven different Philadelphia and New York newspapers on the North Side. His bundle also included one German-language paper that he carried nervously as Hitler rose to power, wondering if the subscriber were a Nazi sympathizer. The man opened his door one day and surprised Dad with doughnuts and hot coffee, then explained how the economic hardships imposed by the West after World War I had made Hitler possible. Dad was skeptical but torn by the kindness the man showed him. The story built toward an awkward confrontation and did not end happily.

I thought to ask Dad if he could point out where that house had been, the one where he delivered the German language newspaper? But I did not, remembering that after that story was published, I asked him why he didn't write more often about his youth, and his answer was that he didn't want to relive it. Too much pain and anguish.

Bethlehem didn't look bad—green, leafy, and somewhat hilly, a restored downtown historic district dating to the Colonial Era, when George Washington stayed at the Sun Inn and Alexander Hamilton had been through town. Mother did three shows, all enthusiastically received. She sold seventy-eight records and tapes. The local paper noted that she drew "a huge crowd" one afternoon, and it quoted a verse from her song about the wayward TV evangelists Jim and Tammy Faye Bakker. In my journal I wrote:

Lehigh is a beautiful campus and possibly the nation's most vertical. Mother grew up on the South Side, in a house on Hillside Avenue, a stone's throw from the university that she could never have hoped to attend.

I took a run from the Hotel Bethlehem across the Hill-to-Hill Bridge, built in 1924 and spanning the Lehigh River, down to the beginning of the steelworks and back across the New St. Bridge and east along Church Street, which passes a long and sylvan cemetery. Brick sidewalks.

At the Philadelphia airport, waiting to board my flight back to Los Angeles, I sat back and allowed my head to fill with the fantasy of returning to Bethlehem to live—a common neurosis of mine whenever and wherever I traveled. In the case of Bethlehem, I had the presence of extended family, even if I didn't know any of them very well. The cost of living would be cheaper, and it was only eighty miles from New York City. I could write my screenplays here, in an apartment somewhere downtown. The Martin guitar factory, where my 1970 D-28 (a graduation gift) was crafted, was in Nazareth, a twenty-minute drive. (We took a tour.) The guitar would also be coming home. The brick sidewalks had character, as did the preserved older buildings. The soot from the steel stacks that my mother remembered coating all the windowsills of her youth was a thing of the past. The ample Lehigh River was recovering from a century of pollution. No smog and no hundred-degree Septembers! And there was the fact that I was born here.

Wouldn't there be some originality (literally) in coming back to reside in the birthplace my parents had yanked me from when I was eighteen months old?

We were not halfway to LA in the air when the fantasy began to recede. Musikfest was great fun, but on further reflection I understood for the first time why my parents had to leave back in 1949. It all came into focus: the narrow possibilities of a small town, the prominence of the church and *churchgoing*, the parochial attitudes, the conformity. What would they have done here? What would

Gene and Lu in retirement
AUTHOR COLLECTION

I have done here? My grandfather, who forbade his dutiful, long-suffering wife to learn the rich and varied cuisine his mother had brought over from the old country, was quick to enforce his lordly dominion over me as a toddler, Dad once told me. Tony ruled his clan with a loud and proud ignorance while referring to my dad with mock respect as "the professor." Of course, Gene and Lu had to get away from him and get out. And how would my life have been different had they stayed?

I preferred to think of the good fortune that befell us the day Dad happened to be in Palmerton or Nesquehoning or whatever the town was north of Bethlehem where he went to sell those Babee Tendas and had to wait for the husband to come home from the mines, allowing him the time to loiter in a drug store and spot that copy of *Holiday* magazine with the word "Texas" on the cover. Whatever its drawbacks, Texas had been a good move for a young working-class couple from a steel town who ended up with jobs and careers that would not have been possible had they stayed in Pennsylvania.

No matter what happened now, the trip was a blessing, allowing us to be here together, the three of us, taking note of where it all began. It wasn't likely the chance would come again.

CHAPTER FORTY-TWO

No *Viva Las Vegas*

BACK AT MY APARTMENT ON THE LOWER EAST SIDE OF BEVERLY HILLS, I was anxious to try out my new life free of the *Herald Examiner* and its discontents. I had cashed out of the *Herald* with a modest pension check and stashed it in the bank, giving me a false confidence that I had a cushion to face the world as an unemployed screenwriter. I was still circulating my script, now retitled *Past Master*, and looking to start work on another.

Docudramas were popular, and I thought my background as a journalist might qualify me for scriptwriting in this new hybrid form combining fiction and nonfiction. The problem for me, the more I thought about it, was that I wasn't sure I believed in the form itself—that is, the veracity of the docudrama. Not that anyone particularly cared about veracity at HBO or CNN, but as a bred-in-the-bone journalist, I cared about it, worried that I wouldn't be able to follow through in good conscience if the rules of drama and structure required bending the truth on some crucial point.

Then I had another idea. C. W. Smith, the former film critic at the *Times Herald*, had published a novel with Atheneum a few years earlier, *The Vestal Virgin Room*, about a husband-and-wife lounge act, playing Holiday Inns on weekends but dreaming of the big time. Charlie and I had become good friends during his stint at the paper, and I regarded him as a top-drawer novelist who was not better known only because he had spent

C.W. Smith in 1975
FARRAR, STRAUS AND GIROUX (GARY BISHOP)

his entire career in the middle of the country.

I had read *The Vestal Virgin Room* when it came out, loved it and now reread it with an eye to how it might be a movie, with me writing the screenplay. Charlie's second novel, *Country Music*, had been optioned by Playboy Productions but never made into a film. This was not uncommon, and Charlie was philosophical about it, glad to get the modest option money and never counting on the bigger payout that would come if a script ever reached production.

I sent him a five-page treatment, or synopsis, of the story as I saw it, sketched in dramatic terms—the sort of thing producers often wanted to see first. He liked my treatment enough to share it with his literary agent in New York, who shared it with a counterpart in Hollywood, who signaled his approval.

I also sent the treatment to Sanford-Pillsbury Productions, run by two women who had produced the recent award-winning independent feature *River's Edge*, about a teenage murder in California. Midge Sanford called one day to tell me how much she liked the treatment and wanted to see the script when I finished it. Of course, I was pleased and thought to myself, I'm getting somewhere: that's a real producer saying that.

Buoyed by the knowledge I had gained from writing *Past Master*, I threw myself into the screenplay, secure in my belief in the story and characters that Charlie had already created. One advantage I thought I held over any established pros attempting an adaptation of *The Vestal Virgin Room* (as several would, for money, in the years ahead) was that I knew Charlie and saw his reflection in Don, the husband and drummer of the story. When I was writing Don's part, I could hear Charlie's voice coming out of Don's mouth.

The novel climaxes in Las Vegas, where Don has snagged a third-rate gig for New Year's Eve playing intermissions at a dreary hotel lounge called The Vestal Virgin Room. I had never been to Las Vegas and figured I better go and have a look.

Las Vegas is a four-and-a-half-hour drive from Los Angeles, east by northeast across the Mojave desert, most of it on Interstate I-15. The city lived up (or down) to my preconceptions of its awfulness. The first thing I noticed were the slot machines at Denny's. Wedding chapels abounded, decorated with marquee messages like "Happy Marriages Start Here." The sun shown down brutally onto harsh concrete streets and Astroturf lawns. People didn't come here for the scenery. They came for what was going on inside the air-conditioned hotels and casinos.

I had promised myself I would not do any serious gambling but figured, as part of my research, I should at least sample the one-armed bandits that lined the corridors of the hotels. I found an available video poker machine and bellied up, noticing the messages "Any malfunction voids all pay and plays" and "You're a winner." I played video poker for thirty minutes, won thirty-five dollars, and decided to quit while I was ahead, taking comfort in knowing I had not contributed to the monthly gross at Caesar's Palace.

After returning to LA, I gave my treatment to a former Style section editor now editing *American Film* magazine, and he offered the disconcerting judgment that the story wasn't complicated enough. In general, movies needed to have more stuff going on than prose fiction. I had learned that by now.

But his verdict notwithstanding, I held to the belief the script I was writing would work onscreen. There was just one sure way to find out, and it was impractical: to hire a director and cast and make it into a film. Robert Towne, the renowned screenwriter of *Chinatown*, told me once, during an interview, that the only way to really learn screenwriting was to see a script you had written turned into a movie and then see what works and what doesn't. "You learn best if it works," he said.

This was not yet an option for me, though things were happening. I finished a first draft and mailed it to Charlie. One night I came back to my apartment on Tower Drive, and the message light was blinking on my answering machine. Charlie had called. He had read the script and sounded elated, adding praise for the changes I'd made and scenes I'd added. I rewound the tape and listened to his message again. It was more than I could have hoped for. I took a long, hot bath and started composing my Oscar acceptance speech in my head, giving credit to Charlie and imploring viewers to seek out his other books. I had trouble getting to sleep that night.

Before long, I got a call from the Hollywood agent who had read the treatment, Ron Bernstein, of the venerable Gersh Agency. By now, Bernstein had read my script as well and liked it enough to say he thought he could "set something up." I wasn't sure what that meant, but it sounded promising. He said, "It's still not a movie yet, but it's got two wonderful characters," then added, "We need to get a director or producer involved" and mentioned the names Bill Forsythe and Jonathan Demme. I pinched myself. He also said Don Johnson was looking for something to do with his new wife, Melanie Griffith (she of DePalma's *Body Double* fame). Don Johnson, the blandly hunky *Miami Vice* star, as Charlie's irascible Don? Not my first choice, but if Don and Melanie could get *The Vestal Virgin Room* off the ground, so be it. I mentioned other actors and actresses I imagined for the roles, but Bernstein flatly rejected all of them. "None of those actors can get a movie made," he huffed, as if I were a schoolkid.

Bernstein asked me to come in for a meeting, and a few days later I drove a half mile down Wilshire to the Gersh offices in the Beverly Hills business district. When I arrived and was shown to his office, I couldn't help but notice a movie poster of George Orwell's *1984* on the wall and thought, damn, I'm in good company here, though in retrospect realized it likely meant that Bernstein or Gersh represented Michael Radford, the writer-director of the recent film adaptation.

Whatever is the opposite of warm and schmoozy, that would describe Ron Bernstein, a thin and intense man, middle-aged and balding, with surviving tendrils of black hair creeping forward toward his glasses. He wore a headset, paced back and forth and occasionally ignored me as he barked something into his mic like "Dante doesn't make Vestron movies," a reference to director Joe Dante (*Twilight Zone: The Movie*) and a film company that David Schmoeller might have worked for. Other celebrity names were dropped—Dennis Quaid, Rob Reiner, Bill Forsythe again, the Scottish director of the terrific *Local Hero*. I assumed he must be a Gersh client. (If so, more good company.)

He asked me if I had other scripts, and I chose to say no, having lost confidence by this time in my prep school murder mystery. I didn't want that script to reveal any shortcomings I had managed to disguise while adapting Charlie's estimable novel.

"We should know something by Thanksgiving or the week after," Bernstein said as he walked me to the door.

It was late afternoon as I strode out onto the sidewalk of Wilshire Boulevard, feeling like I'd just been drafted by the Dodgers and told to report to spring training. Rob Reiner? Bill Forsythe? Don Johnson? These guys were in "the Show," to borrow Kevin Costner's description of the big leagues in the recent film *Bull Durham*. Still, I was left wondering about the prospect of working with someone who brought to mind the title character in *What Makes Sammy Run?* One thing Bernstein had said bothered me. He said, "In the next draft, you have to make them less like losers. I know what sells, and people don't like characters who are losers."

I was encouraged that Bernstein thought there would be another draft, but I didn't envision it ending with Don and Dottie having a hit record and appearing on *The Tonight Show*. That's not who they were. But they were also not losers, not in my mind or in Charlie's mind, I was pretty sure. They were smarter than they were talented perhaps and gained redemption in the end from accepting their limitations and love for one another as preferable to the tawdry status of "making it" in Vegas. Their winning humanity and humor were what made the book so relatable and different, and I worried that Bernstein didn't get that. But then maybe Hollywood wouldn't get it either.

As winter turned into spring, I tried to keep my hopes up for *The Vestal Virgin Room* despite long silences from Bernstein and the occasional report from his office that so-and-so didn't like it, but "they liked the writing." Which could mean any number of things, none of them useful.

One day I got a call from my former headmaster Tom Hartmann, inquiring as to my welfare and progress toward becoming the chief drama critic of the *New York Times*. We hadn't spoken in years. I loved Tom and the difference he had made to my life, but I tried to explain to him, as I had to Gene and Lu, why I did not want to be the drama critic of the *New York Times* and in fact was looking to get out of journalism altogether. I was now a screenwriter, I told him, albeit a screenwriter without portfolio. Journalism was built on expository writing and involved storytelling from time to time, but rarely did it move people emotionally the way dramatic writing could, I said. I wanted to try that now at age forty, even though it required learning a whole new language based on moving pictures. Tom listened sympathetically, but I wasn't sure how much of the subtlety he understood or if he just thought I was nuts.

Around this time, I also heard from Midge Sanford, who was in Vancouver making a movie with James Woods and Elizabeth Mastrantonio. I had sent her the completed script, and she was taking the trouble to call and tell me she "liked the writing, but that not enough happened, especially in the middle." She wouldn't be interested in developing it but wanted to see anything else I might write.

Again, I tried to see the upside of a well-known producer calling me from a set in Canada, even if it represented another rejection. I also began compiling a list of successful movies that were episodic in nature—*Tender Mercies, Annie Hall, Alice Doesn't Live Here Anymore, Rainman*—and wondered if early versions of those scripts were found wanting because not enough happened in the middle?

William Goldman, the screenwriter of *Butch Cassidy and the Sundance Kid*, famously wrote in his book *Adventures in the Screen Trade* about Hollywood, "Nobody knows anything. Not one person in the entire motion picture field knows for a certainty what's going to work. Every time out it's a guess and, if you're lucky, an educated one." Damn straight, Bill. Can I quote you?

One morning Charlie called, early. I wasn't even out of bed yet. He had talked to Ron, who told him that Martin Brest was interested in *The Vestal Virgin Room*. "He said Marty Brest loves your script" were Charlie's exact words, notable for the fact that Martin Brest was an A-list director but best known for the action comedy hit *Beverly Hills Cop*, starring Eddie Murphy. "I'd rather it was Barry Levinson," Charlie said, while passing on the gossip from Ron that Brest was looking to do "a small character piece." OK, whatever. This would be that.

But a month went by and nothing more about Martin Brest. One afternoon Ron calls, the first time I've spoken to him in six months, and he tells me "a well-known television director" named Kim Friedman likes *The Vestal Virgin Room* and wants to meet me. When I speak to Friedman on the phone eventually, she tells me she "likes the script a lot" and wants to discuss it further. A meeting is set up at her home, then cancelled because of her shooting schedule for another TV project. Another month passes, with assistants taking and delivering messages. But Kim Friedman ultimately never meets with me.

Roger Director, the husband of my *Herald Examiner* colleague Jan Cherubin and a former journalist who wrote for the TV shows *NYPD Blue* and *Moonlighting*, remarked to me once about success in Hollywood: "It has a lot to do finally with the force of your personality." I scribbled that sentence into my journal, followed by the words *Uh-oh*.

In my last conversation with Ron months later, I asked him why he thought nothing came of *The Vestal Virgin Room*, a project he once believed in? Immediately he cited the "failure" of *The Fabulous Baker Boys*, a recent movie about a lounge act featuring the brothers Jeff and Beau Bridges (who were, in fact, a rung above Don and Dottie, playing Sheratons and upmarket resorts). The film, written and directed by Steve Kloves, received glowing reviews I thought it well deserved but after three months had not earned back Twentieth Century Fox's modest investment. "A disaster," Ron pronounced it. "It did no business, no business—DOA. I think that movie simply said, no one's interested in this part of the world."

DOA? That was the sound of Hollywood talking. A foreign language to me. I happened to meet Kloves a few years later while doing a story about the movie *The Wonder Boys* that he adapted from a Michael Chabon novel. When I shared with him my experience on *The Vestal Virgin Room* and Bernstein's dismissive comments, Kloves was unfazed. He smiled and said, "Collateral damage."

CHAPTER FORTY-THREE

Life at the *Times*

D ESPITE THE SWAYING PALMS AND MILD CLIMATE,
*this is a tough place. Everyone is on the make, the stakes are high, the
bodies perfect and milk of human kindness in short supply. I think I
have learned a thing or two, been stimulated and forced to re-examine my own
views and talents. Which is essentially the reason for being here. There are still
things I want to express that exceed the bounds of journalism—or newspaper
journalism anyway—and I am experimenting with other forms. The problem, as
you know, is that one must earn a living while trying to be an artist or whatever
we want to call it.*

This, from a letter I wrote to Lud North in my last months at the *Herald.* Lud himself was writing poetry, and he had sent me some. Once joined
as teacher and student, we were bonded now by our mutual love of literature
and our individual efforts to produce it (or some viable alternative), not just
study it. Since St. Mark's, Lud had moved on to private schools in New Jersey
and Michigan, was divorced and remarried, and now was teaching at Wayne
State University in Detroit.

*At some level of consciousness, I revisit that seventh-grade classroom ev-
ery time I sit down at the typewriter or computer. I can't remember whether I ever
told you this, so I thought I would now.*

I want to think he got to read those words. Lud died a few months after
I sent them. He was fifty-four. Throat cancer.

—

DESPITE THE EXPERIENCE OF *THE VESTAL VIRGIN ROOM* (but also because of it), I wanted to write another screenplay. I was thinking about books to option, realizing that the rights were not likely be free this time. And I was out of money. I had started to take freelance assignments to pay the bills, including one from, at long last, the *LA Times.* John Lindsay, the former managing editor at the *Herald*, had gone to the *Times* as its interim *Sunday Magazine* editor, and he called me one day to ask if I would be interested in profiling a trend-setting local ad man named Jay Chiat. I had written off the *Times* as a lost cause and didn't realize Lindsay had noticed and valued my work at the *Herald.* The story would likely be a cover, he said, and involve a trip to New York, where Chiat's agency also had offices.

I was flattered and couldn't turn down the money, but I worried that I was backsliding on my plan to become a screenwriter. Could I do both? The history of literature and Hollywood was rife with stories of writers working other jobs to allow them the time and energy to write creatively. Nathanael West, my Brown literary hero, supposedly worked as a night clerk in a second-rate hotel as he labored away on *Miss Lonelyhearts* and *Day of the Locust*, though it wasn't clear if the hotel was in Los Angeles or New York. In any case, the notion appealed to me, but I lacked the courage to act on it. I was reluctant to surrender whatever status I had earned as a journalist and knowing it would send Dad into a funk. Like it or not, I was a prisoner of respectability and my father's esteem.

Getting into the *LA Times Magazine* was a return to my earlier career trajectory, and when I saw the advance copy of the Jay Chiat issue, I felt a jolt of accomplishment: the West Coast newspaper of record's familiar Old English typeface logo in colored ink over a photo of Chiat and the headline: "Off the Wall On Madison Avenue." And inside, my byline and the credit: "Sean Mitchell is a Los Angeles writer." Maybe I could be a magazine writer *and* write scripts.

The *Magazine* gave me more assignments, including profiles of true crime author Joseph Wambaugh and the best-selling supernaturalist Dean Koontz, both Southern California residents. My Wambaugh story began:

Jamboree Road is one of those Orange County boulevards that looks like it was paved yesterday and scrubbed by hand this morning. Its manicured black-

top climbs a coastal rise past decorator palm trees and a BMW dealership and drops down into the quiet of Newport Beach as neatly as the last line in a song about love being the answer. From Jamboree Road, it's not far to where Joseph Wambaugh lives, on an island of multi-million-dollar homes that have yacht slips in back. Here, surrounded by a harbor full of pleasure boats and the joyful noise of ice cubes kissing the sides of cocktail glasses, Wambaugh goes into a room, alone, seven days a week and contemplates what terrible things human beings are capable of.

Nancy Spiller, who once worked at the *San Jose Mercury News*, arranged to do a regular one-page celebrity Q&A for its magazine each week and invited me to share the load. The magazine's editor, Charles Matthews, had once been an English professor at SMU and an arts critic for the *Iconoclast*. Small world.

Many of the Q&A's were short phoners, easy money, but the *Mercury-News* interview I remember best was the one I did in person with Ray Charles, who lived in LA and had his own recording studio here. Getting forty-five minutes with Ray Charles was prime Q&A territory for anyone interested in the history of rhythm and blues, but it so happened that Charles's availability fell during a week when I was having a chemical face peel (at the behest of a dermatologist) to repair decades of southwestern sun damage to my fair complexion. My face covered with unsightly red blotches, I felt like the Elephant Man and avoided going out in public for weeks. I worried about having to interview anyone looking like this, but when Ray Charles's publicist called, I realized that I could do it because Ray would not be able to see my face or any other part of me. A few days later, when I arrived at his studio in a scrubby block of the Crenshaw district, I was able to leave my self-consciousness in the car and had to explain nothing to Ray. Ray explained a lot to me, including why he performed at the 1984 Republican National Convention in Dallas, regardless of the Republican Party's ongoing "Southern strategy" exploiting racial prejudice. "The check cleared," Ray said.

In thinking about pieces to write that would allow me more of a voice, I decided to invoke the memory of the great press critic A. J. Liebling and examine the humdrum quality of so much Hollywood reporting, tracing the cause to the press-shy paranoia of the stars and the power of the publicists who controlled access to them. I drew on my own experience as a guide, wrote the piece on spec and sent it to the *Washington Journalism Review*, then being edited by Bill Monroe, the former host of NBC's *Meet the Press*. Monroe called me and said he liked it and wanted to run it, with the title "Why the News from Hollywood Always Wears a Tan." Which was perfect. Sometimes things work out.

The essay attracted some attention from journalists, including a columnist at the *New York Daily News* who wrote about it under the headline "Entertainment Writing's Dark and Dirty Side." Deborah Pines, a senior editor at *Premiere*, the glossy new movie monthly, called from New York, wanting to know if I would consider writing for them. Of course, I would (they paid real money) but not quite yet. Unexpectedly I'd gotten more involved with the *LA Times*—not just the magazine but the Calendar (entertainment) section that had once seemed so out of reach. Jack Mathews, the *Times*' movie editor and columnist, had begun offering me regular assignments, and I took them, betraying my vow to put Hollywood journalism behind me but enjoying the additional clout that came with writing for the *Times*. Plus, I liked and admired Jack, who was a top-notch writer and reporter and stood apart from the pack of obsequious Hollywood content providers.

One day John Lindsay, now overseeing all the feature sections, asked me to come downtown and have lunch with him and Jack. Something was up: One of the Hollywood beat reporters was going on maternity leave, and they wanted to offer me a staff position filling in for her for four to six months, maybe more, with the carrot that when she returned, I would be given a "roaming" long-form job on the staff of Sunday Calendar, not unlike my original position at the *Herald Examiner*.

I wasn't keen on the Hollywood beat reporter part, but the Sunday Calendar job was tempting *if I were going to do that sort of thing.* I knew it meant putting my embryonic screenwriting career on hold, but the security was too much to pass up. And once I started, I warmed quickly to the paycheck, benefits, and cachet of being a *Times* staff writer. The lid on the velvet coffin swung open. Maybe I wasn't meant for fiction and the creative life and belonged instead at a nationally prominent newspaper, with a byline and a good salary. Not a bad consolation prize.

By now I had left my Tower Drive apartment and was living with an actress and theatre director named Victoria Ann Lewis in Park LaBrea, a large modernist postwar apartment complex near the Los Angeles County Museum of Art. In my last months at the *Herald*, I had done a story about Lewis and a winning documentary theatre piece she staged at the Mark Taper Forum, using nonactors to dramatize the stories of working people. We later traveled to Australia together when the Australian government invited her to give workshops for disabled playwrights and performers. She was one of those kids of our generation who contracted polio as a child, wore a metal brace on her leg and didn't hide her disability in the recurring role she played on the CBS nighttime soap, *Knots Landing*.

When I was younger, scrambling to make my way at the *Times Herald*, I couldn't imagine taking on the responsibilities of marriage and a family, believing that would have to wait until I had figured out exactly what I wanted to do, where and how. That process had followed me to California and lasted longer than I planned. But I was now forty. The clock was ticking. I sometimes thought of the Jackson Browne song "Ready or Not" about the imperatives of settling down, even though Browne was well short of forty when he wrote it. (*I told her that I'd always lived alone and that I probably always would...*)

That lyric stung and, much as I wanted to deny its relevance, reminded me as the summer wore on that I was not ready to settle down with Victoria Ann Lewis. While reckoning with the conundrum of why I had not found my life partner, I was blindsided by an untimely bulletin from John Lindsay. The reporter I had replaced temporarily, Nina Easton, was coming back from maternity leave early. Very well, I thought. This meant I would be moving on to that Sunday Calendar job Lindsay had promised. But that would have happened only in a world that was fair and rational.

Lindsay's secretary called me at my desk one morning and told me John wanted to see me. His office was about fifty feet across the Calendar section, just past the cubicles of future gossip columnist Nikki Finke and the stuffy British-born feature writer Paul Dean, who once warned me never again to use the term "Brit" to describe any of his countrymen in Hollywood. After closing the door behind me—at Lindsay's request—I took a seat across from him. He began to speak, with less emotion than Mr. Marburger showed when he asked me if I was going to be a crusader editing the *ReMarker*.

"Don't know if you've heard, but Nina's coming back next week, so we're not going to have room for you."

Wait. What about...

"There's a hiring freeze on at Times Mirror" is all he would say by way of explanation. "So, you need to clean out your desk by the end of next week."

I sat there dazed, awaiting a word of apology, under the circumstances, but none was forthcoming. I noticed because how could I not? The omission marked Lindsay forever to me as a man lacking character, empathy, and manners. He might as well have been a Hollywood studio executive.

If this were a screenplay, we'd want to see dramatized all the pressures a boss like Lindsay was under—pressures from *his* bosses to obey the hiring freeze, the pressures not to fire the mediocrities under his supervision who "couldn't write" (his words), the pressures of budgetary shortfalls that were not his fault, the conflict created by promises he had made to other editors and/or to Nina Easton. But this is not a screenplay; it's my life, and the hero just got a shiv when he wasn't looking.

"You can talk to Jack about stories," he said, getting up from his desk. "We still want to use you." Jack Mathews, my immediate supervisor, had given me a stellar performance evaluation only a month earlier ("Everything you've done for us has been first-rate"), leading me to believe we would be working together for years. My name was on the cover of the previous Sunday Calendar section as the author of a long profile of the ranking Mexican American playwright Luis Valdez, on the occasion of his fiftieth birthday, set at his historic Teatro Campesino in northern California. I thought it was one of the best stories I had done.

I assumed there had to be off-camera corporate or departmental politics involved, but on the surface, it made no sense, especially given the culture of the velvet coffin. But there it was: the achievement of becoming a staff writer at the *Los Angeles Times* was being yanked away as quickly as it had been proffered.

CHAPTER FORTY-FOUR

Moving On

A S THE MAN SAID, THEY STILL WANTED MY SER-
VICES. Talk about chutzpah. I was instructed to return to the
freelance queue and await assignments. Angry and demeaned, my
first impulse was to bolt. Just as I was imagining a middle-class future in
California (having passed my seven-year anniversary), I was learning that
the *Times'* admissions office had sent out my acceptance letter by mistake.
I thought back to my close call with *New York Newsday* a few years before
and the prospect of working with Caroline Miller. If I was going to freelance,
I should be doing it in New York, where all the magazines and publishing
houses were, where the theatre really mattered and where, as a journalist,
I could move back in the direction of being a generalist again, maybe even
writing stories that could be adapted into scripts—by me. Lindsay's broken
promise had put me in a New York state of mind. But how would I get there?
And how could I afford it?

First, I needed to save some money, which meant returning to what
I knew how to do for a proven market, on whatever terms were available.
I moved out of Park LaBrea and found a spartan duplex in Los Feliz, near
Griffith Park. I wished never to speak to John Lindsay again, but I needed
income, any income. I could write for *Premiere* and send out more queries
to magazines, but the *Times* was the main game in town, a reliable source
of work for freelancers, albeit at lesser wages than paid to full-time staff.

My stories often got good play, and many people assumed I was still a staff writer when in truth I was a second-class citizen riding in the back of the Calendar Section bus, counting the days until I could move on.

At Thanksgiving, Gene and Lu came out to visit. We cooked a turkey and attended a musical play, *Woody Guthrie's American Song*, performed by the Missouri Repertory Theatre during a tour stop at Pepperdine University in Malibu. Back in my apartment we watched a VHS tape of the Woody Guthrie show Gene and Lu had created for the First Unitarian Church. It was good, and Dad cried, seeing it again.

Their Southwest Airlines flight back to Dallas was cancelled at the last minute, and I had to drive back out to LAX to pick them up. When I arrived, I found my mother alone. "Your dad gets lost in airports," she said.

As I set out to look for him, I thought of the time when, as a tyke, I got lost in a Dallas department store at Christmas. Now, it was me searching for him, scanning the corridors of Los Angeles International for an erudite, white-haired man for whom the world had become an increasingly unfamiliar and threatening place.

"They don't have good signs here," he said when I found him. "Your mother went to the bathroom."

I led him back toward the gate where Mom was waiting, struck by the role reversal taking place. And I was not yet a father, even at forty-two.

I HUNKERED DOWN IN LOS FELIZ, found a new jogging path that took me along the base of Griffith Park and down to Franklin Avenue, where Joan Didion and John Gregory Dunne had once rented the crumbling 1920s mansion she wrote about in *The White Album*. Over the next nine months, I interviewed Richard Dreyfuss, Oliver Stone (again), Penny Marshall, and Martin Sheen, among others, for the *Times* and *USA Today*. I wrote a cover story for the Sunday magazine of *USA Today* about the gratuitous violence in Hollywood movies, a sore subject that I noticed few critics seemed to care about. I flew to North Carolina to meet Kathleen Turner and avoid Tommy Lee Jones. I did an extended Q&A with director Mike Nichols for the British film magazine *Empire*, on the release of *Postcards from the Edge*. We met for breakfast at the Hotel Bel-Air, and I remember him ordering an egg white omelet.

I thought about trying to get into the Arts & Leisure section of the Sunday *New York Times*, the most coveted space in entertainment journalism. I spotted the bylines of Los Angeles freelancers I knew and wondered, why not me? Then I learned that the *New York Times* paid even less for freelance than the lords of Spring Street. When I expressed my surprise about this to an editor in Arts & Leisure, she deigned explain that most freelancers were happy to accept the low wages in exchange for appearing in the prestigious pages of the *Times*. Pardon my innocence but fuck that, I thought. Maybe they didn't need the money. I needed the money. I would accede to this exploitive snobbery some years later but not now.

It did occur to me to ask myself as I advanced toward the more desirable venues for this kind of work, where was it taking me? Even if I got into Arts & Leisure or somehow got to interview, say, Tom Cruise, for, say, *Esquire*, apart from the paycheck and maybe seeing my name on the cover of a national magazine on a newsstand, it was still celebrity journalism. Would it lead to another level of glory or opportunity? A book agent or a table at Ma Maison? Would Mr. North, who had gifted me once with novels by John Hersey and John O'Hara, be proud of me? I was beginning to have my doubts.

Still searching for another book to adapt that might have eluded the Hollywood search engines, I wrote to Thomas Cobb, whose novel *Crazy Heart*, about a boozed-up, over-the-hill country singer, I had enjoyed and believed had potential. Cobb was then teaching creative writing at Rhode Island College in Providence and responded with a nice note, informing me that *Crazy Heart* had already been optioned. (It would be another twenty years before it became an Oscar-win-

ning movie starring Jeff Bridges.)

Under the influence of Cobb's infectious prose and remembering what Richard Matheson said about wishing he had remained a novelist, the idea for anoth-

500 W 111th St. NYC | Author Collection

er murder mystery (in prose) occurred to me. I had long wondered if the prominence of Margo Jones' groundbreaking theatre-in-the-round in Dallas posed an impediment to establishing the Dallas Theater Center in 1959 and how convenient it was for Paul Baker that Jones died in 1955. The cause of death was unusual: Jones had fallen asleep one July night on the carpeted floor of her apartment at the Stoneleigh Hotel and apparently died from inhaling the toxic fumes of chemicals used in a recent carpet cleaning. Visiting artists often stayed at the Stoneleigh, and was it possible that Baker had stayed there while trying to arrange moving his operation north from Waco? Various homicidal scenarios presented themselves, and I thought a plot could be worked out (with the names changed, of course). But that would have to wait. For now, I was preoccupied with getting out of Los Angeles.

In the spring I began to make plans to move to New York. I discovered that the New York girlfriend of a young director who had been in Bill and Taffy's beach volleyball game wanted to move out to LA to be with him and was looking for someone to sublet her studio apartment on West Fifty-sixth Street. The price was right, and we made a deal one weekend she was in town. Six months. I figured that would be enough time for me to scope out New York and its viability for me at age forty-three. I rented a storage space in LA and hired some movers to haul my stuff there.

I would drive to Dallas and fly to New York from there, taking only a suitcase and my guitar (echoes of Paul Simon), plus a new Toshiba PC, for those first six months. Dad flew out to accompany me on the drive. He no longer drove but offered his companionship, which I welcomed. It would be

Arrived on the Upper West Side | AUTHOR COLLECTION

the last time we would have anything like normal conversations. The highlight of the trip came in New Mexico on the second day, picking up a Rangers-Angels game on the radio from Arlington. Nolan Ryan was pitching a no-hitter into the sixth inning, but the signal was so weak, the broadcast was fading in and out every few minutes. Talk about drama. We were headed back to Texas at interstate speed, zooming past the high red mesas of the Southwest at sundown, the radio crackling with the game. It wasn't hard to visualize the action at Arlington Stadium, where we had gone so many times together and with Mom.

Coming through nine hundred miles of static, every word we could understand was precious. In

With Dad visiting Trinity College Dublin, 1985
AUTHOR COLLECTION

the seat next to me, Dad leaned his head closer to the radio to hear that Ryan was striking out 13 . . . 14 . . . 15, as the game went into the ninth. After each strikeout, he would look over at me and smile. I think Ryan lost the no-hitter, but the Rangers won, a victory I would never forget. Not sure about Dad. The next day, as we neared home on Interstate 30, he became disoriented and tried to tell me I was going in the wrong direction. A sign of things to come I'd rather not think about.

Better to remember one of the many occasions he made clear to me how much he loved me, a bond more important than money or success. At the end of my senior baseball season at St. Mark's, the guy who once said, "You're not at St. Mark's to play baseball," drove down to Austin to watch us play a doubleheader in the conference tournament at St. Stephen's School on a hot Saturday in May. I was behind the plate for both games, a true endurance test. We lost the last game in extra innings, and afterward he came into the locker room to console me. As I stripped off my sweat-soaked uniform, he stood there in front of the locker and wanted to know if I remembered my first Little League game when that pop fly to center field missed my glove and hit me on the head? "I wish that coach could have been here today and seen you throw out that runner at second base." Me, too, Dad, I thought. I wasn't going to the major leagues or even to the next level of playing in college, but maybe this was enough, being able to throw out a runner trying to steal second in the Southwest Preparatory Conference.

IT'S JUST AS WELL I DIDN'T HAVE THE FUCK-YOU MONEY that would have allowed me to give Lindsay and the *Times* the finger, because in the months leading up to my departure for New York, I met Kelly Scott, the woman who would become my wife and the mother of our children. Lindsay had poached her from *Newsday* to be his assistant and deputy movie editor, and soon she was handling some of my stories. We worked together well, and I found her attractive, but she was involved in a long-distance relationship at the time, and I didn't pursue her. Later, after I was settled in New York and had graduated from my six-month sublet to a one-bedroom prewar apartment on the Upper West Side, I was invited to a birthday party for her thrown by some of her former *Newsday* colleagues. She was in town for the weekend and seemed unattached, though I wasn't sure. After she had returned to LA, I asked one of those *Newsday* reporters, a good friend of hers, if he happened to know if she was "available." "She's available," he said.

A choice was looming—a big one. New York had lived up to my expectations, and I was enjoying it much more than I did twenty years earlier when I was a clueless media plebe knocking on doors. I was writing features for *New York Newsday* and tagging along with *Variety* critic Jeremy Gerard to Broadway and off Broadway openings. On magazine assignments that took me across the country, I found that without asking, I'd been upgraded to the status of "a New York writer." Funny how that worked. If I got involved with Kelly Scott,

I would be surrendering that credential and moving back to Los Angeles, reentering the universe ruled by John Lindsay. But such practical considerations were no match for matters of the heart given what was at stake.

With Kelly in NYC, 1992 | AUTHOR COLLECTION

I had covered some distance since leaving the bosom of Cincinnati Country Day and lighting out for the territory of newspapers, theatre criticism, and Hollywood. It had been at times a nerve-rattling journey, requiring all the encouragement I could summon from memories of Lud North at St. Mark's, Charles Nichols at Brown, and Anne Crutcher in Washington. The uncertainty of it all still prevailed. I didn't yet know, but everything was about to change. Waiting for me was a second tour in the Valley of Smoke, where my focus would be pulled from journalism and one-on-ones with movie stars to the challenges and joys of raising a family. Nothing about it was going to be easy, nonetheless, I would discover it to be the real prize at the end of the line.

Acknowledgements

GRATEFUL ACKNOWLEDGEMENT to *D Magazine*, where the chapter "My Year in the Underground" was first published under the title "Notes from the Underground."

To Dan Williams at TCU Press for seeing the possibilities of this memoir and for the invaluable suggestions he made that improved the manuscript.

To David Searcy, whose ideas and support were crucial from the beginning.

To Elizabeth Van Vleck, whose keen sense of story helped me find my way.

To Jeff Unger, trusted colleague and correspondent nonpareil whose extensive knowledge of newspapers informed and influenced my own.

To my cousin William Reiser, who provided important details about the history of the family.

To my late mother, Lu Mitchell, for saving the letters I wrote home from college.

Also to the following people whose encouragement and/or recollections of the past were essential to completing this narrative: Barnett Bookatz, Christopher Dunn, Alan Fedman, Gary Goolsby, Michael Hahn, Jeremiah Kelley, Monica MacAdams, Thom Marshall, Gregory Nobles, Eric Nye, Len Reed, Robert Rozelle, Marcia Smith, Gina Spartz, Nancy Spiller, and Richard Wincorn.

To Irina du Quenoy for her sharp-eyed copyediting.

And to Ellen Storeim for her kindness and patience.

SEAN MITCHELL grew up in Dallas, where he was editor of the city's first alternative weekly, then a reporter and cultural critic for the *Dallas Times Herald* before moving to Los Angeles to cover Hollywood for the *Herald Examiner* and *Los Angeles Times*. A graduate of St. Mark's School of Texas and Brown University, he has also worked as an English teacher, videographer, and builder of custom wood fences.

Photo Credit: Kent Barker

www.ingramcontent.com/pod-product-compliance
Lightning Source LLC
Chambersburg PA
CBHW020847020726
47497CB00005B/1292